Sus

The Old Helmet

Vol. 2

SALZWASSER
VERLAG

Susan Warner

The Old Helmet

Vol. 2

Reprint of the original, first published in 1864.

1st Edition 2022 | ISBN: 978-3-75259-318-1

Verlag (Publisher): Salzwasser Verlag GmbH, Zeilweg 44, 60439 Frankfurt, Deutschland
Vertretungsberechtigt (Authorized to represent): E. Roepke, Zeilweg 44, 60439 Frankfurt, Deutschland
Druck (Print): Books on Demand GmbH, In de Tarpen 42, 22848 Norderstedt, Deutschland

THE OLD HELMET.

THE OLD HELMET.

BY

THE AUTHOR OF "WIDE, WIDE WORLD."

IN TWO VOLUMES.

'Nothing before, nothing behind:
The steps of Faith
Fall on the seeming void, and find
The rock beneath."
WHITTIER.

VOL. II.

LONDON:

M.DCCC.LXIV.

THE OLD HELMET.

CHAPTER I.

> "Let no one ask me how it came to pass;
> It seems that I am happy, that to me
> A livelier emerald twinkles in the grass,
> A purer sapphire melts into the sea."

ELEANOR could not stay away from the Wednesday meetings at Mrs. Powlis's house. In vain she had thought she would; she determined she would; when the day came round she found herself drawn with a kind of fascination towards the place. She went; and after that second time never questioned at all about it. She went every week.

It was with no relief to her mental troubles however. She was sometimes touched and moved; often. At other times she felt dull and hopeless. Yet it soothed her to go; and she came away generally feeling inspirited with hope by something she had heard, or feeling at least the comfort that she had taken a step in the right direction. It did not seem to bring her much more comfort. Eleanor did not see how she could be a Christian while her heart was so hard and so full of its own will. She found it perverse, even now, when she was wishing so much to be different. What hope for her?

It was a great help, that during all this time Mrs. Caxton left her unquestioned and uncounselled. She made no remarks about Eleanor's going to class-meeting;

she took it as a perfectly natural thing; never asked her anything about it or about her liking it. A contrary course would have greatly embarrassed Eleanor's action; as it was she felt perfectly free; unwatched, and at ease.

The spring was flushing into mature beauty and waking up all the flowers on the hills and in the dales, when Eleanor one afternoon came out to her aunt in the garden. A notable change had come over the garden by this time; its comparatively barren-looking beds were all rejoicing in gay bloom and sending up a gush of sweetness to the house with every stir of the air that way. From the house to the river, terrace below terrace sloped down, brimfull already of blossoms and fragrance. The roses were making great preparations for their coming season of festival; the mats which had covered some tender plants were long gone. Tulips and hyacinths and polyanthuses and primroses were in a flush of spring glory now; violets breathed everywhere; the snowy-flowered gooseberry and the red-flowered currant, and berberry with its luxuriant yellow bloom, and the almond, and a magnificient Magnolia blossoming out in the arms of its evergreen sister, with many another flower less known to Eleanor, made the garden terraces a little wilderness of loveliness and sweetness. Near the house some very fine auriculas in pots were displaying themselves. In the midst of all this Mrs. Caxton was busy, with one or two people to help her and work under direction. Planting and training and seed-sowing were going on; and the mistress of the place moved about among her floral subjects a very pleasant representation of a rural queen, her niece thought. Few queens have a more queenly presence than Mrs. Caxton had; and with a trowel in hand just as much as if it were a sceptre. And few queens indeed carry such a calm mind under such a calm brow. Eleanor sighed and smiled.

"Among your auriculas, aunty, as usual!"

"Among everything," said Mrs. Caxton. "There is a great deal to do. Don't you want to help, Eleanor? You may plant Gladiolus bulbs—or you may make cuttings—or you may sow seeds. I can find you work."

"Aunty, I am going down to the village."

"O it is Wednesday afternoon!" said Mrs. Caxton. And she came close up to her niece and kissed her, while one hand was full of bulbs and the other held a trowel. "Well go, my dear. Not at peace yet, Eleanor?"

There was so tender a tone in these last words that Eleanor could not reply. She dashed away without making any answer; and all along the way to Plassy she was every now and then repeating them to herself. "Not at peace yet, Eleanor?"—

She was in a tender mood this afternoon; the questions and remarks addressed to the other persons in the meeting frequently moved her to tears, so that she sat with her hand to her brow to hide the watering eyes. She did not dread the appeal to herself, for Mr. Rhys never asked her any troublesome questions; never anything to which she had to make a troublesome answer; though there might be perhaps matter for thought in it. He had avoided anything, whether in his asking or replying, that would give her any difficulty *there*, in the presence of others,—whatever it might do in her own mind and in secret. To-day he asked her, "Have you found peace yet?"

"No," said Eleanor.

"What is the state of your mind—if you could give it in one word?"

"Confusion."

"What is it confused about? Do you understand—clearly—the fact that you are a sinner? without excuse?"

"Fully!"

"Do you understand—clearly—that Christ has suffered

for sins, the just for the unjust, that he might bring us to God?"

"Yes. I understand it."

"Is there any confusion in your mind as to the terms on which the Lord will receive you?—forsaking your sins, and trusting in him to pardon and save you?"

"No—I see that."

"Do you think there is any other condition besides those two?"

"No."

"Why do you not accept them?"

Eleanor raised her eyes with a feeling almost of injustice. "I cannot!"—she said.

"That makes no difference. God never gives a command that cannot with his help be fulfilled. There was a man once brought to Jesus—carried by four men; he was palsied, and lay on a litter or bed, unable to move himself at all. To this man the Lord said, 'Arise, take up thy bed, and walk.' Suppose he had looked up and said, 'I cannot?'"

Eleanor struggled with herself. Was this fair? Was it a parallel case? She could not tell. She kept silence. Mr. Rhys went on, with tones subdued to great gentleness.

"My friend, Jesus invites to no empty board—to no cold reception. On his part all is ready; the unreadiness lies somewhere with you, or the invitation would be accepted. In your case it is not the bodily frame that is palsied; it is the heart; and the command comes to you, sweet as the invitation,—'*Give it to me.*' If you are entirely willing, the thing is done. If it be not done, it is because, somewhere, you are not willing—or do not believe. If you can trust Jesus, as that poor man did, you may rise up and stand upon your feet this very hour. 'Believe ye that I am able to do this?' he asked of the blind man whom he cured."

There was silence for an instant. And again as he turned away from her, Mr. Rhys broke out with the song, that Eleanor thought would break her heart in twain this time,—

"How lost was my condition
Till Jesus made me whole;
There is but one physician
Can cure a sin-sick soul.
There's balm in Gilead—
To make the wounded whole
There's power enough in Jesus
To save a sin-sick soul."

Eleanor had been the last one spoken to; the meeting soon was ended, and she was on her way home. But so broken-spirited and humiliated that she did not know what to do with herself. Could it be possible that she was not *willing*—or that she wanted *faith*—or that there was some secret corner of rebellion in her heart? It humbled her wonderfully to think it. And yet she could not disprove the reasoning. God could not be unfaithful; and if there were not somewhere on her part a failure to meet the conditions, surely peace would have been made before now. And she had thought herself all this while a subject for pity, not for blame; nay, for blame indeed, but not in this regard. Her mouth was stopped now. She rode home broken-hearted; would not see Mrs. Caxton at supper; and spent the evening and much of the night in weeping and self-searching. They were very downcast days that followed this day. Mrs. Caxton looked at her anxiously sometimes; never interfered with her.

Towards the end of the week there was preaching at Glanog, and the family went as usual. Eleanor rode by herself, going and coming, and held no communication with her aunt by the way. But late at night, some time after Mrs. Caxton had gone to bed, a white-robed figure came into her room and knelt down by the bed-side.

"Is that you, Eleanor?"

"Aunt Caxton—it's all gone!"

"What?"

"My trouble. I came to tell you. It's all gone. I am so happy!"

"How is it, my dear child?"

"When Mr. Rhys was preaching to-night, it all came to me; I saw everything clearly. I saw how Jesus loves sinners. I saw I had nothing to do but to give myself to him, and he would do everything. I see how sins are forgiven through his blood; and I trust in it, and I am sure mine are; and I feel as if I had begun a new life, aunt Caxton!"

Eleanor's tears flowed like summer rain. Mrs. Caxton rose up and put her arms round her.

"The Lord be praised!" she said. "I was waiting for this, Eleanor."

"Aunt Caxton, I had been trying and thinking to make myself good first. I thought I was unworthy and unfit to be Christ's servant; but now I see that I can be nothing but unworthy, and only he can make me fit for anything; so I give up all, and I feel that he will do all for me. I am so happy! I was so blind before!"

Mrs. Caxton said little; she only rejoiced with Eleanor so tenderly as if she had been her own mother. Though that is speaking very coolly on the present occasion. Mrs. Powle had never shewed her daughter so much of that quality in her life, as Eleanor's aunt shewed now.

The breakfast next morning was unusually quiet. Happiness does not always make people talkative.

"How do you do, my love?" said Mrs. Caxton when they were left alone. "After being up half the night?"

"More fresh than I have felt for a year, aunt Caxton. Did you hear that nightingale last night?"

"I heard him. I listened to him and thought of you."

"He sang—I cannot tell you what his song sounded like to me, aunt Caxton. I could almost have fancied there was an angel out there."

"There were a great many rejoicing somewhere else. What glory to think of it!" They were silent again till near the end of breakfast; then Mrs. Caxton said,—"Eleanor, I shall be engaged the whole of this morning. This afternoon, if you will, I will go with you into the garden."

"This afternoon—is Wednesday, aunt Caxton."

"So it is. Well, before or after you go to the village, I want you to dress some dishes of flowers for me—will you?"

"With great pleasure, ma'am. And I can get some hawthorn blossoms, I know. I will do it before I go, ma'am."

Was it pleasant, that morning's work? Eleanor went out early to get her sprays of May blossoms; and in the tender beauty of the day and season was lured on and on, and tempted to gather other wild bits of loveliness, till she at last found her hands full, and came home laden with tokens of where she had been. "O'er the muir, amang the heather," Eleanor's walk had gone; and her basket was gay with gorse and broom just opening; but from grassy banks on her way she had brough the bright blue speedwell; and clematis and bryony from the hedges, and from under them wild hyacinth and white campion and crane's-bill and primroses; and a meadow she had passed over gave her one or two pretty kinds of orchis, with daisies and cowslips, and grasses of various kinds. Eleanor was dressing these in flower baskets and dishes, in the open gallery that overlooked the meadows, when Mrs. Caxton passing through on her own business stopped a moment to look at her.

"All those from your walk, my dear! Do you not mean to apply to the garden?"

"Aunty, I could have got a great many more, if I could have gone into the woods—but my walk did not lie that way. Yes, ma'am, I am going into the garden presently, when I have ordered these dishes well. Where are they to go, aunt Caxton?"

"Some in one place and some in another. You may leave them here, Eleanor, when they are done, and I will take care of them. Shall I have the garden flowers cut for you?"

"O no, ma'am, if you please!"

Mrs. Caxton stood a moment longer watching Eleanor; the pretty work and the pretty worker; the confusion of fair and sweet things around her and under her fingers, with the very fine and fair human creature busy about them. Eleanor's face was gravely happy; more bright than Mrs. Caxton had ever seen it; very much of kin to the flowers. She watched her a moment, and then went nearer to kiss Eleanor's forehead. The flowers fell from the fingers, while the two exchanged a look of mute sympathy; then on one part and on the other, business went forward.

Eleanor's work held her all the morning. For after the wild beauties had been disposed to her mind, there was another turn with their more pretentious sisters of the garden. Azaleas and honeysuckles, lilies of the valley, hyacinths and pomponium lilies, with Scotch roses and white broom, and others, made superb floral assemblages, out of doors or in; and Eleanor looked at her work lovingly when it was done.

So went the morning of that day, and Eleanor's ride in the afternoon was a fit continuation. May was abroad in the bursting leaves as well as in opening flowers; the breath of Eden seemed to sweep down the valley of Plassy. Ay, there is a partial return to the lost paradise, for those whom Christ leads thither, even before we get to the everlasting hills.

Eleanor this day was the first person addressed in the meeting. It had never happened so before. But now Mr. Rhys asked her first of all, "How do you do to-day?"

Eleanor looked up and answered, "Well. And all changed."

"Will you tell us how you mean?"

"It was when you were preaching last night. It all came to me. I saw my mistake, when you told about the love of Christ to sinners. I saw I had been trying to make myself good."

"And how is it now?"

"Now,"—said Eleanor looking up again with full eyes,—"I will know nothing but Christ."

The murmur of thanksgiving heard from one or two voices brought her head down. It had nearly overcome her. But she controlled herself, and presently went on; though not daring to look again into Mr. Rhys's face, the expression of whose eyes of gladness was harder to meet than the spoken thanksgivings.

"I see I have nothing, and am nothing," she said. "I see that Christ is all, and will do all for me. I wish to be his servant. All is changed. The very hills are changed. I never saw such colours or such sunlight, as I have seen as I rode along this afternoon."

"A true judgment," said Mr. Rhys. "It has been often said, that the eye sees what the eye brings the means of seeing; and the love of Christ puts a glory upon all nature that far surpasses the glory of the sun. It is a changed world, for those who know that love for the first time! Friends, most of us profess to have that knowledge. Do we have it so that it puts a glory on all the outer world, in the midst of which we live and walk and attend to our business?"

"It does to me, sir," said the venerable old man whom Eleanor had noticed;—"it does to me. Praise the Lord!" Instead of any other answer they broke out singing,—

"O how happy are they
Who the Saviour obey,
And have laid up their treasure above.
Tongue can never express
The sweet comfort and peace
Of a soul in its earliest love."

"The way to keep that joy," said Mr. Rhys returning to Eleanor, "and to know more of it, is to take every succeeding step in the Christian life exactly as you took the first one;—in self-renunciation, in entire dependence. As ye have received Christ Jesus the Lord, so walk ye in him. It is a simple and humble way, the way along which the heavenly light shines. Do everything for Christ—do everything in his strength;—and you will soon know that the secret of the Lord is with them that fear him. Blessed be his name! He giveth power to the faint, and to them that have no might he increaseth strength."

It was easy to see that the speaker made a personal application here, with reference to himself; but after that there was no more said directly to Eleanor. The subject went round the circle, receiving the various testimony of the persons there. Eleanor's heart gave quick sympathy to many utterances, and took home with intent interest the answering counsels and remarks, which in some instances were framed to put a guard against self-deception or mistake. One or two of her neighbours when the exercises were over, came and took her hand, with a warm simple expression of feeling which made Eleanor's heart hot; and then she rode home.

"Did you have a pleasant time?" said her aunt.

"Aunt Caxton, I think that room where we meet is the pleasantest place in the world!"

"What do you think of the chapel at Glanog?"

"I don't know. I believe that is as good or better."

"Are you too tired to go out again?"

"Not at all. Who wants me?"

"Nanny Croghan is very sick. I have been with her all the afternoon; and Jane is going to sit up with her to-night; but Jane cannot go yet."

"She need not. I will stay there myself. I like it, aunt Caxton."

"Then I will send for you early in the morning."

Nanny Croghan lived a mile or two from the farm-house. Eleanor walked there; attended by John with a basket. The place was a narrow dell between two uprising hills covered with heather; as wild and secluded as it is possible to imagine. The poor woman who lived there alone was dying of lingering disease. John delivered the basket, and left Eleanor alone with her charge and the mountains.

It was not a night like that she had spent by the bedside of her old nurse's daughter. Nanny was dying fast; and she needed something done for her constantly. Through all the hours of the darkness Eleanor was kept on the watch or actively employed, in administering medicine, or food, or comfort. For when Nanny wanted nothing else, she wanted that.

"Tell me something I can fix my mind onto," she would say. "It seems slipping away from me, like. And then I gets cold with fear."

Eleanor was new at the business; she had forgotten to bring her Bible with her, and she could find none in the house; "her sister had been there," Nanny said, "and had carried it away." Eleanor was obliged to draw on the slender stores of her memory; and to make the most of those, she was obliged to explain them to Nanny, and go them over and over, and pick them to pieces, and make her rest upon each clause and almost each word of a verse. There were some words that surely Eleanor became well acquainted with that night. For Nanny could sleep very little, and when she could not sleep she wanted talking incessantly. Eleanor urged her to accept the promises and she would have the peace. "The secret of the Lord is with them that fear him."

"Ay, but I never did fear him, you see,—till a bit agone; and now it's all fear. I fear furder'n I can see."

"Nanny, Nanny, the blood of Christ will take all that fear away—if only you will trust in it. He shed it for you—to pay your debts to justice. There is no condemnation to them which are in him."

Nanny did not know exactly what so big a word as condemnation meant; Eleanor was obliged to explain it; then what was meant by being "in Christ." Towards morning Nanny seemed somewhat soothed and fell into a doze. Eleanor went to the cottage door and softly opened it, to see how the night went.

The dawn was breaking fair over the hills, the tops of which shewed the unearthly brightness of coming day. It took Eleanor's eyes and thoughts right up. O for the night of darkness to pass away from this weary earth! Down in the valley the shadows lay thicker; how thick they lay about the poor head just now resting in sleep. How thick they lay but a day or two ago upon Eleanor herself! Now she looked up. The light was flushing upon the mountain tops every moment stronger. The dewy scents of the May morning were filling the air with their nameless and numberless tokens of rich nature's bounty. The voice of a cataract, close at hand, made merry down the rocks along with the song of the blackbird, woodpecker and titmouse. And still, as Eleanor stood there and looked and listened, the rush and the stir of sweet life grew more and more; the spring breeze wakened up and floated past her face bringing the breath of the flowers fresher and nearer; and the hill tops ever kindled into more and more glow. "It is Spring! and it is Day!" thought Eleanor,—"and so it is in my heart. The darkness is gone; the light is like that light,—promising more; my life is full of sweetness I never knew. Surely this month shall be the month of months to me for ever. O for this day—O for this morning—to waken over all the world!"

She stood there, for Nanny still slept, till the sunbeams struck the hills and crept down the sides of them; and till John and Jane came in sight round the angle of the road. John had brought the pony to take Eleanor home; and a few minutes' ride brought her there. Morning prayers were however done, before Eleanor could refresh herself with cold water and a change of dress. When she came down to the sitting-room Mrs. Caxton had stepped out on some business; and in her place, sitting alone with a book, Eleanor was greatly surprised to see Mr. Rhys.

He was not at all surprised to see her; rose up and gave her a very cordial grasp of the hand, and stirred up the wood fire; which, May morning though it was, the thick walls of the old stone house and the neighbourhood of the mountains made useful and agreeable. In silence and with a good deal of skill Mr. Rhys laid the logs together so that a fresh blaze sprang up; then after a remark upon the morning he went back to his book. Eleanor sat down, also silent, feeling very much delighted to see him there, and to think that they would have his company at breakfast; but not at all inclined, nor indeed competent, to open a conversation. She looked into the fire and wondered at the turns that had brought about this meeting; wondered over the past year of her life; remembered her longing for the "helmet of salvation" which her acquaintance with Mr. Rhys had begun; and sang for joy in her heart that now she had it. Yes, it was hers, she believed; a deep rest and peace had taken place of craving and anxiety, such as even now disturbed poor dying Nanny. Eleanor felt very happy, in the midst of all her care for her. The fire burned beautifully.

"I was not aware," said Mr. Rhys looking up from his book, "I was not aware till last night that you lived with Mrs. Caxton."

Very odd, Eleanor thought; most people would have found out; however she took it simply.

"I am her niece."

"So I find,—so I am glad to find. I can wish nothing better for any one, in that kind, than to be connected with Mrs. Caxton."

He sat with his finger between the leaves of his book, and Eleanor again wondered at the silence; till Mrs. Caxton came in. It was not very flattering; but Eleanor was not troubled with vanity; she dismissed it with a thought compounded of good-humour and humility. At breakfast the talk went on pretty briskly; it was all between the other two and left her on one side; yet it was good enough to listen to it. Eleanor was well satisfied. Mr. Rhys was the principal talker; he was telling Mrs. Caxton of different people and things in the course of his labours; which constantly gave a reflex gleam of light upon those labours themselves and upon the labourer. Unconsciously of course, and merely from the necessity of the case; but it was very interesting to Eleanor, and probably to Mrs. Caxton; she looked so. At last she turned to her niece.

"How did you leave Nanny?"

"A little easier towards morning, I think; at least she went to sleep, which all the night she could not do."

"Nor you neither."

"O that's nothing. I don't mind that at all. It was worth watching, to see the dawn."

"Was the woman in so much pain?" Mr. Rhys asked.

"No; not bodily; she was uneasy in mind."

"In what way."

"Afraid of what lies before her; seeing dimly, if at all."

"Was she comforted by what you told her?"

"I had very little to tell her," said Eleanor; "I had no Bible; I had forgotten to take it; and hers was gone. I had to get what I could from memory, for I did not like to give her anything but the words of the Bible itself to ground hope upon."

"Yes, but a good warm testimony of personal experience, coming from the heart, often goes to the heart. I hope you tried that."

Eleanor had *not;* she was silent. The testimony she had given in the class-meeting somehow she had been shy of uttering unasked in the ear of the dying woman. Was that humility—or something else? Again Mr. Rhys had done for her what he so often did for her and for others—probed her thoughts.

"It is a good plan," said Mrs. Caxton, "to have a storehouse in one's memory of such things as may be needed upon occasion; passages of Scripture and hymns; to be brought out when books are not at hand. I was made to learn a great deal out of the Bible when I was a girl; and I have often made a practice of it since; and it always comes into play."

"I never set myself lessons to get by heart," said Mr. Rhys. "I never could learn anything in that way. Or perhaps I should say, I never *liked* to do it. I never did it."

"What is your art, then?" said Mrs. Caxton, looking curious.

"No art. It is only that when anything impresses itself strongly on my feelings, the words seem to engrave themselves in my memory. It is an unconscious and purely natural operation."

Eleanor remembered the multitudinous quoting of the Bible she had at different times heard from Mr. Rhys; and again wondered mentally. All that, all those parts of the Bible, he had not set himself to study, but had *felt* them into his memory! They had been put in like gold letters, with a hot iron.

"Where is this woman?" Mr. Rhys went on.

"She lives alone, in the narrow dell that stretches behind Bengarten Castle—and nearly in a straight line with it, from here. Do not go there this morning—you want rest, and it is too far for you to walk. I am going to take you into my garden, to see how my flowers go."

"Won't you take me into your dairy?"

"If you like it," said Mrs. Caxton smiling.

"I like it exceedingly. It is something like a musical box to me, Miss Powle, to see Mrs. Caxton's cheese-making. It soothes my nerves, the noiseless order of everything. Do you know that wonderful cheese-house, where they stand in ranks like yellow millstones? I never can get over my surprise at going in there. Certainly we, as a nation, are fond of cheese!"

"You think so because you are not," said Mrs. Caxton. "It is too late for the dairy to-day. You shall give me help in my garden, where I want it."

"I understand," says Mr. Rhys. "But it is my business to make flowers grow in the Lords's garden—wherever I can. I wish I could do more of *that* gardening work!"

Eleanor gave a quick glance up at the speaker. His

brow rested on his hand for the moment; she noticed the sharply drawn lines of the face, the thin cheeks, the complexion, which all witnessed to *over*-work already attempted and done. The brow and eyes were marked with lines of watching and fatigue. It was but a glance, and Eleanor's eyes went down again; with an additional lesson of unconscious testimony carried deep home. This man lived as he talked. The good of existence was not one thing in his lips and another in his practice. Eleanor looked at her plate with her heart burning. In her old fancy for studying, or at least reading, hands, she had noticed too in her glance the hand on which the head rested; and with surprise. It was almost a feminine hand in make, with long slim fingers; white withal, and beautifully cared for. Certain refinements were clearly necessary to this man, who was ready to plunge himself into a country of savages nevertheless, where all the refinement would be his own. To some natures it would be easier to part with a hand altogether, than to forego the necessity of having it clean. This was one. And *he* was going to give himself up to Polynesia and its practices. Eleanor eat with the rest of her breakfast and swallowed with her tea, the remembered words of the apostle—"But what things were gain to me, those I counted loss for Christ."—"Neither count I my life dear unto myself, so that I may finish my course with joy, and the ministry, which I have received of the Lord Jesus, to be faithful."—Eleanor's heart swelled. Tears were very near.

After breakfast, a large part of the morning was spent by her aunt and Mr. Rhys in the garden; as Mrs. Caxton had said; and very busy they were. Eleanor was not asked to join them, and she did not choose to volunteer; she watched them from the house. They were very honestly busy; planting and removing and consulting; in real garden work; yet it was manifest their minds had also much more in common, in matters of greater interest; they stood and talked for long intervals when the flowers were forgotten. They were very near each other, those two, evidently, in regard and mutual confidence and probably mutual admiration also. It was very strange Eleanor should never have come to the knowledge of it till to-day. And yet, why should she? She had never mentioned the name of Mr. Rhys to her aunt in any of her stories of Wiglands.

He was away all the afternoon and the evening, and came back again late; a tired and exhausted man. He said nothing, except to officiate at family prayers; but Eleanor was delighted that he was to spend the night at the farm and they would have him at breakfast. Only to see him and hear him talk to others, only the tones of his voice, brought up to her everything that was good and strong and pure and happy. He did not seem inclined to advance at all upon their Wiglands acquaintance. He made no allusion to it. As far as she was concerned, Eleanor thought that there was more reserve in his manner towards her than he had shewed there. No matter. With Mrs. Caxton he was very much at home; and she could study him at her ease all the better for not talking to him.

CHAPTER II.

> "The flush of life may well be seen
> Thrilling back over hills and valleys
> The cowslip startles in meadows green,
> The buttercup catches the sun in its chalice,
> And there's never a leaf or a blade too mean
> To be some happy creature's palace."

"MRS. CAXTON," said Mr. Rhys the next morning, when half the breakfast had been passed in silence, "have you such a thing as a microscope in the house?"

"I am afraid not. Why do you ask?"

"Only, that I have suddenly discovered myself to be very ignorant, in a department of knowledge where it would be very pleasant as well as proper to be otherwise. I have been reading a book on some of the forms of life which are only to be known through the help of glasses; and I find there is a world there I know nothing about. That book has made a boy of me."

"How?" said Mrs. Caxton smiling.

"You think I always retain more or less of that character! Well—it has made me doubly a boy then; in my eagerness to put myself to school, on the one hand, and my desire to see something new on the other. Miss Powle, have you ever studied the invisible inhabitants of pools, and ponds, and sea-weeds?"

"Not at all," said Eleanor.

"You do not know much more than the names, then, of Infusoria, Rotifera, and Pedunculata, and such things?"

"Not so much as the names—except Infusoria. I hope they are better than they sound."

"If the accounts are true—Mrs. Caxton, the world that we do not see, because of the imperfection of our organs, is even far more wonderful than the world that we do see. Perhaps it seems so, because of the finiteness of our own powers. But I never had a single thing give me such a view of the infinite glory of God, as one of the things detailed in that book—one of the discoveries of the microscope."

"His glory in creation," said Mrs. Caxton.

"More than that—There is to be sure the infiniteness of wisdom and of power, that makes your brain dizzy when you think of it; but there is an infinite moral glory also."

"What was the thing that struck you so much?" Eleanor inquired.

"It was a little fellow that lives in the water. He is not bigger than the diameter of the slenderest needle—and that is saying as much as I can for his size. This fellow builds himself a house of bricks, which he makes himself; and under his head he carries a little cup mould in which the bricks are made."

"Mr. Rhys," said Eleanor, "I am wondering what is the slenderest needle of your acquaintance!"

"No," said he laughing, "you are mistaken. I have seen my mother hem thin ruffles of muslin; and you know with what sort of a needle that should be done."

"Aunt Caxton," said Eleanor, "it is inconceivable!"

Mrs. Caxton did not make much answer, and the conversation turned. After breakfast, and after, as Eleanor judged, they had been a good while in the dairy, the two went out together in the car. Eleanor supposed it was to visit Nanny; and so she found when her aunt came home.

"I knew he would go," said Mrs. Caxton; "and then

we made another call. Nanny is hopeful, and comfortable; but the other——Mr. Rhys came away very much agitated. He is not fit for it. I wish I could keep him from work for a few weeks. It's the best economy. But I will keep him here as long as I can, at least."

"Is he going to stay here?"

"Yes; he was not comfortably situated in the village; and now I will have him at the farm, I hope, till he goes. I shall trust you to keep the flowers fresh in his room, Eleanor.—No, my dear; Jane will stay with Nanny to-night."

So Mr. Rhys stayed at the farm, and certainly wanted for no comfort that the mistress of it could secure to him. Neither did Eleanor neglect the flowers. Mr. Rhys made his home there, and went out to his preaching and visiting and teaching as vigorously as ever; and was often a tired man when he came home. Nevertheless he gained ground, to Mrs. Caxton's great satisfaction. He grew stronger; and was less often a silent, prostrated, done-over member of their little circle. At first he was very often that. But when he felt well he was exceedingly social and conversational; and the Plassy farm-house had never been so pleasant, nor the evenings and mornings and meal times so full of interest. In all which however Mrs. Caxton thought Eleanor took a very quiet part.

"You do not do your share, Eleanor," she said one day; "you are become nothing of a talker; and I can bear witness you had a tongue once. Has religion made you silent, my dear?"

"No, aunty," said Eleanor laughing; "but you forget—you have somebody else to talk to now."

"I am sure, and so have you."

"No ma'am—Mr. Rhys does not talk to me generally."

"I would return good for evil, then; and not silence for silence."

"I can't, aunty. Don't you know, there are some people that have a sort of quieting effect upon one?"

"I don't think anybody ever did upon me," said Mrs. Caxton; "and I am sure Mr. Rhys would be shocked if he knew the effect of his presence."

One morning Mrs. Caxton asked Mr. Rhys at breakfast if he had leisure to unpack a box for her. He said yes, with great alacrity; and Mrs. Caxton had the box brought in.

"What is it?" said Mr. Rhys as he began his work. "Am I to take care of china and glass—or to find gardener's plants nicely done up—or best of all, books?"

"I hope, something better yet," said Mrs. Caxton.

"There is a good deal of it, whatever it is," said Mr. Rhys, taking out one and another and another carefully wrapped up bit of something. "Curiosity can go no further!"

He stopped unpacking, and took the wrapping papers off one or two odd-looking little pieces of brass; paused, —then suddenly exclaimed, "Mrs. Caxton!—"

"Well?" said that lady smiling.

"It is just like you! I might have known the other morning what all that talk would end in."

Mrs. Caxton smiled in silence, and the gentleman went on with his unpacking; with added zeal and tenderness now, it was evident. It stood full in view at last, an exquisitely made and mounted microscope of one of the best London makers. Now was Mr. Rhys in his element; and proved how justly he had declared himself a *boy*. He got the microscope all into place and arranged, and then set himself to find out its powers and method of management. There were some prepared objects sent with the instrument, which gave him enough to work with; and over them he was in an absorbed state for hours; not selfishly, however, for he allowed Eleanor to take her full share of the pleasure of looking, when once he had brought objects into view. At last he broke off and hurried away to an engagement.

The next day at breakfast, Eleanor was a good deal surprised to be asked if she would take a walk?

"Now?" said Eleanor. "You mean immediately after breakfast?"

"It is the only time I have to-day. All the time before dinner, I have; but I supposed we should want the whole of it. I am going after objects for the microscope —and I thought it would be selfish to go alone. Besides, we may help one another."

"I shall be very glad to go," said Eleanor laughing; "but don't expect any *help* of me; unless it be in the way of finding out such places as you want."

"I fancy I know those better than you do. Miss Powle, a small basket would be desirable to hold phials of water."

"And phials."

"I will take care of those."

Much amused, and a little excited, Eleanor made ready for the walk, and in the matter of the basket at least proved helpful. It was bright and early when they set out. Among those mountains and valleys, the dew was not off the fields yet, while the air was freshly sweet from roses and wild thyme, and primroses lingering, and numberless other sweet things; for hedgerow and meadow and mountain side were gay and rich with a multitude of flowers. There was a mingling of shadow and sunshine too, at that early time in the morning; and as the two walkers passed along they were sometimes in one, sometimes in the other. There was little conversation at first. Mr. Rhys went not with a lingering step, but as if with some purpose to reach a definite locality. Eleanor was musing to herself over the old walks taken with Julia by her present companion; never but once Eleanor's walking companion till now. How often Julia had gone with him; what a new and strange pleasure it was for herself; and how oddly life changes about things; that the impossible thing at Wiglands should be possible at Plassy.

"What sort of places are you looking for, Mr. Rhys?" Eleanor inquired at last.

"All sorts of places," he said smiling. "All sorts at least of wet places. But I know nothing about it, you know, except what I have read. They say, wherever water is found, some or other species of these minute wonders may be met with; standing pools, and rivers, and ditches all have them; and some particularly beautiful are to be found in bog water; so with, I am afraid you will think, a not very commendable impatience, I am pointing my steps towards a bog that I know—in the wish to get some of the best first."

"That is being very impatient," said Eleanor laughing. "I should be satisfied with almost anything, for the first."

"So you will very probably have to be. I am by no means sure of accomplishing my design. Am I walking too fast for you, in the meanwhile?"

"Not at all. I am thinking, Mr. Rhys, how we are to bring home the bog water when we have found it."

In answer to which, he put his hand in his pocket and brought out thence and deposited in his basket one after another of half a dozen or more little phials, all duly corked. Eleanor was very much amused.

"And what is this stick to do, that you wanted me to bring?"

"You will see."

The bog was reached in due time, after a walk over a most delicious country, for the most part new to Eleanor. Water was found, though not exactly with the conditions Mr. Rhys desired; however a phial of it was dipped up, corked and marked. Then they retraced their steps partially, diverging right and left. Just the right sort of pool was found at last; covered with duck-weed. Here Mr. Rhys stopped and tied one of the phials to the end of the stick. With this he dipped water from the surface, then he dipped from the bottom; he took from one side and from another side, where there was sunshine and where there was shade; pouring each dipping into a fresh phial, while Eleanor in a great state of amusement corked and labelled each as it was filled. At last it was done. Mr. Rhys filled his last phial, looked at Eleanor's face, and smiled.

"You do not think much is going to come of all this?" he said.

"Yes I do," said Eleanor. "At least I hope so."

"I know it. Look through that."

He put a pocket lens into her hand and bade her survey one of the phials with it. Eleanor's scepticism fled. That *something* was there, in pretty active life, was evident. Somethings. The kinds were plural.

"It was like Mrs. Caxton, to order this lens with the microscope," Mr. Rhys went on. "I suppose she made her order general—to include everything that would be necessary for a naturalist in making his observations. I not being a naturalist. Did you ever see the 'Bundle' of Helig?"

"I do not know what it is."

"'Bundle' or 'Bandel'—I do not know how it got the name, I am sure; but I suppose it is a corruption of something. Would you like to go a little out of your way to see it?"

"You can judge better than I, Mr. Rhys!" Eleanor said with her full, rich smile, which that gentleman had not often seen before. He answered it with his own very peculiar one, sober and sweet.

"I will take so much responsibility. You ought not to come so near and miss it."

Turning from the course of their return way, they followed a wild woody dell for a little distance; then making a sudden angle with that, a few steps brought them in sight of a waterfall. It poured over a rocky barrier of considerable height, the face of which was corrugated, as it were, with great projecting ridges of rock. Separated of necessity by these, the waters left the top of the precipice in four or five distinct bands or ribbands of bright wave and foam, soon dashed into whiteness; and towards the bottom of the fall at last found their way all together; which they celebrated with a rush and a dance and a sparkle and a roar that filled all the rocky abyss into which they plunged. The life, the brightness, the peculiar form, the wild surroundings, of this cataract made it a noted beauty. In front of it the rocks closed in so nearly that spectators could only look at it through a wild narrow gap. Above, beyond the top of the fall, the waving branches could be seen of the trees and bushes that stood on the borders of the water; to reach which was a mere impossibility, unless by taking a very long way round. At the foot, the waters turned off suddenly and sought their course where the eye could not follow them.

It was out of the question to talk in the presence of the shout of those glad waters. Mr. Rhys leaned against the rock, and looked at them, so motionless that more than once the eye of Eleanor went from them to him with a little note-taking. When at last he turned away and they got back into the stillness of the glen, he asked her, "how looking at such a thing made her feel?"

"Nothing but surprise and pleasure, I think," said Eleanor; "but a great deal of both those." Then as he still remained silent, she went on,—"To tell the truth, Mr. Rhys, I think my mental eye is only beginning to get educated. I used always to enjoy natural beauty, but I think it was in a superficial kind of way. Since I have been at Plassy—and especially since a few weeks back,—all nature is much more to me than it was."

"It is sure to be so," he said. "Nature without and nature within are made for each other; and till the two are set to the same key, you cannot have a good tune.—There is a fellow who is in pretty good order! Do you hear that blackbird?"

"Sweet!" said Eleanor. "And what is that other note—'chee, chee, chee,' so many times?"

"That is a green wren."

"You are *something* of a naturalist, Mr. Rhys," said Eleanor.

"Not at all! no more than my acquaintance with you and Mrs. Caxton makes me a philosopher."

Eleanor wanted to ask what looking at the cataract made *him* think of; but as she had told her aunt, Mr. Rhys exercised a sort of quieting influence over her. No natural audacity, of which she had an innocent share, remained to her in his company. She walked along in demure silence. And to say the truth, the sun was now growing warm, and the two had walked not a few good miles that morning; which also has a quieting influence. Eleanor queried with herself whether all the bright part of the walk were over.

"I think it is time we varied our attention," said Mr. Rhys breaking silence. "We have been upon one class of subjects a good while;—suppose we try another. Don't you want to rest?"

"I am not tired,—but I have no objection."

"You are not easily tired?"

"Not about anything I like."

"You have struck a great secret of power and usefulness," he said gravely. "What do you think of this bank?—it is dry, and it is pleasant."

It would have been hardly possible to find a spot in all their way that would not have been pleasant; and from this bank they looked over a wide rich valley bordered with hills. It was not the valley where the farmhouse of Plassy stood, with its meadows and river; this was different in its features, and moreover some miles distant. Eleanor and Mr. Rhys sat down on the moss at the foot of the trees, which gave both shade and rest. It was the edge of a piece of woods, and a blackbird was again heard saluting them.

"Now if you want refreshment," said Mr. Rhys, "I can give it to you; but only of one kind."

"I don't know—I should say of several kinds," said Eleanor looking into the basket — "but the quality doubtful."

"Did you think I meant *that?*"

Eleanor laughed at the earnest gravity of this speech. "Mr. Rhys, I saw no other refreshment you had to offer me; but indeed I do not want any—more than I am taking."

"I was going to offer it to you of another kind, but there is no kind like it. What is your way of reading the Bible?"

"I have no particular 'way,'" said Eleanor in some surprise. "I read several chapters a day—or at least always a chapter at morning and another at evening. What 'way' do you mean?"

"There are a great many ways; and it is good to use them all at different times. But what way would be good for a half hour's refreshment, at such a time as this?"

"I am sure, I don't know," said Eleanor. "I have no way but the one."

"Yes, but we should not have seen the 'Bandel' of Helig, if we had not turned aside to look at it; and you would not have heard the blackbird and the wren perhaps, unless you had stopped to listen to them. I suppose we have missed a million of other things, for want of looking."

"Yes, but we could not look at everything all along these miles of our way," said Eleanor, her smile breaking forth again.

"Very true. On the other hand, if we go but a very little way, we can examine all around us. Have you a Bible with you?"

"No. I never carry one."

"I am better off than you. Let us try a little of this —the first chapter of Romans. Will you read the first verse, and consider it."

He handed her his Bible and Eleanor read.

"'Paul, a servant of Jesus Christ, called to be an apostle, separated unto the gospel of God'—"

"What do you find there?" said her companion.

"Not much. This verse seems to be a sort of opening, or introduction to the rest. Paul tells who he is, or what he is."

"And what does he say he is?"

"A servant of Jesus Christ."

"You think that is 'not much?'"

"Certainly it is much, in itself; but here I took it for a mere statement of fact."

"But what a fact. *A servant of Jesus Christ.* Only that! Do you know what a fact that is? What is it, to be a servant of Jesus Christ?"

Without waiting for the answer, which was not ready, Mr. Rhys rose up from his seat and began an abstracted exploration of the bit of woodland at the edge of which they had been sitting; wandering in and out among the trees, and stooping now and then to pluck a flower or a fern or to examine one; apparently too full of his thoughts to be quiet. Eleanor heard him sometimes and watched him when she could; he was very busy; she wished he would give some of his thoughts to her.

"I thought you wanted rest, Mr. Rhys," she said

boldly, when she got a chance. "Please sit down here and take it, along with your other refreshment."

He smiled and came immediately with a bunch of Myosotis in his hand, which he threw into Eleanor's lap; and turning to her he repeated very seriously his question.

"What is it, to be a servant of Jesus Christ?"

"I know very little," said Eleanor timidly. "I am only just beginning to learn."

"You know the words bring for our refreshment only the meaning that we attach to them—except so far as the Holy Spirit answering our prayers and endeavours shews us new meaning and depth that we had not known before."

"Of course—but I suppose I know very little. These words convey only the mere fact to me."

"Let us weigh the words. A servant is a follower. Christ said, 'If a man serve me, let him *follow me.*'"

"Yes,—I know."

"A follower must know where his Master goes. How did Christ walk?"

"He went about doing good."

"He did; but mark, there are different ways of doing that. Get to the root of the matter. The young man who kept all the commandments from his youth, was not following Christ; and when it came to the pinch he turned his back upon him."

"How then, Mr. Rhys? You mean heart-following?"

"That is what the Lord means. Look here—Paul says in the ninth verse,—'Whom I serve *with my spirit* in the gospel'—Following cannot have a different end in view from that of the person followed. And what was Christ's?—'My meat is to do the will of him that sent me, and to finish his work.' Are we servants of Christ after that rule, Miss Powle?"

The question had a singular intonation, as if the questioner were charging it home upon himself. Yet Eleanor knew he could answer it in the affirmative and that she could not; she sat silent without looking up. The old contrast of character recurred to her, in spite of the fact that her own had changed so much. She hung over the book, while her companion half abstractedly repeated,

"'My meat is to do the will of him that sent me.'—That makes a way of life of great simplicity."

"Is it always easy to find?" ventured Eleanor.

"Very!—if his will is all that we desire."

"But that is a very searching, deep question."

"Let it search, then. 'My meat is to do the will of him—' No matter what that may be, Miss Powle; our choice lies in this—that it is his will. And as soon as we set our hearts upon one or the other particular sort of work, or labour in any particular place, or even upon any given measure of success attending our efforts, so that we are not willing to have him reverse our arrangements,—we are getting to have too much will about it."

Eleanor looked up with some effort.

"You are making it a great matter, to be a true servant of Christ, Mr. Rhys."

"Would you have it a little matter?" he said with a smile of great sweetness and brightness. "Let the Lord have all! He was among us 'as one that serveth' —amid discouragements and disappointments, and abuse; and he has warned us that the servant is not greater than his Lord. It is not a little thing, to be the minister of Jesus Christ!"

"Now you are getting out of the general into the particular."

"No—I am not; a 'minister' is but a servant; what we call a minister, is but in a more emphatic degree the servant of all. The rules of service are the same for him and for others. Let us look at another one. Here it is—in John—"

And the fingers that Eleanor had watched the other morning, and with which she had a curious association, came turning over the leaves.

"'Ye call me Master, and Lord: and ye say well; for so I am. If I then, your Lord and Master, have washed your feet; ye also ought to wash one another's feet. For I have given you an example, that ye should do as I have done to you.'—One thing is plain from that, Miss Eleanor—we are not to consider ourselves too good for anything."

"No—" said Eleanor;—"but I suppose that does not forbid a just judgment of ourselves or of others, in respect of their adaptations and qualifications."

"Yes it does," he said quickly. "The only question is, Has the Lord put that work in your hands? If he has, never ask whether your hands are the right ones. He knows. What our Lord stooped to do, well may we!"

Eleanor dared not say any more; she knew of what he was thinking; whether he had a like intuition with respect to her thoughts she did not know, and would not risk them any nearer discovery.

"There is another thing about being a servant of Christ," he presently went on;—"it ensures some kind and degree of persecution."

"Do you think so?" said Eleanor; "in these days? Why it is thought praiseworthy and honourable, is it not, through all the land, to be good? to be a member of the Church, and to fulfil the requirements of religion? Does anybody lose respect or liking from such a cause?"

"No. But he suffers persecution. My dear friend, what are the 'requirements of religion?' We are just considering them. Can you remember a servant of

Christ, such as we have seen the name means, in your knowledge, whom the world allowed to live in peace?"

Eleanor was silent.

"'Remember the word that I said unto you, the servant is not greater than his Lord. If they have persecuted me, they will also persecute you; if they have kept my saying, they will keep yours also.'"

"But in *these* days, Mr. Rhys?" said Eleanor doubtfully.

"I can only say, that if you are of the world, the world will love his own. I know no other way of securing that result. 'Because ye are not of the world,' Jesus said, 'but I have chosen you out of the world, therefore the world hateth you.' And it is declared elsewhere, that all that will live godly in Christ Jesus shall suffer persecution. Can you remember any instance to the contrary?"

Eleanor looked up and gave Mr. Rhys a good view of her honest eyes; they looked very intent now and somewhat sorrowful.

"Mr. Rhys, except in Plassy, I do not know such a person as you ask me about."

"Is it possible!" he said.

"Mr. Rhys, I was thinking the servants of Christ have good need of that 'helmet of salvation' I used to wish for."

"Well, they have it!" he said brightly. "'If any man serve me, let him follow me; *and where I am, there shall also my servant be.*' That is the end of all. But there is another point of service that occurs to me. We have seen that we must not please ourselves; I recollect that in another place Paul says that if he pleased men, he would not be the servant of Christ. There is a point where he and the world would come in contact of opposition."

"But I thought we ought to please everybody as much as we could?"

He smiled, put his hand over and turned two or three leaves of the Bible which she kept open at the first of Romans, and pointed to a word in the fifteenth chapter. "Let every one of us please his neighbour for his good, to edification."

"There is your limit," said he. "So far thou mayest go, but no further. And to do that you will find requires quite sufficiently that you should not please yourself. And now how shall we do all this?—how shall we be all this?"

"You are asking the very question!" said Eleanor gravely.

"We must come to the root and spring of all this service and following—it is our love of the Lord himself. That will do it, and nothing else will. 'What things were gain to me, those I counted loss for Christ.'"

"But suppose," said Eleanor, with some difficulty commanding her voice,—"suppose one is deficient in that very thing? suppose one wants that love?"

"Ay!" he said, looking into her face with his eyes of light,—"suppose one does; what then?"

Eleanor could not bear them; her own eyes fell. "What is one to do?"—Mr. Rhys had risen up before he answered, in his deliberate accents,

"'Seek him, that maketh the seven stars and Orion, and turneth the shadow of night into morning.'"

He paced slowly up and down before Eleanor; then went off upon a rambling search through the wood again; seeming to be busy with little things in his way. Eleanor sat still. After a little he came and stood before her with a bunch of ferns and Melic grass and lilies of the valley, which he was ordering in his hands as he spoke.

"The effect of our following Christ in this way, Miss Powle, will be, that we shall bear testimony to the world that He is our King, and what sort of a king he is. We shall proclaim that Jesus Christ is Lord, to the glory of God the Father. We shall have the invisible army of angels for our fellow-servants and co-workers; and we shall be passing on with the whole redeemed world to the day of full triumph and final restoration; when Christ will come to be glorified in his saints and to be admired in them that believe—because our testimony among you was believed. But now our business is to give the testimony."

He walked up and down, up and down, before Eleanor for some minutes, in a thoughtful, abstracted way. Eleanor felt his manner as much as his words; the subject had clearly gone home to himself. She felt both so much that she did not like to interrupt the silence, nor to look up. At last he stopped again before her and said in quite a different tone, "What are the next words, Miss Powle?"

"'Called to be an apostle.'"

"We shall not get home to dinner, if we go into that," he said smiling.

"You have preached a sermon to me, Mr. Rhys."

"I do that very often to myself," he answered.

"To yourself?" said Eleanor.

"Yes. Nobody needs it more."

"But when you have so much real preaching to do—I should think it would be the last thing you would wish to do in private,—at other times."

"For that very reason. I need to have a sermon always ready, and to be always ready myself. Now, let us get home and look at our 'rotifera'—if we have any."

However, there was to be no microscopical examination that morning.

"The best laid schemes o' mice and men
Gang aft agley."

They had gone but half a mile further homeward when their course was again stopped. They came up with a man and a horse; the horse standing still, the man lying on the ground beside him. At first sight they thought it was a case of drunkenness, for the face of the man was very red and he was unable to give any account of himself; but they were soon convinced it was sudden illness, not intoxication, which was the matter. He had fallen from his horse evidently, and now was not unconscious but in great pain; the red in his face alternating with sudden changes of colour. Apparently his condition was that of a small farmer or upper farm servant, who had been overtaken on some business errand by this attack of severe sickness. His horse stood quietly beside him.

"This is no case for a lancet," said Mr. Rhys after making a slight examination. "It calls for greater skill than mine. How will you do? I must take the horse and ride for it. But the first thing is to find where I ought to go—if I can—"

For this information he sought in the man's pockets; and found presently a pocket-book with one or two bills, which gave the name he wanted. It was a name not unknown to Mr. Rhys; and let him know also the direction in which he must ride; not towards the valley of Plassy.

"What will you do, Miss Powle?—will you be afraid to find your way home alone?"

"I will stay here till you come back."

"Will you? But I may be gone some time—and I must tell you," he said gravely, "the man is very ill."

"There is the more reason then, I am sure. I will stay and do anything for him I can, Mr. Rhys. You go —I will stay here."

Mr. Rhys said nothing more, though Eleanor felt sure from his face that he did not disapprove of her conclusion. He mounted the horse immediately.

"I will send help from the way if I can, though I doubt it. The way is lonely, till I get almost there."

He rode off at a sharp pace, and Eleanor was left quite alone. Her attention came back to the sick person at her feet. So near the light-hearted pleasure of ten minutes ago had been to pain and death! And Mr. Rhys's sermon was nearer still. The first thing to consider, was what she could do for the man.

He had fallen and lay on the grass in the broad sunshine. The sun had mounted high now; its beams fell hot and full on the sufferer's face. At a little distance was a grove of oaks and beeches, and good shelter; but Eleanor's strength could not move the man thither; he was a great, thickset, burly fellow. Yet it was miserable to see the sun beating upon his face where the sweat of pain already stood. Eleanor went to the wood, and with much trouble and searching managed to find or break off two or three sticks of a few feet in length. She planted these for a frame near the sick man's head and spread her light summer shawl over them to make a screen. It was a light screen; nevertheless much better than nothing. Then Eleanor kneeled down by the man to see what more she could do. Red and pale changed fast and fearfully upon his face; big drops stood on the brow and cheeks. Eleanor doubted whether he were conscious, he lay so still. She took her pocket-handkerchief to wipe the wet brow. A groan answered her at that. It startled her, for it was the first sound she had heard the sick person utter. Putting down her face to receive if possible some intimation of a wish, she thought he said or tried to say something about 'drink.' Eleanor rose up and sought to recollect where last and nearest she had seen water. It was some distance behind; a little spring that had crossed their foot-way with its own bright track. Then what could she bring some in? The phials! Quick the precious pond water and bog water was poured out, with one thought of the nameless treasures for Mr. Rhys's microscope that she was spilling upon the ground; and Eleanor took the basket again and set off on the backward way. She was in a hurry, the sun was warm, the distance was a good quarter of a mile; by the time she had found the stream and filled her phials and retraced again her steps to where the sick man lay, she was heated and weary; for every step was hurried with the thought of that suffering which the water might alleviate. This was pure, sparkling, good water with which the phials were now filled. But when Eleanor got back to him, the man could not open his lips to take it. She feared he would die, and suddenly.

It was a wild uncultivated place they were in. No signs of human habitation were to be seen, except far up away on a hillside in the distance, where smoke went up from a farmhouse or some sort of a house; towards which Eleanor looked with earnest longings that the human help which was there could be brought within available distance. It was greatly too far for that. How soon would Mr. Rhys be back? Impossible to say; she could not tell what length of road he might have to travel. And the man seemed dying. Eleanor knelt down again, and with the precious contents of one of the phials bathed the brow and the lips that she thought would never return to their natural colour again. She did it perseveringly; it was all she could do. Perhaps it gave comfort. But Eleanor grew tired, and felt increasingly lonely and desirous that some one should come. No one did come by that way, nor was likely to come, until the return of Mr. Rhys; the place was not near a highway; only on a wild mountain track. It struck Eleanor then that the sufferer's head lay too low, upon the ground. She could not move him to a better position; and finally placing herself on the grass beside him, she contrived with great exertion to lift his head upon her lap.

He could not thank her; she did not know if he were aware of what she did; but then Eleanor had done all. She schooled herself to sit patiently and wipe the brow that lay upon her knee, and wait; knowing that death might come to take her charge before any other arrival relieved her of it. Eleanor had a great many thoughts meanwhile; and as she sat there revolved Mr. Rhys's 'sermon' in her mind over and over, and from one end to the other and back again.

So at last Mr. Rhys found her. He came as he had gone, full speed; jumped off his horse, and took a very grave survey of the group on the ground. It was not early. Mr. Rhys had been a long time away; it seemed half a day's length to Eleanor.

"Have you been there all this time?" was his question.

"O no."

"I will take your place," said he kneeling down and lifting the unconscious head from Eleanor's lap. "There is a waggon coming. It will be here directly."

Eleanor got up, trembling and stiff from her long constrained position. The waggon presently came in sight; a huge covered wain which had need to move slowly. Mr. Rhys had stayed by it to guide it, and only spurred forward when near enough to the place. Into it they now lifted the sick man, and the horses' heads were turned again. Mr. Rhys had not been able to bring a doctor.

"Why here is Powis!" exclaimed Eleanor, as on the waggon coming round she discovered her pony hitched to the back of it. Mr. Rhys unhitched him. Powis was saddled.

"I thought you would have done enough for to-day," said he; "and I went round by the farm to bring him. Now you will ride home as fast as you please."

"But I thought the farm was out of your way?"

"I had time to gallop over there and meet the waggon again; it went so slowly."

"O thank you! But I do not need Powis—I can walk perfectly well. I am sure you need him more than I do, Mr. Rhys. I do not need him at all."

"Come, mount!" said he. "I cannot ride on a side saddle, child."

Eleanor mounted in silence, a little surprised to find that Mr. Rhys helped her not awkwardly; and not knowing exactly whence came a curious warm glow that filled her heart like a golden reflection. But it kept her silent too; and it did not go away even when Mr. Rhys said in his usual manner,

"I beg your pardon, Miss Powle—I live among the hills till I grow unceremonious."

Eleanor did not make any answer, and if she rode home as fast as she pleased, it was her pleasure to ride slowly; for Mr. Rhys walked beside her all the way. But she was too tired perhaps to talk much; and he was in one of his silent moods.

"What have you done with the phials?" said he looking into the basket as they neared home.

"I am very sorry, Mr. Rhys! I had to empty them to get water for that poor man. I wasn't quite sure, but I thought he asked for it."

"Oh!—And where did you go to find water?"

"Back—don't you remember?—some distance back of where we found him, we had passed a little brook of running clear water. I had to go there."

"Yes—I know. Well, we shall have to make another expedition."

CHAPTER III.

"I will have hopes that cannot fade,
For flowers the valley yields!
I will have humble thoughts instead
Of silent, dewy fields!
My spirit and my God shall be
My sea-ward hill, my boundless sea."

THE promised expedition came off; and a number of others; not too frequently however, for Mr. Rhys continued to be one of the world's busy people, and was often engaged and often weary. The walks after natural history came between times; when he was not under the immediate pressure of duty, and felt that he needed recreation to fit him for it. Eleanor was his companion generally, and grew to be as much interested in his objects as he was himself. Perhaps that is saying too much. In the house certainly Mr. Rhys bestowed an amount of patient time and investigation upon his microscopical studies which Eleanor did not emulate; time and pains which made him presently a capital manipulator, and probably stowed away quantities of knowledge under that quiet brow of his. Many an hour Mr. Rhys and his microscope were silent companions, during which he was rapt and absorbed in his contemplations or his efforts—whichever it might be; but then at other times, and before and after these times, Eleanor and Mrs. Caxton were constantly invited to a share in some of the results at least of what was going on.

Perhaps three people rarely enjoy more comfort together in themselves and in each other, than these three did for some weeks following the date of the last chapter. Mr. Rhys was a wonderful pleasant addition to the family. He was entirely at home, and not a person to be trammelled by any ordinary considerations. He was silent when he felt like it; he kept alone when he was busy; he put no unnatural force upon himself when he was fatigued; but silent, or weary, or busy, there was always and at all times where he was, the feeling of the presence of one who was never absent from God. It was in the atmosphere about him; it was in the look that he wore, free and simple as that always was, in its gravity; it was in the straightforward doing of duty, in all little things as much as in great things; the little things never forgotten, the great things never waived. It was an unconscious testimony that Mr. Rhys carried about with him; and which his companions seeing, they moved about with softened steps and strengthened hearts all the while. But he was not always tired and silent; and when he was not, he was a most delightful companion, as free to talk as a child and as full of matter as a wise man; and entirely social and sympathetic too in his whole temper and behaviour. He would not enjoy his natural historical discoveries alone; Mrs. Caxton and Eleanor were made to take their full share. The family circle was, quietly, a very lively one; there was no stagnating anywhere. He and Mrs. Caxton had many subjects and interests in common of which they talked freely, and Eleanor was only too glad to listen. There were books and reviews read aloud sometimes, with very pithy discussion of the same; in fact, there was conversation, truly deserving the name; such as Eleanor had never listened to before she came to Plassy, and which she enjoyed hugely. Then the walks after natural objects were on the whole frequent; and Mr. Rhys was sure to ask her to go along; and they were full of delightful pleasure and of nice talk too, though it never happened that they sat down under a tree again to sermonize and

Mr. Rhys never forgot himself again to speak to her by the undignified appellation he once had given her. But Eleanor had got over her shyness of him pretty well, and was inclined to think it quite honour and pleasure enough to be allowed to share his walks; waited very contentedly when he was wrapped up in his own thoughts; wrapped herself up in hers; and was all ready for the talk when it came. With all this she observed that he never distinguished her by any more familiarity than Mrs. Caxton's niece and his daily neighbour at the table and in the family, might demand from a gentleman and Mrs. Caxton's friend and guest. The hills and the valleys around Plassy were very beautiful that summer.

So was Mrs. Caxton's garden. The roses flushed out into bloom, with all their cotemporaries; the terraces down to the river were aglow with richness and profusion of blossoms, and sweet with many fragrances. The old farmhouse itself had become an object of admiration to Eleanor. Long and low, built of dark red stone and roofed with slate, it was now in different parts wreathed and draped in climbing roses and honeysuckle as well as in the ivy which did duty all winter. To stand under these roses at the back of the house, and look down over the gorgeous terraces, to the river and the bridge and the outspread meadows on the other side, stretching away down and up the valley and reaching to the foot of the hills which rose beyond them; to see all this, was to see a combination of natural features rare even in England, though words may not make it seem so.

Mrs. Caxton and Eleanor were there one evening. It was towards the end of the season of "June roses," though indeed it was later than the month of June. Mr. Rhys had been called away to some distance by business, and been detained a week; and this evening he might be expected home. They had missed him very much, Mrs. Caxton and Eleanor. They had missed him exceedingly at prayer-time; they had missed him desolately at meals. To-night the tea-table was spread where he loved to have it; on the tiled floor under the projecting roof before mentioned. A dish was crowned with red and white strawberries in the middle of the table, and Eleanor stood decorating it slowly with ivy leaves and blossoms of white heath.

"It is not certain, my dear, he will come home to-night," Mrs. Caxton said as she watched her.

"No, aunty,"—said Eleanor with a slight start, but then going on with her occupation. "What about it?"

"Nothing. We will enjoy the flowers ourselves."

"But he thought he would be at home to-night, aunt Caxton?"

"He could not be sure. He might easily be detained. You have got over your fear of Mr. Rhys, Eleanor?"

"Aunt Caxton, I don't think I ever feared him!"

"He used to have a 'quieting influence' upon you," Mrs. Caxton said smiling.

"Well,—he does now, ma'am. At least I am sure Mr. Rhys is one of the persons I should never care to contradict."

"I should think not," said Mrs. Caxton quietly. Eleanor had coloured a little.

"But that is not because, merely, I do not think myself wise; because there are other persons before whom I think myself no wiser, whom I *would* contradict—I mean, in a polite way—if it came into my head."

"We shall miss him when he goes," said Mrs. Caxton with a little bit of a sigh. Eleanor wanted to ask a question, but the words did not come. The ornamenting of the strawberry dish was finished. She turned from it, and looked down where the long train of cows came winding through the meadows and over the bridge. Pretty, peaceful, lovely, was this gentle rural scene; what was the connection that made but a step in Eleanor's thoughts between the meadows of Plassy and some far-off islands in distant Polynesia? Eleanor had changed since some time ago. She could understand now why Mr. Rhys wanted to go there; she could comprehend it; she could understand how it was that he was not afraid to go and did not shrink from leaving all this loveliness at her feet. All that was no mystery now; but her thoughts fastened on her aunt's words—how they would "miss him." She was very still, and so was Mrs. Caxton; till a step brought both heads round to the door.

It was only a servant that came out, bringing letters; one for Eleanor, one for Mrs. Caxton. Standing where she was, Eleanor broke hers open. It was from her mother, and it contained something both new and unexpected; an urgent injunction on her to return immediately home. The family were going at once to Brighton, the letter said; Mrs. Powle wished Eleanor to lose no time, in order that her wardrobe might be properly cared for. Thomas was sent with the letter, and her mother desired that Eleanor would immediately on the receipt of it, "without an hour's delay," set off to come home with him. Reasons for this sudden proceeding there were none given; and it came with the suddenness of a hurricane upon Eleanor. Up to this time there had been no intimation of her mother's wish to have her at home again ever; an interval of several weeks had elapsed since any letters; now Mrs. Powle said "she had been gone long enough," and they all wanted her, and must have her at once to go to Brighton. So suddenly affectionate?

Eleanor stood looking at her letter some time after she had ceased to read it, with a face that shewed turmoil. Mrs. Caxton came up to her. Eleanor dropped the letter in her hand, but her eye avoided her aunt's.

"What is all this haste, Eleanor?" Mrs. Caxton said gravely.

"I don't know, ma'am."

"At any rate, my child, you cannot leave me to-night. It is too late."

"Yes, ma'am."

"Does your mother assign no reason for this sudden demand of you? She gives me none."

"She gives me none, ma'am."

"Eleanor——"

It brought Eleanor's eye up, and that brought her head down on Mrs. Caxton's shoulder. Her aunt clasped her tenderly for a moment, and then said,

"Had you not better see your mother's servant, my dear, and give your orders?—and then we will have tea."

Eleanor steadied herself immediately; went out and had an interview with old Thomas, which however brought her no enlightenment; made her arrangements with him, and returned to her aunt. Mrs. Caxton ordered tea; they would not wait for Mr. Rhys any longer. The aunt and niece sat down to the table behind the honeysuckle drapery of the pillars; the sunlight had left the landscape; the breath of the flowers floated up cool and sweet from the terraced garden and waved about them with every stir of the long rose and honeysuckle sprays. Eleanor sat by the table and looked out. Mrs. Caxton poured out the tea and looked at her.

"Aren't you going to take some strawberries, my love?"

"Shall I give you some, aunt Caxton?"

"And yourself, my dear."

She watched while Eleanor slowly broke up the heath and ivy adornment of the strawberry dish, and carefully afterwards replaced the sprays and leaves she had dislodged. It is no harm for a lady's hand to be white;

but travelling from the hand to the face, Mrs. Caxton's eye found too little colour there. Eleanor's cheeks were not generally wanting in a fine healthy tinge. The tinge was fainter than usual to-night. Nevertheless she was eating strawberries with apparent regularity.

"Eleanor, I do not understand this sudden recall. Have you any clue?"

"No ma'am, not the least."

"What arrangements have you made, my dear?"

"For to-morrow morning, ma'am. I had no choice."

"No, my dear, you had not; and I have not a word to say. I hope Mr. Rhys will come back before you go."

Absolute silence on Eleanor's part.

"You would like to bid him good bye before you leave Plassy."

There was a cessation of any attention to the strawberries, and Eleanor's hand took a position which rather hindered observations of her face. You might have heard a slight little sigh come from behind Mrs. Caxton's tea-pot.

"Eleanor, have you learned that the steps of a good man are ordered by the Lord? My love they are not left to our own disposal, and we should not know how to manage it. You are going to do the Lord's work, are you not, wherever you may be?"

"I hope so."

"Then trust him to place you where he wants the work to be done. Can you, Eleanor?"

Eleanor left her seat, came round and knelt down by Mrs. Caxton's side, putting her face in her lap.

"It is not like a good soldier, dear, to wish to play general. You have something now to do at home—perhaps not more for others than for yourself. Are you willing to do it?"

"Don't ask me if I am willing, aunt Caxton! I have been too happy——But I shall be willing."

"That is all we live for, my dear—to do the Lord's work; and I am sure that in service as in everything else, God loves a cheerful giver. Let us give him that now, Eleanor; and trust him for the rest. My child, you are not the only one who has to give up something."

And though Mrs. Caxton said little more than that word on the subject of what Eleanor's departure cost herself, she manifested it in a different way by the kind incessant solicitude and care with which she watched over Eleanor and helped her and kept with her that night and the next morning. Eleanor made her preparations and indulged in very few words. There was too much to think of, in the last evening's society, the last night in her happy room, the last morning hours. And yet Eleanor did very little thinking. She was to go immediately after breakfast. The early prayers were over, and the aunt and niece were left by themselves a moment before the meal was served.

"And what shall I say to Mr. Rhys?" enquired Mrs. Caxton, as they stood silent together. Eleanor hesitated, and hesitated; and finally said,

"I believe, nothing, ma'am."

"You have given me messages for so many other people, you know," said Mrs. Caxton quietly.

"Yes, ma'am. I don't know how to make a message for him."

"I think he will feel it," said Mrs. Caxton in the same manner.

Then she saw, for her eyes were good, the lightning flash of emotion which worked in Eleanor's face. Proud self-control kept it down, and she stood motionless, though it did not prevent the perceptible paling of her cheek which Mrs. Caxton had noticed last night. She stood silent, then she said slowly,—

"If I thought *that*—You may give him any message for me that you think good, aunt Caxton."

The breakfast arrived, and few more words passed on any topic. Another hour, and Eleanor was on her journey.

She felt in a confusion of spirits and would not let herself think, till they reached her stopping place for the night. And then, instead of thinking, Eleanor to say the truth could do nothing but weep. It was her time for tears; to-morrow would end such an indulgence. At an early hour the next day she met her father's carriage which had been sent so far for her.; and the remaining hours of her way Eleanor did think. Her thoughts are her own. But at the bottom of some that were sorrowful lay one deep subject of joy. That she was not going helmet-less into the fight which she felt might be before her. Of that she had an inward presentiment, though what form it would take she was entirely uncertain.

Julia was the first person that met her, and that meeting was rapturous.

"O Nell! it has been so dreadful and dull since you have been gone! I'm so glad to have you home! I'm so glad to have you home!"—she repeated with her arms round Eleanor's neck.

"But what are you going to Brighton for?" said Eleanor after the first salutations had satisfied the first eagerness of the sisters.

"O I don't know. Papa isn't just well, I believe; and mamma thought it would do him good. Mamma's in here."

It was to Eleanor's relief that her reception in this quarter also was perfectly cordial. Mrs. Powle seemed to have forgotten, or to be disposed to forget, old causes of trouble; and to begin again as if nothing had happened.

"You look well, Eleanor. Bless me, I never saw your complexion better! but how your hair is dressed! That isn't the way now; but you'll get to rights soon. I've got a purple muslin for you that will be beautiful. Your whole wardrobe will want attention, but I have everything ready—dress-maker and all—only waiting for you. Think of your being gone seven months and more! But never mind—we'll let bygones be bygones. I am not going to rake up anything. We'll go to Brighton and have everything pleasant."

"How soon, mamma?"

"Just as soon as I can get you dressed. And Eleanor! I wish you would immediately take a review of all your wardrobe and all I have got for you, and see if I have omitted anything."

"What has put you into the notion of Brighton, mamma?"

"Everybody is there now—and we want a change. I think it will do your father good."

To see her father was the next thing; and here there was some comfort. The squire was undoubtedly rejoiced to see his daughter and welcomed her back right heartily. Made much of her in his way. He was the only one too who cared much to hear of Mrs. Caxton and her way of life and her farm. The squire did care. Eleanor was kept a long time answering questions and giving details. It cost her some hard work.

"She is a good woman, is my sister Caxton," said the Squire; "and she has pluck enough for half a dozen. The only thing I have against her is her being a Methodist. She hasn't made a Methodist of you, hey, Eleanor?"

"I don't think she has, papa," Eleanor answered slowly.

"That's the only fault *I* have to find with her," the Squire went on; "but I suppose women must have an empty corner of their heads, where they will stick fancies if they don't stick flowers. I think flowers are the most becoming of the two. Wears a brown gown always, don't she?"

"No, sir."

"I thought they did," said the Squire; "but she's a clever woman, for all that, or she wouldn't carry on that business of the farm as she does. Your mother don't like the farm; but I think my sister is right. Better be independent and ask leave of nobody. Well, you must get dressed, must you. I am glad to have you home, child!"

"Why are we going to leave home, papa?"

"St. George and the Dragon! Ask your mother."

So Eleanor did not get much wiser on the subject till dinner-time; nor then either, though it was nearly the only thing talked about, both directly and indirectly. A great weariness came over her, as the contrast rose up of Mrs. Caxton's dinner-table and the three faces round it; with the sweet play of talk, on things natural or philosophical, religious or civil, but always sensible, fresh, and original and strong. Always that; the party might lapse into silence; if one of them was tired it often did; but when the words came again, they came with a ready life and purpose—with a sort of perfume of love and purity—that it made Eleanor's heart ache now to think of. Her mother was descanting on lodgings, on the people already at Brighton, or coming there; on dresses ready and unready; and to vary this topic the Squire complained that his wine was not cooled properly. Eleanor sank into silence and then into extreme depression of spirits; which grew more and more, until she caught her little sister's eye looking at her wistfully. Julia had hardly said a word all dinner-time. The look smote Eleanor's conscience. "Is this the way I am doing the work given me?" she thought; "this selfish forgetting of all others in myself? Am I standing in my post like a good soldier? Is *this* 'pleasing all men for their good?'" Conscience thumped like a hammer; and Eleanor roused up, entered into what was going, talked and made herself pleasant to both father and mother, who grew sunshiny under the influence. Mrs. Powle eat the remainder of her dinner with more appetite; and the Squire declared Eleanor had grown handsome and Plassy had done her no harm. But Julia looked and listened and said never a word. It was very hard work to Eleanor, though it brought its reward as she went along, not only in comments but in the sense of duty performed. She would not run away from her post; she kept at it; when her father had gone away to smoke she stayed by her mother; till Mrs. Powle dropped off into her usual after dinner nap in her chair. Eleanor sat still a minute or two longer, then made an escape. She sought her old garden, by the way of her old summer parlour. Things were not changed there, except that the garden was a little neglected. It brought painful things back, though the flowers were sweet and the summer sunset glow was over them all. So it used to be in old times. So it used to be in nearer times, last summer. And now was another change. Eleanor paced slowly down one walk and up another, looking sorrowfully at her old friends, the roses, carnations and petunias, which looked at her as cheerfully as ever; when a hand touched hers and she found Julia at her side.

"Eleanor," she said wistfully, "are you *sorry* to be at home again?"

"I am glad to see you, darling; and papa, and mamma."

"But you don't look glad. Was it so much pleasanter where you have been?"

Eleanor struggled with herself.

"It was very different, Julia—and there were things that you and I both love, that there are not here."

"What?"

"Here all is for the world, Julia; there, at Plassy, nothing is for the world. I feel the difference just at first—I suppose I shall get a little used to it presently."

"I have not thought so much about all that," said Julia soberly, "since Mr. Rhys went away. But you must have loved aunt Caxton very much, Eleanor, to make you sorry to come home."

Julia spoke almost sadly. Eleanor felt bitterly reproached. Was there not work at home here for her to do! Yet she could hardly speak at first. Putting her arm round Julia she drew her down beside her on a green bank and took her little sister in her arms.

"You and I will help each other, Julia, will we not?"

"In what?"

"To love Christ, and please him."

"Why, do you love him?" said Julia. "Are you like Mr. Rhys."

"Not much. But I do love the same Master he loves, Julia; and I have come home to serve him. You will help me?"

"Mamma don't like all that," remarked Julia.

Eleanor sighed. The burden on her heart seemed growing heavy. Julia half rose up and putting both arms round her neck covered her lips with kisses.

"You don't seem like yourself!" she said; "and you look as grave as if you had found us all dead. Eleanor —are you afraid?" she said with an earnest look.

"Afraid of what, dear?"

"Of that man—afraid of Mr. Carlisle?"

"No, I am not afraid of him, or of anything. Besides, he is hundreds of miles away, in Switzerland or somewhere."

"No he isn't; he is here."

"What do you mean by 'here?'"

"In England, I mean. He isn't at the Priory; but he was here at the Lodge the other day."

Eleanor's heart made two or three springs one way and another.

"No dear, I am not afraid of him," she repeated, with a quietness that was convincing; and Julia passed to other subjects. Eleanor did not forget that one; and as Julia ran on with her talk, she pondered it, and made a secret thanksgiving that she was so escaped both from danger and from fear. Nevertheless she could not help hinking about the subject. It seemed that Mr. Carlisle's wound had healed very rapidly. And moreover she had not given him credit for finding any attraction in that house, beyond her own personal presence in it. However, she reflected that Mr. Carlisle was busy in politics, and perhaps cultivated her father. They went in again, to take up the subject of Brighton.

And what followed? Muslins, flowers, laces, bonnets and ribbands. They were very irksome days to Eleanor, that were spent in getting ready for Brighton; and the thought of the calm purity of Plassy with its different occupations sometimes came over her and for the moment unnerved her hands for the finery they had to handle. Once Eleanor took a long rambling ride alone on her old pony; she did not try it again. Business and bustle was better, at least was less painful, than such a time for thinking and feeling. So the dresses were made, and they went to Brighton.

CHAPTER IV.

"In the world's broad field of battle,
In the bivouac of Life,
Be not like dumb, driven cattle!
Be a hero in the strife!

ELEANOR was at once plunged into a whirl of engagements, with acquaintances new and old. And the former class multiplied very rapidly. Mrs. Powle's fair curls hung on either side of her face with almost their full measure of complacency, as she saw and beheld her daughter's successful attractions. It was true. Eleanor was found to have something unique about her; some said it was her beauty, some said it was her manners; some insisted it was neither, but had a deeper origin; at any rate she was fresh. Something out of the common line and that piqued curiosity, was delightful; and in despite of her very moderate worldly advantages, compared with many others who were there, Eleanor Powle seemed likely to become in a little while the belle of Brighton. Certain rumours which were afloat no doubt facilitated and expedited this progress of things. Happily Eleanor did not hear them.

The rush of engagements and whirl of society at first was very wearying and painful to her. No heart had Eleanor to give to it. Only by putting a force upon herself, to please her father and mother, she managed to enter with some spirit into the amusements going forward, in which she was expected to take an active part. Perhaps this very fact had something to do with the noble and sweet disengagedness of manner which marked her unlike those about her, in a world where self-interest of some sort is the ruling motive. It was not Eleanor's world; it had nothing to do with the interests that were dear in her regard; and something of that carelessness which she brought to it conferred a grace that the world imitates in vain. Eleanor found however after a little, that the rush and hurry of her life and of all the people about her had a contagion in it; her own thoughts were beginning to be absorbed in what absorbed everybody; her own cherished interests were getting pushed into a corner. Eleanor resolved to make a stand then, and secure time enough to herself to let her own inner life have play and breathing room. But it was very difficult to make such a stand. Mrs. Powle ever stood like a watchman at the door to drive Eleanor out when she wanted to be in. Time! there seemed to be no time.

Eleanor had heard that Mr. Carlisle was expected at Brighton; so she was not greatly surprised one evening to find herself in the same room with him. It was at a public assembly. The glances that her curiosity cast, found him moving about among people very like, and in very exactly the manner of his old self. No difference that she could see. She wondered whether he would have the audacity to come and speak to her. Audacity was not a point in which Mr. Carlisle was failing. He came; and as he came others scattered away; melted off, and left her alone.

He came with the best air in the world; a little conscious, a little apologetic, wholly respectful, not altogether devoid of the old familiarity. He offered his hand; did not to be sure detain hers, which would have been inconvenient in a public assembly; but he detained *her*, falling into talk with an ease or an effrontery which it was impossible not to admire. And Eleanor admired him involuntarily. Certainly this man had capacities. He did not detain her too long; passed away as easily as he had come up; but returned again in the course of the evening to offer her some civility; and it was Mr. Carlisle who put her mother and herself into their carriage. Eleanor looked for a remark from her mother on the subject during their drive home; but Mrs. Powle made none.

The next evening he was at Mrs. Powle's rooms, where a small company was gathered every Tuesday. He might be excused if he watched, more than he wished to be seen watching, the sweet unconscious grace and ease with which Eleanor moved and spoke. Others noticed it, but Mr. Carlisle drew comparisons; and found to his mystification that her six months on a cheese farm had returned Eleanor with an added charm of eye and manner, for which he could not account; which he could not immediately define. She was not expecting to see him this time, for she started a little when he presented himself. He came with the same pleasant expression that he had worn last night.

"Will you excuse me for remarking, that your winter has done you good?" he said.

"Yes. I know it has," Eleanor answered.

"With your old frankness, you acknowledge it?"

"Willingly."

Her accent was so simple and sweet, the attraction was irresistible. He sat down by her.

"I hope you are as willing as I am to acknowledge that all our last winter's work was not good. We ex changed letters."

"Hardly, Mr. Carlisle."

"Will you allow me to say, that I am ashamed of my part in that transaction. Eleanor, I want you to forget it, and to receive me as if it had not happened."

Eleanor was in a mixture of astonishment and doubt, as to how far his words might be taken. In the doubt, she hesitated one instant. Another person, a lady, drew near, and Mr. Carlisle yielded to her the place he had been occupying. The opportunity for an answer was gone. And though he was often near her during the evening, he did not recur again to the subject, and Eleanor could not. But the little bit of dialogue left her something to think of.

She had occasion often to think of it. Mr. Carlisle was everywhere, of course, in Brighton; at least he was in Eleanor's everywhere; she saw him a great deal, and was a little struck and puzzled by his manner. He was very often in her immediate company; often attending upon her; it constantly happened, she could not tell how, that his arm was the one to which she was consigned, in walks and evening escorts. In a measure, he assumed his old place beside her; his attentions were constant, gracefully and freely paid; they just lacked the expression which would have obliged and enabled her to throw them off. It was rather the manner of a brother than of a lover; but it was familiar and confidential beyond what those assume that are not brothers. Whatever it meant, it dissatisfied Eleanor. The world, perhaps the gentleman himself, might justly think if she permitted this state of things that she allowed the conclusions naturally to be drawn from it. She determined to withdraw herself. It was curiously and inexplicably difficult. Too easily, too gracefully, too much as a matter of course, things fell into train, for Eleanor often to do anything to alter the train. But she was determined.

"Eleanor, do you know everybody is waiting?" Mrs. Powle exclaimed one morning bursting into Eleanor's room. "There's the whole riding party—and you are not ready!"

"No, mamma. I am not going."

"Not going! Just put on your riding habit as quick as you can—Julia, get her hat!—you said you would go, and I have no notion of disappointing people like that. Get yourself ready immediately—do you hear me?"

"But mamma—"

"Put on your habit!—then talk if you like. It's all nonsense. What are you doing? studying? Nonsense! there's time enough for studying when you are at home. Now be quick!"

"But mamma—"

"Well? Put your hair lower, Eleanor; that will not do."

"Mamma, isn't Mr. Carlisle there?"

"Mr. Carlisle? What if he is? I hope he is. You are well in that hat, Eleanor."

"Mamma, if Mr. Carlisle is there,—"

"Hold your tongue, Eleanor!—take your whip and go. They are all waiting. You may talk to me when you come back, but now you must go. I should think Mr. Carlisle would like to be of the party, for there isn't such another figure on the ride. Now kiss me and go. You are a good girl."

Mrs. Powle said it with some feeling. She had never found Eleanor so obediently tractable as since her return; she had never got from her such ready and willing coöperation, even in matters that her mother knew were not after Eleanor's heart, as now when her heart was less in them than ever. And at this moment she was gratified by the quiet grave obedience rendered her, in doing what she saw plainly enough Eleanor did not like to do. She followed her daughter down stairs with a proud heart.

It happened again, as it was always happening, that Mr. Carlisle was Eleanor's special attendant. Eleanor meditated possible ways of hindering this in future; but for the present there was no remedy. Mr. Carlisle put her on her horse; it was not till she was taking the reins in her left hand that something struck her with a sense of familiarity.

"What horse is this?" she asked.

"No other than your old friend and servant—I hope you have not forgotten her. She has not forgotten you."

Eleanor perceived that. As surely as it was Black Maggie, Maggie knew her; and displeased though Eleanor was with the master, she could not forbear a little caress of recognition to the beautiful creature he had once given her. Maggie was faultless; she and Eleanor were accustomed to each other; it was an undeniable pleasure to be so mounted again, as Eleanor could not but acknowledge to herself during the first few dainty dancing steps that Maggie made with her wonted burden. Nevertheless it was a great deal too much like old times that were destroyed; and glancing at Mr. Carlisle Eleanor saw that he was on Tippoo, and furthermore that there was a sparkle in his eye which meant hope, or triumph. Something put Eleanor on her mettle; she rode well that day. She rode with a careless grace and ease that even drew a compliment from Mr. Carlisle; but beyond that, his companion at first gave him little satisfaction. She was grave and cold to all his conversational efforts. However, there she was on his black mare; and Mr. Carlisle probably found an antidote to whatever discouragement she threw in his way. Chance threw something else in his way.

They had turned into one of the less frequented streets of the town, in their way to get out of it, when Eleanor's eye was seized by a figure on the sidewalk. It startled her inexpressibly; and before she could be sure her eyes did not deceive her the figure had almost passed, or they had almost passed the person. But in passing he had raised his hat; she knew then he had recognized her, as she had known him; and he had recognized her in such company. And he was in Brighton. Without a moment for thought or delay, Eleanor wheeled her horse's head sharply round and in one or two smart steps brought herself alongside of Mr. Rhys. He stopped, came up to her stirrup and shook hands. He looked grave, Eleanor thought. She hastened to speak.

"I could not pass you, Mr. Rhys. I had to leave Plassy without bidding you good bye."

"I am glad to meet you now," he said,—"before I go."

"Do you leave Brighton very soon?"

"To-morrow. I go up to London, and in a few days I expect to sail from there."

"For —?"

"Yes,—for my post in the Southern Ocean. I have an unexpected opportunity."

Eleanor was silent. She could not find anything to say. She knew also that Mr. Carlisle had wheeled his horse after her, and that Tippoo was taking steps somewhere in her close neighbourhood. But she sat motionless, unable to move as well as to speak.

"I must not detain you," said Mr. Rhys. "Do you find it as easy to live well at Brighton as at Plassy?"

Eleanor answered a low and grave "no;" bending down over her saddlebow.

"Keep that which is committed to thy charge," he said gently. "Farewell—and the Lord bless you!"

Eleanor had bared her gauntleted hand; he gave it the old earnest grasp, lifted his hat, and went on his way. Eleanor turned her horse's head again and found herself alongside of Mr. Carlisle. She rode on briskly, pointing out to him how far ahead were the rest of the party.

"Was not your friend somebody that I know?" he enquired as soon as there was a convenient pause.

"I am sure I do not know," said Eleanor. "I do not

know how good your memory may be. He is the gentleman that was my brother's tutor at home—some time ago."

"I thought I remembered. Is he tutoring some one else now?"

"I should think not. He just tells me he is about to sail for the South Seas. Mr. Carlisle, Maggie has a very nice mouth."

"Her mistress has a very nice hand," he answered, bending forward to Maggie's bridle so that he could look up in Eleanor's face. "Only you let her rein be too slack, as of old. You like her better than Tippoo?"

"Tippoo is beyond my management."

"I am not going to let you say that. You shall mount Tippoo next time, and become acquainted with your own powers. You are not afraid of anything?"

"Yes, I am."

"You did not use it."

"Well I have not grown cowardly," said Eleanor; "but I am afraid of mounting Tippoo; and what I am afraid of, Mr. Carlisle, I will not do."

"Just the reverse maxim from that which I should have expected from you. Do you say your friend there is going to the South Seas?"

"Mr. Rhys?" said Eleanor, turning her face full upon him.

"If that is his name—yes. Why does he not stick to tutoring?"

"Does anybody stick to tutoring that can help it?"

"I should think not; but then as a tutor he would be in the way of better things; he could mount to something higher."

"I believe he has some expectation of that sort in going to the Pacific," said Eleanor. She spoke it with a most commonplace coolness.

"Seems a very roundabout road to promotion," said

Mr. Carlisle, watching Eleanor's hand and stealthily her face; "but I suppose he knows best. Your friend is not a Churchman, is he?"

"No."

"I remember him as a popular orator of great powers. What is he leaving England for?"

"You assume somewhat too much knowledge on my part of people's designs," said Eleanor carelessly. "I must suppose that he likes work on the other side of the world better than to work here;—for some reason or other."

"How the reason should be promotion, puzzles me," said her companion; "but that may be owing to prejudice on my part. I do not know how to conceive of promotion out of the regular line. In England and in the Church. To be sent to India to take a bishopric seems to me a descent in the scale. Have you this feeling?"

"About bishoprics?" said Eleanor smiling. "They are not in my line, you know."

"Don't be wicked! Have you this feeling about England?"

"If a bishopric in India were offered me?—"

"Well, yes! Would you accept it?"

"I really never had occasion to consider the subject before. It is such a very new thought, you see. But I will tell you, I should think the humblest curacy in England to be chosen rather,—unless for the sake of a wider sphere of doing good."

"Do you know," said Mr. Carlisle, looking very contented and coming up closer, "your bridle hand has improved? It is very nearly faultless. What have you been riding this winter?"

"A wiry little pony."

"Honour, Eleanor!" said Mr. Carlisle laughing and bringing his hand again near enough to throw over a lock of Maggie's mane which had fallen on the wrong side. "I am really curious."

"Well I tell you the truth. But Mr. Carlisle, I wonder you people in parliament do not stir yourselves up to right some wrongs. People ought to live, if they are curates; and there was one where I was last winter—an excellent one—living, or starving, I don't know which you would call it, on thirty pounds a year."

Mr. Carlisle entered into the subject; and questions moral, legislative, and ecclesiastical, were discussed by him and Eleanor with great earnestness and diligence; by him at least with singular delight. Eleanor kept up the conversation with unflagging interest; it was broken by a proposal on Mr. Carlisle's part for a gallop, to which she willingly agreed; held her part in the ensuing scamper with perfect grace and steadiness, and as soon as it was over, plunged Mr. Carlisle deep again into reform.

"Nobody has had such honour as I to-day," he assured her as he took her down from her horse. "I shall see you to-night, of course?"

"Of course. I suppose," said Eleanor.

It cannot be said that Eleanor made any effort to change the "of course," though the rest of the day as usual was swallowed up in a round of engagements. There was no breathing time, and the evening occasion was a public one. Mrs. Powle was in a great state of satisfaction with her daughter to-day; Eleanor had shunned no company nor exertion, had carried an unusual spirit into all; and a minute with Mr. Carlisle after the ride had shewed him in a sort of exultant mood. She looked over Eleanor's dress critically when they were about leaving home for the evening's entertainment. It was very simple indeed; yet Mrs. Powle in the depth of her heart could not find that anything was wanting to the effect.

Nor could a yet more captious critic, Mr. Carlisle;

who was on the ground before them and watched and observed a little while from a distance. Admiration and passion were roused within him, as he watched anew what he had already seen in Eleanor's manner since she came to Brighton; that grace of absolute ease and unconsciousness, which only the very highest breeding can successfully imitate. No Lady Rythdale, he was obliged to confess, that ever lived, had better advanced the honours of her house, than would this one; could she be persuaded to accept the position. This manner did not use to be Eleanor's; how had she got it on the borders of Wales? Neither was the sweetness of that smile to be seen on her lip in the times gone by; and a little gravity was wanting then, which gave a charm of dignity to the exquisite poise which whether of character or manner was so at home with her now. Was she too grave? The question rose; but he answered it with a negative. Her smile came readily, and it was the sweeter for not being always seen. His meditations were interrupted by a whisper at his elbow.

"She will not dance!"

"Who will not?" said he, finding himself face to face with Mrs. Powle.

"Eleanor. She will not. I am afraid it is one of her new notions."

Mr. Carlisle smiled a peculiar smile. "Hardly a fault, I think, Mrs. Powle. I am not inclined to quarrel with it."

"You do not see any faults at all, I believe," said the lady. "Now I am more discerning."

Mr. Carlisle did not speak his thoughts, which were complimentary only in one direction, to say truth. He went off to Eleanor, and prevented any more propositions of dancing for the rest of the evening. He could not monopolize her, though. He was obliged to see her attention divided in part among other people, and to take a share which though perfectly free and sufficiently gracious, gave him no advantage in that respect over several others. The only advantage he could make sure of was that of attending Eleanor home. The evening left him an excited man, not happy in his mind.

Eleanor, having quitted her escort, went slowly up the stairs; bade her mother good night; went into her own room and locked the door. Then methodically she took off the several parts of her evening attire and laid them away; put on a dressing-gown, threw her window open, and knelt down by it.

The stars kept watch over the night. A pleasant fresh breeze blew in from the sea. They were Eleanor's only companions, and they never missed her from the window the whole night long. I am bound to say, that the morning found her there.

But nights so spent make a heavy draft on the following day. In spite of all that cold water could do in the way of refreshment, in spite of all that the morning cup of tea could do, Eleanor was obliged to confess to a headache.

"Why Eleanor, child, you look dreadfully!" said Mrs. Powle, who came into her room and found her lying down. "You are as white!—and black rings under your eyes. You will never be able to go with the riding party this morning."

"I am afraid not, mamma. I am sorry. I would go if I could; but I believe I must lie still. Then I shall be fit for this evening, perhaps."

She was not; but that one day of solitude and silence was all that Eleanor took for herself. The next day she joined the riders again; and from that time held herself back from no engagement to which her mother or Mr. Carlisle urged her.

Mr. Carlisle felt it with a little of his old feeling of pride. It was the only thing in which Eleanor could be said to give the feeling much chance; for while she did not reject his attendance, which she could not easily do, nor do at all without first vanquishing her mother; and while she allowed a certain remains of the old wonted familiarity, she at the same never gave Mr. Carlisle any reason to think that he had regained the least power over her. She received him well, but as she received a hundred others. He was her continual attendant, but he never felt that it was by Eleanor's choice; and he knew sometimes that it was by her choice that he was thrown out of his office. She bewildered him with her sweet dignity, which was more utterly unmanageable than any form of pride or passion. The pride and passion were left to be Mr. Carlisle's own. Pride was roused, that he was stopped by so gentle a barrier in his advances; and passion was stimulated, by uncertainty not merely, but by the calm grace and indefinable sweetness which he did not remember in Eleanor, well as he had loved her before. He loved her better now. That charm of manner was the very thing to captivate Mr. Carlisle; he valued it highly; and did not appreciate it the less because it baffled him.

"He's ten times worse than ever," Mrs. Powle said exultingly to her husband. "I believe he'd go through fire and water to make sure of her."

"And how's she?" growled the Squire.

"She's playing with him, girl-fashion," said Mrs. Powle chuckling. "She is using her power."

"What is she using it for?" said the Squire threateningly.

"O to enjoy herself, and make him value her properly. She will come round by and by."

How was Eleanor? The world had opportunities of judging most of the time, as far as the outside went; yet there were still a few times of the day which the world did not intrude upon; and of those there was an hour before breakfast, when Eleanor was pretty secure against interruption even from her mother. Mrs. Powle was a late riser. Julia, who was very much cast away at Brighton and went wandering about like a rudderless vessel, found out that Eleanor was dressed and using the sunshine long before anybody else in the house knew the day was begun. It was a golden discovery. Eleanor was alone, and Julia could have her to herself a little while at least. Even if Eleanor was bent on reading or writing, still it was a joy to be near her, to watch her, to smooth her soft hair, and now and then break her off from other occupations to have a talk.

"Eleanor," said Julia one day, a little while after these oases in time had been discovered by her, "what has become of Mr. Rhys? do you know?"

"He has gone," said Eleanor. She was sitting by her open window, a book open on her lap. She looked out of the window as she spoke.

"Gone? Do you mean he has gone away from England? You don't mean that?"

"Yes."

"To that dreadful place?"

"What dreadful place?"

"Where he was going, you know,—somewhere. Are you sure he has gone, Eleanor?"

"Yes. I saw it in the paper—the mention of his going—He and two others."

"And has he gone to that horrible place?"

"Yes, I suppose so. That is where he wished to go."

"I dont see how he could!" said Julia. "How could he! where the people are so bad!—and leave England?"

"Why Julia, have you forgotten? Don't you know whose servant Mr. Rhys is?"

"Yes," said Julia mutteringly,— "but I should think he would be afraid. Why the people there are as wicked as they can be."

"That is no reason why he should be afraid. What harm could they they do to him?"

"Why!—they could kill him, easily," said Julia.

"And would that be great harm to Mr. Rhys?" said Eleanor looking round at her. "What if they did, and he were called quick home to the court of his King,—do you think his reception there would be a sorrowful thing?"

"Why Nell," said Julia, "do you mean heaven?"

"Do you not think that is Mr. Rhys's home?"

"I haven't thought much about it at all," said Julia laying her head down on Eleanor's shoulder. "You see, nobody talked to me ever since he went away; and mamma talks everything else."

"Come here in the mornings, and we'll talk about it," said Eleanor. Her voice was a little husky.

"Shall we?" said Julia rousing up again. "But Eleanor, what are your eyes full for? Did *you* love Mr. Rhys too?"

It was an innocent question; but instead of answering, Eleanor turned again to the window. She sat with her hand pressed upon her mouth, while the full eyes brimmed and ran over, and filled again; and drop after drop plashed upon the window-sill. It was impossible to help it, for that minute; and Julia looked on wonderingly.

"O Nell," she repeated almost awe-struck, "what is it? What has made you sorry too?—" But she had to wait a little while for her answer.

"He was a good friend to me," said Eleanor at last, wiping her eyes; "and I suppose it is not very absurd to cry for a friend that is gone, that one will never see again."

"Maybe he will come back some time," said Julia sorrowfully.

"Not while there is work there for him to do," said

Eleanor. She waited a little while. There was some difficulty in going on. When she did speak her tone was clear and firm.

"Julia, shall we follow the Lord as Mr. Rhys does?"

"How?"

"By doing whatever Jesus gives us to do."

"What has he given us to do?" said Julia.

"If you come to my room in the mornings, we will read and find out. And we will pray, and ask to be taught."

Julia's countenance lightened and clouded with alternate changes.

"Will you, Eleanor! But what have we got to do?"

"Love Jesus."

"Well I—O I did use to, Eleanor! and I think I do now; only I have forgotten to think about anything, this ever so long."

"Then if we love him, we shall find plenty of things to do for him."

"What, Eleanor? I would like to do something."

"Just whatever he gives us, Julia. Come, darling,—have you not duties?"

"Duties?—"

"Have you not things that it is your duty to do?—or not to do?"

"Studies!" said Julia. "But I don't like them."

"For Jesus' sake?"

Julia burst into tears. Eleanor's tone was so loving and gentle, it reached the memories that had been slumbering.

"How can I do them for him, Eleanor?" she asked, half perversely still.

"'Whatsoever ye do, do all in the name of the Lord Jesus.' So he has told us."

"But my studies, Eleanor? how can I?"

"Who gave you the opportunity, Julia?"

"Well—I know."

"Well, if God has given you the opportunity, do you think he means it for nothing? He has work for you to do, Julia, some time, for which you will want all these things that you have a chance of learning now; if you miss the chance, you will certainly not be ready for the work."

"Why, Eleanor!—that's funny."

"What is it?"

"Why I never thought of such a thing."

"What did you think?"

"I thought I had French and German to study, for instance, because everybody else learned French and German. I did not think there was any use in it."

"You forgot who had given you them to learn."

"No, mamma would have it. Just her notion. Papa didn't care."

"But dear Julia, you forget who has made it your duty to please mamma's notions. And you forget who it is that has given you your place in the world. You might have been born in poverty, with quite other lessons to learn, and quite other work in the world."

"You talk just as queer as if you were Mr. Rhys himself," said Julia. "I never heard of such things. Do you suppose all the girls who are learning French and German at school—all the girls in England—have the same sort of work to do? that they will want it for?"

"No, not all the same. But God never gives the preparation without the occasion."

"Then suppose they do not make the preparation?"

"Then when the occasion comes, they will not be ready for it. When their work is given them to do, they will be found wanting."

"It's so queer!" said Julia.

"What?"

"To think such things about lessons.

"You may think such things about everything. Whatever God gives you, he gives you to use in some way for him."

"But how can I possibly know *how*, Eleanor?"

"Come to me in the mornings, and you and I will try to find out."

"Did you say, I must please all mamma's notions?"

"Certainly—all you can."

"But I like papa's notions a great deal better than mamma's."

"You must try to meet both," said Eleanor smiling.

"I do not like a great many of mamma's notions. I don't think there is any sense in them."

"But God likes obedience, Julia. He has bid you honour mamma and papa. Do it for him."

"Do *you* mean to please all mamma's notions?" said Julia sharply.

"All that I can, certainly."

"Well it is one of her notions that Mr. Carlisle should get you to the Priory after all. Are you going to let her? Are you going to let him, I mean?"

"No."

"Then if it is your duty to please mamma's notions, why mustn't you please this one?"

"Because here I have my duty to others to think of."

"To whom?" said Julia as quick as lightning.

"To myself—and to Mr. Carlisle."

"Mr. Carlisle!" said Julia. "I'll be bound he thinks your duty to him would make you do whatever he likes."

"It happens that I take a different view of the subject."

"But Eleanor, what work do you suppose I have to do in the world, that I shall want French and German for? real work, I mean?"

"I can't tell. But I know *now* you have a beautiful example to set?

"Of what? learning my lessons well?"

"Of whatever is lovely and of good report. Of whatever will please Jesus."

Julia put her arms round her sister's neck and hid her face there.

"I am going to give you a word to remember today; keep it with you dear. 'Whatsoever ye do, do all in the name of the Lord Jesus.' Just think of that, whether you are busy or not busy. And we will ask the Lord to make us so full of his love, that we cannot help it."

They knelt and prayed together; after which Julia gave her sister a great many earnest caresses; and they went down to breakfast a much comforted pair.

CHAPTER V.

"London makes mirth! but I know God hears
The sobs i' the dark, and the dropping of tears."

THE morning meetings were kept up. Julia had always been very fond of her sister; now she almost worshipped her. She would get as close as possible, put her arm round Eleanor's waist, and sometimes lay her head on her shoulder; and so listen to the reading and join in the talking. The talks were always finished with prayer; and at first it not seldom happened that Eleanor's prayer became choked with tears. It happened so often that Julia remarked upon it; and after that it never happened again.

"Eleanor, can you see much use in my learning to dance?" was a question which Julia propounded one morning.

"Not much."

"Mamma says I shall go to dancing school next winter."

"Next winter! What, at Brompton?"

"O we are going to London after we go from here. So mamma says. Why didn't you know it?"

Eleanor remained silent.

"Now what good is that going to do?" Julia went on. "What work is that to fit me for, Eleanor?—dancing parties?"

"I hope it will not fit you for those," the elder sister replied gravely.

"Why not? don't you go to them?"

"I am obliged to go sometimes—I never take part."

"Why not Eleanor? Why don't you? you can dance."

"Read," said Eleanor, pointing to the words. Julia read.

"'Whatsoever ye do, do all in the name of the Lord Jesus; giving thanks to God and the Father by him.'—Well Eleanor?"

"I cannot find anything I can do in the Lord's service at such places, except to stand by and say by my manner that I do not enjoy them nor approve of them."

"That won't hinder other people enjoying them, though."

"I do not think people enjoy them much. You and I have a hundred times as much fun in one good scamper over the moor. Dear old moor! I wish we were back again. But other people's doing is not my business."

"Then what makes you go, Eleanor?"

"Mamma would be so exceedingly vexed if I did not. I mean to get out of it soon—as soon as I can."

"Do you think you will, in London?"

Eleanor was silent, and thoughtful.

"Well, I know one thing," said Julia,—"I am not going to dancing school. Mamma says it will make me graceful; and I think I am as graceful as other people now—as most other people. I don't think I am as graceful as you are. Don't you think so, Eleanor?"

Eleanor smiled, soberly enough.

"Eleanor, must I go to dancing school?"

"Why do you wish not to go?"

"Because you think it is wrong."

"Darling, you cannot displease mamma for such a reason. You must always honour every wish of hers, except you thought that honouring her would be to dishonour or displease the Lord."

The words were spoken and listened to with intense feeling and earnestness on both sides; and the tears came back in Eleanor's prayer that morning.

With the world at large, things maintained a very unaltered position during the rest of the stay at Brighton. Mr. Carlisle kept his position, advancing a little where it seemed possible. Eleanor kept hers; neither advancing nor retreating. She was very good to Mr. Carlisle; she did not throw him off; she gave him no occasion to complain of an unready talker or an unwilling companion. A little particular kindness indeed she had for him, left from the old times. Julia would have been much mystified by the brightness and life and spirit Eleanor shewed in company, and in his company especially; which her little sister did not see in their private intercourse alone. Nevertheless, Mr. Carlisle's passion was rather stimulated by difficulty than fed by hope; though hope lived high sometimes. All that Eleanor gave him she gave him readily, and as readily gave to others; she gave coolly too, as coolly as she gave to others. Mr. Carlisle took in many things the place of an accepted suitor; but never in Eleanor's manner, he knew. It chafed him, it piqued him; it made him far more than ever bent on obtaining her hand; her heart he could manage then. Just now it was beyond his management; and when Mrs. Powle smiled congratulation, Mr. Carlisle bit his lip. However, he had strong aids; he did not despair. He hoped something from London.

So they all went to London. Eleanor could gain no satisfactory explanation why. Only her mother asserted that her father's health must have the advice of London physicians. The Squire himself was not much more explicit. That his health was not good, however, was true; the Squire was very unlike his hearty, boisterous, independent self. He moped, and he suffered too. Eleanor could not help thinking he would have suffered less, as he certainly would have moped less, at home; and an unintelligible grunt and grumble now and then seemed to confirm her view of the case; but there they were, fixed in London, and Eleanor was called upon to enter into all sorts of London gayeties, of which always Mr. Carlisle made part and parcel.

Eleanor made a stand, and declined to go to places where she could not enjoy nor sympathize with what was done. She could not think it duty to go to the opera, or the theatre, or to great routs, even to please her mother. Mrs. Powle made a stand too, and insisted, and was very angry; but Eleanor stood firm; and the end was, she gained her point. Mr. Carlisle was disappointed, but counselled acquiescence; and Mrs. Powle with no very good grace acquiesced; for though a woman, she did not like to be foiled. Eleanor gained one point only; she was not obliged to go where she could not go with a good conscience. She did not thereby get her time to herself. London has many ways of spending time; nice ways too; and in one and another of these Eleanor found hers all gone. Day by day it was so. Nothing was left but those hours before breakfast. And what was worse, Mr. Carlisle was at her elbow in every place; and Eleanor became conscious that she was in spite of herself appearing before the world as his particular property, and that the conclusion was endorsed by her mother. She walked as straight as she could; but the days grew o be heavy days.

She devoted herself to her father as much as possible; and in that found a refuge. The Squire was discontented and unwell; a good deal depressed in spirits as a consequence; he delighted to have Eleanor come and sit with him and read to him after dinner. She escaped many an engagement by that means. In vain Mrs. Powle came in with her appeal, about Eleanor's good requiring him to do without her; the Squire listened, struggled, and selfishness got the better.

"St. George and the Dragon!" he exclaimed,—"she shall do as she likes, and as I like, for one hour in the twenty-four. You may haul her about the rest of the time—but from dinner for a while or so you may spare her. I choose she shall be with me."

The "while" was often three hours. Eleanor enjoyed repose then, and enjoyed ministering to her father; who speedily became exceedingly wedded to her services, and learned to delight in her presence after a new manner. He would have her read to him; she might read everything she pleased except what had a religious bearing. That he disposed of at once, and bade her seek another book. He loved to have her brush his hair, when his head ached, by the half hour together; at other times he engaged her in a game of chess and a talk about Plassy. The poor Squire was getting a good deal tamed down, to take satisfaction in such quiet pleasures; but the truth was that he found himself unable for what he liked better. Strength and health were both failing; he was often suffering; drives in the park wearied him almost as much as sitting alone in his room; he swore at them for the stupidest entertainment man ever pleased himself with. What he did with the lonely hours he spent entirely by himself, nobody knew; Eleanor knew that he was rejoiced every time to see her come in. His eye brightened when she opened the door, and he settled himself in his easy chair to have a good time; and then even the long columns of the newspaper, read from one end to the other, up and down, were pleasant to Eleanor too. It was soothing repose, in contrast with the whirl of all the rest of her life. Until the time came when Mr. Carlisle began to join the party. How he did it Eleanor hardly knew; but he did it. He actually contrived to make one at those evening entertainments, which admitted but two others; and with his usual adroitness and skill he made his presence so acceptable that Eleanor felt it would be quite in vain to attempt to hinder him. And so her rest was gone, and her opportunity; for she had cherished fond hopes of winning not only her own way into her father's heart, but with that, in time, a hearing for truths the Squire had always pushed out of his path.

Mr. Carlisle was very pleasant; there was no question. He did not at all usurp her office, nor interfere with it. But when he saw her getting weary of a parliamentary discussion, or a long discourse on politics or parties, his hand would gently draw away the paper from hers and his voice carry on the reading. And his voice was agreeable to her father; Eleanor saw it; the Squire would turn his head a little towards the new reader, and an expression of anything but dissatisfaction steal over his features. Eleanor sat by, half mortified, half feeling real good will towards Mr. Carlisle for his grace and kindness. Or if a game of chess were on foot, Mr. Carlisle would sit by, he generally declined playing himself, and make the play very lively with his talk; teaching Eleanor, whose part he invariably took, and keeping a very general's watch over her as if she had been a subordinate officer. Mr. Powle liked that too; it made his fighting better fun; he chuckled a good deal over Mr. Carlisle's play by proxy. Eleanor could not help it, nor withdraw herself. She knew what brought Mr. Carlisle there, and she could not avoid him, nor the very easy familiar terms on which they all sat round the chess table. She was admirably quiet and cool; but then it is true she felt no unkindness towards Mr. Carlisle, and sometimes she feared she shewed kindness too frankly. It was very difficult to help that too. Nevertheless it was plain the gentleman did not dare trust anything to his present power over her, for he never tried it. He evidently relied on somewhat else in his advances. And Eleanor felt that the odds were rather hard against her. Father and mother, and such a suitor!

She was cut off from her evening refreshment; and the next step was, that her morning pleasure with Julia was also denied her. Mrs. Powle had been in a state of gratulation with reference to Julia's improvement; Julia had become latterly so docile, so decorous, and so diligent. One unlucky day it came to Mrs. Powle's knowledge that Julia objected to going to dancing school; objected to spending money on the accomplishment, and time on the acquisition; and furthermore, when pressed, avowed that she did not believe in the use of it when attained. It seemed to Mrs. Powle little less than a judgment upon her, to have the second of her daughters holding such language; it was traced to Eleanor's influence of course; and further and diligent questioning brought out the fact of the sisters' daily studies in company. They should happen no more, Mrs. Powle immediately decided. Julia was forbidden to go to her sister's room for such purposes; and to make matters sure she was provided with other and abundant occupation to keep her engaged at the dangerous hour. With Eleanor herself Mrs. Powle held no communication on the subject; having for certain reasons an unwillingness to come into unnecessary collision with her; but Eleanor found her little sister's society was no more to be had. Mrs. Powle would assuredly have sent Julia quite out of the house to get her away from mischievous influences, but that she could not prevail on her husband. No daughter of his, he declared, should be made a fool of in a boarding-school, while he had a foot above ground to prevent it.

"Why Mrs. Powle," he said, "don't you know yourself that Eleanor is the only sensible girl in London? That's growing up at home, just as you didn't want."

"If she only had not some notions—" said Mrs. Powle dubiously. For between her husband and Mr. Carlisle she was very much *held in* on Eleanor's subject; both insisting that she should let her alone. It was difficult for Eleanor to be displeased with Mr. Carlisle in these times; his whole behaviour was so kind and gentlemanly. The only fault to be found with him was his pursuit of her. That was steady and incessant; yet at the same time so brotherly and well-bred in manner that Eleanor sometimes feared she gave him unconsciously too much encouragement. Feeling really grateful to him, it was a little hard not to shew it. For although Mr. Carlisle was the cause of her trouble, he was also a shield between her and its more active manifestations. He favoured her not dancing; *that* was like a jealous man, Mrs. Powle said. He smiled at Eleanor's charities, and would have helped them if he could. He would not have her scolded on the score of religious duties; he preferred administering the antidote to them as quietly as possible.

"Eleanor!" said Mrs. Powle, putting her head out of the drawing-room door one Sunday evening as she heard somebody come in—"Eleanor! is that you? come here. Where have you been? Here is Mr. Carlisle waiting this hour to go with you to hear the Bishop of London preach."

Eleanor came into the room. She was dressed with extreme plainness, and looking so calm and sweet that it was no wonder Mr. Carlisle's eyes rested on her as on a new object of admiration. Few of his acquaintance looked so; and Eleanor did not use it, in times past.

"Now here you are, child, almost too late. Make haste and get yourself ready. Where have you been?"

"She cannot be more ready than she is," remarked the other member of the party.

"I think, mamma, I will not go to-night. I am a little tired."

"That's nonsense, Eleanor! When were you ever too unwell to go to church, *this* winter? Go and get ready. What Mr. Carlisle says is all very well, but he does not see you with my eyes."

"I shall not take her if she is tired," said Mr. Carlisle gently. And Eleanor sat still.

"Where have you been then, child, to tire yourself? You do try me, Eleanor. What can you have found to do?"

"All London, mamma," said Eleanor pleasantly.

"All London! I should like to know what that means. All wrong, I suppose, according to you. Well, what part of London have you been attacking to-day? *I* should think the best thing for London would be to hear its Bishop. What have you been about, Eleanor?"

"Only to school, mamma—Sunday school."

"But you went there this morning?"

"That was another."

Mrs. Powle looked appealingly to Mr. Carlisle, as saying, How long would you let this go on? Turned her dissatisfied face again to Eleanor,

"What school is this, mistress? and where?"

"Mamma, if I tell you where it is, I am afraid you will be frightened. It is a Ragged school."

"A Ragged school! What does that mean, Eleanor? What is a Ragged school?"

"A school to teach ragged children, mamma. Or rather, for ragged people—they are not most of them children; and perhaps I should not say they are ragged; for though some of them are, others of them are not. They are some of the wretchedest of the ragged class at any rate."

"And Eleanor Powle can find nothing more suitable to do, than to go and teach such a set! Why you ought to have a policeman there to take care of you."

"We have several."

"Policemen!"

"Yes, ma'am."

"And it is not safe without them!"

"It is safe with them, mamma."

"Mr. Carlisle, what do you think of such doings?" said Mrs. Powle appealing in despair.

"They move my curiosity," he said quietly. "I hope Eleanor will go on to gratify it."

"And can you really find nothing better than that to do, of a Sunday?" her mother went on.

"No, mamma, I do not think I can."

"What do they learn?" Mr. Carlisle inquired.

"A little reading, some of them; but the main thing to teach them is the truths of the Bible. They never heard them before, anywhere,—nor can hear them anywhere else."

"Do you think they will hear them there?"

"I am sure they do."

"And remember?"

The tears filled Eleanor's eyes, as she answered, "I am sure some of them will."

"And suppose you lose your life in this Ragged teaching?" said Mrs. Powle. "You might catch your death of some horrid disease, Eleanor. Do you think that is right?"

"Mamma, there was One who did lay down his life for you and for me. I am not going to offer mine needlessly. But I do not think it is in any danger here. Many go besides me."

"She is a confirmed Methodist!" said Mrs. Powle turning to Mr. Carlisle. He smiled.

"Where does your school meet, Eleanor?"

"I am afraid of terrifying mamma, if I tell you."

"We will take care of her in case she faints. I am in no danger."

"It is the Field-Lane school, Mr. Carlisle."

"The Field-Lane? Won't you enlighten me?"

"Carter's Field-Lane; but it is only called Field-Lane. Did you never hear of it? It was in a wretched place in Saffron Hill at first—now it is removed to an excellent room in a better street."

"Where?"

"You know where Clerkenwell is?"

This name gave no intelligence whatever to Mrs. Powle, but Mr. Carlisle looked enlightened. His face changed and grew dark with something very like horror and alarm.

"Do you know that is one of the worst parts of London?" he said.

"Pretty bad," said Eleanor, "and the school used to be. It is wonderfully improved now."

"There, you see, Eleanor, Mr. Carlisle thinks it is a very improper place for you to be; and I hope you will go there no more. I do not mean you shall."

Eleanor was silent, looking a little anxious, though not cast down. Mr. Carlisle marked her.

"It is not safe for you, Eleanor," he said.

"It is perfectly safe," she answered with a smile that had a curious brightness in it. "I run no risk whatever."

"You are a bold creature," said her mother, "and always were; but that is no reason why you should be allowed to go your own crazy ways. I will have no more of this, Eleanor."

"Mamma, I am perfectly safe. I have nothing at all to fear. I would not fail of going for anything in the world." She spoke with an earnest and shadowed face now. She felt it.

"Who goes with you? or do you go alone?"

"No, ma'am—Thomas is with me always."

"How came you to get into such a strange place?"

"I heard of it—and there is sure to be more to do in

such a work than there are hands for. I know one or two of the gentlemen that teach there also."

"Methodists, I suppose?" said Mrs. Powle sneeringly.

"One of them is, mamma; the other is a Churchman."

"And do you *teach* there?"

"Yes, ma'am—a large class of boys." Eleanor's smile came again—and went.

"I'll have no more of it, Eleanor. I will not. It is just absurdity and fanaticism, the whole thing. Why shouldn't those boys go to the regular schools, instead of your giving your time and risking your life to teach them Sundays? *You* indeed!"

"You do not know what sort of boys they are, mamma; or you would not ask that."

"I suppose they have learned some things too well already?" said Mr. Carlisle.

"Well, I'll have no more of it!" said Mrs. Powle. "I am disgusted with the whole thing. If they are not good boys, the House of Correction is the best place for them. Mr. Carlisle, do you not say so?"

Mr. Carlisle's knowledge of the limits of Houses of Correction and the number of boys in London who were not good boys, forbade him to give an affirmative answer; his character as a reformer also came up before him. More than all, Eleanor's face, which was somewhat sad.

"Mrs. Powle, I am going to petition you to suspend judgment, and reconsider the case of the Ragged schools. I confess to a selfish motive in my request—I have a desire to go there myself and see this lady with her scholars around her. The picturesque effect, I should say, must be striking."

Mrs. Powle looked at him as a very unwise and obstinate man, who was bewitched into false action.

"If you have a fancy for such effects," she said; "I suppose you must do as you please. To me the effect is striking and not picturesque. Just look at her!"

Mr. Carlisle did so, and the expression on his face was so unsatisfactory that Mrs. Powle gave up the matter; laughed, and went out of the room.

"I will be less striking," said Eleanor, "if you will excuse me." And she left the room to change her dress. But when she came back an hour after, Mr. Carlisle was still there.

"Eleanor," said he, coming and standing before her, "may I go with you the next time you go to Field-Lane?"

"No, I think not. You would not know what to do in such a place, Mr. Carlisle."

"Do you think so?"

"They are a set of people whom you do not like; people who you think ought to be fined—and imprisoned—and transported; and all that sort of thing."

"And what do you think ought to be done with them?"

"I would try a different regimen."

"Pray what would it be?"

"I would tell them of the love of One who died for them. And I would shew them that the servants of that One love them too."

She spoke quietly, but there was a light in her eye.

"How, for heaven's sake, Eleanor?"

"Mr. Carlisle, I would never condemn a man or boy very severely for stealing, when I had left him no other way to live."

"So you would make the rest of the world responsible?"

"Are they not? These fellows never heard a word of right or of truth—never had a word of kindness—never were brought under a good influence,—until they found it in the Ragged school. What could you expect? May I illustrate?"

"Pray do."

"There is a boy in a class neighbouring to mine in the room, whose teacher I know. The boy is thirteen or fourteen years old now; he came to the school first some four or five years ago, when he was a little bit of a fellow. Then he had already one brother transported for stealing, and another in prison for stealing—both only a little older than he. They had often no other way of getting food but stealing it. The father and mother were both of them drunkards and swallowed up everything in liquor. This little fellow used to come to the morning school, which was held every day, without any breakfast; many a time. Barefooted, over the cold streets, and no breakfast to warm him. But after what he heard at the school he promised he would never do as his brothers had done; and he had some very hard times in keeping his promise. At last he came to his teacher and asked him for a loan of threepence; if he had a loan of threepence he thought he could make a living."

Mr. Carlisle half turned on his heel, but instantly resumed his look and attitude of fixed attention.

"Mr. Morrison lent him threepence. And Jemmy has supported himself respectably ever since, and is now in honest employment as an errand boy."

"I hope you can tell me how he managed it? I do not understand doing business on such a capital."

"The threepence bought twelve boxes of matches. Those were sold for a halfpenny each—doubling his capital at once. So he carried on that business for two years. All day he went to school. In the end of the day he went out with twelve boxes of matches and hawked them about until they were disposed of. That gave him threepence for the next day's trade, and threepence to live upon. He spent one penny for breakfast, he said; another for dinner, and another for supper. So he did for two years; now he does better."

"He deserves it, if anybody in London does. Is not this a strange instance, Eleanor?—on honour?"

"If you like—but not solitary."

"What has been done for the mass of these boys in these schools? what has been accomplished, I mean?"

"I have given you but one instance out of many, many individual instances."

"Then you can afford to be generous and give me another."

Perhaps he said this only because he wanted to have her go on talking; perhaps Eleanor divined that; however she hesitated a moment and went on.

"Lord Cushley, with some other friends, has just provided for the emigration to Australia of near a dozen promising cases of these boys."

"Was Eleanor Powle another of the friends?"

"No; I had not that honour. These are reclaimed boys, mind; reclaimed from the very lowest and most miserable condition; and they are going out with every prospect of respectability and every promise of doing well. Do you want to know the antecedents of one among them?"

"By all means!"

"Notice them. First, slavery under two drunken people, one of them his mother, who sent him out to steal for them; and refused him even the shelter of their wretched home if he came to it with empty hands. At such times, thrust out houseless and hungry, to wander where he could, he led a life of such utter wretchedness, that at length he determined to steal for himself, and to go home no more. Then came years of struggling vagrancy—during which, Mr. Carlisle, the prison was his pleasantest home and only comfortable shelter; and whenever he was turned out of it he stood in London streets helpless and hopeless but to renew his old ways of thieving and starvation. Nobody had told him better; no one had shewed the child kindness; was he to blame?"

"Somebody shewed him kindness at last," said Mr. Carlisle, looking into the lustrous eyes which were so full of their subject.

"Who, do you think?"

"Impossible for me to guess—since you were not here."

"One of the most noted thieves in London went to one of the city missionaries and told him of the boy and recommended him to his kindness."

"Impelled by what earthly motive?"

"The misery of the case."

"Why did he not teach him his own trade?"

"The question the missionary put to him. The thief answered that he knew a thief's life too well."

"I should like to see you before a committee of the House of Commons," said Mr. Carlisle, taking two or three steps away and then returning. "Well?"

"Well—the missionary put the child with some decent people, where he was washed and clothed. But it is impossible for me to tell, as it was too bad to be told to me, the state to which squalor, starvation, and all that goes with it, had brought the child. He went to school; and two years after was well, healthy, flourishing, intelligent, one of the best and most useful lads at the establishment where he was employed. Now Lord Cushley has sent him to Australia."

"Eleanor, I will never say anything against Ragged schools again."

"Then I have not spoken in vain," said Eleanor rising.

He took her hand, held it, bowed his lips to it, held it still, too firmly for Eleanor to disengage it without violence.

"Will you grant me one little favour?"

"You take without asking, Mr. Carlisle!"

He smiled and kissed her hand again, not releasing it, however.

"Let me go with you to Field-Lane in future."

"What would you do there?"

"Take care of you."

"As I do not need it, you would be exceedingly bored; finding yourself without either business or pleasure."

"Do you think that what interests you will not interest me?"

A change came over her face—a high grave light, as she answered,—"Not till you love the Master I do. Not till his service is your delight, as it is mine.—Mr. Carlisle, if you will allow me, I will ring the bell for tea."

He rang the bell for her instantly, and then came to her side again, and waited till the servant was withdrawn.

"Eleanor, seriously, I am not satisfied to have you go to that place alone."

"I do not. I am always attended."

"By a servant. Have you never been frightened?"

"Never."

"Do you not meet a very ugly sort of crowd sometimes, on your way?"

"Yes—sometimes."

"And never feel afraid?"

"No. Mr. Carlisle, would you like a cup of tea, if you could get it?"

She had met his questions with a full clear look of her eyes, in which certainly there lay no lurking shadow. He read them, and drank his tea rather moodily.

"So, Eleanor," said Mrs. Powle the next day, "you have enlisted Mr. Carlisle on your side as usual, and he will have you go to your absurd school as you want to do. How did people get along before Ragged schools were invented, I should like to know?"

"You would not like to know, mamma. It was in

misery and ignorance and crime, such as you would be made sick to hear of."

"Well, they live in it yet, I suppose; or are they all reclaimed already?"

"They live in it yet—many a one."

"And it is among such people you go! Well, I wash my hands of it. Mr. Carlisle will not have you molested. He must have his own way."

"What has he to do with it, mamma?" Eleanor asked, a little indignantly.

"A good deal, I should say. You are not such a fool as not to know what he is with you all the time for, Eleanor."

A hot colour came up in Eleanor's cheeks.

"It is not by my wish, mamma."

"It is rather late to say so. Don't you like him, Eleanor?"

"Yes ma'am—very much—if only he would be content with that."

"Answer me only one thing. Do you like any one else better? He is as jealous as a bear, and afraid you do."

"Mamma," said Eleanor, a burning colour again rising to her brow,—"you know yourself that I see no one that I favour more than I do Mr. Carlisle. I do not hold him just in the regard he wishes, nevertheless."

"But do you like any one else better? tell me that. I just want that question answered."

"Mamma, why? Answering it will not help the matter. In all England there is not a person out of my own family whom I like so well;—but that does not put Mr. Carlisle in the place where he wishes to be."

"I just wanted that question answered," said Mrs. Powle.

CHAPTER VI.

> "Still all the day the iron wheels go onward,
> Grinding life down from its mark;
> And the children's souls, which God is calling sunward,
> Spin on blindly in the dark."

"She declares there is not anybody in the world she likes better than she does you—nor so well."

Mrs. Powle's fair curls hung on either side of a perplexed face. Mr. Carlisle stood opposite to her. His eye brightened and fired, but he made no answer.

"It is only her absurd fanaticism that makes all the trouble."

"There will be no trouble to fear, my dear madam, if that is true."

"Well I asked her the question, and she told me in so many words; and you know Eleanor. What she says she means."

Mr. Carlisle was silent, and Mrs. Powle went on. He was seldom loquacious in his consultations with her.

"For all that, she is just as fixed in her ways as a mountain; and I don't know how to manage her. Eleanor always was a hard child to manage; and now she has got these fanatical notions in her head she is worse than ever."

There was a slight perceptible closing in of the fingers of Mr. Carlisle's hand, but his words were quiet.

"Do not oppose them. Fanaticism opposed grows rigid, and dies a martyr. Let her alone; these things will all pass away by and by. I am not afraid of them."

"Then you would let her go on with her absurd Ragged schools and such flummery? I am positively afraid she will bring something dreadful into the house, or be insulted herself some day. I do think charity begins at home. I wish Lord Cushley, or whoever it is, had been in better business. Such an example of course sets other people wild."

"I will be there myself, and see that no harm comes to Eleanor. I think I can manage that."

"Eleanor of all girls!" said Mrs. Powle. "That *she* should be infected with religious fanaticism! She was just the girl most unlike it that could possibly be; none of these meek tame spirits, that seem to have nothing better to do."

"No, you are wrong," said Mr. Carlisle. "It is the enthusiastic character, that takes everything strongly, that is strong in this as in all the rest. Her fanaticism will give me no trouble—if it will once let her be mine!"

"Then you would let her alone?" said Mrs. Powle.

"Let her alone."

"She is spoiling Julia as fast as she can; but I stopped that. Would you believe it? the minx objected to taking lessons in dancing, because her sister had taught her that dancing assemblies were not good places to go to! But I take care that they are not together now. Julia is completely under her influence."

"So am I," said Mr. Carlisle laughing; "so much that I believe I cannot bear to hear any more against her than is necessary. I will be with her at Field-Lane next Sunday."

He did not however this time insist on going with her. He went by himself. It is certain that the misery of London disclosed to him by this drive to Field-Lane, the course of which gave him a good sample of it, did almost shake him in his opinion that Eleanor ought to be let alone. Mr. Carlisle had not seen such a view of London in his life before; he had not been in such a district of crime and wretchedness; or if by chance he had touched upon it, he had made a principle of not seeing what was before him. Now he looked; for he was going where Eleanor was accustomed to go, and what he saw she was obliged to meet also. He reached the building where the Field-Lane school was held, in a somewhat excited state of mind.

He found at the door several policemen, who warned him to guard well and in a safe place anything of value he might have about his person. Then he was ushered up stairs to the place where the school was held. He entered a very large room, looking like a factory room, with bare beams and rough sides, but spacious and convenient for the purpose it was used for. Down the length of this room ran rows of square forms, with alleys left between the rows; and the forms were in good measure filled with the rough scholars. There must have been hundreds collected there; three-fourths of them perhaps were girls, the rest boys and young men, from seven years old and upwards. But the roughness of the scholars bore no proportion to the roughness of the room. *That* had order, shape, and some decency of preparation. The poor young human creatures that clustered within it were in every stage of squalor, rags, and mental distortion. With a kind of wonder Mr. Carlisle's eye went from one to another to note the individual varieties of the general character; and as it took in the details, wandered horror-stricken, from the nameless dirt and shapeless rags which covered the person, to the wild or stupid or cunning or devilish expression of vice in the face. Beyond description, both. There were many there who had never slept in a bed in their lives; many who never had their clothes off from one month's end to another; the very large proportion lived day and night by a course of wickedness. There they were gathered now, these wretches, eight or ten in a form, listening with more or less of interest to the instructions of their teachers who sat before them; and many, Mr. Carlisle saw, were shewing deep interest in face and manner. Others were full of mischief, and shewed that too. And others, who were interested, were yet also restless; and would manifest it by the occasional irregularity of jumping up and turning a somerset in the midst of the lesson. That frequently happened. Suddenly, without note or warning, in the midst of the most earnest deliverances of the teacher, a boy would leap up and throw himself over; come up all right; and sit down again and listen, as if he had only been making himself comfortable; which was very likely the real state of the case in some instances. When however a general prevalence of somersets throughout the room indicated that too large a proportion of the assemblage were growing uneasy in their minds, or their seats, the director of the school stood up and gave the signal for singing. Instantly the whole were on their feet, and some verse or two of a hymn were shouted heartily by the united lungs of the company. That seemed to be a great safety valve; they were quite brought into order, and somersets not called for, till some time had passed again.

In the midst of this great assemblage of strange figures, small and large, Mr. Carlisle's eye sought for Eleanor. He could not immediately find her, standing at the back of the room as he was; and he did not choose the recognition to be first on her side, so would not go forward. No bonnet or cloak there recalled the image of Eleanor; he had seen her once in her school trim, it is true, but that signified nothing. He had seen her only, not her dress. It was only by a careful scrutiny that he was able to satisfy himself which bonnet and which outline of a cloak was Eleanor's. But once his attention had alighted on the right figure, and he was sure, by a kind of instinct. The turns of the head, the fine proportions of the shoulders, could be none but her's; and Mr. Carlisle moved somewhat nearer and took up a position a little in the rear of that form, so that he could watch all that went on there.

He scanned with infinite disgust one after another of the miserable figures ranged upon it. They were well-grown boys, young thieves some of them, to judge by their looks; and dirty and ragged so as to be objects of abhorrence much more than of anything else to his eye. Yet to these squalid, filthy, hardened looking little wretches, scarcely decent in their rags, Eleanor was most earnestly talking; there was no avoidance in her air. Her face he could not see; he could guess at its expression, from the turns of her head to one and another, and the motions of her hands, with which she was evidently helping out the meaning of her words; and also from the earnest gaze that her unpromising hearers bent upon her. He could hear the soft varying play of her voice as she addressed them. Mr. Carlisle grew restless. There was a more evident and tremendous gap between himself and her than he had counted upon. Was she doing this like a Catholic, for penance, or to work out good deeds to earn heaven like a philanthropist? While he pondered the matter, in increasing restlessness, mind and body helping each other; for the atmosphere of the room was heavy and stifling from the foul human beings congregated there, and it must require a very strong motive in anybody to be there at all; he could hardly bear it himself; an incident occurred which gave a little variety to his thoughts. As he stood in the alley, leaning on the end of a form where no one sat, a boy came in and passed him; brushing so near that Mr. Carlisle involuntarily shrank back. Such a looking fellow-creature he had never seen until that day. Mr. Carlisle had lived in the other half of the world. This was a half-grown boy, inexpressibly forlorn in his rags and wretchedness. An old coat hung about him, much too large and long, that yet did not hide a great rent in his trowsers which shewed that there was no shirt beneath. But the face! The indescribable brutalized, stolid, dirty, dumb look of badness and hardness! Mr. Carlisle thought he had never seen such a face. One round portion of it had been washed, leaving the dark ring of dirt all circling it like a border, where the blessed touch of water had not come. The boy moved on, with a shambling kind of gait, and to Mr. Carlisle's horror, paused at the form of Eleanor's class. Yes,—he was going in there, he belonged there; for she looked up and spoke to him; Mr. Carlisle could hear her soft voice saying something about his being late. Then came a transformation such as Mr. Carlisle would never have believed possible. A light broke upon that brutalized face; actually a light; a smile that was like a heavenly sunbeam in the midst of those rags and dirt irradiated it; as a rough thick voice spoke out in answer to her—"Yes—if I didn't come, I knowed you would be disappointed."

Evidently they were friends, Eleanor and that boy; young thief, young rascal, though Mr. Carlisle's eye pronounced him. They were on good terms, even of affection; for only love begets love. The lesson went on, but the gentleman stood in a maze till it was finished. The notes of Eleanor's voice in the closing hymn, which he was sure he could distinguish, brought him quite back to himself. Now *he* might speak to her again. He had felt as if there were a barrier between them. Now he would test it.

He had to wait yet a little while, for Eleanor was talking to one or two elderly gentlemen. Nobody to move his jealousy however; so Mr. Carlisle bore the delay with what patience he could; which in that stifling atmosphere was not much. How *could* Eleanor endure it? As at last she came down the room, he met her and offered his arm. Eleanor took it, and they went out together.

"I did not know you were in the school," she said.

"I would not disturb you. Thomas is not here—Mrs. Powle wanted him at home."

Which was Mr. Carlisle's apology for taking his place. Or somewhat more than Thomas's place; for he not only put Eleanor in a carriage, but took a seat beside her. The drive began with a few moments of silence.

"How do you do?" was his first question.

"Very well."

"Must I take it on trust? or do you not mean I shall see for myself?" said he. For there had been a hidden music in Eleanor's voice, and she had not turned her face from the window of the carriage. At this request however she gave him a view of it. The hidden sweetness was there too; he could not conceive what made her look so happy. Yet the look was at once too frank and too deep for his personal vanity to get any food from it; no surface work, but a lovely light on brow and lip that came from within. It had nothing to do with him. It was something though, that she was not displeased at his being there; his own face lightened.

"What effect does Field-Lane generally have upon you?" said he.

"It tires me a little—generally. Not to-day."

"No, I see it has not; and how you come out of that den, looking as you do, I confess is a incomprehensible thing to me. What has pleased you there?"

A smile came upon Eleanor's face, so bright as shewed it was but the outbreaking of the light he had seen there before. His question she met with another.

"Did nothing there please you?"

"Do you mean to evade my inquiry?"

"I will tell you what pleased me," said Eleanor. "Perhaps you remarked—whereabouts were you?"

"A few feet behind you and your scholars."

"Then perhaps you remarked a boy who came in when the lesson was partly done—midway in the time—a boy who came in and took his seat in my class."

"I remarked him—and you will excuse me for saying, I do not understand how pleasure can be connected in anybody's mind with the sight of him."

"Of course you do not. That boy has been a most notorious pickpocket and thief."

"Exactly what I should have supposed."

"Did you observe that he had washed his face?"

"I think I observed how imperfectly it was done."

"Ah, but it is the first time probably in years that it has touched water, except when his lips touched it to drink. Do you know, that is a sign of reformation?"

"Water?"

"Washing. It is the hardest thing in the world to get them to forego the seal and the bond of dirt. It is a badge of the community of guilt. If they will be brought to wash, it is a sign that the bond is broken—that they are willing to be out of the community; which will I suppose regard them as suspected persons from that time. Now you can understand why I was glad."

Hardly; for the fire and water sparkling together in Eleanor's eyes expressed so much gladness that it quite went beyond Mr. Carlisle's power of sympathy. He remained silent a few moments.

"Eleanor, I wish you would answer one question, which puzzles me. Why do you go to that place?"

"You do not like it?"

"No, nor do you. What takes you there?"

"There are more to be taught than there are teachers for," said Eleanor looking at her questioner. "They want help. You must have seen, there are none too many to take care of the crowds that come; and many of those teachers are fatigued with attendance in the week."

"Do *you* go in the week?"

"No, not hitherto."

"You must not think of it! It is as much as your life is worth to go Sundays. I met several companies of most disorderly people on my way—do you not meet such?"

"Yes."

"What takes you there, Eleanor, through such horrors?"

"I have no fear."

"No, I suppose not; but will you answer my question?"

"You will hardly be able to understand me," said Eleanor hesitating. "I like to go to these poor wretches, because I love them. And if you ask me why I love them,—I know that the Lord Jesus loves them; and he is not willing they should be in this forlorn condition; and so I go to try to help get them out of it."

"If the Supreme Ruler is not willing there should be this class of people, Eleanor, how come they to exist?"

"You are too good a philosopher, Mr. Carlisle, not to know that men are free agents, and that God leaves them the exercise of their free agency, even though others as well as themselves suffer by it. I suppose, if those a little above them in the social scale had lived according to the gospel rule, this class of people never would have existed."

"What a reformer you would make, Eleanor!"

"I should not suit you? Yes—I do not believe in any radical way of reform but one."

"And that is, what?—counsellor."

"Do unto others as you would that others should do unto you."

"Radical enough! You must reform the reformers first, I suppose you know."

"I know it."

"Then, hard as it is for me to believe it, you do not go to Field-Lane by way of penance?"

"The penance would be, to make me stay away."

"Mrs. Powle will do that, unless I contrive to disturb the action of *her* free agency; but I think I shall plunge into the question of reform, Eleanor. Speaking of that, how much reformation has been effected by these Ragged institutions?"

"Very much; and they are only as it were beginning, you must remember."

"Room for amendment still," said Mr. Carlisle. "I never saw such a disorderly set of scholars in my life before. How do you find an occasional somersault helps a boy's understanding of his lesson?"

"Those things were constant at first; not occasional," said Eleanor smiling; "somersaults, and leaping over the forms, and shouts and catcalls, and all manner of uproarious behaviour. That was before I ever knew them. But now, think of that boy's washed face!"

"That was the most partial reformation I ever saw rejoiced in," said Mr. Carlisle.

"It gives hope of everything else, though. You have no idea what a bond that community of dirt is. But there are plenty of statistics, if you want those, Mr. Carlisle. I can give you enough of them; shewing what has been done."

"Will you shew them to me to-night?"

"To-night? it is Sunday. No, but to-morrow night, Mr. Carlisle; or any other time."

"Eleanor, you are very strict!"

"Not at all. That is not strictness; but Sunday is too good to waste upon statistics."

She said it somewhat playfully, with a shining of her old arch smile, which did not at all reassure her companion.

"Besides, Mr. Carlisle, you like strictness a great deal better than I do. There is not a law made in our Queen's reign or administered under her sceptre, that you would not have fulfilled to the letter—even down to the regulations that keep little boys off the grass. It is only the laws of the Great King which you do not think should be strictly kept."

She was grave enough now, and Mr. Carlisle swallowed the reproof as best he might.

"Eleanor, you are going to turn preacher too, as well as reformer? Well, I will come to you, dear, and put myself under your influences. You shall do what you please with me."

Too much of a promise, and more of a responsibility than Eleanor chose to take. She went into the house with a sober sense that she had a difficult part to play; that between Mr. Carlisle and her mother, she must walk very warily or she would yet find herself entangled before she was aware. And Mr. Carlisle too had a sober sense that Eleanor's religious character was not of a kind to exhale, like a volatile oil, under the sun of prosperity or the breezes of flattery. Nevertheless, the more hard to reach the prize, the more of a treasure when reached. He never wanted her more than now; and Mr. Carlisle had always, by skill and power, obtained what he wanted. He made no doubt he would find this instance like the others.

For the present, the thing was to bring a bill into parliament "for the reformation of juvenile offenders"—and upon its various provisions Mr. Carlisle came daily to consult Eleanor, and take advice and receive information.

Doubtless there was a great deal to be considered about the bill, to make it just what it should be; to secure enough and not insist upon too much; its bearings would be very important, and every point merited well the deepest care and most circumspect management. It enlisted Eleanor's heart and mind thoroughly; how should it not? She spent hours and hours with Mr. Carlisle over it; wrote for him, read for him, or rather for those the bill wrought for; talked and discussed and argued, for and against various points which she felt would make for or against its best success. Capital for Mr. Carlisle. All this brought him into constant close intercourse with her, and gave him opportunities of recommending himself. And not in vain. Eleanor saw and appreciated the cool, clear business head; the calm executive talent, which seeing its ends in the distance, made no hurry but took the steps and the measures surest to attain them, with patient foresight. She admired it, and sometimes also could almost have trembled when she thought of its being turned towards herself. And was it not, all the while? Was not Eleanor tacitly, by little and little, yielding the ground she fought so hard to keep? Was she not quietly giving her affirmative to the world's question,—and to Mr. Carlisle's too? To the former, yes; for the latter, she knew and Mr. Carlisle knew that she shewed him no more than the regard that would not satisfy him. But then, if this went on indefinitely, would not he, and the world, and her mother, all say that she had given him a sort of pre scriptive right to her? Ay, and Eleanor must count her father too now as among her adversaries' ranks. She saw it and felt it somewhat bitterly. She had begun to gain his ear and his heart; by and by he might have listened to her on what subject she pleased, and she might have won him to the knowledge of the truth that she held dearest. Now, she had gained his love certainly, in a measure, but so had Mr. Carlisle. Gently, skilfully, almost unconsciously it seemed, he was as much domiciled in her father's room as she was; and even more acceptable. The Squire had come to depend on him, to look for him, to delight in him; and with very evident admission that he was only anticipating by a little the rights and privileges of sonship. Eleanor could not absent herself neither; she tried that; her father would have her there; and there was Mr. Carlisle, as much at home, and sharing with her in filial offices as a matter of rule, and associating with her as already one of the family. It is true, in his manner to Eleanor herself he did not so step beyond bounds as to give her opportunity to check him; yet even over this there stole insensibly a change; and Eleanor felt herself getting deeper and deeper in the toils. Her own manner meanwhile was nearly perfect in its simple dignity. Except in the interest of third party measures, which led her sometimes further than she wanted to go, Eleanor kept a very steady way, as graceful as it was steady. So friendly and frank as to give no cause of umbrage; while it was so cool and self-poised as to make Mr. Carlisle very uneasy and very desperate. It was just the manner he admired in a woman; just what he would like to see in his wife, towards all the rest of the world. Eleanor charmed him more by her high-bred distance, than ever she had done by the affection or submissiveness of former days. But he was pretty sure of his game. Let this state of things go on long enough, and she would have no power to withdraw; and once his own, let him have once again the right to take her to his breast and whisper love or authority, and he knew he could win that fine sweet nature to give him back love as well as obedience,—in time. And so the bill went on in its progress towards maturity. It did not go very fast.

All this while the sisters saw very little of each other. One morning Eleanor waylaid Julia as she was passing her door, drew her in, and turned the key in the lock. The first impulse of the two was to spring to each other's arms for a warm embrace.

"I never have a chance to speak to you, darling," said the elder sister. "What has become of you?"

"O I am so busy, you see—all the times except when you are gone out, or talking in the drawing-room to people, or in papa's room. *Then* I am out, and you are out too; somewhere else."

"Out of what?"

"Out of my studies, and teachers, and governesses. I must go now in two minutes."

"No you must not. Sit down; I want to see you. Are you remembering what *we* have learnt together?"

"Sometimes—and sometimes it is hard, you see. Everything is so scratchy. O Eleanor, are you going to marry Mr. Carlisle?"

"No. I told you I was not."

"Everybody says you are, though. Are you *sure* you are not?"

"Quite sure."

"I amost wish you were; and then things would go smooth again."

"What do you mean by their being 'scratchy'? that is a new word."

"Well, everything goes cross. I am in ever so many dictionaries besides English—and shut up to learn 'em—and mamma don't care what becomes of me if she can only keep me from you; and I don't know what you are doing; and I wish we were all home again!"

Eleanor sighed.

"I call it *scratchy*," said Julia. "Everybody is trying to do what somebody else don't like."

"I hope you are not going on that principle,"—said

her sister: with a smile which made Julia spring to her neck again and load her lips with kisses over and over.

"I'll try to do what you like, Eleanor—only tell me what. Tell me something, and I will remember it."

"Julia, are you going to be a servant of Christ? have you forgotten that you said you loved him?"

"No, and I do, Eleanor! and I want to do right; but I am so busy, and then I get so vexed!"

"That is not like a servant of Jesus, darling."

"No. If I could only see you, Eleanor! Tell me something to remember, and I will keep it in my head, in spite of all the dictionaries."

"Keep it in your life, Julia. Remember what Jesus said his servants must be and how they must do—just in this one little word—'And ye yourselves like them that wait for their Lord.'"

"How, Eleanor?"

"That is what we are, dear. We are the Lord's servants, put here to work for him, put just in the post where he wishes us to be, till he comes. Now let us stand in our post and do our work, 'like them that wait for their Lord.' You know how that would be."

Julia again kissed and caressed her, not without some tears.

"I know," she said; "it is like Mr. Rhys, and it is like you; and I don't believe it is like anybody else."

"Shall it be like you, Julia?"

"Yes, Eleanor, yes! I will never forget it. O Eleanor, are you sure you are not going to Rythdale?"

"What makes you ask me?"

"Why everybody thinks so, and everybody says so; and you—you are with Mr. Carlisle all the time, talking to him."

"I have so many thoughts to put into his head," said Eleanor gravely.

"What are you so busy with him about?"

"Parliament business. It is for the poor of London, Julia. Mr. Carlisle is preparing a bill to bring into the House of Commons, and I know more about the matter than he does; and so he comes to me."

"Don't you think he is glad of his ignorance?" said Julia shrewdly. Eleanor leaned her head on her hand and looked thoughtfully down.

"What do you give him thoughts about?"

"My poor boys would say, 'lots of things.' I have to convince Mr. Carlisle that it would cost the country less to reform than to punish these poor children, and that reforming them is impossible unless we can give them enough to keep them from starvation; and that the common prison is no place for them; and then a great many questions besides these and that spring out of these have to be considered and talked over. And it is important beyond measure; and if I should let it alone,—the whole might fall to the ground. There are two objections now in Mr. Carlisle's mind—or in other people's minds—to one thing that ought to be done, and must be done; and I must shew Mr. Carlisle how false the objections are. I have begun; I must go through with it. The whole might fall to the ground if I took away my hand; and it would be such an incalculable blessing to thousands and thousands in this dreadful place——"

"Do you think London is a dreadful place?" said Julia doubtfully.

"There are very few here who stand 'like them tha wait for their Lord,'"—said Eleanor, her face taking a yearning look of thoughtfulness.

"There aren't anywhere, *I* don't believe. Eleanor—aren't you happy?"

"Yes!"

"You don't always look—just—so."

"Perhaps not. But to live for Jesus makes happy days—be sure of that, Julia; however the face looks."

"Are you bothered about Mr. Carlisle?"

"What words you use!" said Eleanor smiling. "'Bother,' and 'scratchy.' No, I am not bothered about him—I am a little troubled sometimes."

"What's the difference?"

"The difference between seeing one's way clear, and not seeing it; and the difference between having a hand to take care of one, and not having it."

"Well why do you talk to him so much, if he troubles you?" said Julia, reassured by her sister's smile.

"I must," said Eleanor. "I must see through this business of the bill—at all hazards. I cannot let that go. Mr. Carlisle knows I do not compromise myself."

"Well, I'll tell you what," said Julia getting up to go,—"mamma means you shall go to Rythdale; and she thinks you are going."

With a very earnest kiss to Eleanor, repeated with an emphasis which set the seal upon all the advices and promises of the morning, Julia went off. Eleanor sat a little while thinking; not long; and met Mr. Carlisle the next time he came, with precisely the same sweet self-possession, the unchanged calm cool distance, which drove that gentleman to the last verge of passion and patience. But he was master of himself and bided his time, and talked over the bill as usual.

It was not Eleanor alone who had occasion for the exercise of admiration in these business consultations. Somewhat to his surprise, Mr. Carlisle found that his quondam fair mistress was good for much more than a plaything. With the quick wit of a woman she joined a patience of investigation, an independent strength of judgment, a clearness of rational vision, that fairly met him and obliged him to be the best man he could in the business. He could not get her into a sophistical maze; she found her way through immediately; he could not puzzle her, for what she did not understand one day she had studied out by the next. It is possible that Mr. Carlisle would not have fallen in love with this clear intelligence, if he had known it in the front of Eleanor's qualities; for he was one of those men who do not care for an equal in a wife; but his case was by this time beyond cure. Nay, what might have alienated him once, bound him now; he found himself matched with Eleanor in a game of human life. The more she proved herself his equal, the nobler the conquest, and the more the instinct of victory stirred within him; for pride, a poor sort of pride, began to be stirred as well as love.

So the bill went on; and prisons and laws and reformatory measures and penal enactments and industrial schools, and the question of interfering with the course of labour, and the question of offering a premium upon crime, and a host of questions, were discussed and rediscussed. And partly no doubt from policy, partly from an intelligent view of the subject, but wholly moved thereto by Eleanor, Mr. Carlisle gradually gave back the ground and took just the position (on paper) that she wished to see him take.

CHAPTER V.

> "Why how one weeps
> When one's too weary! Were a witness by,
> He'd say some folly—"

So the bill went on. And the season too. Winter merged into spring; the change of temperature reminded Eleanor of the changing face of the earth out of London; and even in London the parks gave testimony of it. She longed for Wiglands and the Lodge; but there was no token of the family's going home at present. Parliament was in session; Mr. Carlisle was busy there every night almost; which did not in the least hinder his being busied with Eleanor as well. Where she and her mother went, for the most part he went; and at home he was very much at home indeed. Eleanor began to feel that the motions of the family depended on him; for she could find no sufficient explanation in her father's health or her mother's pleasure for their continued remaining in town. The Squire was much as he had been all winter; attended now and then by a physician, and out of health and spirits certainly; yet Eleanor could not help thinking he would be better at home, and somewhat suspected her father thought so. Mrs. Powle enjoyed London, no doubt; still, she was not a woman to run mad after pleasure, or after anything else; not so much but that the pleasure of her husband would have outweighed hers. Nevertheless, both the Squire and she were as quietly fixed in London, to judge by all appearance, as if they had no other place to go to; and the rising of parliament was sometimes hinted at as giving the only clue to the probable time of their departure.

Did you ever lay brands together on a hearth, brands with little life in them too, seemingly; when with no breath blown or stirring of air to fan them, gradually, by mere action and reaction upon each other, the cold grey ends began to sparkle and glow, till by and by the fire burst forth and flame sprang up? Circumstances may be laid together so, and with like effect.

Everything went on in a train at the house in Cadogan Square; nobody changed his attitude or behaviour with respect to the others, except as by that most insensible, unnoticeable, quiet action of elements at work; yet the time came when Eleanor began to feel that things were drawing towards a crisis. Her place was becoming uncomfortable. She could not tell how, she did not know when it began, but a change in the home atmosphere became sensible to her. It was growing to be oppressive. Mother, father, and friends seemed by concert to say that she was Mr. Carlisle's; and the gentleman himself began to look it, Eleanor thought, though he did not say it. A little tacit allowance of this mute language of assignment, and either her truth would be forfeited or her freedom. She must make a decided protest. Yet also Eleanor felt that quality in the moral atmosphere which threatened that if any clouds came up they would be stormy clouds; and she dreaded to make any move. Julia's society would have been a great solace now; when she never could have it. Julia comforted her, whenever they were together in company or met for a moment alone, by her energetic whisper—"I remember, Eleanor!—" but that was all. Eleanor could get no further speech of her. At the Ragged school Mr. Carlisle was pretty sure to be, and generally attended her home. Eleanor remonstrated with her mother, and got a sharp answer, that it was only thanks to Mr. Carlisle she went there at all; if it were not for him Mrs. Powle certainly would put a stop to it. Eleanor pondered very earnestly the question of putting a stop to it herself; but it was at Mr. Carlisle's own risk; the poor boys in the school wanted her ministrations; and the "bill" was in process of preparation. Eleanor's heart was set on that bill, and her help she knew was greatly needed in ts construction; she could not bear to give it up. So she let matters take their course; and talked reform diligently to Mr. Carlisle all the time they were driving from West-Smithfield home.

At last to Eleanor's joy, the important paper was drawn up according to her mind. It satisfied her. And it was brought to a reading in the House and ordered to be printed. So much was gained. The very next day Mr. Carlisle came to ask Eleanor to drive out with him to Richmond, which she had never seen. Eleanor coolly declined. He pressed the charms of the place, and of the country at that season. Eleanor with the same coolness of manner replied that she hoped soon to enjoy the country at home; and that she could not go to Richmond. Mr. Carlisle withdrew his plea, sat and talked some time, making himself very agreeable, though Eleanor could not quite enjoy his agreeableness that morning; and went away. He had given no sign of understanding her or of being rebuffed; and she was not satisfied. The next morning early her mother came to her.

"Eleanor what do you say to a visit to Hampton Court to-day?"

"Who is going, mamma?"

"Half the world, I suppose—there or somewhere else—such a day; but with you, your friend in parliament."

"I have several friends in parliament."

"Pshaw, Eleanor! you know I mean Mr. Carlisle.

You had better dress immediately, for he will be here for you early. He wants to have the whole day. Put on that green silk which becomes you so well. How it does, I don't know; for you are not blonde; but you look as handsome as a fairy queen in it. Come, Eleanor!"

"I do not care about going, mamma."

"Nonsense, child; you do care. You have no idea what Bushy Park is, Eleanor. It is not like Rythdale—though Rythdale will do in its way. Come, child, get ready. You will enjoy it delightfully."

"I do not think I should, mamma. I do not think I ought to go with Mr. Carlisle."

"Why not?"

"You know, mamma," Eleanor said calmly, though her heart beat; "you know what conclusions people draw about me and Mr. Carlisle. If I went to Hampton Court or to Richmond with him, I should give them, and him too, a right to those conclusions."

"What have you been doing for months past, Eleanor? I should like to know."

"Giving him no right to any conclusions whatever, mamma, that would be favorable to him. He knows that."

"He knows no such thing. You are a fool, Eleanor. Have you not said to all the world all this winter, by your actions, that you belonged to him? All the world knows it *was* an engagement, and you have been telling all the world that it *is*. Mr. Carlisle knows what to expect."

Eleanor coloured.

"I cannot fulfil his expectations, mamma. He has no right to them."

"I tell you, you have given him a right to them, by your behaviour these months past. Ever since we were at Brighton. Why how you encouraged him there!"

A great flush rose to Eleanor's cheeks.

"Mamma,—no more than I encouraged others. Grace given to all is favour to none."

"Ay, but there was the particular favour in his case of a promise to marry him."

"Broken off, mamma."

"The world did not know that, and you did not tell them. You rode, you walked, you talked, you went hither and thither with Mr. Carlisle, and suffered him to attend you."

"Not alone, mamma; rarely alone."

"Often alone, child; often of evenings. You are alone with a gentleman in the street, if there is a crowd before and behind you."

"Mamma, all those things that I did, and that I was sorry to do, I could hardly get out of or get rid of; they were Mr. Carlisle's doing and yours."

"Granted; and you made them yours by acceptance. Now Eleanor, you are a good girl; be a sensible girl. You have promised yourself to Mr. Carlisle in the eye of all the world; now be honest, and don't be shy, and fulfil your engagements."

"I have made none," said Eleanor getting up and beginning to walk backwards and forwards in the room. "Mr. Carlisle has been told distinctly that I do not love him. I will never marry any man whom I have not a right affection for."

"You did love him once, Eleanor."

"Never! not the least; not one bit of real—Mamma, I *liked* him, and I do that now; and then I did not know any better; but I will never, for I ought never, to marry any man upon mere liking."

"How come you to know any better now?"

Eleanor's blush was beautiful again for a minute; then it faded. She did not immediately speak.

"Is Mr. Carlisle right after all, and has he a rival?"

"Mamma, you must say what you please. Surely it

does not follow that a woman must love all the world because she does not love one."

"And *you* may say what you please; I know you like Mr. Carlisle quite well enough, for you as good as told me so. This is only girl's talk; but you have got to come to the point, Eleanor. I shall not suffer you to make a fool of him in my house; not to speak of making a fool of yourself and me, and ruining—forever ruining—all your prospects. You can't do it, Eleanor. You have said yea, and you can't draw back. Put on your green gown and go to Hampton Court, and come back with the day fixed—for that I know is what Mr. Carlisle wants."

"I cannot go, mamma."

"Eleanor, you would not forfeit your word?"

"I have not given it."

"Do not contradict me! You have given it all these months. Everybody has understood it so. Your father looks upon Mr. Carlisle as his son already. You would be everlastingly disgraced if you play false."

"I will play true, mamma. I will not say I give my heart where I do not give it."

"Give your hand then. All one," said Mrs. Powle laughing. "Come! I order you to obey me, Eleanor!"

"I must not, mamma. I will not go to Hampton Court with Mr. Carlisle."

"What is the reason?"

"I have told you."

"Do you mean, absolutely, that you will not fulfil your engagement, nor obey me, nor save us all from dishonour, nor make your friend happy?"

Eleanor grew paler than she had been, but answered, "I mean not to marry Mr. Carlisle, mamma."

"I understand it then," said Mrs. Powle rising. "It is not your heart but your head. It is your religious fanaticism. I will put that out of the way!"

And without another word she departed.

Eleanor was much at a loss what would be the next move. Nevertheless she was greatly surprised when it came. The atmosphere of the house was heavy that day; they did not see Mr. Carlisle in the evening. The next day, when Eleanor went to her father's room after dinner she found, not Mr. Carlisle, but her mother with him. "Waiting for me"—thought Eleanor. The air of Mrs. Powle said so. The squire was gathered up into a kind of hard knot, hanging his head over his knees. When he spoke, and was answered by his daughter, the contrast of the two voices was striking, and in character; one gruff, the other sweet but steady.

"What's all this, Eleanor? what's all this?" he said abruptly.

"What, papa?"

"Have you refused Mr. Carlisle?"

"Long ago, sir."

"Yes, that's all past; and now this winter you have been accepting him again; are you going to throw him over now?"

"Papa—"

"Only one thing!" roared the Squire,—"are you going to say no to him? tell me that."

"I must, papa."

"I command you to say yes to him! What do you say now?"

"I must say the same, sir. If you command me, I must disobey you."

"You will disobey me, hey?"

"I must, papa."

"Why won't you marry him? what's the reason?" said the Squire, looking angry and perplexed at her, but very glum.

"Papa—"

"I have seen you here myself, all winter, in this very

room; you have as good as said to him every day that you would be his wife, and he has as good as said to you that he expected it. Has he not, now?"

"Yes, sir,—but—"

"Now why won't you have him, hey?"

"Papa, I do not like him well enough to marry him. That is reason enough."

"Why did you tell him all the winter that you *did?*"

"Sir, Mr. Carlisle knows I did not. He has never been deceived."

"Why don't you like him well enough, then? that's the question; what fool's nonsense! Eleanor, I am going to have you at the Priory and mistress of it before the world is three months older. Tell me that you will be a good girl, and do as I say."

"I cannot, papa. That is all past. I shall never be at the Priory."

"What's the reason?" roared her father.

"I have told you, sir."

"It's a lie! You do like him. I have seen it. It's some fool's nonsense."

"Let me ask one question," said Mrs. Powle, looking up and down from her work. "If it had not been for your religious notions, Eleanor, would you not have married Mr. Carlisle more than a year ago? before you went to Wales?"

"I suppose I should, mamma."

"And if you had no religious notions, would you have any difficulty about marrying him now? You will speak the truth, I know."

"Mamma—"

"Speak!" the Squire burst out violently—"speak! truth or falsehood, whichever you like. Speak out, and don't go round about. Answer your mother's question."

"Will you please to repeat it, mamma?" Eleanor said, a little faintheartedly.

"If you had never been in a Methodist Chapel, or had anything to do with Methodists,—would you have any difficulty now about being the wife of Mr. Carlisle, and lady of Rythdale?"

Eleanor's colour rose gradually and grew deep before she ceased speaking.

"If I had never had anything to do with Methodists, mamma, I should be so very different from what I am now, that perhaps, it would be as you say."

"That's enough!" said the Squire, in a great state of rage and determination. "Now Eleanor Powle, take notice. I am as good as the Methodists any day, and as well worth your minding. You'll mind me, or I'll have nothing to do with you. Do you go to their chapels?"

"Sometimes."

"You don't go any more! St. George and the Dragon fly away with all the Methodist Chapels that ever were built! they shall hold no daughter of mine. And hark ye,—you shall give up this foolery altogether and tell me you will marry Mr. Carlisle, or I won't have you in *my* family. You may go where you like, but you shall not stay with me as long as *I* live. I give you a month to think of it, Eleanor;—a month? what's to-day?—the tenth? Then I give you till the first of next month. You can think of it and make up your mind to give yourself to Mr. Carlisle by that time; or you shall be no daughter of mine. St. George and the Dragon! I have said it, and you will find I mean it. Now go away."

Eleanor went, wondering whether her ears had served her right; so unnaturally strange seemed this turn of affairs. She had had no time to think of it yet, when passing the drawing-room door a certain impulse prompted her to go in. Mr. Carlisle was there, as something had told her he might be. Eleanor came in, looking white, and advanced towards him with a free steady step eyeing him fully. She was in a mood to meet anything.

"Mr. Carlisle," she said, "you are the cause of all the trouble that has come upon me."

He did not ask her what trouble. He only gently and gravely disclaimed the truth of her assertion.

"Mr. Carlisle," said Eleanor facing him, "do you want the hand without the heart?" There was brave beauty in her face and air.

"Yes!" he said. "You do not know yourself, Eleanor —you do not see yourself at this moment—or you would know better how impossible it is to give other than one answer to such a question."

His look had faced hers as frankly; there was no evil expression in it. Eleanor's head and her gaze sank a little. She hesitated, and then turned away. But Mr. Carlisle with a quick motion intercepted her.

"Eleanor, have you nothing kind to say to me?" he asked, taking her hand. And he said it well.

"Not just now," said Eleanor slowly; "but I will try not to think unkindly of you, Mr. Carlisle."

Perhaps he understood that differently from her meaning; perhaps he chose to misinterpret it; at all events he stooped forward and kissed her. It brought a flash of colour into Eleanor's face, and she went up stairs much more angry with her suitor than her last words had spoke her. The angry mood faded fast when she reached her own room and could be alone and be still. She sat down and thought how, while he stood there and held her hand, there had been a swift presentation to her mind, swift and clear, of all she would be giving up when she turned away from him. In one instant the whole view had come; the rank, the ease, the worldly luxury, the affection; and the question came too, waywardly, as impertinent questions will come, whether she was after all giving it up for sufficient cause? She was relinquishing if she quitted him, all that the world values. Not quite that, perhaps; if turned out from her father's family even, she was in no danger of wanting food or shelter or protection; for she would be sure of those and more in Mrs. Caxton's house. But looking forward into the course of future years that might lie before her, the one alternative offered for her choice presented all that is pleasant in worldly estimation; and on the other side there was a lonely life, and duty, and the affection of one old woman. But though the two views came with startling clearness before Eleanor just at this moment, the more attractive one brought no shadow of temptation with it. She saw it, that was all, and turned away from it to consider present circumstances.

Would her father keep to his word? It seemed impossible; yet coolly reflecting, Eleanor thought from what she knew of him that he would; so far at least as to send her into immediate banishment. That such banishment would be more than temporary she did not believe. Mr. Carlisle would get over his disappointment, would marry somebody else; and in course of time her mother and father, the latter of whom certainly loved her, would find out that they wanted her at home again. But how long first? That no one could tell, nor what might happen in the interval; and when she had got so far in her thoughts, Eleanor's tears began to flow. She let them flow; it relieved her; and somehow there was a good fountain head of them. And again those two pictures of future life rose up before her; not as matters of choice, to take one and leave the other—but as matters of contrast, in somewhat that entered the spring of tears and made them bitter. Was something gone from her life, that could never be got back again? had she lost something that could never be found again? Was there a "bloom and fragrance" waving before her on the one hand, though unattainable, which the other path of life with all its beauty did not offer? To judge by Eleanor's tears she had some such thoughts. But after a time the tears cleared away, and her bowed face looked up as fair as a blue sky after a storm. And Eleanor never had another time of weeping during the month.

It was a dull month to other people. It would have been a dreary one to her, only that there is a private sunshine in some hearts that defies cloudy weather. There is an anchor of the soul, sure and steadfast, by which one rides contentedly in rough water; there is a hope of glory, in the presence of which no darkness can abide; and there is a word with which Eleanor dried her tears that day and upon which she steadied her heart all the days after. It was written by one who knew trouble. "The Lord is my portion, saith my soul; therefore will I hope in him." It is hard to take that portion away from a man, or to make him poor while he has it.

Eleanor had little else the remaining twenty-one days of that month. What troubled her much, she could by no means see Julia; and she found that her sister had been sent home, to the Lodge at Wiglands, under charge of a governess; Mrs. Powle averring that it was time she should be in the country. London was not good for Julia. Was it good for any of them, Eleanor thought? But parliament was still sitting; Mr. Carlisle was in attendance; it was manifest they must be so too. Everything went on much as usual. Eleanor attended her father after his early dinner, for Mr. Powle would not come into London hours; and Mr. Carlisle as usual shared her office with her, except when he was obliged to be in the House. When he was, Mrs. Powle now took his place. The Squire was surly and gloomy; only brought out of those moods by Mr. Carlisle himself. That gentleman held his ground, with excellent grace and self-control, and made Eleanor more than ever feel his power. But she kept her ground too; not without an effort and a good deal of that old arm of defence which is called "all-prayer;" yet she kept it; was gentle and humble and kind to them all, to Mr. Carlisle himself, while he was sensible her grave gentleness had no yielding in it. How he admired her, those days! how he loved her; with a little fierce desire of triumph mingling, it must be confessed, with his love and admiration, and heightened by them; for now pride was touched, and some other feeling which he did not analyze. He had nobody to be jealous of, that he knew; unless it were Eleanor herself; yet her indifference piqued him. He could not brook to be baffled. He shewed not a symptom of all this; but every line of her fine figure, every fold of her rich, beautiful hair, every self-possessed movement, at times was torment to him. Her very dress was a subject of irritation. It was so plain, so evidently unworldly in its simplicity, that unreasonably enough, for Eleanor looked well in it, it put Mr. Carlisle in a fume every day. She should not dress so when he had control of her; and to get the control seemed not easy; and the dress kept reminding him that he had it not. On the whole probably all parties were glad when the sweet month of May for that season came to an end. Even Eleanor was glad; for though she had made up her mind what June would bring her, it is easier to grasp a fear in one's hand, like a nettle, than to touch it constantly by anticipation. So the first of June came.

CHAPTER VIII.

"Come spur away!
I have no patience for a longer stay,
But must go down,
And leave the changeable noise of this great town·
I will the country see,
Where old simplicity,
Though hid in grey,
Doth look more gay
Than foppery in plush and scarlet clad."

ALTHOUGH Eleanor's judgment had said what the issue would be of that day's conference, she had made no preparation to leave home. That she could not do. She could not make certain before it came the weary foreboding that pressed upon her. She went to her father's room after dinner as usual, leaning her heart on that word which had been her walking-staff for three weeks past. "The Lord is my portion, saith my soul; therefore will I hope in him!"

Mrs. Powle was there, quietly knitting. The Squire had gathered himself up into a heap in his easy chair, denoting a contracted state of mind; a'ter that curious fashion which bodily attitudes have, of repeating the mental. Eleanor took the newspaper and sat down.

"Is there anything there particular?" growled the Squire.

"I do not see anything very particular, sir. Here is the continuation of the debate on—"

"How about that bill of yours and Mr. Carlisle's?" broke in Mrs. Powle.

"It was ordered to be printed, mamma—it has not reached the second reading yet. It will not for some time."

"What do you suppose will become of it then?"

"What the Lord pleases. I do not know," said Eleanor with a pang at her heart. "I have done my part—all I could—so far."

"I suppose you expect Mr. Carlisle will take it up as his own cause, after it has ceased to be yours?"

Eleanor understood this, and was silent. She took up the paper again to find where to read.

"Put that down, Eleanor Powle," said her father who was evidently in a very bad humour, as he had cause, poor old gentleman; there is nobody so bad to be out of humour with as yourself;—"put that down! until we know whether you are going to read to me any more or no. I should like to know your decision."

Eleanor hesitated, for it was difficult to speak.

"Come!—out with it. Time's up. Now for your answer. Are you going to be an obedient child, and give Mr. Carlisle a good wife? Hey? Speak!"

"An obedient child, sir, in everything but this. I can give Mr. Carlisle nothing, any more than he has."

"Any more than he has? What is that?"

"A certain degree of esteem and regard, sir—and perhaps, forgiveness."

"Then you will not marry him, as I command you?"

"No—I cannot."

"And you won't give up being a Methodist?"

"I cannot help being what I am. I will not go to church, papa, anywhere that you forbid me."

She spoke low, endeavouring to keep calm. The Squire got up out of his chair. He had no calmness to keep, and he spoke loud.

"Have you taught your sister to think there is any harm in dancing?"

"In dancing parties, I suppose I have."

"And you think they are wicked, and won't go to them?"

"I do not like them. I cannot go to them, papa; for I am a servant of Christ; and I can do no work for my Master there at all; but if I go, I bear witness that they are good."

"Now hear me, Eleanor Powle—" the Squire spoke with suppressed rage—"No such foolery will I have in my house, and no such disrespect to people that are better than you. I told you what would come of all this if you did not give it up—and I stand to my word. You come here to-morrow morning, prepared to put your hand in Mr. Carlisle's and let him know that you will be his obedient servant—or, you quit my house. To-morrow morning you do one thing or the other. And when you go, you will stay. I will never have you back, except as Mr. Carlisle's wife. Now go! I don't want your paper any more."

Eleanor went slowly away. She paused in the drawing-room; there was no one there this time; rang the bell and ordered Thomas to be sent to her. Thomas came, and received orders to be in readiness and have everything in readiness to attend her on a journey the next day. The orders were given clearly and distinctly as usual; but Thomas shook his head as he went down from her presence at the white face his young mistress had worn. "She don't use to look that way," he said to himself, "for she is one of them ladies that carry a hearty brave colour in their cheeks; and now there wasn't a bit of it." But the old servant kept his own counsel and obeyed directions.

Eleanor went through the evening and much of the night without giving herself a moment to think. Packing occupied all that time and the early hours of the next day; she was afraid to be idle, and even dreaded the times of prayer; because whenever she stopped to think, the tears would come. But she grew quiet; and was only pale still, when at an early hour in the morning she left the house. She could not bear to go through a parting scene with her father; she knew him better than to try it; and she shrank from one with her mother. She bid nobody good-bye, for she could not tell anybody that she was going. London streets looked very gloomy to Eleanor that morning as she drove through them to the railway station.

She had still another reason for slipping away, in the fear that else she would be detained to meet Mr. Carlisle again. The evening before she had had a note from him, promising her all freedom for all her religious predilections and opinions—leave to do what she would, if she would only be his wife. She guessed he would endeavour to see her, if she staid long enough in London after the receipt of that note. Eleanor made her escape.

Thomas was sorry at heart to see her cheeks so white yet when they set off; and he noticed that his young mistress hid her face during the first part of the journey. He watched to see it raised up again; and then saw with content that Eleanor's gaze was earnestly fixed on the things without the window. Yes, there was something there. She felt she was out of London; and that whatever might be before her, one sorrowful and disagreeable page of life's book was turned over. London was gone, and she was in the midst of the country again, and the country was at the beginning of June. Green fields and roses and flowery hedge-rows, and sweet air, all wooed her back to hopefulness. Hopefulness for the moment stole in. Eleanor thought things could hardly continue so bad as they seemed. It was not natural. It could not be. And yet—Mr. Carlisle was in the business, and mother and father were set on her making a splendid match and being a great lady. It might be indeed, that there would be no return for Eleanor, that she must remain in banishment, until Mr. Carlisle should take a new fancy or forget her. How long would that be? A field for calculation over which Eleanor's thoughts roamed for some time.

One comfort she had promised herself, in seeing Julia on the way; so she turned out of her direct course to go to Wiglands. She was disappointed. Julia and her governess had left the Lodge only the day before to pay a visit of a week at some distance. By order, Eleanor could not help suspecting it had been; of set purpose, to prevent the sisters meeting. This disappointment was bitter. It was hard to keep from angry thoughts. Eleanor fought them resolutely, but she felt more desolate than she had ever known in her life before. The old place of her home, empty and still, had so many reminders of childish and happy times; careless times; days when nobody thought of great marriages or settlements, or when such thoughts lay all hidden in Mrs. Powle's mind. Every tree and room and book was so full of good and homely associations of the past, that it half broke Eleanor's heart. Home associations now so broken up; the family divided, literally and otherwise; and worst of all, and over which Eleanor's tears flowed bitterest, her own ministrations and influence were cut off from those who most needed them and whom she most wished to benefit. Eleanor's day at home was a day of tears; it was impossible to help it. The roses with their sweet faces looked remonstrance at her; the roads and walks and fields where she had been so happy invited her back to them; the very grey tower of the Priory rising above the trees held out worldly temptation and worldly reproof, with a mocking embodiment of her causes of trouble. Eleanor could not bear it; she spent one night at home; wrote a letter to Julia which she entrusted to a servant's hands for her; and the next morning set her face towards Plassy. Julia lay on her heart. That conversation they had held together the morning when Eleanor waylaid her—it was the last that had been allowed. They had never had a good talk since then. Was that the last chance indeed, for ever? It was impossible to know.

In spite of June beauty it was a dreary journey to her from home to her aunt's; and the beautiful hilly outlines beyond Plassy rose upon her view with a new expression. Sterner, and graver; they seemed to say, "It is life work, now, my child; you must be firm, and if necessary rugged, like us; but truth of action has its own beauty too, and the sunlight of Divine favour rests there always." A shadowless sunlight lay on the crowns and shoulders of the mountains as Eleanor drew near. She got out of the carriage to walk the last few steps and look at the place. Plassy never was more lovely. An aromatic breath, pure and strong, came from the hills and gathered the sweetness of the valleys. Roses and honeysuckles and jessamines and primroses, with a thousand others, loaded the air with their gifts to it, from Mrs. Caxton's garden and from all the fields and hedgerows around. And one after another bit of hilly outline reminded Eleanor that off *there* went the narrow valley that led to the little church at Glanog; *there* went the road to the village, where she and Powis had gone so often of Wednesday afternoons; and in *that* direction lay the little cot where she had watched all night by the dying woman. Not much time for such remembrances was just now; for the farmhouse stood just before her. The dear old farmhouse! looking as pretty as everything else in its dark red stone walls and slate roof; stretching along the ground at that rambling, picturesque, and also opulent style. Eleanor would not knock now, and the door was not fastened to make her need it. Softly she opened it, went in, and stood upon the tiled floor.

No sound of anything in particular; only certain tokens of life in the house. Eleanor went on, opened the door of the sitting parlour and looked in. Nobody there; the room in its summer state of neatness and coolness as she had left it. Eleanor's heart began to grow warm. She would not yet summon a servant; she left that part of the house and wound about among the passages till she came to the back door that led out into the long tiled porch where supper was wont to be spread. And there was the table set this evening; and the wonted glow from the sunny west greeted her there, and a vision of the gorgeous flower-garden. But Eleanor hardly saw the one thing or the other; for Mrs. Caxton was there also, standing by the tea-table, alone, putting something on it. Eleanor moved forward without a word. Her voice would not come out of her throat very well.

"Eleanor!" exclaimed Mrs. Caxton. "My dear love! what has given me this happiness?"

Very strong language for Mrs. Caxton to use. Eleanor felt it, every word of it, as well as the embrace of those kind arms and her aunt's kisses upon her lips; but she was silent.

"How come you here, my darling?"

"They have sent me away from home."

Mrs. Caxton saw that there was some difficulty of speech, and she would not press matters. She put Eleanor into a seat, and looked at her, and took off her bonnet with her own hands; stooped down and kissed her brow. Eleanor steadied herself and looked up.

"It is true, aunt Caxton. I come to you because I have nowhere else to be."

"My love, it is a great happiness to have you, for any cause. Wait, and tell me what the matter is by and by."

She left Eleanor for a moment, only a moment; gave

some orders, and returned to her side. She sat down and took Eleanor's hand.

"What is it, my dear?"

And then Eleanor's composure, which she had thought sure, gave way all of a sudden; and she cried heartily for a minute, laying her head in its old resting-place. But that did her good; and then she kissed Mrs. Caxton over and over before she began to speak.

"They want me to make a great match, aunty; and will not be satisfied with anything else."

"What, Mr. Carlisle?"

"Yes."

"And is that all broken off?" said Mrs. Caxton, a little tone of eagerness discernible under her calm manner.

"It was broken off a year ago," said Eleanor—"more than a year ago. It has always been broken since."

"I heard that it was all going on again. I expected to hear of your marriage."

"It was not true. But it is true, that the world had a great deal of reason to think so; and I could not help that."

"How so, Eleanor?"

"Mamma, and papa, and Mr. Carlisle. They managed it."

"But in such a case, my dear, a woman owes it to herself and to her suitor and to her parents too, to be explicit."

"I do not think I compromised the truth, aunt Caxton," said Eleanor, passing her hand somewhat after a troubled fashion over her brow. "Mr. Carlisle knew I never encouraged him with more favour than I gave others. I could not help being with him, for mamma and he had it so; and they were too much for me. I could not help it. So the report grew. I had a difficult part to play," said Eleanor, repeating her troubled gesture and seeming ready to burst into tears.

"In what way, my love?"

Eleanor did not immediately answer; sat looking off over the meadow as if some danger existed to self-control; then, still silent, turned and met with an eloquent soft eye the sympathizing yet questioning glance that was fixed on her. It was curious how Eleanor's eye met it; how her eye roved over Mrs. Caxton's face and looked into her quiet grey eyes, with a kind of glinting of some spirit fire within, which could almost be seen to play and flicker as thought and feeling swayed to and fro. Her eye said that much was to be said, looked into Mrs. Caxton's face with an intensity of half-speech,—and the lips remained silent. There was consciousness of sympathy, consciousness of something that required sympathy; and the seal of silence. Perhaps Mrs. Caxton's response to this strange look came half unconsciously; it came wholly naturally.

"Poor child!"—

"The colour rose on Eleanor's cheek at that; she turned her eyes away.

"I think Mr. Carlisle's plan—and mamma's—was to make circumstances too strong for me; and to draw me on by degrees. And they would, perhaps, but for all I learned here."

"For what you learned here, my dear?"

"Yes aunty; if they could have got me into a whirl of society—if they could have made me love dancing parties and theatres and the opera, and I had got bewildered and forgotten that a great worldly establishment is not the best thing—perhaps temptation would have been too much for me.—Perhaps it would. I don't know."

There was a little more colour in Eleanor's cheeks than her words accounted for, as Mrs. Caxton noticed.

"Did you ever feel in danger from the temptation, Eleanor?"

"Never, aunty. I think it never so much as touched me."

"Then Mr. Carlisle has been at his own risk," said Mrs. Caxton. "Let us dismiss him, my love."

"Aunt Caxton, I have a strange homeless, forlorn feeling."

For answer to that, Mrs. Caxton put her arms round Eleanor and gave her one or two good strong kisses. There was reproof as well as affection in them; Eleanor felt both, even without her aunt's words.

"Trust the Lord. You know who has been the dwelling-place of his people, from all generations. They cannot be homeless. And for the rest, remember that whatever brings you here brings a great boon to me. My love, do you wish to go to your room before you have tea?"

Eleanor was glad to get away and be alone for a moment. How homelike her old room seemed!—with the rose and honeysuckle breath of the air coming in at the casements. How peaceful and undisturbed the old furniture looked. The influence of the place began to settle down upon Eleanor. She got rid of the dust of travel, and came down presently to the porch with a face as quiet as a lamb.

Tea went on with the same soothing influence. There was much to tell Eleanor, of doings in and about Plassy the year past; for the fact was, that letters had not been frequent. Who was sick and who was well; who had married, and who was dead; who had set out on a Christian walk, and who were keeping up such a walk to the happiness of themselves and of all about them. Then how Mrs. Caxton's own household had prospered; how the dairy went on; and there were some favourite cows that Eleanor desired to hear of. From the cows they got to the garden. And all the while the lovely meadow valley lay spread out in its greenness before

Eleanor; the beautiful old hills drew the same loved outline across the sunset sky; the lights and shadows were of June; and the garden at hand was a rich mass of beauty sloping its terraced sweetness down to the river. Just as it was a year ago, when the summons came for Eleanor to leave it; only the garden seemed even more gorgeously rich than then. Just the same; even to the dish of strawberries on the table. But that was not wreathed with ivy and myrtle now.

"Aunt Caxton, this is like the very same evening that I was here last."

"It is almost a year," said Mrs. Caxton.

Neither added anything to these two very unremarkable remarks; and silence fell with the evening light, as the servants were clearing away the table. Perhaps the mountains with the clear paling sky beyond them, were suggestive. Both the ladies looked so.

"My dear," said Mrs. Caxton then, "let me understand a little better about this affair that gives you to me. Do you come, or are you sent?"

"It is formal banishment, aunt Caxton. I am sent from them at home; but sent to go whither I will. So I come, to you."

"What is the term assigned to this banishment?"

"None. It is absolute—unless or until I will grant Mr. Carlisle's wishes, or giving up being, as papa says, a Methodist. But that makes it final—as far as I am concerned."

"They will think better of it by and by.

"I hope so," said Eleanor faintly. "It seems a strange thing to me, aunt Caxton, that this should have happened to me—just now when I am so needed at home. Papa is unwell—and I was beginning to get his ear,—and I have great influence over Julia, who only wants leading to go in the right way. And I am taken away from all that. I cannot help wondering why."

"Let it be to the glory of God, Eleanor; that is all your concern. The rest you will understand by and by."

"But that is the very thing. It is hard to see how it can be to his glory."

"Do not try," said Mrs. Caxton smiling. "The Lord never puts his children anywhere where they cannot glorify him; and he never sends them where they have ot work to do or a lesson to learn. Perhaps this is your lesson, Eleanor—to learn to have no home but in him."

Eleanor's eyes filled very full; she made no answer.

But one thing is certain; peace settled down upon her heart. It would be difficult to help that at Plassy. We all know the effect of going home to the place of our childhood after a time spent in other atmosphere; and there is a native air of the spirit, in which it feels the like renovating influence. Eleanor breathed it while they sat at the table; she felt she had got back into her element. She felt it more and more when at family prayer the whole household were met together, and she heard her aunt's sweet and high petitions again. And the blessing of peace fully settled down upon Eleanor when she was gone up to her room and had recalled and prayed over her aunt's words. She went to sleep with that glorious saying running through her thoughts—"Lord, thou hast been our dwelling-place in all generations."

CHAPTER IX.

"But there be million hearts accurst, where no sweet sunbursts shine,
And there be million hearts athirst for Love's immortal wine,
This world is full of beauty, as other worlds above;
And if we did our duty, it might be full of love."

PEACE had unbroken reign at Plassy from that time. Eleanor threw herself again eagerly into all her aunt's labours and schemes for the good and comfort of those around her. There was plenty to do; and she was Mrs. Caxton's excellent helper. Powis came into requisition anew; and as before, Eleanor traversed the dales and the hills on her various errands, swift and busy. That was not the only business going. Her aunt and she returned to their old literary habits, and read books and talked; and it was hard if Eleanor in her rides over the hills and over the meadows and along the streams did not bring back one hand full of wild flowers. She dressed the house with them, getting help from the garden when necessary; botanized a good deal; and began to grow as knowing in plants almost as Mrs. Caxton herself. She would come home loaded with wild thyme and gorse and black bryony and saxifrage and orchis flowers, having scoured hill and meadow and robbed the hedgerows for them, which also gave her great tribute of wild roses. Then later came crimson campion and eyebright, dog roses and honeysuckles, columbine and centaury, grasses of all kinds, and harebell, and a multitude impossible to name; though the very naming is pleasant. Eleanor lived very much out of doors, and was likened by her aunt to a rural Flora or Proserpine that summer; though when in the house she was just the most sonsy, sensible, companionable little earthly maiden that could be fancied. Eleanor was not under size indeed; but so much like her own wild flowers in pure simpleness and sweet natural good qualities that Mrs. Caxton was sometimes inclined to bestow the endearing diminutive upon her; so sound and sweet she was.

"And what are all these?" said Mrs. Caxton one day stopping before an elegant basket.

"Don't you like them?"

"Very much. Why you have got a good many kinds here."

"That is Hart's Tongue, you know—that is wall spleenwort, and that is the other kind; handsome things, are they not?"

"And this?"

"That is the forked spleenwort. You don't know it? I rode away, away up the mountain for it yesterday. That is where I got those Woodsia's too—aren't they beautiful. I was gay to find those; they are not common."

"No. And this is not common, to me."

"Don't you know it, aunt Caxton? It grows just in the spray of a waterfall—this and this; they are polypodies. That is another—that came from the old round tower."

"And where did you get these?—these waterfall ferns?"

"I got them at the Bandel of Helig."

"There? My dear child! how could you, without risk?"

"Without much risk, aunty."

"How did you ever know the Bandel?"

"I have been there before, aunt Caxton."

"I think I never shewed it to you?"

"No ma'am;—but Mr. Rhys did."

His name had scarcely been mentioned before since Eleanor had come to the farm. It was mentioned now with a cognizance of that fact. Mrs. Caxton was silent a little.

"Why have you put these green things here without a rose or two? they are all alone in their greenness."

"I like them better so, aunty. They are beautiful enough by themselves; but if you put a rose there, you cannot help looking at it."

Mrs. Caxton smiled and turned away.

One thing in the midst of all these natural explorations, remained unused; and that a thing most likely, one would have thought, to be applied to for help. The microscope stood on one side apparently forgotten. It always stood there, in the sitting parlour, in full view; but nobody seemed to be conscious of its existence. Eleanor never touched it; Mrs. Caxton never spoke of it.

From home meantime, Eleanor heard little that was satisfactory. Julia was the only one that wrote, and her letters gave painful subjects for thought. Her father was very unlike himself, Julia said, and growing more feeble and more ill every day; though by slow degrees. She wished Eleanor would write her letters without any religion in them; for she supposed *that* was what her mother would not let her read; so she never had the comfort of seeing Eleanor's letters for herself, but Mrs Powle read aloud bits from them. "Very little bits too," added Julia, "I guess your letters have more relig ion in them than anything else. But you see it is no use." Eleanor read this passage aloud to Mrs. Caxton.

"Is that true, Eleanor?"

"No, ma'am. I write to Julia of everything that I do, all day long, and of everything and everybody that interests me. What mamma does not like comes in, of course, with it all; but I do very little preaching, aunt Caxton."

"I would go on just so, my dear. I would not alter the style of my letters."

So the flowers of June were replaced by the flowers of July; and the beauties of July gave place to the purple "ling" of August, with gentian and centaury and St. John's wort; and then came the Autumn changes, with the less delicate blossoms of that later time, amidst which the eclipsed meadow-sweet came quite into favour again. Still Eleanor brought wild things from the hills and the streams, though she applied more now to Mrs. Caxton's home store in the garden; wild mints and Artemisias and the Michaelmas daisy still came home with her from her rides and walks; the rides and walks in which Eleanor was a ministering angel to many a poor house, many an ignorant soul and many a failing or ailing body.

Then came October; and with the first days of October the news that her father was dead.

It added much bitterness to Eleanor's grief, that Mrs. Powle entirely declined to have her come home, even for a brief stay. If she chose to submit to conditions, her mother wrote, she would be welcome; it was not too late; but if she held to her perversity, she must bear the consequences. She did not own her nor want her. She gave her up to her aunt Caxton. Her remaining daughter was in her hands, and she meant to keep her there. Eleanor, she knew, if she came home would come to sow rebellion. She should not come to do that, either then or at all.

Mildly quiet and decided Mrs. Powle's letter was; very decided, and so cool as to give every assurance the decision would be persisted in. Eleanor felt this very much. She kept on her usual way of life without any variation; but the radiant bright look of her face was permanently saddened. She was just as sweet and companionable an assistant to her aunt as ever; but from month to month Mrs. Caxton saw that a shadow lay deep upon her heart. No shadow could have less of anything like hard edges.

They had been sitting at work one night late in the winter, those two, the aunt and the niece; and having at last put up her work Eleanor sat gravely poring into the red coals on the hearth; those thought-provoking, life-stirring, strange things, glowing and sparkling between life and death like ourselves. Eleanor's face was very sober.

"Aunt Caxton," she said at length,—"my life seems such a confusion to me!"

"So everything seems that we do not understand," Mrs. Caxton said.

"But is it not, aunty? I seem taken from everything that I ought most naturally to do—papa, Julia, mamma. I feel like a banished person, I suppose; only I have the strange feeling of being banished from my place in the world."

"What do you think of such a life as Mr. Rhys is leading?"

"I think it is straight, and beautiful,"—Eleanor answered, looking still into the fire. "Nothing can be further from confusion. He is in *his* place."

"He is in a sort of banishment, however."

"Not from that! And it is voluntary banishment—for his Master's sake. *That* is not sorrowful, aunt Caxton."

"Not when the Lord's banished ones make their home in him. And I do not doubt but Mr. Rhys does that."

"Have you ever heard from him, aunt Caxton."

"Not yet. It is almost time, I think."

"It is almost a year and a half since he went."

"The communication is slow and uncertain," said Mrs. Caxton. "They do not get letters there, often, till they are a year old."

"How impossible it used to be to me," said Eleanor, "to comprehend such a life; how impossible to understand, that anybody should leave home and friends and comfort, and take his place voluntarily in distance and danger and heathendom. It was an utter enigma to me."

"And you understand it now?"

"O yes, aunty," Eleanor went on in the same tone; and she had not ceased gazing into the coals;—"I see that Christ is all; and with him one is never alone, and under his hand one can never be in danger. I know now how his love keeps one even from fear."

"You are no coward naturally."

"No, aunt Caxton—not about ordinary things, except when conscience made me so, some time ago."

"That is over now?"

Eleanor took her eyes from the fire, to give Mrs. Caxton a smile with the words—"Thank the Lord!"

"Mr. Rhys is among scenes that might try any natural courage," said Mrs. Caxton. They are a desperate set of savages to whom he is ministering."

"What a glory, to carry the name of Christ to them!"

"They are hearing it, too," said Mrs. Caxton. "But there is enough of the devil's worst work going on there to try any tender heart; and horrors enough to shock stout nerves. So it has been. I hope Mr. Rhys finds it better."

"I don't know much about them," said Eleanor "Are they much worse than savages in general, aunt Caxton?"

"I think they are,—and better too, in being more intellectually developed. Morally, I think I never read of a lower fallen set of human beings. Human life is of no account; such a thing as respect to humanity is unknown, for the eating of human bodies has gone on to a most wonderful extent, and the destroying them for that perpose. With all that, there is a very careful respect paid to descent and rank; but it is the observance of fear. That one fact gives you the key to the whole. Where a man is thought of no more worth than to be killed and eaten, a woman is not thought worth anything at all; and society becomes a lively representation of the infernal regions, without the knowledge and without the remorse."

"Poor creatures!" said Eleanor.

"You comprehend that there must be a great deal of trial to a person of fine sensibilities, in making a home amongst such a people, for an indefinite length of time."

"Yes, aunty,—but the Lord will make it all up to him."

"Blessed be the name of the Lord!" it was Mrs. Caxton's turn to answer; and she said it with deep feeling and emphasis.

"It seems the most glorious thing to me, aunt Caxton, to tell the love of Christ to those that don't know it. I wish I could do it."

"My love, you do."

"I do very little, ma'am. I wish I could do a thousand times more!"

The conversation stopped there. Both ladies remained very gravely thoughtful a little while longer and then separated for the night. But the next evening when they were seated at tea alone, Mrs. Caxton recurred to the subject.

"You said last night, Eleanor, that you wished you could do a great deal more work of a certain kind than you do."

"Yes, ma'am."

"Did your words mean, my love, that you are discontented with your own sphere of duty, or find it too narrow?"

Eleanor's eyes opened a little at that. "Aunt Caxton, I never thought of such a thing. I do not remember that I was considering my own sphere of duty at all. I was thinking of the pleasure of preaching Christ—yes, and the glory and honour—to such poor wretches as those we were talking of, who have never had a glimpse of the truth before."

"Then for your part you are satisfied with England?"

"Why yes, ma'am. I am satisfied, I think,—I mean to be,—with any place that is given me. I should be sorry to choose for myself."

"But if you had a clear call, you would like it, to go to the Cape of Good Hope and teach the Hottentots?"

"I do not mean that, aunty," said Eleanor laughing a little. "Surely you do not suspect me of any wandering romantic notion about doing the Lord's work in one place rather than in another. I would rather teach English people than Hottentots. But if I saw that my place was at the Cape of Good Hope, I would go there. If my place were there, some way would be possible for me to get there, I suppose."

"You would have no fear?" said Mrs. Caxton.

"No aunty; I think not. Ever since I can say 'The Lord is my Shepherd—' I have done with fear."

"My love, I should be very sorry to have you go to the Cape of Good Hope. I am glad there is no prospect of it. But you are right about not choosing. As soon as we go where we are not sent, we are at our own charges."

The door here opened, and the party and the tea-table received an accession of one to their number. It was an elderly, homely gentleman, to whom Mrs. Caxton gave a very cordial reception and whom she introduced to Eleanor as the Rev. Mr. Morrison. He had a pleasant face, Eleanor saw, and as soon as he spoke, a pleasant manner.

"I ought to be welcome, ma'am," he said rubbing his hands with the cold as he sat down. "I bring you letters from Brother Rhys."

"You are welcome without that, brother, as you know," Mrs. Caxton answered. "But the letters are welcome. Of how late date are they?"

"Some pretty old—some not more than nine or ten months ago; when he had been stationed a good while."

"How is he?"

"Well, he says; never better."

"And happy?"

"I wish I was as happy!" said Mr. Morrison.—"He had got fast hold of his work already."

"He would do that immediately."

"He studied the language on shipboard, all the way out; and he was able to hold a service in it for the natives only a few weeks after he had landed. Don't you call that energy?"

"There is energy wherever he is," said Mrs. Caxton.

"Yes, you know him pretty well. I suppose they never have it so cold out there as we have it to-night," Mr. Morrison said rubbing his hands. "It's stinging! That fire is the pleasantest thing I have seen to-day."

"Where is Mr. Rhys stationed?"

"I forget—one of the islands down there, with an unintelligible name. Horrid places!"

"Is the place itself disagreeable?" Eleanor asked.

"The place itself, ma'am," said Mr. Morrison, his face stiffening from its genial unbent look into formality as he turned to her,—"the place itself I do not understand to be very disagreeable; it is the character of the population which must make it a hard place to live in. They are exceedingly debased. Vile people!"

"Mr. Rhys is not alone on his station?" said Mrs. Caxton.

"No, he is with Mr. and Mrs. Lefferts. His letters will tell you."

For the letters Mrs. Caxton was evidently impatient; but Mr. Morrison's refreshment had first to be attended to. Only fair; for he had come out of his way on purpose to bring them to her; and being one of a certain Committee he had it in his power to bring for her perusal and pleasure more than her own letters from Mr. Rhys, and more than Mr. Rhys's own letters to the Committee. It was a relief to two of the party when Mr. Morrison's cups of tea were at last disposed of, and the far-come despatches were brought out on the green tablecloth under the light of the lamp.

With her hand on her own particular packet of letters, as if so much communication with them could not be put off, Mrs. Caxton sat and listened to Mr. Morrison's reading. Eleanor had got her work. As the particular interest which made the reading so absorbing to them may possibly be shared in a slight degree by others, it is fair to give a slight notion of the character of the news contained in those closely written pages. The letters Mr. Morrison read were voluminous; from different persons on different stations of the far-off mission field. They told of difficulties great, and encouragements greater; of their work and its results; and of their most pressing wants; especially the want of more men to help. The work they said was spreading faster than they could keep up with it. Thousands of heathen had given up heathenism, who in miserable ignorance cried for Christian instruction; children as wild as the wild birds, wanted teaching and were willing to have it; native teachers needed training, who had the will without the knowledge to aid in the service. Thirty of them, Mr. Lefferts said, he had under his care. With all this, they told of the wonderful beauty of the regions where their field of labour was. Mr. Lefferts wrote of a little journey lately taken to another part of his island, which had led him through almost every variety of natural luxuriance. Mountains and hills and valleys, rivers and little streams, rich woods and mangrove swamps. Mr. Lefferts' journey had been, like Paul's of old, to establish the native churches formed at different small places by the way. There he married couples and baptized children and met classes and told the truth. At one place where he had preached, married several couples, baptized over thirty, young and old, and met as many in classes, Mr. Lefferts told of a walk he took. It led him to the top of a little hill, from which a rich view was to be had, while a multitude of exquisite shrubs in flower gave another refreshment in their delicious fragrance. A little stream running down the side of the hill was used by the natives to water their plantations of taro, for which the side hill was formed into terraced beds. Paroquets and humming birds flew about, and the sun was sinking brilliantly in the western ocean line as he looked. So far, everything was fair, sweet, lovely; a contrast to what he met when he reached the lower grounds again. There the swarms of mosquitos compelled Mr. Lefferts to retreat for the night within a curtain canopy for protection; and thither he was followed by a fat savage who shared the protection with him all night long. Another sort of experience! and another sort of neighbourhood from that of the starry white *Gardenia* flowers on the top of the hill.

Nevertheless, of a neighbouring station Mr. Rhys wrote that the people were at war, and the most horrible heathen practices were going on. At the principal town, he said, more people were eaten perhaps than anywhere else in the islands. The cruelties and the horrors were impossible to be told. A few days before he wrote, twenty-eight persons had been killed and eaten in one day. They had been caught fishing—taken prisoners and brought home—half killed, and in that state thrown into the ovens; still having life enough left to try to get away from the fire.

"The first time I saw anything of this kind," wrote Mr. Rhys, "was one evening when we had just finished a class-meeting. The evening was most fair and peaceful as we came out of the house; a fresh air from the sea had relieved the heat of the day; the leaves of the trees were glittering in the sunlight; the ocean all sparkling under the breeze; when word came that some bodies of slain people were bringing from Lauthala. I could hardly understand the report, or credit it; but presently the horrible procession came in sight, and eleven dead bodies were laid on the ground immediately before us. Eleven only were brought to this village; but great numbers are said to have been killed. Their crime was the killing of one man; and when they would have submitted themselves and made amends, all this recompence of death was demanded by the offended chief. The manner in which these wretched creatures were treated is not a thing to be described; they were not handled with the respect which we give to brute animals. The natives have looked dark upon us since that time, and give us reason to know that as far as they are concerned our lives are not safe. But we know in whose hands our lives are; they are the Lord's; and he will do with them what he pleases—not what the heathen please. So we are under no concern about it."

That storm appeared to have passed away; for in later letters Mr. Rhys and Mr. Lefferts spoke of acceptable services among the people and an evidently manifested feeling of trust and good will on their part towards the missionaries. Indeed these were often able to turn the natives from their devilish purposes and save life.

Not always. The old king of that part of the country had died, and all the influence and all the offers of compensation made by the missionaries, could not prevent the slaughter of half a dozen women, his wives, to do him honour in his burial. The scene as Mr. Lefferts described it was heart-sickening.

As he drew near the door of the king's house, with the intent to prevail for the right or to protest against the wrong, he saw the biers standing ready; and so knew that all the efforts previously made to hinder the barbarous rites had been unavailing. The house as he entered was in the hush of death. One woman lay strangled. Another sitting on the floor, covered with a large veil, was in the hands of her murderers. A cord was passed twice round her neck, and the ends were held on each side of her by a group of eight or ten strong men, the two groups pulling opposite ways. She was dead, the poor victim underneath the veil, in a minute or two after the missionaries entered; and the veil being taken off they saw that it was a woman who had professed Christianity. Her sons were among those who had strangled her. Another woman came forward with great shew of bravery when her name was called; offered her hand to the missionaries as she passed them; and with great pride of bearing submitted herself to the death which probably she knew she could not avoid. Everybody was quiet and cheerful, and the whole thing went on with the undisturbed order of a recognized and accustomed necessity; only the old king's son, the reigning chief for a long time back, was very uneasy at the part he was playing before the missionaries; he was the only trembling or doubtful one there. Yet he would not yield the point. Pride before all; his father must not be buried without the due honours of his position. Mr. Rhys and Mr. Lefferts had staid to make their protest and offer their entreaties and warnings, to the very last; and then heart-sick and almost faint with the disgusting scene, had returned home.

Yet the influence of the truth was increasing and the good work was spreading and growing around them, steadily and in every direction. A great many had renounced heathenism; not a small number were earnest Christians and shewed the truth of their religion in their changed lives. A great number of reports proved this.

"It is work that tries what stuff men's hearts are of, however," remarked Mr. Morrison as he folded up one packet of letters. Neither of his hearers made him any answer. Mrs. Caxton sat opposite to him, deeply attentive but silent, with her hand always lying upon her own particular packet. Eleanor had turned a little away and sat with her side face towards Mr. Morrison, looking into the fire. Her work was dropped; she sat motionless.

"I have a letter to read you now of a later date," Mr. Morrison went on,—"from Mr. Rhys, which shews how well he has got hold of the people and how much he is regarded by them already. It shews the influence gained by the truth, too, which is working there fast."

After giving some details of business and of his labours, Mr. Rhys wrote—"My last notable piece of work, has been in the character of an ambassador of peace—not heavenly but earthly. News was brought four or five days ago that the heathen inhabitants of two neighbouring districts had engaged in open hostilities. Home business claimed me one day; the next morning I set out on my mission, with one or two Christian natives. The desolations of war soon met our eyes, in destroyed crops and a deserted village. Nobody was to be seen. I and those who were with me sat down in the shade of some trees, while a native went to find the inhabitants who had hid themselves in a thicket of mangroves. As soon as the chief heard that I was there, and what I had come for, he declared he would be a Christian forthwith; and four or five of his principal men followed his example. They came to me, and entered fully into my object; and it was decided that we should go on immediately to the fortress where those who wished to carry on war had intrenched themselves. We got there just as the sun was setting; and from that time till midnight I was engaged in what I saw now for the first time; a savage council of war. Grim black warriors covered with black powder sat or stood about, on a little clear spot of ground where the moon shone down; muskets and clubs and spears lay on the grass and were scattered about among the boles of the trees; a heathen-looking scene. Till midnight we talked, and hard talking too; then it was ended as I had prayed it might. The party with whom I was had suffered already in battle and had not had their revenge; it was difficult to give that up; but at last the chief got up and put his hand in mine. "I should like to be a heathen a little longer," he said, "but I will *lotu* as you so earnestly entreat me." *Lotu* is their name for embracing Christianity. Another young warrior joined him; and there under the midnight moon, we worshipped God; those two and those who were with me. In another part of the village a dozen women for the first time bowed the knee in the same worship.

"So far was well; but it yet remained to induce the opposite hostile party to agree to peace; you understand only one side was yet persuaded. Early the next morning I set about it. Here a difficulty met me. The Christian chiefs made no objection to going with me to parley with their enemies; but I wanted the company also of another, the chief of this district; knowing it very important. And he was afraid to go. He told me so plainly. 'If I do as you ask me,' said he, 'I am a dead man this day.' I did my best to make him think differently; a hundred men declared that they would die in defence of him; and at last I gained my point. Tui Mbua agreed to go to the neighbourhood of the hostile town, if I would bring its principal men to meet him at an appointed place. So we went. This chosen place was a fine plot of ground enclosed by magnificent chestnut trees. I went on to the town, with a few unarmed men. The people received us well; but it was difficult to make the old heathen, brought up on treachery and falsehood, believe that I was to be trusted. But in the end the chief and twenty of his men consented to go with us, and left their arms at home. They did it with forebodings, for I overheard an old man say, as we set out from the place,—'We shall see death to-day.' I lifted my voice and cried, 'To-day we live!' They took up the words, and heart at the same time, and repeated, 'To-day we live'—to encourage themselves, I suppose, as we went towards the chestnut-tree meeting ground.

"I felt that the peace of the whole region depended on what was to be done there, and for my part went praying that all might go well. It was an anxious moment when we entered the open place; any ill-looks in either party would chase away trust from the other. As we went in I watched the chief who accompanied me. He gently bowed to Tui Mbua and approached him with due and evidently honest respect. My heart leaped at that moment. Tui Mbua looked at him keenly, sprang to his feet, and casting his arms about his enemy's neck gave him a warm embrace. The people around shouted for joy; I was still, I believe, for the very depth of mine. One of the Christian chiefs spoke out and cried, 'We thank thee, O Lord, for thus bringing thy creatures into the way of life;' and he wept aloud for very gladness.

"After that we had speechifying; and I returned home very full of thankful joy."

This was the last letter read. Mr. Morrison folded up his packet amid a great silence. Mrs. Caxton seemed thoughtful; Eleanor was motionless.

"He is doing good work," remarked Mr. Morrison; "but it is hard work. He is the right sort of man to go there—fears nothing, shirks nothing. So are they all, I believe; but almost all the rest of them have their wives with them. How came Rhys to go alone?"

"He does not write as if he felt lonely," said Mrs. Caxton.

"It is better for a man to take a wife, though," said Mr. Morrison. "He wants so much of comfort and home as that. They get tired, and they get sick, and to have no woman's hand about is something to be missed at such times. O we are all dependent. Mr. Rhys is domesticated now with Brother Lefferts and his family. I suppose he feels it less, because he has not had a home of his own in a good while; that makes a difference."

"He knows he has a home of his own too," said Mrs. Caxton; "though he has not reached it yet. I suppose the thought of that makes him content."

"Of course. But in a heathen land, with heathen desolation and dark faces all around one, you have no idea how at times one's soul longs for a taste of England. Brother Rhys too is a man to feel all such things. He has a good deal of taste, and what you might call sensitiveness to externals."

"A good deal," said Mrs. Caxton quietly. "Then he has some beautiful externals around him."

"So they say. But the humanity is deplorable. Well, they will get their reward when the Master comes. A man leaves everything indeed when he goes to the South Seas as Rhys has done. He would have been very popular in England."

"So he will in the islands."

"Well so it seems," said Mr. Morrison. "He has got

the ear of those wild creatures evidently. That's the man."

It was time for evening prayers; and afterwards the party separated; Mrs. Caxton carrying off with her her packet of letters unbroken. The morning brought its own business; the breakfast was somewhat hurried; Mr. Morrison took his departure; and nothing more was said on the subject of South Sea missionaries till the evening. Then the two ladies were again alone together.

"Are you well to-day, Eleanor?" was Mrs. Caxton's first question at the tea-table.

"Some headache, aunt Caxton."

"How is that? And I have noticed that your eyes were heavy all day."

"There is no harm, ma'am. I did not sleep very well."

"Why not?"

"I think the reading of those letters excited me, aunt Caxton."

Mrs. Caxton looked at a line of faint crimson which was stealing up into Eleanor's cheeks, and for a moment stayed her words.

"My dear, there is as good work to be done here, as ever in Polynesia."

"I do not know, aunt Caxton," said Eleanor leaning her head on her hand in thoughtful wise. "England has had the light a great while; it must be grand to be the first torch-bearers into the darkness."

"So Mr. Rhys feels. But then, my dear, I think we are to do the work given us—one here and one there;—and let the Lord place his servants, and our service, as he will.

"I do not think otherwise, aunt Caxton."

"Would you like to hear some of what Mr. Rhys has written to me? there is a little difference between what is sent to a Committee and what is for the private eye of a friend."

"Yes ma'am, I would like it," Eleanor said; but she did not say so at all eagerly; and Mrs. Caxton looked at her once or twice before she changed the subject and spoke of something else. She held to her offer, however; and when the green cloth and the lamp were again in readiness, she brought out the letters. Eleanor took some work and bent her head over it.

"This is one of the latest dates," Mrs. Caxton said as she opened the paper; "written after he had been there a good many months and had got fairly acquainted with the language and with the people. It seems to me he has been very quick about it."

"Yes, I think so," Eleanor answered; "but that is his way."

Mrs. Caxton read.

"'MY DEAR FRIEND,

"In spite of the world of ocean rolling between us, I yet have a strange and sweet feeling of taking your hand, when I set myself to write to you. Spirit and matter seem at odds; and far away as I am, with the vegetation and the air of the tropics around me, as soon as I begin upon this sheet of paper I seem to stand in Plassy again. The dear old hills rear their wild outlines before me; the green wealth of vegetation is at my feet, but cool and fresh as nothing looks to me under the northerly wind which is blowing now; and your image is so distinct, that I almost can grasp your hand, and almost hear you speak; *see* you speak, I do. Blessed be the Lord for imagination, as well as for memory! Without it, how slowly we should mount to the conception of heavenly things and the understanding of himself; and the distance between friends would be a sundering of them indeed. But I must not waste time or paper in telling you what you know already.

"By which you will conclude that I am busy. I am

as busy as I can possibly be. That is as I wish it. It is what I am here for. I would not have a moment unused. On Sunday I have four or five services, of different sorts. Week days I have an English school, a writing school, one before and the other after mid-day; and later still, a school for regular native instruction. Every moment of time that is free, or would be, is needed for visiting the sick, whose demands upon us are constant. But this gives great opportunity to preach the gospel and win the hearts of the people.

"Some account of a little preaching and teaching journey in which I took part some few months ago, I have a mind to give you. Our object was specially an island between one and two hundred miles away, where many have become Christians, and not in name only; but where up to this time no missionary has been stationed. We visit them when we can. This time we had the advantage of a brig to make the voyage in; the mission ship was here with the Superintendent and he desired to visit the place. We arrived at evening in the neighbourhood; at a little island close by, where all the people are now Christian. Mr. Lefferts went ashore in a canoe to make arrangements; and the next day we followed. It was a beautiful day and as beautiful a sight as eyes could see. We visited the houses of the native teachers, who were subjects of admiration in every respect; met candidates for baptism and examined them; married a couple; and Bro. Griffiths preached. There is a new chapel, of very neat native workmanship; with a pulpit carved out of a solid piece of wood, oiled to give it colour and gloss. In the chapel the whole population of the island was assembled, dressed in new dresses, attentive, and interested. So were we, you may believe, when we remembered that only two years ago all these people were heathens. O these islands are a glorious place now and then, in spots where the devil's reign is broken. I wish you could have seen us afterwards, my dear friend, at our native feast spread on the ground under the trees; you who never saw a table set but with exact and elegant propriety. We had no table; believe me, we were too happy and hungry to mind that. I do not think you would have quarrelled with our dishes; they were no other and no worse than the thick broad glossy leaves of the banana. No fault could be found with their elegance; and our napkins were of the green rind of the same tree. Cocoanut shells were our substitute for flint glass, and I like it very well; especially when cocoanut milk is the refreshment to be served in them. Knives and forks we had none! What would you have said to that? Our meat was boiled fowls and baked yams and fish dressed in various ways; and the fingers of the natives, or our own, were our only dividers. But I have seen less pleasant entertainments; and I only could wish you had been there,—so you might have whisked back to England the next minute after it was over, on some convenient fairy carpet such as I used to read of in Eastern tales when I was a boy. For us, we had to make our way in haste back to the ship, which lay in the offing, and could not come near on account of the reef barrier. We got on board safely, passing the reefs where once an American ship was wrecked and her crew killed and eaten by the people of these parts.

"The next day we made the land we sought; and got ashore through a tremendous surf. Here we found the island had lately been the seat of war—some of the heathen having resolved to put an end by violence to the Christian religion there, or as they call it, the *lotu*. The Christians had gained the victory, and then had treated their enemies with the utmost kindness; which had produced a great effect upon them. The rest of the day after our landing was spent in making thorough inquiry into this matter; and in a somewhat extended preaching service. At night we slept on a mat laid for us, or tried to sleep; but my thoughts were too busy; and the clear night sky was witness to a great many restless movements, I am afraid, before I lost them in forgetfulness. The occasion of which, I suppose, was the near prospect of sending letters home to England by the ship. At any rate, England and the South Seas were very near together that night; and I was fain to remember that heaven is nearer yet. But the remembrance came, and with it sleep. The next day was a day of business. Marrying couples (over forty of them) baptizing converts, preaching; then meeting the teachers and class-leaders and examining them as to their Christian experience, etc. From dawn till long past mid-day we were busy so; and then were ready for another feast in the open air like that one I described to you—for we had had no breakfast. We had done all the work we could do at that time at Ono, and sought our ship immediately after dinner; passing through a surf too heavy for the canoes to weather.

"Let me tell you some of the testimony given by these converts from heathenism; given simply and heartily, by men who have not learned their religion by book nor copied it out of other men's mouths. It was a very thrilling thing to hear them, these poor enterers into the light, who have but just passed the line of darkness. One said, 'I love the Lord, and I know he loves me; not for anything in me, or for anything I have done; but for Christ's sake alone. I trust in Christ and am happy. I listen to God, that he may do with me as he pleases. I am thankful to have lived until the Lord's work has begun. I feel it in my heart! I hold Jesus! I am happy! My heart is full of love to God!'

"Another said, 'One good thing I know,—the sacred blood of Jesus. I desire nothing else.'

"Another,—'I know that God has justified me

through the sacred blood of Jesus. I know assuredly that I am reconciled to God. I know of the work of God in my soul. The sacred Spirit makes it clear to me. I wish to preach the gospel, that others also may know Jesus.'

"All these have been engaged the past year in teaching or proclaiming the truth in various ways. Another of their number who was dying, one or two of us went to see. One of us asked him if he was afraid to die? 'No,' he said, 'I am sheltered. The great Saviour died for me. The Lord's wrath is removed. I am his.' And another time he remarked, 'Death is a fearfully great thing, but I fear it not. There is a *Saviour* below the skies.'

"So there is a helmet of salvation for the poor Fijian as well as for the favoured people at home. Praise be to the Lord. Did I tell you, my dear friend, I was restless at the thought of sending letters home? Let me tell you now, I am happy; as happy as I could be in any place in the world; and I would not be in any other place, by my own choice, for all the things in the world. I need only to be made more holy. Just in proportion as I am that, I am happy and I am useful. I want to be perfectly holy. But there is the same way of trusting for the poor Fijian and for me; and I believe in that same precious blood I shall be made clean, even as they. I want to preach Christ a thousand times more than I do. I long to make his love known to these poor people. I rejoice in being here, where every minute may tell actively for him. My dear friend, when we get home, do what we will, we shall not think we have done enough.

"Our life here is full of curious contrasts. Within doors, what our old habits have stereotyped as propriety, is sadly trenched upon. Before the ship came, Mrs. Lefferts' stock of comfort in one line was reduced to a single tea-cup; and in other stores, the demands of the natives had caused us to run very short. You know it is only by payment of various useful articles that we secure any service done or purchase any native produce. Money is unknown. Fruit and vegetables, figs, fish, crabs, fowls, we buy with iron tools, pieces of calico, and the like; and if our supply of these gives out, we have to draw upon the store of things needed by ourselves; and blankets and hardware come to be minus. Then, forgetting this, which it is easy to do, all the world without is a world of glorious beauty. How I wish I could shew it to you! These islands are of very various character, and many of them like the garden of Eden for natural loveliness; shewing almost every kind of scenery within a small area. Most of them are girdled more or less entirely by what is called a *barrier reef*—an outside and independent coral formation, sometimes narrow, sometimes miles in width, on the outer edge of which the sea breaks in an endless line of white foam. Within the reef the lagoon, as it is called, is perfectly still and clear; and such glories of the animal and vegetable world as lie beneath its surface I have no time to describe to you now. I have had little time to examine them; but once or twice I have taken a canoe and a piece of rest, gliding over this submarine garden, and rejoicing in the Lord who has made everything so beautiful in its time. My writing hour is over for to-day. I am going five or six miles to see a man who is said to be very ill.

"Feb. 16. The man had very little the matter with him. I had my walk for nothing, so far as my character of doctor or nurse was concerned.

"I will give you a little notion of the beauty of these islands, in the description of one that I visited a short time ago. It is one of our out-stations—too small to have a teacher given it; so it is visited from time to time by Mr. Lefferts and myself. With a fair wind the distance is hardly a day's journey; but sometimes as in this case it consumes two days. The voyage was made in a native canoe, manned by native sailors, some Christian, some heathen. They are good navigators, for savages; and need to be, for the character of the seas here, threaded with a network of coral reefs, makes navigation a delicate matter. Our voyage proceeded very well, until we got to the entrance of the island. That seems a strange sentence; but the island itself is a circle, nearly; a band of volcanic rock, not very wide, enclosing a lake or lagoon within its compass. There is only a rather narrow channel of entrance. Here we were met by difficulty. The surf breaking shorewards was tremendously high; and meeting and struggling with it came a rush of the current from within. Between the two opposing waters the canoe was tossed and swayed like a reed. It was, for a few moments, a scene to be remembered, and not a little terrific. The shoutings and exertions of the men, who felt the danger of their position, added to the roar and the power of the waters, which tossed us hither and thither as a thing of no consequence, made it a strange wild minute,—till we emerged from all that struggle and roar into the still beautiful quiet of the lagoon inside. Imagine it, surrounded with its border of rocky land covered with noble trees, and spotted with islets covered in like manner. The whole island is of volcanic formation, and its rocks are of black scoria. The theory is, I believe, that a volcano once occupied the whole centre of such islands; which sinking afterwards away left its place to the occupancy of a lake instead. However produced, the effect is singular in its wild beauty. The soil of this island is poor for any purpose but growing timber; the inhabitants consequently are not many, and they live on roots and fish and what we should think still poorer food—a great wood maggot, which is found in plenty. There are but four villages, two of them Christian. I staid there one night and the next day, giving them all I could; and it was a good time to me. The day after I returned home. O sweet gospel of Christ! which is lighting up these dark places; and O my blessed Master, who stands by his servants and gives them his own presence and love, when they are about his work and the world is far from them, and men would call them lonely. There is no loneliness where Christ is. I must finish this long letter with giving you the dying testimony of a Tongan preacher who has just gone to his home. He came here as a missionary from his own land, and has worked hard and successfully. He said to Mr. Calvert the day before his death, 'I have long *enjoyed* religion and felt its *power*. In my former illness I was happy; but now I am greatly blessed. The Lord has come down with mighty power into my soul, and I feel the blessedness of *full rest of soul* in God. I feel religion to be peculiarly sweet, and my rejoicing is great. I see more fully and clearly the truth of the word and Spirit of God, and the suitableness of the Saviour. The whole of Christianity I see as exceedingly excellent.'

"With this testimony I close, my dear friend. It is mine; I can ask no better for you than that it may be yours."

Mrs. Caxton ended her reading and looked at Eleanor. She had done that several times in the course of the reading. Eleanor was always bent over her work, and busily attentive to it; but on each cheek a spot of colour had been fixed and deepening, till now it had reached a broad flush. Silence fell as the reading ceased; Eleanor did not look up; Mrs. Caxton did not take her eyes from her niece's face. It was with a kind of subdued sigh that at last she turned from the table and put her papers away.

"Mr. Morrison is not altogether in the wrong," she remarked at length. "It is better for a man in those far-off regions, and amidst so many labours and trials, to have the comfort of his own home."

"Do you think Mr. Rhys writes as if he felt the want?"

"It is hard to tell what a man wants, by his writing. I am not quite at rest on that point."

"How happened it that he did not marry, like everybody else, before going there?"

"He is a fastidious man," said Mrs. Caxton; "one of those men that are rather difficult to please, I fancy; and that are apt enough to meet with hindrances because of the very nice points of their own nature."

"I don't think you need wish any better for him, aunt Caxton, than to judge by his letters he has and enjoys as he is. He seems to me, and always did, a very enviable person."

"Can you tell why?"

"Good—happy—and useful," said Eleanor. But her voice was a little choked.

"You know grace is free," said Mrs. Caxton. "He would tell you so. Ring the bell, my dear. And a sinner saved in England is as precious as one saved in Fiji. Let us work where our place is, and thank the Lord!"

CHAPTER X.

> "Speak, is't so?
> If it be so, you have wound a goodly clue;
> If it be not, forswear't: howe'er, I charge thee,
> As heaven shall work in me for thine avail,
> To tell me truly."

Mr. Morrison's visit had drifted off into the distance of time; and the subject of South Sea missions had passed out of sight, for all that appeared. Mrs. Caxton did not bring it up again after that evening, and Eleanor did not. The household went on with its quiet ways. Perhaps Mrs. Caxton was a trifle more silent and ruminative, and Eleanor more persistently busy. She had been used to be busy; in these weeks she seemed to have forgotten how to rest. She looked tired accordingly sometimes; and Mrs. Caxton noticed it.

"What became of your bill, Eleanor?" she said suddenly one evening. They had both been sitting at work some time without a word.

"My bill, ma'am? What do you mean, aunt Caxton?"

"Your Ragged school bill."

"It reached its second reading, ma'am; and there it met with opposition."

"And fell through?"

"I suppose so—for the present. Its time will come, I hope; the time for its essential provisions, I mean."

"Do you think Mr. Carlisle could have secured its passage?"

"From what I know and have heard of him, I have no doubt he could."

"His love is not very generous," remarked Mrs. Caxton.

"It never was, aunt Caxton. After I left London I had little hope of my bill. I am not disappointed."

"My dear, are you weary to-night?"

"No ma'am! not particularly."

"I shall have to find some play-work for you to do. Your voice speaks something like weariness."

"I do not feel it, aunt Caxton."

"Eleanor, have you any regret for any part of your decision and action with respect to Mr. Carlisle?"

"Never, aunt Caxton. How can you ask me?"

"I did not know but you might feel weariness now at your long stay in Plassy and the prospect of a continued life here."

Eleanor put down her work, came to Mrs. Caxton, kneeled down and put her arms about her; kissing her with kisses that certainly carried conviction with them.

"It is the most wicked word I ever heard you say, aunt Caxton. I love Plassy beyond all places in the world, that I have ever been in. No part of my life has been so pleasant as the part spent here. If I am weary, I sometimes feel as if my life were singularly cut off from its natural duties, and stranded somehow, all alone; but that is an unbelieving thought, and I do not give it harbour at all. I am very content—very happy."

Mrs. Caxton brought her hand tenderly down the side of the smooth cheek before her, and her eyes grew somewhat misty. But that was a rare occurrence, and the exhibition of it immediately dismissed. She kissed Eleanor and returned to her ordinary manner.

"Talking about stranded lives," she said; "to take another subject,—you must forgive me for that one, dear,—I think of Mr. Rhys very often."

"His life is not stranded," said Eleanor; "it is under full sail."

"He is alone, though."

"I do not believe he feels alone, aunt Caxton."

"I do not know," said Mrs. Caxton. "A man of a sensitive nature must feel, I should think, in his circumstances, that he has put an immense distance between himself and all whom he loves."

"But I thought he had almost no family relations left?"

"Did it never occur to you," said Mrs. Caxton, "when you used to see him here, that there was somebody, somewhere, who had a piece of his heart?"

"No, ma'am,—never!" Eleanor said with some energy. "I never thought he seemed like it."

"I did not know anything about it," Mrs. Caxton went on slowly, "until a little while before he went away—some time after you were here. Then I learned that it was the truth."

Eleanor worked away very diligently and made no answer. Mrs. Caxton furtively watched her; Eleanor's head was bent down over her sewing, but when she raised it to change the position of her work, Mrs. Caxton saw a set of her lips that was not natural.

"You never suspected anything of the kind?" she repeated.

"No, ma'am,—and it would take strong testimony to make me believe it."

"Why so, pray?"

"I should have thought—but it is no matter what I thought about it!"

"Nay, if I ask you, it is matter. Why should it be hard to believe, of Mr. Rhys especially?"

"Nothing; only—I should have thought, if he liked any one, a woman,—that she would have gone with him."

"You forget where he was bound to go. Do you think many women would have chosen to go with him to such a home—perhaps for the remainder of their lives? I think many would have hesitated."

"But *you* forget for what he was going; and any woman whom he would have liked, would have liked his object too."

"You think so," said Mrs. Caxton; "but I cannot wonder at his having doubted. There are a great many questions about going such a journey, my dear."

"And did the lady refuse to go?" said Eleanor bending over her work and speaking huskily.

"I do not think he ever asked her. I almost wish he had."

"*Almost*, aunt Caxton? Why he may have done her the greatest wrong. She might like him without his knowing it; it was not fair to go without giving her the chance of saying what she would do."

"Well, he is gone," said Mrs. Caxton; "and he went alone. I think men make mistakes sometimes."

Eleanor sewed on nervously, with a more desperate haste than she knew, or than was in the least called for by the work in hand. Mrs. Caxton watched her, and turned away to the contemplation of the fire.

"Did the thought ever occur to you, Eleanor," she went on very gravely, "that he fancied *you?*"

Eleanor's glance up was even pitiful in its startled appeal.

"No, ma'am, of course not!" she said hastily. "Except—O aunt Caxton, why do you ask me such a thing!"

"*Except*,—my dear?"

"Except a foolish fancy of an hour," said Eleanor in overwhelmed confusion. "One day, for a little time—aunt Caxton, how can you ask me such a thing?"

"I had a little story to tell you, my dear; and I wanted to make sure that I should do no harm in

VOL .II.

telling it. What is there so dreadful in such a question?"

But Eleanor only brushed away a hot tear from her flushed face and went on with her sewing. Or essayed to do it, for Mrs. Caxton thought her vision seemed to be not very clear.

"What made you think so that time, Eleanor? and what is the matter, my dear?"

"It hurts me, aunt Caxton, the question. You know we were friends, and I liked him very much, as I had reason; but I *never* had cause to fancy that he thought anything of me—only once I fancied it without cause."

"On what occasion, my love?"

"It was only a little thing—a nothing—a chance word. I saw immediately that I was mistaken."

"Did the thought displease you?"

"Aunt Caxton, why should you bring up such a thing now?" said Eleanor in very great distress.

"Did it displease you, Eleanor?

"No aunty"—said the girl; and her head dropped in her hands then.

"My love," Mrs. Caxton said very tenderly, "I knew this before; I thought I did; but it was best to bring it out openly, for I could not else have executed my commission. I have a message from Mr. Rhys to you, Eleanor."

"A message to me?" said Eleanor without raising her head.

"Yes. You were not mistaken."

"In what?"

Eleanor looked up; and amidst sorrow and shame and confusion, there was a light of fire, like the touch the summer sun gives to the mountain tops before he gets up. Mrs. Caxton looked at her flushed tearful face, and the hidden light in her eye; and her next words were as gentle as the verv fall of the sunbeams themselves.

"My love, it is true."

"What, aunt Caxton?"

"You were not mistaken."

"In what, ma'am?"

"In thinking what you thought that day, when something—a mere nothing—made you think that Mr. Rhys liked you."

"But aunty," said Eleanor, a scarlet flood refilling the cheeks which had partially faded,—"I had never the least reason to think so again."

"That is Mr. Rhys's affair. But you may believe it now, for he told me; and I give it to you on his own testimony."

It was curious to Mrs. Caxton to see Eleanor's face. She did not hide it; she turned it a little away from her aunt's full view and sat very still, while the intense flush passed away and left only a nameless rosy glow, that almost reminded Mrs. Caxton of the perfume as well as of the colour of the flower it was likened to. There was a certain unfolding sweetness in Eleanor's face, that was most like the opening of a rosebud just getting into full blossom; but the lips, unbent into happy lines, were a little shame-faced, and would not open to speak a word or ask another question. So they both sat still; the younger and elder lady.

"Do you want me to tell you any more, Eleanor?"

"Why do you tell me this at all now, aunt Caxton?" Eleanor said very slowly and without stirring.

"Mr. Rhys desired I should."

"Why, aunt Caxton?"

"Why do gentlemen generally desire such things to be made known to young ladies?"

"But ma'am!"—said Eleanor, the crimson starting again.

"Well, my dear?"

"There is the whole breadth of the earth between us."

"Ships traverse it," said Mrs. Caxton coolly.

"Do you mean that he is coming home?" said Eleanor. Her face was a study, for its changing lights; too quick, too mingled, too subtle in their expression, to be described. So it was at this instant. Half eager, and half shame-faced; an unmistakeable glow of delight, and yet something that was very like shrinking.

"No, my love," Mrs. Caxton made answer—"I do not mean that. He would not leave his place and his work, even for you."

"But then, ma'am—"

"What all this signifies? you would ask. Are you sorry—do you feel any regret—that it should be made known to you?"

"No, ma'am," said Eleanor low, and hanging her head.

"What it signifies, I do not know. That depends upon the answer to a very practical question which I must now put to you. If Mr. Rhys were stationed in England and could tell you all this himself, what would you say to him in answer?"

"I could give him but one, aunt Caxton," said Eleanor in the same manner.

"And that would be a grant of his demand?"

"You know it would, ma'am, without asking me."

"Now we come to the question. He cannot leave his work to come to you. Is your regard for him enough to make you go to Fiji?"

"Not without asking, aunt Caxton," Eleanor said, turning away.

"Suppose he has asked you."

"But dear aunt Caxton," Eleanor said in a troubled voice, "he never said one word to me of his liking for me, nor to draw out my feeling towards him."

"Suppose he has said it."

"How, ma'am? By word, or in writing?"

"In writing."

Eleanor was silent a little, with her head turned away; then she said in a subdued way, "May I have it, aunt Caxton?"

"My dear, I was not to give them to you except I found that you were favourably disposed towards the object of them. If you ask me for them again, it must be upon that understanding."

"Will you please to give them to me, aunt Caxton," Eleanor said in the same subdued tone.

Mrs. Caxton rose and went to a secretary in the room for one or two papers, which she brought and put in Eleanor's hand. Then folding her arms round her, stooped down and kissed the turned-away face. Eleanor rose up to meet the embrace, and they held each other fast for a little while, neither in any condition to speak.

"The Lord bless you, my child!" said Mrs. Caxton as she released her. "You must make these letters a matter of prayer. And take care that you do the Lord's will in this business—not your own."

"Aunt Caxton," said Eleanor presently, "why was this not told me long ago—before Mr. Rhys went away?" She spoke the words with difficulty.

"It is too long a story to tell to-night," Mrs. Caxton said after hesitating. "He was entirely ignorant of what your feeling might be towards him—ignorant too how far you might be willing to do and dare for Christ's sake—and doubtful how far the world and Mr. Carlisle might be able to prevail with you if they had a fair chance. He could not risk taking a wife to Fiji who had not fairly counted the cost."

"He was so doubtful of me, and yet liked me?" said Eleanor.

"My love, there is no accounting for these things," Mrs. Caxton said with a smile.

"And he left these with you to give to me?"

"One was left—the other was sent. One comes from Fiji. I will tell you about them to-morrow. It is too long a story for to-night; and you have quite enough to think about already. My dear Eleanor!"

They parted without more words, only with another speaking embrace, more expressive than words; and without looking at the other each went to her own room. Eleanor's was cosy and bright in winter as well as in summer; a fire of the peculiar fuel used in the region of the neighbourhood, made of cakes of coal and sand, glowed in the grate, and the whole colouring of the drapery and the furniture was of that warm rich cast which comforts the eye and not a little disposes the mind to be comfortable in conformity. The only wood fire used in the house was the one in the sitting parlour. Before her grate-full of glowing coals Eleanor sat down; and looked at the two letters she held in her hand. Looked at the handwriting too, with curious scrutiny, before she ventured to open and read either paper. Wondered too, with an odd side thought, why her fingers should tremble so in handling these, when no letter of Mr. Carlisle's writing had ever reminded her that her fingers had nerves belonging to them. One was a little letter, which Mrs. Caxton had told her was the first to be read; it was addressed, "In the hand of Mrs. Caxton, for Miss Eleanor Powle." That note Eleanor's little fingers opened with as slight tearing of the paper as might be. It was in few words indeed.

"Although I know that these lines will never meet the eye of her for whom they are written, unless she be favourably inclined both to them and to me; yet in the extreme doubt which possesses me whether that condition will be ever fulfilled, and consequently whether I am not writing what no one will ever read, I find it very difficult to say anything. Something charges me with foolhardiness, and something with presumption; but there is a something else, which is stronger, that overthrows the charges and bids me go on.

"If you ever see these lines, dear Eleanor, you will know already what they have to tell you; but it is fit you should have it in my own words; that—not the first place in my heart—but the second—is yours; and yours without any rivalry. There is one thing dearer to me than you—it is my King and his service; after that, you have all the rest.

"What is it worth to you? anything? and what will you say to me in reply?

"When you read this I shall be at a distance—before I can read your answer I shall be at the other side of the globe. I am not writing to gratify a vague sentiment, but with a definite purpose—and even, though it mocks me, a definite hope. It is much to ask—I hardly dare put it in words—it is hardly possible—that you should come to me. But if you are ready to do and venture anything in the service of Christ—and if you are willing to share a life that is wholly given to God to be spent where and how he pleases, and that is to take up its portion for the present, and probably for long, in the depths of South Sea barbarism—let your own heart tell you what welcome you will receive.

"I can say no more. May my Lord bless and keep you. May you know the fulness of joy that Jesus can give his beloved. May you want nothing that is good for you.

"R. RHYS."

The other letter was longer. It was dated "Island Vulanga, in the South Seas, March, 18—.

MY DEAR ELEANOR:—

"I do not know what presumption moves me to address you again, and from this far-away place. I say to myself that it is presumption; and yet I yield to the impulse. Perhaps it is partly the wish to enjoy once at least even this fancied communion with you, before some news comes which may shut me off from it for ever. But I yield to the temptation. I feel very far from you to-day; the tops of the bread-fruit trees that I see from my window, the banana tree with its bunches of fruit and broad bright leaves just before my door—this very hot north wind that is blowing and making it so difficult to do anything and almost to breathe—all remind me that I am in another land; and by the very force of contrast, the fresh Welsh mountains, the green meadows, the cool sweet air of Plassy—and your face—come before me. Your face, most of all. My mind can think of nothing it would be so refreshing to see. I will write what I please; for you will never read it if the reading would be impertinent; and something tells me you *will* read it.

"This is one of the hot months, when exertion is at times very difficult. The heat is oppressive and takes away strength and endurance. But it is for my Master. That thought cures all. To be weary for Christ, is not to be weary; it is better than any delights without him. So each day is a boon; and each day that I have been able to fill up well with work for God, I rejoice and give thanks. There is no limit here to the work to be done; it presses upon us at all points. We cannot teach all that ask for teaching; we can hardly attend to the calls of the sick; hundreds and hundreds stand stretching out their hands to us with the prayer that we would come and tell them about religion, and we cannot go! Our hands are already full; our hearts break for the multitudes who want the truth, to whom we cannot give it. We wish that every talent we have were multiplied. We wish that we could work all night as well as all day. Above all *I* want to be more like my Lord. When I am all Christ's, *then* I shall be to the praise of his glory, who called me out of darkness into his marvellous light. I want to be altogether holy; then I shall be quite happy and useful, and there is no other way. Are you satisfied with less, Eleanor? If you are, you are satisfied with less than satisfies Christ. Find out where you stand. Remember, it is as true for you as it was for Paul to say, 'Through Christ I can do all things.'

"There are a few native Christians here who are earnestly striving to be holy. But around them all is darkness—blacker than you can even conceive. Where the Sun of righteousness has shined, there the golden beams of Fiji's morning lie; it is a bright spot here and there; but our eyes long for the day. We know and believe it is coming. But when? I understand out here the meaning of that recommendation—'Pray ye therefor the Lord of the harvest, that he would send forth labourers into the harvest.' You can hardly understand it in England. Do you pray that prayer, Eleanor?"

Before I left England I wrote you a note. Amid the exquisite pleasure and pain of which lurked a hope—without which it would not have been written, but which I now see to have been very visionary. It is possible that circumstances may be so that the note may have been read by you; in that case Mrs. Caxton will give you this; but at the distance of space and time that intervenes now, and with cooler thoughts and better knowledge, I feel it to be scarcely possible that you should comply with the request I was daring enough to make to you. I do not expect it. I have ceased to allow myself to hope for it. I think I was unreasonable to ask—and I will never think you unreasonable for refusing—so extravagant a demand. Even if you were willing, your friends would not allow it. And I would not disguise from you that the difficulties and dangers to be met in coming here, are more and greater than can possibly have been represented to you. Humanly speaking, that is; I have myself no fear, and never have felt any. But the evils that surround us—that come to our knowledge and under our very eyes—are real and tangible and dreadful. So much the more reason for our being here;—but so much the less likely that you, gently reared and delicately cared for, will be allowed to risk your delicate nurture in this land of savages. There is cannibalism here, and to the most dreadful extent; there is all the defilement of life and manners that must be where human beings have no respect for humanity; and all this must come more or less under the immediate knowledge and notice of those that live here. The Lord God is a sun and shield; we dwell in him and not in the darkness; nevertheless our eyes see what our hearts grieve over. I could not shield you from it entirely were you here; you would have to endure what in England you could not endure. There are minor trials many and often to be encountered; some of which you will have learned from other letters of the mission.

The heathen around us are not to be trusted, and will occasionally lay their hands upon something we need very much, and carry it off. Not long ago the house of Mr. Thomas, on a neighbouring station, was entered at night and robbed of almost all the wearing apparel it contained. The entrance was effected silently, by cutting into the thin reed and grass wall of the house; and nobody knew anything of the matter till next morning. Then the signs shewed that the depredators had been prepared to commit violence if resisted. I do not know—but I am inclined to think such a thing would not happen in my house. I have been enabled to gain the good will of the people very generally, by kindness to the sick, &c; and two or three of the most powerful chiefs in this vicinity have declared themselves each formally my 'friend'—a title of honour which I scrupulously give and take with them. Nevertheless they are not to be relied upon. What of that? The eternal God is our refuge! After all I come back into feeling how safe we are, rather than how exposed.

"Yet all I have told you is true, and much more. Let no one come here who does not love Christ well enough to suffer the loss of all things for his sake, if necessary· for it may be demanded of him. He wants the helmet of salvation on his head; but with that, it does not matter where we are—glory to the Captain of our salvation! Fiji is very near heaven, Eleanor; nearer than England; and if I dared, I would say, I wish you were here;—but I do not dare. I do not know what is best. I leave you to your own judgment of what you ought to do, and to that better direction which will tell you. For me, I know that I shall not want; not so but that I can find my supply; and soon I shall be where I shall not want at all. Meanwhile every day is a glad day to me, for it is given to my Lord; and Jesus is with me. The people hear the word gladly, and with some fruit of it continually our hearts are cheered. I would not be anywhere else than I am. My choice would be, if I had my choice, to live and die in Fiji."

"I dare not trust myself to say the thoughts that come surging up for utterance; it is wiser not. If my first note to you was presumptuous, this at least is the writing of a calmer and wiser man. I have resigned the expectations of a moment. But it is no harm for me to say I love you as well as ever; *that* I shall do, I think, till I die; although I shall never see you again, and dare not promise myself I shall ever again write to you. It may be it will be best not, even as a friend, to do that. Perhaps as a friend I could not. It is not as a friend, that I sign myself now,

"ROWLAND RHYS."

Poor Eleanor! She was of all people in the world the least given to be sentimental or soft-hearted in a foolish way; but strong as she was, there was something in these letters—or some mixture of things—that entered her heart like an arrow through the joints of an armour, and found her as defenceless. Tears came with that resistless, ceaseless, measureless flow, as when the secret nerve of tenderness has been reached, and every barrier of pride or self-consideration is broken down or passed over. So keen the touch was to Eleanor, that weeping could not quiet it. After all it was only a heavy summer shower—not a winter storm. Eleanor hushed her sobs at last to begin her prayers; and there the rest of the night left her. The morning was dawning grey in the east, when she threw herself upon her bed for an hour's sleep. Sleep came then without waiting.

Perhaps Mrs. Caxton had not been much more reposeful than her niece; for she was not the first one down stairs. Eleanor was there before her; Mrs. Caxton watched her as she came in; she was ceremoniously putting the fire in best burning condition, and brushing up the ashes from the hearth. As Mrs. Caxton came near, Eleanor looked up and a silent greeting passed between them; very affectionate, but silent evidently of purpose. Neither of them was ready to speak. The bell was rung, the servants were gathered; and immediately after prayers breakfast was brought in. It was a silent meal for the first half of it. Mrs. Caxton still watched Eleanor, whose eyes did not readily meet hers. What about her? Her manner was as usual, one would have said, yet it was *not;* nor was she. A little delicate undefined difference made itself felt; and that Mrs. Caxton was studying. A little added grace; a little added deftness and alacrity; Mrs. Caxton had seen it in that order taken of the fire before breakfast; she saw it and read it then. And in Eleanor's face correspondingly there was the same difference; impossible to tell where it lay, it was equally impossible not to perceive it. Though her face was grave enough, there was a beauty in the lines of it that yesterday had not seen; a nameless witness in the corners of her mouth, that told tales the tongue would not. Mrs. Caxton looked on and saw it and read it, for half the breakfast time, before she spoke. Maybe she had a secret sigh or two to cover; but at any rate there was nothing like that in her look or her voice when she spoke.

"So you will go, Eleanor!"

Eleanor started, and coloured; then looked down at her plate, the blush growing universal.

"Have you decided, my love?"

Eleanor leaned her head upon her hand, as if with the question came the remembrance of last night's burden of thoughts; but her answer was a quiet low "yes."

"May I know—for I feel myself responsible to a degree in this matter,—may I know, on what ground?"

Eleanor's look was worth five hundred pounds. The little glance of surprise and consciousness—the flash of hidden light, there was no need to ask from what magazine, answered so completely, so involuntarily. She cast down her eyes immediately and answered in words sedate enough—

"Because I am unable to come to any other decision, ma'am."

"But Eleanor, my dear," said Mrs. Caxton,—"do you know, Mr. Rhys himself would be unwilling you should come to him for his own sake alone—in Fiji."

Eleanor turned away from the table at that and covered her face with her hands; a perfect rush of confusion bringing over face and neck and almost even over the little white fingers, a suffusing crimson glow. She spoke presently.

"I cannot say anything to that, aunt Caxton. I have

tried myself as well as I can. I think I would go anywhere and do anything where I saw clearly my work and my place were put for me. I do not know anything more about it."

"My love, that is enough. I believe you. I entirely approve your decision. I spoke, because I needed to ask the question *he* would have asked if he had been here. Mr. Rhys has written to me very stringently on the subject.

"So he has to me, ma'am."

"If you have settled that question with your conscience, my dear, there is no more necessary to be said about it. Conscience should be clear on that point, and the question settled securely. If it is not, you had better take time for thought and self-searching."

"I do not need it, aunt Caxton."

Mrs. Caxton left her place and came round to Eleanor, for the sole purpose of taking her in her arms and kissing her. Grave, earnest kisses, on brow and cheek, speaking a heart full of sympathy, full of tenderness, full of appreciation of all that this decision of Eleanor's involved, full of satisfaction with it too. A very unusual sort of demonstration from Mrs. Caxton, as was the occasion that called for it. Eleanor received it as the seal of the whole business between them. Her aunt's arms detained her lovingly while she pressed her lips to every part of Eleanor's face; then Mrs. Caxton went back to her place and poured herself out another cup of coffee. Sentiment she had plenty; she was not in the least bit sentimental. She creamed her coffee thoughtfully and broke bread and eat it, before she came out with another question.

"When will you go, Eleanor?"

Eleanor looked up doubtfully. "Where, aunt Caxton?"

"To Fiji."

There seemed to be some irresolution or uncertainty in the girl's mind; for she hesitated.

"Aunt Caxton, I doubt much—my mother will oppose my going."

"I think she will. But I think also that her opposition can be overcome. When will you write to her?"

"I will write to-day, ma'am."

"We must have an answer before we send any other letters. Supposing she does not oppose, or that her opposition is set aside, I come back to my question. When will you go?"

Eleanor looked up doubtfully again. "I don't know, ma'am—I suppose opportunities of going only occur now and then.

"That is all—with long intervals sometimes. Opportunities for *your* going would come only rarely. You must think about it, Eleanor; for we must know what we are to tell Mr. Rhys."

Eleanor was silent; her colour went and came.

"You must think about it, my dear. If you write to Mr. Rhys to-day and send it, we may get an answer from him possibly in twenty months—possibly in twenty-four months. Then if you wait four or five months for an opportunity to make the voyage, and have a reasonably good passage, you may see your friend in three years from now. But it might well happen that letters might be delayed, and that you might wait much longer than four or five months for a ship and company in which you could sail; so that the three years might be nearer four."

"I have thought of all that, aunt Caxton," Eleanor said, while the colour which had been varying in her cheeks fixed itself in two deep crimson spots.

Mrs. Caxton was now silent on her part, slowly finishing her coffee and putting the cups together on the tray. She left it for her niece to speak next.

"I have thought of all that, aunt Caxton," Eleanor repeated after a little while,—"and—"

"Well, my love?"

"Aunt Caxton," said the girl, looking up now while her cheeks and brow were all one crimson flush—"is it unmaidenly in me—would it be—to go so, without being asked?"

"Has he not asked you?"

"Yes ma'am. But—"

"What?"

"Not since he got there."

"Have you reason to think his mind is altered on the subject?"

"No ma'am," said Eleanor, drooping her head.

"What does your own feeling bid you do, my love?"

"I have thought it all over, aunt Caxton," said the girl slowly,—"I did that last night; I have thought of everything about it; and my feeling was—"

"Well, my love?"

"My feeling, as far as I am concerned—was to take the first good opportunity that offered."

"My love, that is just what I thought you would do. And what I would have you do, if you go at all. It is not unmaidenly. Simple honest frankness, is the most maidenly thing in the world, when it is a woman's time to speak. The fact that your speaking must be action does not alter the matter. When it takes two years for people to hear from each other, life would very soon be spent in the asking of a few questions and getting the answers to them. I am a disinterested witness, Eleanor; for when you are gone, all I care for in this world is gone. You are my own child to me now."

Eleanor's head bent lower.

"But I am glad to have you go, nevertheless, my child. I think Mr. Rhys wants you even more than I do; and I have known for some time that you wanted something. And besides—I shall only be separated from you in body."

Eleanor made no response.

"What are you going to do now?" was Mrs. Caxton's qnestion in her usual calm tone.

"Write to mamma."

"Very well. Do not send your letter to her without etting mine go with it."

"But aunt Caxton," said Eleanor lifting up her head, —"my only fear is—I am quite satisfied in my own mind, and I do not care for people—my only fear is, lest Mr. Rhys himself should think I come too easily. You know, he is fastidious in his notions." She spoke with great difficulty and with her face a flame.

"Your fear will go away when you have heard my story," said Mrs. Caxton tranquilly. "I will give you that to-night. He is fastidious; but he is a sensible man."

Quieted with which suggestion, Eleanor went off to her desk.

CHAPTER XI.

"But never light and shade
Coursed one another more on open ground,
Beneath a troubled heaven, than red and pale
Across the face of Enid hearing her.

VARIOUS letters were written that day. In the evening the two ladies came together again cheerfully. The time between had not all been spent in letter-writing, for the world does not stand still for love matters. Eleanor had been out the whole afternoon on visits of kindness and help to sick and poor people. Mrs. Caxton had been obliged to attend to the less interesting company of one or two cheese-factors. At the tea-table the subject of the morning came back.

"You posted your letter and mine, Eleanor?"

"Yes, ma'am. But I cannot think mamma's answer will be favourable. I cannot fancy it."

"Well, we shall see. The world is a curious world; and the wind does not always blow from the quarter whence we expect it. We must wait and pray."

"I am puzzled to imagine, aunt Caxton," Eleanor said after some pause, "how you came to know all about this matter in the first place. How came you to know what I never knew?"

"That is my story," said Mrs. Caxton. "We will let the table be cleared first, my dear."

So it was done. But Eleanor left her work by her side to-night, and looked into her aunt's face to listen.

"I never should have known about it, child, till you

had, if you had been here. You remember how you went away in a hurry. Who knows? Perhaps, but for that, none of us would have been any wiser to-day on the subject than we were then. It is very possible."

"How, ma'am?"

"You disappeared, you know, in one night, and were gone. When Mr. Rhys came home, the next day or the same day, I saw that he was very much disappointed. That roused my suspicions of him; they had been only doubtful before. He is not a person to shew what he thinks, unless he chooses."

"So I knew; that made me surprised."

"I saw that he was very much disappointed, and looked very sober; but he said hardly anything about it, and I was forced to be silent. Then in a little while —a few weeks, I think—he received his appointment, with the news that he must sail very soon. He had to leave Plassy then in a very few days; for he wanted some time in London and elsewhere. I saw there was something more than leaving Plassy, upon his mind; he was graver than that could make him, I knew; and he was giving up something more than England, I knew by his prayers.

"One night we were sitting here by the fire—it was a remarkably chill evening and we had kindled a blaze in the chimney and shut the windows. Mr. Rhys sat silent, watching the fire and keeping up the blaze; too busy with his own thoughts to talk to me. I was taken with a spirit of meddling which does not very often possess me; and asked him how much longer he had to stay. He said how long, in so many words; they were short, as pain makes words.

"'How comes it,' I asked, plunging into the matter, 'that you do not take a wife with you? like everybody else.'

"He answered, in dry phrases, 'that it would be presumption in him to suppose that anybody would go with him, if he were to ask.'

"I said quietly, I thought he was mistaken; that anybody who was worthy of him would go; and it could not be *presumption* to ask anybody else.

"'You do not realize, Mrs. Caxton, how much it would be asking of any one,' he said; 'you do not know what sacrifices it would call for.'

"'Love does not care for sacrifices,' I reminded him.

"'I have no right to suppose that anybody has such a degree of regard for me,' he said.

"I can't tell what in his manner and words told me there was more behind. They were a little short and dry; and his ordinary way of speaking is short sometimes, but never with a sort of edge like this—a hard edge. You know it is as frank and simple when he speaks short as when his words come out in the gentlest way. It hurt me, for I saw that something hurt him.

"I asked if there was not anybody in England good enough for him? He said there were a great many too good.

"'Mr. Rhys,' said I,—I don't know what possessed me to be so bold,—'I hope you are not going to leave your heart behind with somebody, when you go to Fiji?'

"He got up and walked once or twice through the room, went out and presently came back again. I was afraid I had offended him, and I was a good deal troubled; but I did not know what to say. He sat down again and spoke first.

"'Mrs. Caxton,' said he, 'since you have probed the truth, I may as well confess it. I am going to do the unwise thing you have mentioned.'

"'Who are you going to leave your heart with, Mr. Rhys?' I asked.

"'With the lady who has just left you.'

"'Eleanor?'

"'Yes,' he said.

"'Have you told her, Mr. Rhys?' I asked.

"He said no.

"'You are not going to do her the injustice to go and *not* speak to her?'

"'Why should I tell her?' he said.

"'There might be several answers given to that,' I said; 'but the best one at present seems to be, why should you *not?*'

"'For several reasons,' he said. 'In the first place I do not know at all whether Miss Powle has that degree of love to Christ that she would be willing to forsake all her earthly prospects—home and friends—for hard work in his service. In the second place, even if she have that, I have not the slightest reason to believe that she —that she cares enough for me to go with me at my asking.'

"'And do you mean to go in ignorance?' I said.

"'Yes—I must.'

"I waited a little, and then I told him I thought he was wrong.

"'Why?' he asked quickly.

"'People cannot see each other's hearts,' I said. 'Suppose that she have the same secret feeling towards you that you have towards her. She cannot speak; you will not; and so both would be unhappy for nothing.

"'I never saw the least thing like it,' he said.

"'I suppose she might say the same of you—might she not?'

"'Yes and with truth; for knowing the uncertainties —or rather the certainties—of my position, I have not given her the least cause.'

"'You could hardly expect demonstrations from her in that case,' I said.

"'There is no chance, Mrs. Caxton, even if it were according to your supposition. Her friends would never permit her to marry a man with my lot in life;—and I do not know that I ought to ask her, even if they would. She has a very fair prospect for this world's happiness.'

"'What do you think of your own lot in life?' I asked him.

"'I would not exchange it, you know,' he said, "for any other the world could offer me. It is brighter and better.'

"'It strikes me you are selfish,—' I told him.

"He laughed a little, for the first time; but he grew as grave as possible immediately after.

"'I have not meant to be selfish,' he said. 'But I could not take a woman to Fiji, who had not thoroughly considered the matter and counted the cost. That could not be done in a little while. The world has a fair chance now to see if it can weaken Miss Powle's principles or overcome her faithfulness to them. It is better that she should try herself perhaps, before having such a question asked of her.

"'And suppose she comes clear out of the trial?' I said.

"'Then I shall be in Fiji.'

"We were both silent a while. He began then.

"'Mrs. Caxton, without invading any confidences or seeking to know anything that should not be known,—may I ask you a question?'

"'Certainly,' I said. 'I reserve the discretion of answering.'

"'Of course. Your words look like a rebuke of the attitude I have taken towards this subject. Is it proper for me to ask, whether you have any foundation for them beyond your general knowledge of human nature and your good will towards me? I mean—whether you, as a friend, see any ground of hope for me?'

"'If you were going to stay in England,' I said, 'I would answer no such question. Every man must make his own observations and run his own risk. But these circumstances are different. And appealed to as a friend —and answering on my own observations simply—I should say, that I think your case not hopeless.'

"I could see the colour rise in his cheek; but he sat quite still and did not speak, till it faded again.

"'I have never heard a word on the subject,' I told him. 'I do not say I am certain of anything. I may mistake. Only, seeing you are going to the other end of the world, without the chance of finding out anything for yourself, I think it fair to tell you what, as a woman, I should judge of the case.'

"'Why do you tell me?' he said quickly.

"'I am but answering your question. You must judge whether the answer is worth anything.'

"He half laughed again, at himself; at least I could see the beginning of a smile; but he was too terribly in earnest to be anything but serious. He sat silent; got up and fidgetted round the room; then came and stood by the chimney piece looking down at me.

"'Mrs. Caxton,' he said, 'I am going to venture to ask something from you—to fulfil a contingent commission. When I am gone, if Miss Powle returns to you, or when you have otherwise opportunity,—will you, if you can, find out the truth of her feeling on these subjects, which I have failed to find out? You tempt me beyond my power of self-abnegation.'

"'What shall I do with the truth, if I find it, Mr. Rhys?"

"'In that case,' he said,—'if it is as you suppose it possible it may be, though I dare not and do not hope it;—if it be so, then you may tell her all I have confessed to you to-night.'

"'Why?'

"'You are uncommonly practical to-night,' he said. 'I could have but one motive in discovering it to her.'

"'To ask her to follow you to Fiji?'

"'I dare not put it in words. I do not believe the chance will ever come. But I am unable to go and leave the chance changed into an impossibility.'

"'We are talking of what *may* be,' I said. 'But you do not suppose that she could follow you on my report of your words alone?'

"'I shall be too far off to speak them myself.'

"'You can write then,' I said.

"'Do you remember what the distances are, and the intervals of time that must pass between letter and letter? When should I write?'

"'Now—this evening. I am not thinking of such courtship as took place in the antediluvian days.'

"'I cannot write on such an utter uncertainty. I have not hope enough; although I cannot bear to leave the country without enlisting you to act for me.'

"'I shall reconsider the question of acting,' I said, 'if I have no credentials to produce. I cannot undertake to tell anything to Eleanor merely to give her pleasure—or merely to give her pain.'

"'Would you have me write to her here—now?' he asked.

"'Yes, I would,' I told him.

"He sat pondering the matter a little while, making up the fire as you did this morning—only with a very different face; and then with a half laugh he said I was making a fool of him, and he went off. I sat still—and in a few minutes he came down and handed me that note for you."

Eleanor's cheeks would have rivalled the scarlet Lobelia or Indian Mallow, or anything else that is brilliant. She kept profound silence. It was plain enough what Mr. Rhys expected her to do—that is, supposing he had any expectations. Now her question was, what would her mother say? And Eleanor in her secret heart looked at the probability of obstinate opposition in that quarter; and then of long, long waiting and delay; perhaps never to be ended but with the time and the power of doing what now her heart longed to do. The more she thought of it, the less she could imagine that her mother would yield her consent; or that her opposition would be anything but determined and unqualified. Then what could she do? Eleanor sighed.

"No," said Mrs. Caxton. "Have patience, my dear, and believe that all will go right—*however it goes*, Eleanor. We will do our part; but we must be content with our part. There is another part, which is the Lord's; let him do that, and let us say it is well, Eleanor. Till we have learnt that, we have not learnt our lesson."

"I do say it, and will, aunt Caxton," said the girl. But she said nothing more that night.

To tell the truth, they were rather silent days that followed. Mrs. Powle's letters of answer did not come speedily; indeed no one knew at Plassy just where she might be at this time, nor how far the Plassy letters might have to travel in order to reach her; for communication was not frequent between the two families. And till her answer came, Eleanor could not forget that the question of her life was undecided; nor Mrs. Caxton, that the decision might take away from her, probably for ever, the only living thing that was very dear to her. That was Eleanor now. They were very affectionate to each other those days, very tender and thoughtful for each other; not given to much talking. Eleanor was a good deal out of the house; partly busy with her errands of kindness, partly stilling her troublesome and impatient thoughts with long roamings on foot or on horseback over the mountains and moors.

"The spring has come, aunt Caxton," she said, coming in herself one day, fresh enough to be spring's impersonation. "I heard a blackbird and a wheat-ear: and I have found a violet for you."

"You must have heard blackbirds before. And you have got more than violets there."

"Yes ma'am—not much. I found the Nepeta and the ivy-leaved Veronica under the hedge; and whitlow grass near the old tower. That's the willow catkin you know of course—and sloe. That's all—but it's spring."

A shade came over the faces of both. Where might another spring find her.

"I have got something more for you," said Mrs. Caxton.

"My letter, ma'am!—Had you one, aunt Caxton?"

"Yes."

Eleanor could not tell from her aunt's answer what the letter might be. She went off with her own, having parted suddenly with all the colour she had brought in with her. It returned again however soon.

Mrs. Powle declared that according to all *her* experience and power of judging of the world, her daughter and her sister Mrs. Caxton were both entirely crazy. She had never, in her life, heard of anything so utterly absurd and ridiculous as the proposition upon which they had required her to give an opinion. Her opinion found no words in the English language strong enough in which to give it. That Eleanor should be willing to forego every earthly prospect of good or pleasure, was like Eleanor; that is, it was like the present Eleanor; an entirely infatuated, blind, fanatical, unreasonable thing. Mrs. Powle had given up the expectation of anything wiser or better from her, until years and the consequences of her folly should have taught her when it would be too late. Why Eleanor, if she wished to throw herself away, should pitch upon the South Seas for the place of her retirement, was a piece of the same mysterious fatuity which marked the whole proceeding. Why she could think of no pleasanter wedding journey than a voyage of twelve thousand miles in search of a husband, was but another incomprehensible point. Mrs. Powle had a curiosity to know what Eleanor expected to live upon out there, where she presumed the natives practised no agriculture and wheaten flour was a luxury unknown? And what she expected to *do?* However, having thus given her opinion, Mrs. Powle went on to say, that she must quite decline to give it. She regarded Eleanor as entirely the child of her aunt Caxton, as she understood was also Mrs. Caxton's own view; most justly, in Mrs. Powle's opinion, since conversion and adoption to Mrs. Caxton's own family and mind must be amply sufficient to supersede the accident of birth. At any rate, Mrs. Powle claimed no jurisdiction in the matter; did not choose to exercise any. She felt herself incompetent. One daughter she had still remaining, whom she hoped to keep her own, guarding her against the influences which had made so wide a separation between her eldest and the family and sphere to which she belonged. Julia, she hoped, would one day do her honour. As for the islands of the South Seas, or the peculiar views and habits of life entertained by those white people who chose them for their residence, Mrs. Powle declared she was incapable from very ignorance of understanding or giving judgment about them. She made the whole question, together with her daughter, over to her sister Mrs. Caxton, who she did not doubt would do wisely according to her notions. But as they were not the notions of the world generally, they were quite incomprehensible to the writer, and in a sphere entirely beyond and without her cognizance. She hoped Eleanor would be happy—if it were not absurd to hope an impossibility.

But on one point the letter was clear, if on no other.

Eleanor should not come home. She had ruined her own prospects; Mrs. Powle could not help that; she should not ruin Julia's. Whether she stayed in England or whether she went on her fool's voyage, *this* was a certain thing. She should not see Julia, to infect her. Mrs. Powle desired to be informed of Eleanor's movements; that if she went she herself might meet her in London before she sailed. But she would not let her see Julia either then or at any time.

This cruel letter broke Eleanor down completely. It settled the question of her life indeed; and settled it according to her wish and against her fears; but for all that, it was a letter of banishment and renunciation. With something of the feeling which makes a wounded creature run to shelter, Eleanor gathered up her papers and went down to Mrs. Caxton; threw them into her lap, and kneeling beside her put herself in her arms.

"What is it, my child?" said Mrs. Caxton. "What does your mother say to you?"

"She gives her consent—but she gives me up to you, aunt Caxton. She counts me your child and not hers."

"My love, I asked her to do so. You have been mine, in my own mind, for a long time past. My Eleanor!"—And Mrs. Caxton's kiss and her warm clasping arms spoke more than her words.

"But she renounces me—and she will not let me see Julia."—Eleanor was in very great distress.

"She will by and by. She will not hold to that."

"She says she will not at all. O aunt Caxton, I want to see Julia again!"—

"Were you faithful to Julia while you were with her?"

"Yes—I think so—while I could. I had hardly any chance the last winter I was at home; we were never together; but I seized what I could."

"Your mother kept you apart?"

"I believe so."

"My child, remember, as one day is with the Lord as a thousand years, so one word is as a thousand words; he can make it do his work. All we have to do is to be faithful, and then trust. You recollect the words of that grand hymn on the Will of God—

"'I do the little I can do,
And leave the rest to thee.'"

"I don't think I know it."

Mrs. Caxton went on.

"'When obstacles and trials seem
Like prison walls to be,
I do the little I can do,
And leave the rest to thee.

"'I know not what it it is to doubt;
My heart is ever gay;
I run no risk, for, come what will,
Thou always hast thy way.

"'I have no cares, O blessed will!
For all my cares are thine.
I live in triumph, Lord, for thou
Hast made thy triumphs mine.'"

Eleanor lifted up her face and pressed a long kiss on her aunt's lips. "But I want to see Julia!"

"My love, I think you will. It will be some time yet before you can possibly leave England. I think your mother will withdraw her prohibition before that time. Meanwhile—"

Eleanor lay with her head on Mrs. Caxton's bosom, her brown eyes looking out with a sweet and sorrowful wistfulness towards the light. Mrs. Caxton read them.

"This gift would be very precious to me, my child," she said, tightening the pressure of the arms which still were wrapped round Eleanor,—"if I were not obliged so soon to make it over to somebody else. But I will not be selfish. It is unspeakably precious to me now. It gives me the right to take care of you. I asked your mother for it. I am greatly obliged to her. Now what are you going to do to-day?"

"Write—to Fiji," said Eleanor slowly and without moving.

"Right; and so will I. And do not you be overmuch concerned about Julia. There is another verse of that hymn, which I often think of—

"'I love to see thee bring to nought,
The plans of wily men;
When simple hearts outwit the wise,
O thou art loveliest then!'"

CHAPTER XII.

> "If Proteus like your journey, when you come,
> No matter who's displeas'd when you are gone;
> I fear me he will scarce be pleas'd withal."

THE way was clear, and Eleanor wrote to Fiji as she had said. She could not however get rid of her surprise that her mother had permitted the tenor of these letters to be what it was. What had moved Mrs. Powle, so to act against all her likings and habits of action? How came she to allow her daughter to go to the South Seas and be a missionary?

Several things which Eleanor knew nothing of, and which so affected the drift of Mrs. Powle's current of life that she was only, according to custom, sailing with it and not struggling against it. When people seem to act unlike themselves, it is either that you do not know themselves, or do not know some other things which they know. So in this case. For one thing, to name the greatest first, Mr. Carlisle was unmistakeably turning his attention to another lady, a new star in the world of society; an earl's daughter and an heiress. Whether heart-whole or not, which was best known to himself, Mr. Carlisle was prosecuting his addresses in this new quarter with undoubted zeal and determination. It was not the time for Eleanor now to come home! Let her do anything else,—was the dictate of pride. *Now* to come home, or even not to come home, remaining Eleanor Powle, was to confess in the world's eye a lamentably lost game; to take place as a rejected or vainly ambitious girl; the *would-have-been* lady of Rythdale. Anything but that! Eleanor might almost better die at once. She would not only have ruined her own prospects, but would greatly injure those of Julia, on whom her mother's hopes and pride were now all staked. Alfred was taken from her and put under guardians; Mrs. Powle did not build anything on him; he was a boy, and when he was a man he would be only Alfred Powle. Julia promised to be a beauty; on her making a fine match rested all Mrs. Powle's expectations from this world; and she was determined to spare no pains, expense, nor precautions. Therefore she resolved that the sisters should not be together, cost what it might. Good bye to all her cares or hopes on Julia's behalf, looking to a great establishment, if Julia became a Methodist! She might go on a farm like her aunt and sell cheeses. The thought of those cheeses froze the blood in Mrs. Powle's veins; that was a characteristic of good blood, she firmly believed. Therefore on every account, for every reason, nothing better could happen than that Eleanor should go to the South Seas. She would escape the shame of coming home; Julia would be out of danger of religious contamination; and she herself would be saved from the necessary odium of keeping one daughter in banishment and the other in seclusion; which odium she must incur if both of them remained in England and neither of them ever saw the other. All this would be cleverly saved. Then also, if Eleanor married a missionary and went to the other end of the world, her case could be very well dismissed as one of a religious enthusiasm—a visionary, fanatical excitement. Nay, there could be made even a little *éclat* about it. There would be no mortification, at any rate, comparable to that which must attend supposed overthrown schemes and disappointed ambition. Eleanor had chosen her own course, backed by her wealthy relation, Mrs. Caxton, who had adopted her; and whose views were entirely not of this world. Mrs. Powle deplored it, of course, but was unable to help it. Besides, Mrs. Caxton had answered, on her own knowledge, for the excellent character and superior qualities of the gentleman Eleanor was to marry; there was no fault to be found with him at all, except that he was a fanatic; and as Eleanor was a fanatic herself, that was only a one-sided objection.

Yes, Mrs. Caxton had answered for all that, on her own knowledge, of many years' standing; and she had said something more, which also weighed with Mrs. Powle and which Mrs. Powle could also mention among the good features of the case, without stating that it had had the force of an inducement with herself. Mrs. Caxton had asked indeed to be permitted to consider Eleanor her own, and had promised in that case to make Eleanor entirely her own care, both during Mrs. Caxton's life and afterwards; leaving Mrs. Powle free to devote all her fortune to Julia that would have been shared with Julia's sister. Mrs. Powle's means were not in her estimation large; she wanted every penny of them for the perfecting and carrying out of her plans which regarded her youngest daughter; she consented that the elder should own another mother and guardian. Mrs. Powle agreed to it all. But not satisfied with any step of the whole affair nevertheless, which all displeased her, from beginning to end, her own action included, she expressed her determination to Eleanor in terms which half broke Eleanor's heart; and left a long, lingering, sore spot there. To Mrs. Caxton Mrs. Powle's writing was much better worded; civil if not kind, and well mannered if not motherly.

The thing was done, at all events; Eleanor was formally made over to another mother and left free to do whatever her new guardian pleased. Letters of a different sort of temper were sent off upon their long journey to the South Seas; and there began a busy time at Plassy, in anticipation of Eleanor's following them. It was still very uncertain when that might be; opportunities must be waited for; such an opportunity as would satisfy Mrs. Caxton. In the mean while a great deal of business was on hand. Mrs. Caxton even made a journey up to London and took Eleanor with her; for the sake of inquiries and arrangements which could not be attended to from a distance. For the sake of purchases too, which could be made nowhere but in London. For Mrs. Caxton was bent, not only on supplying Eleanor with all that could be be thought of in the way of outfit; but also on getting together to accompany or precede her everything that could be sent that might be useful or helpful to Mr. Rhys or comfortable in the household; in short, to transfer England as nearly as possible to Fiji. As freights of course were expensive, all these matters must be found and compressed in the smallest compass they could possibly know as their limits; and Mrs. Caxton was very busy. London did not hold them but a fortnight; the rest of the time work was done at Plassy.

And the months rolled on. Cheeses were turned off as usual, and Mrs. Caxton's business was as brisk as ever. Eleanor's outfit gradually got ready; and before and after that was true, Eleanor's visits among her neighbours and poor people were the same as ever. She had strength and spirit enough for all calls upon either; and her sweet diligence seemed to be even more than ever, now that work at Plassy was drawing towards a close. Still Eleanor gathered the spoils of the moors and the hedge-rows, as she went and came on her errands; climbed the mountain on Powis and explored the rocks and the waterfalls on her way. As usual her hands came home full. The house was gay with broom again in its season; before that the violets and wood anemone had made the tea-table and the breakfast table sweet with their presence. Blue-bells and butter-cups and primroses had their time, and lovely they looked, helped out by the yellow furze blossoms which Eleanor was very fond of. Then the scorpion grass, of both kinds, proclaimed that it was summer; and borage was bright in the sitting-room. Eleanor could hardly look at it without an inward smile and sigh, remembering the cheering little couplet which attached to it by old usage; and Julia from whose lips she had first heard it; and the other lips that had given it to Julia. Corn-marigold was gay again in July, and the white blackberry blossoms came with crane's bill and flax, campion and willow-herb, speedwell and vetchling. Any one well acquainted with the wild things that grow and blossom in the land, might have known any day what time of the year it was by going into Mrs. Caxton's sitting parlour and using his eyes. Until the purple ling and loosestrife, gave place to mint and maiden pink and late meadow sweet; and then the hop vine and meadow saffron proclaimed that summer was over. But ferns had their representatives at all times.

Summer was over; and no chance for Eleanor's sailing had yet presented itself. Preparations were all made; and the two ladies lived on in waiting and in the enjoyment of each other, and doubtless with a mixture of thoughts that were not enjoyment. But a very sweet even glow of love and peace and patience filled the house. Letters were written; and once and again letters had arrived, even from Mr. Rhys. They told of everything going on at his station; of his work and pleasures; of the progress the truth was making; and the changes coming even while he looked, upon the population of the islands, their manners and character. There never were letters, I suppose, more thoroughly read and studied and searched out in every detail, than all those letters were by Eleanor; for every fact was of importance to her; and the *manner* of every word told her something. They told her what made her eyes fill and her pulse beat quick. But among them there was not a word to herself. No, and not even a word about herself. In vain Eleanor hoped for it and searched for it. There was not even an allusion that looked her way.

"Do you want to know what I am doing?" Mr. Rhys wrote in one of these letters. "You see by my date that I am not in the place I last wrote from. I am alone on this island, which has never had a resident missionary and which has people enough that need the care of one; so it has been decided that I should pitch my tent here for some months. There is not a large population—not quite five hundred people in the whole island; but almost all of them that are grown up are professing Christians—members of the church, and not disgracing their profession. The history of the church in this place is wonderful and even of romantic interest. One of their chiefs, being in another part of Fiji, fell in with a chief who was a Christian. From him he learned something of the new religion, and carried back to Ono thus much of truth—that Jehovah is the only God and that all worship and praise is his due. Further than this, and the understanding that the seventh day should be especially spent in his service, the Ono chief knew nothing. Was not that a little seed for a great tree to grow from? But his island had just been ravaged by disease and by war; in their distress the people had applied in vain to their old gods to save them; they were convinced now from what they heard that help is in the Lord alone, and they resolved to seek him. But they knew not the Lord, nor his ways, and there was no one to teach them. Fancy that company of heathens renouncing heathenism—setting apart the seventh day for worship, preparing food beforehand so that the day might be hallowed, putting on their best dresses and fresh oil, and meeting to seek the unknown God! Oh kingdom of Christ, come, come!—

"When they were met, they did not know how to begin their service. However, as old custom referred them to their priests for intercourse with heaven, they bethought them to apply to one now, and told him what they wanted. I do not understand what influenced the man; but however, heathen priest of a heathen god as he was, he consented to officiate for this Christian service. The priest came; the assembly sat down; and the priest made a prayer, after this fashion as it has been reported to me. *He* did not then renounce heathenism, you understand.

"Lord, Jehovah! here are thy people; they worship thee. I turn my back on thee for the present, and am on another tack, worshipping another god. But do thou bless these thy people; keep them from harm, and do them good."

That was the beginning; and doubtless the Lord hearkened and heard it. For awhile they went on as they had begun; then wanting something more, they sent messengers to Tonga to beg for teachers. Now, as I said, the people are nearly all Christians, and not in name only; and all the children are brought to be taught. Here am I; don't you think I am in a good place? But I am here only for a little while; more cannot be spared to so small a population at this time.

"To get here one has to shoot something such a gulf as I described to you at Vulanga. The barrier reef has a small opening. At particular times of tide a boat can go through; but with the rush of waves from without, meeting the tremendous current from within, it is an exciting business; somewhat dangerous as well as fearful. The ships cannot get inside the barrier. The night I came, canoes came out to meet me, bringing a present.

of yams as their contribution to our fund; they brought as many as the vessel could find room for. In the canoe with the Ono people I felt myself with friends; I had visited the place before, and they knew me. The current made fearfully hard work for them; but it was love's labour; they felt about me, I suppose, something as the Galatians did towards Paul. The next day was Sunday. I preached to an attentive congregation, and had a happy time. Now I will give you a notion of my run of employments at the present time.

First. Playing bookbinder. Fact. One has to play all sorts of things here—and the more the better! My work was to stitch, fold, (fold first) and cover, so many copies of the New Testament as I had brought with me—printed, but in sheets. I did them strong! more than that I will not answer for; but I wish I could send you a copy. It would be only a curiosity in art, though; you could not read it. It is an admirable translation in Fijian. As I have had but very slight previous practice in bookbinding, my rate of progress was at first somewhat slow; and after a few days of solitary labour I was glad to accept the offer of help from four or five native apprentices—some of our local preachers. They took to the work kindly; and in five weeks we finished the edition—sixty copies. I could do the next sixty quicker. These are the first Fijian testaments in Ono, and you can understand—or you can*not*—what a treasure. The natives who came to purchase them found no fault with the binding, I assure you. So you see I have been bookseller as well as the other thing; and I received pay for my testaments in *sinnet*—you know what that is. It is as good as money for the mission use here in Fiji. During these bookbinding weeks I was making excursions hither and thither, to preach and baptize. Twice a week I took a time to see the local preachers and teachers and examine them and hear them read and talk to them and be talked to by them. Every Tuesday and Friday I did this. The whole course of the week's work is now something like the following:

"Sunday begins with a prayer-meeting. Afterwards old and young have a catechism exercise together. Morning and afternoon, preaching.

"Monday, the morning there is a children's school, and the afternoon a school for grown people. I question both classes on the sermons of the preceding day; and I hope English people have as good memories. The afternoon school is followed by a prayer-meeting. Tuesdays and Fridays I have the teachers' meeting in addition.

"Wednesday I preach, have leaders' meeting, and give out work for the week to come.

"Thursdays, preaching at one of the neighbouring towns, and a sort of young class-meeting.

"Friday I have said what I do.

"Saturday has a prayer-meeting.

"So much for the regular work. Then there are the sick to look after, and my own private studies; and there is not a minute to spare. A few that cannot be spared are claimed by the mosquitos, which hold their high court and revel here at Ono; of all places on the earth that I know, their headquarters. When I was here before with Brother Lefferts and others, two of them could not sit still to read something that wanted to be read; they walked the floor, one holding the candle, the other the paper; both fighting mosquitos with both hands. I am of a less excitable temperament—for I contrive to live a little more quietly.

"Shall I tell you some of these native testimonies of Christians who a little while ago worshipped idols? At our love-feast lately some thirty or forty spoke. They did my heart good. So may they yours. These people said but few words, full of feeling; my report cannot at all give the effect. I wish it could.

"One old chief who could hardly speak for feeling, said, 'These are new things to me in these days;' (he meant the love-feasts) 'I did not know them formerly. My soul is humbled. I rejoice greatly in the Lord. I rejoice greatly for sending his servants.'

"A Tongan teacher—'I desire that God may rule over me,' (i. e. direct me) 'I desire not to govern myself. I know that I am a child of God: I know that God is my father. My friends wrote for me to go to Tonga; but I wondered at it. I wish to obey the Father of my soul.'

"A local preacher—'I know that God is near, and helps me sometimes in my work. I love all men. I do not fear death; one thing I fear, the Lord."

"Leva Soko, a female class-leader, a very holy woman, said,—this is but a part of what she said,—'My child died, but I loved God the more. My body has been much afflicted, but I love him the more. I know that death would only unite me to God.'

"A teacher, a native of Ono, who had gone to a much less pleasant place to preach the gospel, and was home on a visit, spoke exceedingly well. 'I did not leave Ono that I might have more food. I desired to go that I might preach Christ. I was struck with stones twice while in my own house; but I could bear it. When the canoes came, they pillaged my garden; but my mind was not pained at it: I bore it only.'

"A local preacher—'I am a very bad man; there is no good thing in me; but I know the love of God. There are not two great things in my mind; there is one only,—the love of God for the sake of Christ. I know that I am a child of God. I wish to repent and believe every day till I die.'

"These are but a specimen, my dear friend. The

other day in our teachers' meeting we were reading the nineteenth chapter of John. An old teacher read the eighteenth verse in his turn—the words, 'Where they crucified him, and two other with him, on either side one, and Jesus in the midst.' He could hardly get through it, and then burst into tears and wept aloud. This man was a cannibal once. And now his life speaks for the truth of his tears.

"Good night. The mosquitos are not favourable to epistle writing. I am well. Remember me, as I remember you." R. R.

"Aunt Caxton," said Eleanor after reading this letter for the second or third time,—"have we a supply of mosquito netting among my boxes? I could get the better of the mosquitos, I think."

"How would you like to help bind books?" said Mrs. Caxton. "Or translate? Mr. Rhys seems to be about that business, by what he says in the other letter."

"He would not want help in that," said Eleanor, musing and flushing. "Aunt Caxton—is it foolish in me to wish I could hear once more from Mr. Rhys before I go?"

"Only a little foolish, my love; and very natural."

"Then why is it foolish?"

"Because reason would tell you that it is simply impossible your letters could receive an answer by this time. They have perhaps but barely got to Mr. Rhys this minute. And reason would tell you further that there is no ground for supposing he is in any different mind from that expressed when he wrote to you."

"But—you know—since then he does not say one word about it, nor about me," said Eleanor flushing pretty deep.

"There is reason for that, too. He would not allow himself to indulge hope; and therefore he would not act as if he had any. That sight of you at Brighton threw him off a good deal, I judge."

"He told you he saw me?"

"He wrote to me about it."

"Did he tell you how he saw me?"

"Yes."

"What more?"

"He said he thought there was little chance I would have any use for his letters; he saw the world was closing its nets around you fast: how far they were already successful he could not know; but he was glad he had seen what forbade him in time to indulge vain anticipations."

"Oh aunt Caxton!" said Eleanor—"Oh aunt Caxton! what a strange world this is, for the way people's lives cross each other, and the work that is done without people's knowing it! If you knew—what that meeting cost me!—"

"My dear child! I can well believe it."

"And it aroused Mr. Carlisle's suspicions instantly, I knew. If I made any mistake—if I erred at all, in my behaviour with regard to him, it was then and in consequence of that. If I had faltered a bit then—looked grave or hung back from what was going on, I should have exposed myself to most cruel interpretation. I could not risk it. I threw myself right into whatever presented itself—went into the whirl—welcomed everybody and everything—only, I hoped, with so general and impartial a welcome as should prove I preferred none exclusively."

Eleanor stopped and the tears came into her eyes.

"My child! if I had known what danger you were in, I should have spent even more time than I did in praying for you."

"I suppose I was in danger," said Eleanor thoughtfully. "It was a difficult winter. Then do you think—Mr. Rhys gave me up?"

"No," said Mrs. Caxton smiling. "You remember he wrote to you after that, from Fiji; but I suppose he tried to make himself give you up, as far as hope went."

"For all that appears, I may be here long enough yet to have letters before I go. We have heard of no opportunity that is likely to present itself soon. Aunt Caxton, if my feeling is foolish, why is it natural?"

"Because you are a woman, my dear."

"And foolish?"

"Not at all; but feeling takes little counsel of reason in some cases. I am afraid you will find that out again before you get to Mr. Rhys—*after* that, I do not think you will."

The conversation made Eleanor rather more anxious than she had been before to hear of a ship; but October and November passed, and the prospect of her voyage was as misty as ever.

Again and again, all summer, both she and Mrs. Caxton had written begging that Mrs. Powle would make a visit to Plassy, and bring or send Julia. In vain. Mrs. Powle would not come. Julia could not.

CHAPTER XIII.

> "A wild dedication of yourselves
> To unpath'd waters, undream'd shores; most certain,
> To miseries enough."

In a neat plain drawing-room in a plain part of London, sat Mrs. Caxton and Eleanor. Eleanor however soon left her seat and took post at the window; and silence reigned in the room unbroken for some length of time except by the soft rustle of Mrs. Caxton's work. Her fingers were rarely idle. Nor were Eleanor's hands often empty; but to-day she stood still as a statue before the window, while now and then a tear softly rolled down and dropped on her folded hands. There were no signs of the tears however, when the girl turned round with the short announcement,

"She's here."

Mrs. Caxton looked up a little bit anxiously at her adopted child; but Eleanor's face was only still and pale. The next moment the door opened, and for all the world as in old times the fair face and fair curls of Mrs. Powle appeared. Just the same; unless just now she appeared a trifle frightened. The good lady felt so. Two fanatics. She hardly knew how to encounter them. And then, her own action, though she could not certainly have called it fanatical, had been peculiar, and might be judged divers ways. Moreover, Mrs. Powle was Eleanor's mother.

There was one in the company who remembered that;

witness the still close embrace which Eleanor threw around her, and the still hiding of the girl's face on her mother's bosom. Mrs. Powle returned the embrace heartily enough; but when Eleanor's motionless clasp had lasted as long as she knew how to do anything with it and longer than she felt to be graceful, Mrs. Powle whispered,

"Won't you introduce me to your aunt, my dear,—if this is she."

Eleanor released her mother, but sobbed helplessly for a few minutes; then she raised her head and threw off her tears; and there was to one of the two ladies an exquisite grace in the way she performed the required office of making them known to each other. The gentleness of a chastened heart, the strength of a loving one, the dignity of an humble one, made her face and manner so lovely that Mrs. Caxton involuntarily wished Mr. Rhys could have seen it. "But he will have chance enough," she thought, somewhat incongruously, as she met and returned her sister-in-law's greetings. Mrs. Powle made them with ceremonious respect, not make believe, and with a certain eagerness which welcomed a diversion from Eleanor's somewhat troublesome agitation. Eleanor's agitation troubled no one any more, however; she sat down calm and quiet; and Mrs. Powle had leisure, glancing at her from time to time, to get into smooth sailing intercourse with Mrs. Caxton. She took off her bonnet, and talked about indifferent things, and sipped chocolate; for it was just luncheon time. Ever and anon her eyes came back to Eleanor; evidently as to something which troubled her and which puzzled her; and Mrs. Caxton saw, which had also the effect of irritation too. Very likely, Mrs. Caxton thought! Conscience on one hand not satisfied, and ambition on the other hand disappointed, and Eleanor the point of meeting for both uneasy feelings to concentrate their forces.

It would come out in words soon, Mrs. Caxton knew. But how lovely Eleanor seemed to her. There was not even a cloud upon her brow now; fair as it was pure and strong.

"And so you are going?" Mrs. Powle began at last, in a somewhat constrained voice. Eleanor smiled.

"And *when* are you going?"

"My letter said. Next Tuesday the ship sails."

"And pray, Eleanor, you are not going alone?"

"No, mamma. A gentleman and his wife are going the whole voyage with me."

"Who are they?"

"A Mr. Amos and his wife."

"*What* are they then? missionaries?"

"Yes, ma'am."

"Going to that same place?"

"Yes, ma'am—very nicely for me."

"Pray how long do you expect the voyage will take you?"

"I am not certain—it is made, or can be made, in four or five months; but then we may have to stop awhile at Sydney."

"Sydney? what Sydney? Where is that?"

"Australia, mamma," said Eleanor smiling. "New South Wales. Don't you know?"

"*Australia!* Are you going there? To Botany Bay?"

"No, mamma; not to Botany Bay. And I only take Australia by the way. I go further."

"*Further* than Botany Bay?"

"Yes, ma'am."

"Well certainly,' said Mrs. Powle with an accent of restrained despair, "the present age is enterprising beyond what was ever known in my young days. What do you think, sister Caxton, of a young lady taking a voyage five months long after her husband, instead of her husband taking it for her? He ought to be a grateful man, I think!"

"Certainly; but not too grateful," Mrs. Caxton answered composedly; "for in this case necessity alters the rule."

"I do not understand such necessities," said Mrs. Powle; "at least if a thing cannot be done properly, I should say it was better not to do it at all. However, I suppose it is too late to speak now. I would not have *my* daughter hold herself so lightly as to confer such an honour on any man; but I gave her to you to dispose of, so no doubt it is all right. I hope Mr. What's-his-name is worthy of it."

"Mamma, let me give you another cup of chocolate," said Eleanor. And she served her with the chocolate and the toast and the hung beef, in a way that gave Mrs. Caxton's heart a feast. There was the beautiful calm and high grace with which Eleanor used to meet her social difficulties two years ago, and baffle both her trials and her tempters. Mrs. Caxton had never seen it called for. Her face shewed not the slightest embarrassment at her mother's words; not a shade of rising colour did dishonour to Mr. Rhys by proving that she so much as even felt the slurs against him or the jealousy professed on her own behalf. Eleanor's calm sweet face was an assertion both of his dignity and her own. Perhaps Mrs. Powle felt herself in a hopeless case.

"What do you expect to live on out there?" she said, changing her ground, as she dipped her toast into chocolate. "You won't have this sort of thing."

"I have never thought much about it," said Eleanor smiling. "Where other people live and grow strong, I suppose I can."

"No, it does not follow at all," replied her mother. "You are accustomed to certain things, and you would feel the want of them. For instance, will you have bread like this out there? wheat bread?"

"I shall not want chocolate," said Eleanor. "The climate is too hot."

"But bread?"

"Wheat flour is shipped for the use of the mission families," said Mrs. Caxton. "It is known that many persons would suffer without it; and we do not wish unnecessary suffering should be undergone."

"Have they cows there?"

"Mamma!" said Eleanor laughing.

"Well, have they? Because Miss Broadus or somebody was saying the other day, that in New Zealand they never had them till we sent them out. So I wondered directly whether they had in this place."

"I fancy not, mamma. You will have to think of me as drinking my tea without cream."

"So you will take tea there with you?"

"Why not?"

"I have got the impression," said Mrs. Powle, "somehow, that you would do nothing as other people do. You will drink tea, will you? I'll give you a box."

"Thank you, mamma," said Eleanor, but the colour flushed now to the roots of her hair,—"aunt Caxton has given me a great stock already."

"And coffee?"

"Yes, mamma—for great occasions—and concentrated milk for that."

"Do tell me what sort of a place it is, Eleanor."

"It is a great many places, mamma. It is a great many islands, large and small, scattered over some hundreds of miles of ocean; but they are so many and so near each other often, and so surrounded with interlacing coral reefs, that navigation there is in a kind of network of channels. The islands are of many varieties, and of fairy land beauty; rich in vegetation and in all sorts of natural stores."

"Not cows."

"No, ma'am. I meant, the things that grow out of the ground," said Eleanor smiling again. "Cows and sheep and horses are not among them."

"Nor horses either? How do you go when you travel?"

"In a canoe, I suppose."

"With savages?" exclaimed Mrs. Powle.

"Not necessarily. Many of them are Christians."

"The natives?"

"Yes, ma'am."

"Then I don't see what you are going for. Those that are Christians already might teach those that are not. But Eleanor, who will marry you?"

A bright rose-colour came upon the girl's cheeks. "Mamma, there are clergymen enough there."

"*Clergymen?* of the Church?"

"I beg your pardon, mamma; no. That is not essential?"

"Well, that is as you look at things. I know you and my sister Caxton have wandered away,—but for me, I should feel lost out of the Church. It would be very essential to me. Are there no Church people in the islands at all?"

"I believe not, mamma."

"And what on earth do you expect to do there, Eleanor?"

"I cannot tell you yet, mamma; but I understand everybody finds more than enough."

"What, pray?"

"The general great business, you know, is to carry light to those that sit in darkness."

"Yes, but you do not expect to preach, do you?"

Eleanor smiled, she could not help it, at the bewildered

air with which this question was put. "I don't know, mamma. Do not you think I could preach to a class of children?"

"But Eleanor! such horrid work. Such work for *you!*"

"Why, mamma?"

"Why? With your advantages and talents and education. Mr.—no matter who, but who used to be a good judge, said that your talents would give anybody else's talents enough to do;—and that you should throw them away upon a class of half-naked children at the antipodes!"——

"There will be somebody else to take the benefit of them first," Mrs. Caxton said very composedly. "I rather think Mr. Rhys will see to it that they are not wasted."

"Mamma, I think you do not understand this matter," Eleanor said gently. "Whoever made that speech flattered me; but I wish my talents were ten times so much as they are, that I might give them to this work."

"To this gentleman, you mean!" Mrs. Powle said tartly.

A light came into Eleanor's eyes; she was silent a minute and then with the colour rising all over her face she said, "He is abundantly worthy of all and much more than I am."

"Well I do not understand this matter, as you said," Mrs. Powle answered in some discomfiture. "Tell me of something I do understand. What society will you have where you are going, Eleanor?"

"I shall be too busy to have much time for society, mamma," Eleanor answered good-humouredly.

"No such thing—you will want it all the more. Sister Caxton, is it not so?"

"People do not go out there without consenting to forego many things," Mrs. Caxton answered; "but there is One who has promised to be with his servants when they are about his work; and I never heard that any one who had that society, pined greatly for want of other."

Mrs. Powle opened her eyes at Mrs. Caxton's quiet face; she set this speech down in her mind as uncontaminated fanaticism. She turned to Eleanor.

"Do the people there wear clothes?"

"The Christians clothe themselves, mamma; the heathen portion of the people hardly do, I believe. The climate requires nothing. They have a fashion of dress of their own, but it is not much."

"And can you help seeing these heathen?"

"No, of course not."

"Well you *are* changed!" said Mrs. Powle. "I would never have thought you would have consented to such degradation."

"I go that I may help mend it, mamma."

"Yes, you must stoop yourself first."

"Think how Jesus stooped—to what degradation—for us all."

Mrs. Powle paused, at the view of Eleanor's glistening eyes. It was not easy to answer, moreover.

"I cannot help it," she said. "You and I take different views on the subject. Do let us talk of something else; I am always getting on something where we cannot agree. Tell me about the place, Eleanor."

"What, mamma? I have not been there."

"No, but of course you know. What do you live in? houses or tents?"

"I do not know which you would call them; they are not stone or wood. There is a skeleton frame of posts to uphold the building; but the walls are made of different thicknesses of reeds, laid different ways and laced together with sinnet."

"What's *sinnet*?"

"A strong braid made of the fibre of the cocoanut—of the husk of the cocoanut. It is made of more and less size and strength, and is used instead of iron to fasten a great many sorts of things; carpentry and boat building among them."

"Goodness! what a place. Well go on with your house."

"That is all," said Eleanor smiling; "except that it is thatched with palm leaves, or grass, or cane leaves. Sometimes the walls are covered with grass; and the braid work done in patterns, so as to have a very artistic effect."

"And what is inside?"

"Not much beside the people."

"Well tell me what, for instance. There is something, I suppose. The walls are not bare?"

"Not quite. There are apt to be mats, to sit and lie on;—and pots for cooking, and baskets and a chest perhaps, and a great mosquito curtain."

"Are you going to live in a house like that, Eleanor?"

Mrs. Powle's face expressed distress. Eleanor laughed and declared she did not know.

"It will have some chairs for her to sit upon," said Mrs. Caxton; "and I shall send some china cups, that she may not have to drink out of a cocoanut shell."

"But I should like that very well," said Eleanor; "and I certainly think a Fijian wooden dish, spread with green leaves, is as nice a vessel for food as can be."

Mrs. Powle rose up and began to arrange her shawl, with an air which said, "I do not understand it!"

"Mamma, what are you about?"

"Eleanor, you make me very uncomfortable."

"Do I? Why should I, mamma?"

"It is no use talking." Then suddenly facing round on Eleanor she said, "What are you going to do for servants in that dreadful place?"

"Mr. Rhys says he has a most faithful servant—who

is much attached to him, and does as well as he can desire."

"One of those native savages?"

"He was; he is a Christian now, and a good one."

Mrs. Powle looked as if she did not know how to believe her daughter.

"Aren't you afraid of what you are about, Eleanor—to venture among those creatures? and to take all that voyage first, alone? Are you not afraid?"

There was that in the very simpleness and quietness of Eleanor's answer that put her negative beyond a question. Mrs. Powle sat down again for very bewilderment.

"Why are you not afraid?" she said. "You never were afraid of little things, I know; but those houses—Are there no thieves among those heathen?"

"A good many."

"What is to keep them out of your house? Anybody could cut through a reed wall with a knife—and make no noise about it. Where is your security?"

Alas, in the one face there was such ignorance, in the other such sorrowful consciousness of that ignorance, that the two faces at first looked mutely into each other across the gulf between them.

"Mamma," said Eleanor, "why will you not understand me? Do you not know,—the Eternal God is our refuge!"

The still, grand expression of faith Mrs. Powle could not receive; but the speaking of Eleanor's eyes she did. She turned from them.

"Good morning, sister Caxton," she said. "I will go. I cannot bear it any longer to-day."

"You will come to-morrow, sister Powle?"

"Yes. O yes. I'll be here to-morrow. I will get my feelings quieted by that time. Good bye, Eleanor."

"Mamma," said the girl trembling, "when will you bring Julia?"

"Now Eleanor, don't let us talk about anything more that is disagreeable. I do not want to say anything about Julia. You have taken your way—and I do not mean to unsettle you in it; but Julia is in another line, and I cannot have you interfere with her. I am very sorry it is so,—but it is not my doing. I cannot help it. I do not want to give you pain—"

Mrs. Powle departed. Eleanor came back from attending her to the door, stopped in the middle of the room, and her cheeks grew white as she spoke.

"I shall never see her again!"

"My love," said Mrs. Caxton pityingly,—"I hardly know how to believe it possible."

"I knew it all along," said Eleanor. She sat down and covered her face. Mrs. Caxton sighed.

"It is as true now as it was in the old time," she said, —"He that will live godly in Christ Jesus, shall suffer persecution.' So surely as we walk like Christ, so surely the world will call us odd and strange and fanatical, and treat us accordingly."

Eleanor's head was bent low.

"And Jesus is our only refuge—and our sufficient consolation."

"O yes!—but—"

"'And he can make our silent witness-bearing bring fruits for his glory, and for our dear ones' good, as much as years of talking to them, Eleanor."

"You are good comfort, aunt Caxton," said the girl putting her arms around her and straining her close;—"but—this is something I cannot help just now—"

It was a natural sorrow not to be struggled with successfully; and Eleanor took it to her own room. So did Mrs. Caxton take it to hers. But the struggle was ended then and there. No trace of it remained the next day.

Eleanor met her mother most cheerfully, and contrived admirably to keep her from the gulf of discussion into which she had been continually plunging at her first visit. With so much of grace and skill, and of that poise of her own mind which left her free to extend help to another's vacillations and uncertainties, Eleanor guided the conversation and bore herself generally that day, that Mrs. Powle's sighing commentary as she went away, was, "Ah, Eleanor!—you might have been a duchess!"

But the paleness of sorrow came over her duchess's face again so soon as she was gone. Mrs. Caxton saw that if the struggle was ended, the pain was not; and her heart bled for Eleanor. These were days not to be prolonged. It was good for everybody that Tuesday, the day of sailing, was so near.

They were heavy, the hours that intervened. In spite of keeping herself close and making no needless advertisement of her proceedings, Eleanor could not escape many an encounter with old friends or acquaintances. They heard of her from her mother; learned her address; and then curiosity was enough, without affection, to bring several; and affection mingled with curiosity to bring a few. Among others, the two Miss Broadus's, Eleanor's friends and associates at Wiglands ever since she had been a child, could not keep away from her and could not be denied when they came; though they took precious time, and though they tried Eleanor sorely. They wanted to know everything; if their wishes had sufficed, they would have learned the whole history of Mr. Rhys's courtship. Failing that, their inquiries went to everything else, past and future, to which Eleanor's own knowledge could be supposed to extend. What she had been doing through the year which was gone, and what she expected the coming year would find her to do; when she would get to her place of destination, and what sort of a life she would have of it when once there.

Houses, and horses, and cows and sheep, were as interesting to these good ladies as they were to Mrs. Powle; and feeling less concern in the matter they were free to take more amusement, and so no side feeling or hidden feeling disturbed their satisfaction in the flow of information they were receiving. For Eleanor gratified them patiently, in all which did not touch immediately herself; but when they were gone she sighed. Even Mrs. Powle was less trying; for her annoyances were at least of a more dignified kind. Eleanor could meet them better.

"And this is the end of you!" she exclaimed the evening before Eleanor was to sail. "This is the end of your life and expectations! To look at you and think of it!" Despondency could no further go.

"Not the end of either, mamma, I hope," Eleanor responded cheerfully.

"The expectation of the righteous shall be for ever, you forget," said Mrs. Caxton smiling. "There is no fall nor failure to that."

"O yes, I know!" said Mrs. Powle impatiently; "but just look at that girl and see what she is. She might be presented at Court now, and reigning like a princess in her own house; yes, she might; and to-morrow she is going off as if she were a convict, to Botany Bay!"

"No, mamma," said Eleanor smiling. "I never can persuade you of Australian geography."

"Well it's New South Wales, isn't it?" said Mrs. Powle.

Eleanor assented.

"Very well. The girl that brings you your luncheon when you get there, may be the very one that stole my spoons three years ago. It's all the same thing. And you, Eleanor, you are so handsome, and you have the manners of a queen—Sister Caxton, you have no notion what admiration this girl excited, and what admiration she could command!"

Mrs. Caxton looked from the calm face of the girl, certainly handsome enough, to the vexed countenance of the mother; whose fair curls failed to look complacent for once.

"I suppose Eleanor thinks of another day," she said; "when the Lord will come to be admired in his saints and to be glorified in all them that believe. *That* will be admiration worth having—if Eleanor thinks so, I confess I think so too."

"Dear sister Caxton," said Mrs. Powle restraining herself, "what has the one thing to do with the other?"

"Nothing," said Mrs. Caxton. "To seek both is impossible."

"*Do* you think it is wicked to receive admiration? I did not think you went so far."

"No," said Mrs. Caxton, with her genial smile. "We were talking of seeking it."

Mrs. Powle was silent, and went away in a very ill humour.

CHAPTER XIV.

"The sun came up upon the left,
Out of the sea came he!
And he shone bright, and on the right
Went down into the sea."

And the Tuesday came, and was fair; and under a bright sky the steamer ran down to Gravesend with Eleanor and her friends on board. Not Julia; Eleanor had given up all hopes of that; but Mrs. Caxton was beside her, and on the other side of her was Mrs. Powle. It was a terribly disagreeable journey to the latter; every feeling in her somewhat passionless nature was in a state of fretful rebellion. The other stronger and deeper characters were ready for the time and met it bravely. Met it cheerfully too. The crisping breeze that curled the waters of the river, the blue sky and fair sunlight, the bright and beautiful of the scene around them, those two saw and tasted; with hopeful though very grave hearts. The other poor lady saw nothing but a dirty steamboat and a very unpropitious company. Among these however were Eleanor's fellow-voyagers, Mr. Amos and his wife; and she was introduced to them now for the first time. Various circumstances had prevented their meeting in London.

"A very common-looking man,"—whispered Mrs. Powle to Eleanor.

"I don't know, mamma,—but very *good*," Eleanor returned.

"You are mad on goodness!" said Mrs. Powle. "Don't you see anything else in a man. or the want of anything else? I do; a thousand things; and if a man is ever so good, I want him to be a gentleman too."

"So do I," said Eleanor smiling. "But much more, mamma, if a man is ever so much a gentleman, I want him to be good. Isn't that the more important of the two?"

"No!" said Mrs. Powle. "I don't think it is; not for society."

Eleanor thought of Paul's words—"Henceforth know I no man after the flesh"—What was the use of talking? she and her mother must have the same vision before they could see the same things. And she presently forgot Mr. Amos and all about him; for in the distance she discerned signs that the steamer was approaching Gravesend; and knew that the time of parting drew near.

It came and was gone, and Eleanor was alone on the deck of the "Diana;" and in that last moment of trial Mrs. Powle had been the most overcome of the three. Eleanor's sweet face bore itself strongly as well; and Mrs. Caxton was strong both by life-habit and nature; and the view of each of them was far above that little ship-deck. Mrs. Powle saw nothing else. Her distress was very deep.

"I wish I had taken Julia to her!" was the outburst of her penitent relentings; and Mrs. Caxton was only thankful, since they had come too late, that they were uttered too late for Eleanor to hear. *She* went home like a person whose earthly treasure is all lodged away from her; not lost at all, indeed, but yet only to be enjoyed and watched over from a distance. Even then she reckoned herself rich beyond what she had been before Eleanor ever came to her.

For Eleanor, left on the ship's deck, at first it was hard to realize that she had any earthly treasure at all. One part of it quitted, perhaps for ever, with the home and the country of her childhood; the other, so far, so vague, so uncertainly grasped in this moment of distraction, that she felt utterly broken-hearted and alone. She had not counted upon this; she had not expected her self-command would so completely fail her; but it was so; and although without one shadow of a wish to turn back or in any wise alter her course, the first beginning of her journey was made amidst mental storms. Julia was the particular bitter thought over which her tears poured; but they flooded every image that rose of home things, and childish things and things at Plassy. Mr. Amos came to her help.

"It is nothing," Eleanor said as well as she could speak,—"it is nothing but the natural feeling which will have its way. Thank you—don't be concerned. I don't want anything—if I only could have seen my sister!—"

"Mrs. Amos is about as bad," said her comforter with a sigh. "Ah well! feeling must have its way, and better it should. You will both be better by and by, I hope."

They were worse before they were better. For in a few hours sickness took its place among present grievances; and perhaps on the whole it acted as a relief by effecting a diversion from mental to bodily concerns. It seemed to Eleanor that she felt them both together; nevertheless, when at the end of a few days the sea-sickness left her and she was able to get up again, it was with the sweet fresh quietness of convalescence in mind as well as in body. She was herself again. Things took their place. England was behind indeed—but Fiji was forward—and Heaven was over all.

As soon as she was able to be up she went upon deck. Strength came immediately with the fresh breeze. It was a cool cloudy day; the ship speeding along under a good spread of canvas; the sea in a beautiful state of life, but not boisterous. Nobody was on deck but some of the sailors. Eleanor took a seat by the guards, and began to drink in refreshment. It stole in fast, on mind as well as body, she hardly knew how; only both were braced up together. She felt now a curious gladness that the parting was over, the journey begun, and England fairly out of sight. The going away had been like death; a new life was rising upon her now; and Eleanor turned herself towards it with the same sweet readiness as the good ship whose head is laid upon a new course.

There is a state of mind in which the soul may be aptly called the garden of the Lord; when answering to his culture it brings forth flowers and fruits for his pleasure. In such a state, the paradise which Adam lost is half reëntered again; the moral victory is won over "the works of the devil" which Christ came to destroy. The body is dead, no doubt, because of sin; but the spirit is life, because of righteousness. The air of that garden is peace; no hurricanes blow there; the sunshine dwells therein; the odours of sweet things come forth, and make known all abroad whose garden it is.

Eleanor had sat awhile very still, very busy looking over into the sea, when she heard a step near her on the deck. She looked up, and saw a man whom she recognized as the master of the vessel. A rather hard-featured man, tall and strong set, with a pair of small eyes that did not give forth their expression readily. What there was struck her as not pleasant.

"So you've got up!" said he, in a voice which was less harsh than his looks. "Do you feel better?"

"Much better, thank you."

"Hearty, eh?"

"Pretty well," said Eleanor smiling, "since I have got this salt air into my lungs."

"Ah! you'll have enough of that. 'Tother lady is down yet, eh? She has not got up."

"No."

"Are you all going to the same place?"

"I believe so."

"Missionaries, eh?"

"Yes."

"Think you'll get those dark fellows to listen to you?"

"Why not?" said Eleanor brightly.

"It's all make-believe. They only want to get your axes and hatchets, and such things."

"Well, we want their yams and potatoes and fish and labour," said Eleanor; "so it is a fair bargain; and no make-believe on either side."

"Why don't you stay in the Colonies? there is work enough to be done; people enough that need it; and a fine country. Everything in the world that you need; and not so far from home either."

Eleanor made no answer.

"Why don't you stay in the Colonies?"

"One can only be in one place," said Eleanor lightly.

"And that must always be the place where somebody else is," said the captain maliciously. "That's the way people will congregate together, instead of scattering where they are wanted."

"Do you know the Colonies well?" said Eleanor coolly in answer to this rude speech.

"I ought. I have spent about a third of my life in them. I have a brother at Melbourne too, as rich in flocks and herds almost as Job was. That's the place! That's a country! But you are going to Sydney?"

"Yes."

"Friends there?"

"I have one friend there who expects me."

"Who's he? Maybe I know him."

"Egbert Esthwaite is his name."

"Don't know him, though. And so you have left England to find yourself a new home in the wilderness?"

"Yes."

"Pretty tough change you'll find it. Don't you find it already?"

"No. Don't you know," said Eleanor giving him a good look, "when one's real home is in heaven, it does not make so much difference?"

The captain would have answered the words fast enough; but in the strong sweet eye that had looked into his so full, there was something that silenced him. He turned off abruptly, with the internal conviction—"*That* girl thinks what she says, anyhow!"

Eleanor's eyes left contemplating the waters, and were busy for some time with the book which had lain in her lap until her colloquy with the captain. Somebody came and sat down beside her.

"Mr. Amos! I am glad to see you," said Eleanor.

"I am glad to see you, sister," he replied; "and glad to see you able to be here. You look well again."

"O I am."

"Mrs. Amos cannot raise her head. What are you doing?—if I may ask so blunt a question upon so short an acquaintance."

"This is the first time I have been on deck. I was studying the sea, in the first place;—and then something drove me to study the Bible."

"Ah, we are driven to that on every hand," he answered. "Now go on, and tell me the point of your studies, will you?"

There was something in the utmost genial and kind in his look and way; he was not a person from whom one would keep back anything he wanted to know; as also evidently he was not one to ask anything he should not. The request did not even startle Eleanor. She looked thoughtfully over the heaving sea while she answered.

"I had been taking a great new view of the glory of creation—over the ship's side here. Then I had the sorrow to find—or fear—that we have an unbeliever in our captain. From that, I suppose, I took hold of Paul's reasoning—how without excuse people are in unbelief; how the invisible things of God from the creation of the world are clearly seen, being understood by the things that are made; even his eternal power and Godhead. And those glorious last words were what my heart fixed upon."

"'His eternal power and Godhead.'"

Eleanor looked round without speaking; a look full of the human echo to those words; the joy of weakness, the strength of ignorance, the triumph of humility.

"What a grand characterizing Paul gives in those other words," said Mr. Amos—'the King eternal, immortal, invisible, the only wise God.' Unto him be honour and glory forever!"

"And then those other words," said Eleanor low,—"'The eternal God is thy refuge.'"

"That is a good text for us to keep," said Mr. Amos. "But really, with that refuge, I don't see what we should be afraid of."

"Not even of want of success," said Eleanor.

"No. If faith didn't fail. Paul could give thanks that he was made always to triumph in Christ,—and by the power that wrought with him, so may we." He spoke very gravely, as if looking into himself and pondering his own responsibilities and privileges and shortcomings. Eleanor kept silence.

"How do you like this way of life?" Mr. Amos said presently.

"The sea is beautiful. I have hardly tried the ship."

"Haven't you?" said Mr. Amos smiling. "That speaks a candid good traveller. Another would have made the first few days the type of the whole."

And he also took to his book, and the silence lasted this time.

Mrs. Amos continued prostrated by sea-sickness; unable to raise her head from her pillow. Eleanor could do little for her. The evil was remediless, and admitted of very small amelioration. But the weather was very fine and the ship's progress excellent; and Eleanor spent great part of her time on deck. All day, except when she was at the side of Mrs. Amos, she was there. The sailors watched the figure in the dark neat sea-dress and cloak and the little close straw bonnet with chocolate ribbands; and every now and then made pretences to get near and see how the face looked that was hidden under it. The report of the first venturers was so favourable that Eleanor had an unconscious sort of levee the next day or two; and then, the fresh sweet face that was so like a flower was found to have more attractions when known than it had before when unknown. There was not a hand on board but seized or made opportunities every day and as often as he could to get near her; if a chance offered and he could edge in a word and have a smile and word in answer, that man went away esteemed both by himself and his comrades a lucky fellow. Eleanor awoke presently to the sense of her opportunities, though too genuinely humble to guess at the cause of them; and she began to make every one tell for her work. Every sailor on board soon knew what Eleanor valued more than all other things; every one knew, "sure as guns," as he would have expressed it, that if she had a chance of speaking to him, she would one way or another contrive before it was ended to make him think of his duty and to remember to whom it was owed; and yet—strange to say—there was not one of them that for any such reason was willing to lose or to shun one of those chances. "If all were like she"—was the comment of one Jack tar; and the rest were precisely of his opinion. The captain himself was no exception. He could not help frequently coming to Eleanor's side, to break off her studies or her musings with some information or some suggestion of his own and have a bit of a talk. His manners mended. He grew thoroughly civil to her.

Meanwhile the vessel was speeding southwards. Fast, fast, every day they lowered their latitude. Higher and higher rose the sun; the stars that had been Eleanor's familiars ever since she had eyes to see them, sank one by one below the northern horizon; and the beauty of the new, strange, brilliant constellations of the southern sky began to tell her in curious language of her approach to her new home. They had a most magical charm for Eleanor. She studied and watched them unweariedly; they had for her that curious interest which we give to any things that are to be our life-companions. Here Mr. Amos could render her some help; but with or without help, Eleanor nightly studied the southern stars, watched and pondered them till she knew them well; and then she watched them because she knew them, as well as because she was to know them all the rest of her life.

By day she studied other things; and the days were not weary. The ocean was a storehouse of pleasure for her; and Captain Fox declared his ship had never carried such a clever passenger; "a girl who had plenty of stuff, and knew what to do with herself." Certainly the last piece of praise was true; for Eleanor had no weary moments. She had interests on board, as well as outside the ship. She picked up the sailors' legends and superstitions; ay, and many a little bit of life history came in too, by favour of the sympathy and friendliness they saw in those fine brown eyes. Never a voyage went better; and the sailors if not the captain were very much of the mind that they had a good angel on board.

"Well how do you like *this?*" said Mr. Amos coming up one day. N. B. It was the seventh day of a calm in the tropics.

"I would like a wind better," Eleanor said smiling.

"Can you possess your soul in patience?"

"Yes," she said, but gently and with a slight intonation that spoke of several latent things.

"We are well on our way now,—if a wind would come!"

"It will come."

"I have never asked you," said Mr. Amos. "How do you expect to find life in the islands?"

"In what respect? In general, I should say, as unlike this as possible."

"Of course. I understand there is no stagnation there. But as to hardships—as to the people?"

"The people are part Christianized and part unchristianized; that gives every variety of experience among them, I suppose. The unchristianized are as bad as they can be, very nearly; the good, very good. As to hardships, I have no expectation."

"You have not data to form one?"

"I cannot say that; but things are so different according to circumstances; and there is so great a change going on continually in the character of the people."

"How do you feel about leaving behind you all the arts and refinements and delights of taste in the old world?"

"Will you look over the side of the ship, Mr. Amos? —down below there—do you see anything?"

"Dolphin—," said Mr. Amos.

"What do you think of them?"

"Beautiful!" said Mr. Amos. "Beautiful, undoubtedly! as brilliant as if they had just come out of the jeweller's shop, polished silver. How clear the water is! I can see them perfectly—far below."

"Isn't the sea better than a jeweller's shop?"

"I never thought of it before," said Mr. Amos laughing; "but it certainly is; though I think it is the first time the comparison has been made."

"Did you ever go to Tenby?"

"I never did."

"Nor I; but I have heard the sea-caves in its neighbourhood described as more splendid in their natural treasures of vegetable and animal growth, than any jeweller's shop could be—were he the richest in London."

"*Splendid?*" said Mr. Amos.

"Yes—for brilliance and variety of colour."

"Is it possible? These are things that I do not know."

"You will be likely to know them. The lagoons around the Polynesian islands—the still waters within the barrier-reefs, you understand—are lined with most gorgeous and wonderful displays of this kind. One seems to be sailing over a mine of gems—only not in the rough, but already cut and set as no workman of earth could do them."

"Ah," said Mr. Amos, "I fancy you have had advantages of hearing about these islands, that I have not enjoyed."

Eleanor was checked, and coloured a little; then rallied herself.

"Look now over yonder, Mr. Amos—at those clouds."

"I have looked at them every evening," he said.

Their eyes were turned towards the western heavens, where the setting sun was gathering his mantle of purple and gold around him before saying good night to the world. Every glory of light and colouring was there, among the thick folds of his vapourous drapery; and changing and blending and shifting softly from one hue of richness to another.

"I suppose you will tell me now," said Mr. Amos with a smile of some humour, "that no upholsterer's hangings can rival that. I give up—as the schoolboys say. Yet we do lose some things. What do you say to a land without churches?"

"O it is not," said Eleanor. "Chapels are rising everywhere—in every village, on some islands; and very neat ones."

"I am afraid," said Mr. Amos with his former look of quiet humour, "you would not be of the mind of a lady I heard rejoicing once over the celebration of the church service at Oxford. She remarked, that it was a subject of joyful thought and remembrance, to know that praise so near perfection was offered somewhere on the earth. There was the music, you know, and the beautiful building in which we heard it, and all the accessories. You will have nothing like that in Fiji."

"She must have forgotten those words," said Eleanor —"'Where is the house that ye build unto me, and where is the place of my rest? . . . *to this man* will I look, even to him that is poor and of a contrite spirit, and trembleth at my word.' You will find *that* in Fiji."

"Ah," said Mr. Amos,—"I see. My friend will have a safe wife in you. Do you know, when I first saw you I stood in doubt. I thought you looked like—Well, never mind! It's all right."

"Right!" said Captain Fox coming up behind them. "I am glad somebody thinks so. Right!—lying broiling here all day, and sleeping all night as if we were in port and had nothing to do—when we're a long way from that. Drove you down to-day, didn't it?" said he turning to Eleanor.

"It was so hot; I could not get a bit of permanent shade anywhere. I went below for a little while."

"And yet it's all right!" said the captain. "I am afraid you are not in a hurry to get to the end of the voyage."

Mr. Amos smiled and Eleanor blushed. The truth was, she never let herself think of the end of the voyage. The thought would come—the image standing there would start up—but she always put it aside and kept to the present; and that was one reason certainly why Eleanor's mind was so quiet and free and why the enjoyable and useful things of the hour were not let slip and wasted. So her spirits maintained their healthy tone; no doubt spurred to livelier action by the abiding consciousness of that spot of brightness in the future towards which she would not allow herself to look in bewildering imaginations.

Meanwhile the calm came to an end, as all things will; the beneficent trade wind took charge of the vessel again, and they sped on, south, south; till the sky over Eleanor's head was a new one from that all her life had known, and the bright stars at night looked at her as strangers. For study them as she would, she could not but feel theirs were new faces. The captain one day shewed her St. Helena in the distance; then the Cape of Good Hope was neared—and rounded—and in the Indian Ocean the travellers ploughed their way eastward. The island of St. Paul was passed; and still the ship sailed on and on to the east.

Eleanor had observed for a day or two that there was an unusual degree of activity among the sailors. They seemed to be getting things into new trim; clearing up and cleaning; and the chain cable one day made its appearance on deck, where room had been made for it. Eleanor looked on at the proceedings, with a half guess at their meaning that made her heart beat.

"What is it?" she asked Captain Fox.

"What's all this rigging up? Why we expect to see land soon. You like the sea so well, you'll be sorry."

"How soon?"

"I shouldn't wonder, in a day or two. You will stop in Sydney till you get a chance to go on?"

"Yes."

"I wish I could take you the whole way, I declare! but I would not take an angel into those awful islands.

Why if you get shipwrecked there, they will kill and eat you."

"There would be little danger of that now, Captain Fox; none at all in most of the islands. Instead of killing and eating, they relieve and comfort their shipwrecked countrymen."

"Believe that?" said the captain.

"I know it. I know instances."

"Whereabouts are you going among them?" said he looking at her. "If I get driven out of my reckoning ever and find myself in those latitudes, I'd like to know which way to steer. Where's your place?"

He was not uncivil; but he liked to see, when he could manage to bring it, that beautiful tinge of rose in Eleanor's cheeks which answered such an appeal as this.

CHAPTER XV.

> "And the magic charm of foreign lands,
> With shadows of palms, and shining sands,
> Where the tumbling surf
> O'er the coral reefs of Madagascar,
> Washes the feet of the swarthy 'Lascar.'—"

It was but the next day, and Eleanor was sitting as usual on deck looking over the waters in a lovely bright morning, when a sound was heard which almost stopped her heart's beating for a moment. It was the cry, rung out from the mast-head, "Land, ho!"

"Where is it?" she said to the captain, who was behind her. "I do not see it anywhere."

"You will see it in a little while. Wait a bit. If you could go aloft I could shew it you now."

"What land? do you know?"

"Australia—the finest land the sun shines upon!"

"I suppose you mean, besides England."

"No, I don't, begging your pardon. England is very well for those who can take the ripe side of the cherry; poorer folks had better come here, if they want any chance at all."

The lucky sailor was coming down from the mast-head, and the captain went off to join those who were giving him sundry rewarding tokens of their joy for his news. Eleanor looked over the waste of waters eastward, feeling as if her breath had been taken away.

So much of her journey done! The rest seemed, and was, but little. Australia was almost—*home*. And what sort of a home? And could Mr. Rhys possibly be at

Sydney to meet her? Eleanor knew he could not; yet the physical possibility would assert itself in spite of all the well-allowed moral impossibility. But at any rate at Sydney she would find letters; at Sydney she would find, perhaps very soon, the means of making the remainder of her voyage; at Sydney she could no longer prevent herself from *thinking*. Eleanor had staved off thought all the way by wisely saying and insisting to herself, "Time enough when I get to Sydney." Yes; she was nearing home now. So deep, so engrossing, were her meditations and sensations, that Mr. Amos who had come up to congratulate her on the approaching termination of the voyage, spoke to her once and again without being heard. He could not see her face, but the little straw bonnet was as motionless as if its wearer had been in a dream. He smiled and went away.

Then appeared on the distant horizon somewhat like a low blue cloud, which gathered distinctness and strength of outline by degrees. It was the land, beyond doubt; the coast of New Holland itself, as the captain informed Eleanor; and going on and passing through Bass's Strait the vessel soon directed her course northward. Little remained then before reaching port.

It was under a fair and beautiful sunlight morning that they were at last approaching Sydney. Mr. Amos was on deck as well as Eleanor, the captain standing with them; for a pilot had come on board; the captain had given up his charge, and was in command no longer. Before the watching three stretched a low unpromising shore of sandstone cliffs and sand.

"It is good to see it," said Mr. Amos; "but in this first view it don't shew for much."

"Don't shew for anything," said Captain Fox. "Wait till we get inside the Heads. It don't shew for anything; but it's the most glorious land the sun shines on!"

"In what particular respects?" said Mr. Amos.

"In every respect of making a living and enjoying it," said the captain. "That makes a good land, don't it?"

Mr. Amos allowed that it did.

"It's the most beautiful country, if you come to that," Captain Fox went on;—"that's what Miss Powle thinks of. I wish this was Melbourne we were coming to, instead of Sydney. I'd like to have her look at it."

"Better than this?" said Mr. Amos, for Eleanor was silent.

"A better colony, for beauty and riches," said the captain. "It's the most glorious country, sir, you ever saw! hundreds of square miles of it are as handsome as a duke's park; and good for something, which a duke's park ain't. There's a great tract of country up round Mt. Macedon—thirty or forty miles back into the land—its softly rolling ground without a stone on it, as nice as ever you saw; and spotted with the trees they call she-oaks—beautiful trees; and they don't grow in a wood, but just stand round in clumps and ones or twos here and there, like a picture; and then through the openings in the ground you can see miles off more of just the same, till it gets blue in the distance; and mountains beyond all. And when you put here and there a flock of thousands of sheep spotting the country with their white backs—I ain't poetical, sir, but I tell you! when I saw that country first, I thought maybe I was; but it's likely I was mistaken," said the captain laughing, "for the fit has never come back since. Miss Powle thinks there's as much poetry in the water as on the land."

Still Eleanor did not move to answer; and Mr. Amos, perhaps for her sake, went on.

"What is it that country is so good for? gold? or sheep?"

"Sheep, sir, sheep! the gold grows in another part. There's enough of that too; but I'd as lieve make my money some other way. Victoria is the country for wool-growing, sir. I've a brother there—Stephen Fox—he went with little more than nothing; and now he has a flock of sheep—well, I'm afraid to say how many; but I know he needs and uses a tract of twelve thousand acres of land for them."

"That is being a pretty large land-owner, as well as sheep-owner," Mr. Amos said with a smile.

"O he don't own it. That wouldn't do, you know. The interest of the money would buy all the wool on his sheep's backs."

"How then?"

"He has the use of it,—that's all. Don't you know how they work it? He pays a license fee to Government for the privilege of using the land for a year—wherever he pitches upon a place; then he stocks it, and goes on occupying by an annual license fee, until he has got too many neighbours and the land is getting all taken up in his neighbourhood. Then some one comes along who has money and don't want the plague of a new settlement; and he sells off his stock and claim to him, packs up his traps, pokes off through the bush with his compass till he has found a new location somewhere; then he comes back, pays a new license fee, and stocks the new place with flocks and shepherds and begins again. And I never saw in my life anything so fine as one of those Victoria sheep or cattle farms."

"Why don't you go into it?"

"Well—it's best to divide the business just now. I can be of use to Stephen and he can be of use to me. And I'm a little of this lady's opinion."

"How is it in this colony we are coming to?"

"Well, they are very prosperous; it's a good place to get rich. They have contrived to get along with their gold mines without ruining every other interest, as the other colonies have done for a time. But I think Victoria is the queen of them all; Victoria sends home more wool than either of the others; and she has gold, and she has other mines; different. She has copper equal to Burra-Burra—and she has coal, within a few miles of Melbourne, and other things; but the coal is a great matter here, you see."

The ship all the while was rapidly approaching the Heads, which mark, and make, the entrance to the harbour of Port Jackson. They assumed more dignity of elevation and feature as they were nearer seen; the rocks rising some two or three hundred feet high, with the sea foaming at their foot. Passing swiftly onward, the vessel by and by doubled Bradley's Head, and the magnificent sheet of water that forms the harbour was suddenly revealed to the strangers gaze. Full of islands, full of sailing craft, bordered with varying shores of "promontory, creek, and bay," pleasantly wooded, and spotted along its woody shores with spots of white that marked where people had pretty country homes, the quiet water glittering in the light; the view to the sea-tossed travellers was nothing short of enchanting. Mrs. Amos had come on deck, though scarce able to stand; a quiet, gentle, sweet-looking person; her eyes were full of tears now. Her husband's arm was round her, supporting her strength that she might keep up; his face was moved and grave. Eleanor was afraid to shew anybody her face; yet it was outwardly in good order enough; she felt as if her heart would never get back to its accustomed beat. She sat still, breathlessly drinking in the scene, rejoicing and trembling at once. She heard Mrs. Amos's softly whispered, 'Praise the Lord!—' and her husband's firm 'Amen!' It had like to have overset her. She pressed her hands tight together to keep her heart still.

"They know we are coming," said the captain.

"Who?" said Eleanor quickly.

Mr. Amos pressed his wife's arm; the captain's eyes twinkled.

"Is there anybody there on the look-out for you?" he asked.

"I suppose there may be," said Eleanor calmly.

"Well, he has got notice then, some hours ago," said the captain. "The pilot telegraphed to the South Head, and from the South Head the news has gone all over Sydney and Paramatta. Pretty good-looking city, is Sydney."

It was far more than that. It had been the point of the travellers' attention for some time. From the water up, one height above another, the white buildings of the town rose and spread; a white city; with forts and windmills, and fair looking country seats in its neighbourhood.

"Where is Paramatta?" said Eleanor, "and what is it?"

"It's a nice little pleasure place, up the Paramatta river; fifteen miles above Sydney. Fine scenery; it's as good as going to Richmond," added the captain.

"What is that splendid large white building?" Mrs. Amos asked, "on the hill?"

"No great things of a hill," said the captain. "That's the Government-house. Nice gardens and pleasure grounds there too."

"How beautiful it is!" said Mrs. Amos almost with a sigh.

"It is almost like a Scottish lake!" said her husband. "I remember one that this scene reminds me of at this moment."

"A little of this is worth all Scotland," said the captain. "There's pretty much everything here that a man wants—and not hard to come by, either. O you'll stay in Sydney! why should'nt you? There's people enough here that want teaching, worse than the savages. I declare, I think they do."

"Somebody else will have to teach them," said Mr. Amos. "What an array of ships and sails of all sorts! This gives one an idea of the business of the place."

"Business, and growing business," said the captain. "Sydney is getting ahead as fast as it can."

"How sweet the air is!" said Eleanor.

"Ay!" said the captain. "Now you smell green things again. I'll wager you won't want to put to sea any more, after you once get a firm foot on land. Why this is the very place for you. Enough to do, and every luxury a man need want, at hand when your work is done."

"When is one's work done?" said Eleanor.

"*I* should say, when one has worked enough and got what one is after," said the captain. "That's my idea. I never was for working till I couldn't enjoy."

"What are we after? do you think—" said Eleanor looking round at him.

"What everybody else is!" the captain answered somewhat shortly.

"Luxury, namely?"

"Yes! it comes to that. Everybody is seeking happiness in his own way; and when he has got it, then it is luxury."

Eleanor only looked at him; she did not say anything further, and turned again to the contemplation of the scene they had in view. The captain bustled off and was gone a few minutes.

"I wish you'd sing, sister Powle," said Mr. Amos in that interval.

"Do!" said his wife. "Please do!"

Whether Eleanor was precisely in a singing mood or no, she began as desired. Mr. Amos joined her, in somewhat subdued tones, and Mrs. Amos gave a still gentler seconding; while the rich notes of her own voice filled the air; so mellow that their full power was scarcely recognized; so powerful that the mellow sound seemed to fill the ship's rigging. The sailors moved softly. They were accustomed to that music. All the way out, on every Sunday service or any other that was held, Eleanor had served for choir to the whole company, joined by here and there a rough voice that broke in as it could, and just backed by Mr. Amos's steady support. There was more than one in that ship's company to whom memory would never cease to bring a reminder that 'there is balm in Gilead;' for some reason or other that was one of Eleanor's favourite songs. Now she gave another—sweet, clear, and wild;—the furthest-off sailors stood still to hearken. They had heard it often enough to know what the words were.

"O who's like Jesus!
From sins and fears he frees us.
He died for you,
He died for me,
He died to set poor sinners free.
O who's like Jesus!"

The chorus floated all over after each verse of the hymn was ended; it went clear to the ship's bows; but Eleanor sat quite still in her old position, clasping her hands fast on the rail and not moving her head. During the singing the captain came back and stood behind them listening; while people on the vessels that they passed, suspended their work and looked up to hear. Just as the singing was finished, a little boat was seen swiftly coming alongside; and in another minute they were boarded by the gentleman who had been its solitary passenger. The captain turned to meet him. He was a man rather under middle size, black hair curling all round his head, eyes quick and bright, and whole appearance handsome at once and business-like. He came forward briskly, and so he spoke.

"Have you got anybody here that belongs to me?" he said. "Captain, is there a Miss Powle on board of your ship?"

Captain Fox silently stepped on one side and made a motion of his hand towards Eleanor. Eleanor hearing herself called, slowly rose and faced the new-comer. There was a second's pause, as the two confronted each other; then the gentleman bowed very low and advanced to touch the lady's hand, which however when he touched he held.

"Is this Miss Powle? Miss *Eleanor* Powle?"

"Yes."

"I am honoured in having such a cousin! I hope you have heard somebody speak of a Mr. Esthwaite in these parts?"

"I have heard Mrs. Caxton speak of Mr. Esthwaite—very often."

"All right!" said the gentleman letting go Eleanor's hand. "Identity proved. Captain, I am going to take charge of this lady. Will you see that her luggage, personal effects and so on, are brought on deck?"—then turning to Eleanor with real deference and cordiality in his manner, he went on,—"Mrs. Esthwaite is longing to see you. It is such a pleasure to have a cousin come from England, as you can but feebly appreciate; she hopes to learn the new fashions from you, and all that sort of thing; and she has been dressing your room with flowers, I believe, for these three months past. If you please, we will not wait for the ship's slow motions, but I will carry you straight to land in my boat; and glad you will be! Will you signify your assent to this arrangement?—as I perceive the captain is a servant of yours and will do nothing without you bid him."

"Thank you," said Eleanor,—"I will go with you;—

but what will be done with all my boxes in the hold?" This enquiry was addressed to the captain.

"Don't you fear anything," said Mr. Esthwaite, "now you have overcome so many troubles and got to this haven of rest. We will take care of your boxes. I suppose you have brought enough to stock the whole Navigator's group—or Fiji, is it, you are going to? I would go to any other one rather—but never mind; the boxes shall be stored; and maybe you'll unpack them here after all. Captain, what about that luggage?—"

Eleanor went down to give directions, and presently came on deck again, all ready to go ashore. There was a little delay on account of the baggage; and meanwhile Mr. Esthwaite was introduced to Mr. and Mrs. Amos.

"I am very much obliged to you for taking care of this cousin of mine," he said to them. "I am sure she is worth taking care of. And now I should like to take care of you in turn. Will you go to my house, and make us happy?"

They explained that they were going elsewhere.

"Well, come and see her then; for she will be wanting to see somebody. We will do the best for her we can; but still—you know—absent friends have the best claim. By the way! didn't I hear some sweet Methodist singing as I came up? was it on this ship? You haven't got any Methodists on board, captain; have you?"

"I've been one myself, this voyage!" said the captain.

"I wouldn't," said Mr. Esthwaite. "The Church service is the only one to be used at sea. Every other sounds—I don't know how—incompatible. There is something in the gentle swell of the rolling waves, and in the grandeur of the horizon, that calls for the finest form of words mortals could put together; and when you have got such a form, why not use it?"

"You did not like the form of the singing then?" said Mr. Amos smiling.

"No," said Mr. Esthwaite drily,—"it struck me that if there had been a cathedral roof over it, one of those voices would have lifted the rafters and gone on; and that would not have been reverential, you know. Now, my young cousin!—"

"Mr. Amos," said Eleanor aside to him and colouring deeply, "if there are any letters for me at the house where you are going, or at the post-office, will you send them to me?"

"I will certainly make it my care, and bring them to you myself."

"I'll send for anything you want," said Mr. Esthwaite. "What's that? letters? We'll get all there is in Sydney, and there is a good deal, waiting for this young lady. I've had one floor of my warehouse half full for some months back already. No use of it for myself."

At last they got off; and it was not quickly, for Eleanor had to give a good bye to everybody on board. Mr. Esthwaite looked on smiling, until he was permitted to hand her down the vessel's side, and lodged her in the wherry.

"Now you are out of the ship," said he looking keenly at her. "Aren't you glad?"

"I have some good friends in her," said Eleanor.

"Friends! I should think so. Those were salt tears that were shed for your coming away. Positively, I don't think a man of them could see clear to take his last look at you."

Neither were Eleanor's feelings quite unmixed at this moment. She expected to see Mr. and Mrs. Amos again; with the rest her intercourse was finished; and it had been of that character which leaves longing and tender memories behind. She felt all that now. And she felt much more. With the end of her voyage in the "Diana" came, at least for the present, an end to her inward tranquillity. Now there were letters awaiting her; letters for which she had wished nervously so long; now she was near Fiji and her new life; now she dared to realize, she could not help it, what all the voyage she had refused to think of, as still in a hazy distance of the future. Here it was, nigh at hand, looming up through the haze, taking distinctness and proportions; and Eleanor's heart was in a state of agitation to which that sound little member was very little accustomed. However, the outward effect of all this was to give her manner even an unwonted degree of cool quietness; and Mr. Esthwaite was in a state between daunted and admiring. Both of them kept silence for a little while after leaving the ship, while the wherry pulled along in the beautiful bay, passing among a crowd of vessels of all sorts and descriptions, moving and still. The scene was lively, picturesque, pleasant, in the highest degree.

"How does my cousin like us on a first view?"

"It is a beautiful scene!" said Eleanor. "What a great variety of vessels are here!"

"And isn't this just the finest harbour in the world?"

"I have heard a great deal of Port Philip," said Eleanor smiling. "I understand there is a second Bay of Naples there."

"I don't care for the Bay of Naples! We have sunk all that. We are in a new world. Wait till you see what I will shew you to-morrow. Now look at that wooded point, with the white houses spotting it; those are fine seats; beautiful view and all that; and at Sydney you can have everything you want, almost at command."

"You know," said Eleanor, "that is not absolutely a new experience to me. In England, we have not far to seek."

"O *you* say so! Much you know about it. You have been in such a nest of a place as my cousin Caxton spreads her wings over. *I* never was in a nest, till I made one for myself. How is my good cousin?"

The talk ran upon home things now until they reached the town and landed at a fine stone quay. Then to the Custom House, where business was easily despatched; then Mr. Esthwaite put Eleanor into a cab and they drove away through the streets for his house in the higher part of the city. Eleanor's eyes were full of business. How strange it was! So far away from home, and so long living on the sea, now on landing to be greeted by such a multitude of familiar sounds and sights. The very cab she was driving in; the omnibuses and carts they passed; the English-cut faces; the same street cries; the same trades revealing themselves, as she had been accustomed to in London. But now and then there came a difference of Australasia. There would be a dray drawn by three or four pair of bullocks; London streets never saw that turn-out; and then Eleanor would start at seeing a little group of the natives of the country, dressed in English leavings of costume. Those made her feel where she was; otherwise the streets and houses and shops had very much of a home air. Except indeed when a curious old edifice built of logs peeped in among white stone fronts and handsome shop windows; the relics, Mr. Esthwaite told her, of that not so very far distant time when the town first began to grow up, and the "bush" covered almost all the ground now occupied by it. Eleanor was well pleased to be so busied in looking out that she had little leisure for talking; and Mr. Esthwaite sat by and smiled in satisfaction. But this blessed immunity could not last. The cab stopped before a house in George street.

"Has she come?" exclaimed a voice as the door opened; and a head full of curls put itself out into the hall;—"have you brought her? Oh delightful! How glad I am?—" and the owner of the curls came near to be introduced, hardly waiting for the introduction, and to give Eleanor the most gleeful sort of a welcome.

"And she was on that ship, the 'Diana,' Egbert? how nice! Just as you thought; and I was so afraid it was nothing but another disappointment. I was afraid to look out when the cab came. Now come up stairs, cousin Eleanor, and I will take you to your room. You must be tired to death, are you not?"

"Why should I?" said Eleanor as she tripped up stairs after her hostess. "I have done nothing for four months."

"Look here!" shouted Mr. Esthwaite from the hall—"Louisa, don't stop to talk over the fashions now—it is dinner-time. How soon will you be down?"—

"Don't mind him," said pretty Mrs. Esthwaite, leading the way into a light pleasant room overlooking the bay;—"sit down and rest yourself. Would you like anything before you dress? Now just think you are at home, will you? It's too delightful to have you here!"

Eleanor went to the window, which overlooked a magnificent view of the harbour. Very oddly, the thought in her mind at that moment was, how soon an opportunity could be found for her to make the rest of her voyage. Scarce landed, she wanted to see the means of getting away again. Her way she saw, over the harbour; where was her conveyance? While she stood looking, her new-found cousin was considering her; the erect beautiful figure, in all the simplicity of its dress; the close little bonnet with chocolate ribbands, the fine grave face under it, lastly the little hand which rested on the back of the chair, for Eleanor's sea-glove was off. And a certain awe grew up in Mrs. Esthwaite's mind.

"Cousin Eleanor," said she, "shall I leave you to dress? Dinner will be ready presently, and Egbert will be impatient, I know, till you come down stairs again."

"Thank you. I will be but a few minutes. How beautiful this is! O how beautiful,—to my eyes that have seen no beauty but sea beauty for so long. And the air is so good."

"I am glad you like it. Is it prettier than England?"

"Prettier than England!" Eleanor looked round smiling. "Nothing could be that."

"Well I didn't know. Mr. Esthwaite is always running down England, you see, and I don't know how much of it he means. I came away when I was so little, I don't remember anything of course—"

Here came such a shout of "Louisa!—Louisa!"—from below, that Mrs. Esthwaite laughing was obliged to obey it and go, and Eleanor was left. There was not much time then for anything; yet a minute Eleanor was held at the window by the bay with its wooded shores and islands glittering in the evening light; then she turned from it to pray, for her heart needed strength, and a great sense of loneliness had suddenly come over her. Fighting this feeling, and dressing, both eagerly, in a little time she was ready to descend and encounter Mr. Esthwaite and dinner.

An encounter it was to Mr. Esthwaite. He had put himself in very careful order; though that, to do him justice, was an habitual weakness of his; and he met his guest when she appeared with a bow of profound recognition and appreciation. Yet Eleanor was only in the simplest of all white dresses; without lace or embroidery. No matter. The rich hair was in perfect arrangement; the fine figure and fine carriage in their unconscious ease were more imposing than anything pretentious can ever be, even to such persons as Mr. Esthwaite. He measured his young guest correctly and at once. His wife took the measure of Eleanor's gown meanwhile, and privately studied what it was that made it so graceful; a problem she had not solved when they sat down to dinner.

The dinner was sumptuous, and well served. Mr. Esthwaite took delight evidently in playing his part of host, and some pride both housekeeping and patriotic in shewing to Eleanor all the means he had to play it with. The turtle soup he declared was good, though she might have seen better; the fish from Botany Bay, the wild fowl from the interior, the game of other kinds from the Hunter river, he declared she could not have known surpassed anywhere. Then the vegetables were excellent; the potatoes from Van Dieman's Land, were just better than all others in the world; and the dessert certainly in its abundance of treasures justified his boasting that Australia was a grand country for anybody that liked fruit. The growth of the tropics and of the cooler latitudes of England met together in confusion of beauty and sweetness on Mr. Esthwaite's table. There were oranges and pineapples on one hand, peaches, plums, melons, from the neighbouring country; with all sorts of English-grown fruits from Van Dieman's Land; gooseberries, pears and grapes. Native wines also he pressed on his guest, assuring her that some of them were as good as Sauterne, and others very fair claret and champagne. Eleanor took the wines on credit; for the rest, her eyes enabled her to give admiration where her taste fell short. And admiration was expected of her. Mr. Esthwaite was in a great state of satisfaction, having very much to do in the admiring way himself.

"Did Louisa keep you up stairs to begin upon the fashions?" said he, as he pulled a pineapple to pieces.

"I see you have very little appreciation of that subject," said Eleanor.

"Yes!" said Mrs. Esthwaite,—"just ask him whether he thinks it important that *his* clothes should be cut in the newest pattern, and how many good hats he has thrown away because he got hold of something new that he liked better. Just ask him! He never will hear me."

"I am going to ask her something," said Mr. Esthwaite. "See here;—you are not going to those savage and inhospitable islands, are you?"

Eleanor's smile and answer were as cool as if her whole nature had not been in a stir of excitement.

"What in the world do *you* expect to do there?" said her host with a strong tone of disapprobation. "'Wasting sweetness on the desert air' is nothing to it; this is positive desecration!"

Eleanor let the opinion pass, and eat the pineapple which he gave her with an apparently unimpaired relish.

"You don't know what sort of a place it is!" he insisted.

"I cannot know, I suppose, without going."

"Suppose you stay here," said Mr. Esthwaite; "and we'll send for anybody in the world you please! to make you comfortable. Seriously, we want good people in this colony; we have got a supply of all other sorts, but those are in a deficient minority."

"In that case, I think everybody that stays here is bound to supply one."

"See here—who is that gentleman that is so fortunate as to be expecting you? what is his name?"

"Mr. Esthwaite! for shame!" said his wife. "I think you are a very presuming cousin."

Mr. Esthwaite knew quite well that he was, but he smiled to himself with satisfaction to see the answer his question had called up into Eleanor's cheeks. The rich dye of crimson was pretty to behold; her words were delayed long enough to mark either difficulty of speaking or displeasure at the necessity for it. Mr. Esthwaite did not care which it was. At last Eleanor answered, with calm distinctness though without facing him.

"Do you not know the name?"

"I—I believe Mrs. Caxton must have mentioned it in one of her letters. She ought, and I think she did."

An impatient throb of displeasure passed through Eleanor's veins. It did not appear. She said composedly, "The name is Rhys—it is a Welsh name—spelled R, h, y, s."

"Hm! I remember. What sort of a man is he?"

Eleanor looked up, fairly startled with the audacity of her host; and only replied gravely, "I am unable to say."

Mr. Esthwaite at least had a sense of humour in him; for he smiled, and his lips kept pertinaciously unsteady for some time, even while he went on talking.

"I mean—is he a man calculated for savage, or for civilized life?"

"I hope so," said Eleanor wilfully.

"Mr. Esthwaite! you astonish me!" said his wife.

Mr. Esthwaite seemed however highly amused. "Do you know what savage life is?" he said to Eleanor. "It is not what you think. It is not a garden of roses, with a pineapple tucked away behind every bush. Now if you would come here—here is a grand opening. Here is every sort of work wanting you—and Mr. Rhys—whatever the line of his talents may be. We'll build him a church, and we'll go and hear him, and we'll make much of you. Seriously, if my good cousin had known what she was sending you to, she would have wished the 'Diana' should sink with you on board, rather than get to the end of her voyage. It is quite self-denial enough to come here—when one does not expect to gain anything by it."

"Mr. Esthwaite! Egbert!" cried his wife. "Now you are caught! Self-denial to come here! That is what you mean by all your talk about the Colonies and England!"

"Don't be—silly,—my dear," said her husband. "These people would think it so. *I* don't; but I am addressing myself to their prejudices. Self-denial is what they are after."

"It is not what I am after," said Eleanor laughing. "I must break up *your* prejudices."

"What are you after, then. Seriously, what *are* you going to those barbarous islands for—putting friendship and all such regards out of the question? What takes you there,—without humbug? You must excuse me—but you are a very extraordinary person to look at,—as a missionary."

Eleanor could hardly help laughing. She doubted whether or no this was a question to be answered; discerning a look of seriousness, as she thought, beneath the gleam in her host's eyes, she chose to run the risk of answering. She faced him, and them, as she spoke.

"I love Jesus. And I love to do his work, wherever he gives it to me; or, as I am a woman and cannot do much, I am glad to help those who can."

Mr. Esthwaite was put out a little. He had words on his lips that he did not speak; and piled Eleanor's plate with various fruit dainties, and drank one or two glasses of his Australian claret before he said anything more; an interval occupied by Eleanor in cooling down after her last speech, which had flushed her cheeks prodigiously.

"That's a sort of work to be done anywhere," he said finally, as if Eleanor had but just spoken. "I am sure it can be done here, and much better for you. Now see here—I like you. Don't you suppose, if you were to try, you could persuade this Mr. Rhys to quit those regions of darkness and come and take the same sort of work at Sydney that he is doing there?"

"No."

"Seems decided!—" said Mr. Esthwaite humourously,

looking towards his wife. "I am afraid this gentleman is a positive sort of character. Well!—there is no use in struggling against fate. My dear, take your cousin off and give her some coffee. I will be there directly."

The ladies left him accordingly; and in the pretty drawing-room Mrs. Esthwaite plied Eleanor with questions relating to her voyage, her destination, and above all, the England of which she had heard so much and knew so little. Her curiosity was huge, and extended to the smallest of imaginable details; and one thing followed another with very little of congruous nature between them. And Eleanor answered, and related, and described, and the while thought—where her letters were? Nevertheless she gave herself kindly to her hostess's gratification, and patiently put her own by; and the evening ended with Mrs. Esthwaite being in a state of ecstatic delight with her new-found relation. Mr. Esthwaite had kept silence and played the part of listener for the larger portion of the evening, using his eyes and probably his judgment freely during that time. As they were separating, he asked Eleanor whether she could get up at six o'clock?

Eleanor asked what for?

"Do, for once; and I will take you a drive in the Domain?"

"What Domain? yours, do you mean?"

"Not exactly. I have not got so far as that. No; it's the Government Domain—everybody rides and drives there, and almost everybody goes at six o'clock. It's worth going; botanical gardens, and all that sort of thing."

Eleanor swiftly thought, that it was scarce likely Mr. Amos would have her letters for her, or at least bring them, so early as that; and she might as well indulge her host's fancy if not her own. She agreed to the proposal, and Mrs. Esthwaite went rejoicing with her to her room.

"You'll like it," she said. "The botanical gardens are beautiful, and I dare say you will know a great deal more about them than I do. O it's delightful to have you here! I only cannot bear to think you must go away again."

"You are very kind to me," said Eleanor gratefully. "My dear aunt Caxton will be made glad to know what friends I have found among strangers."

"Don't speak about it!" said Mrs. Esthwaite, her eyes fairly glistening with earnestness. "I am sure if Egbert can do anything he will be too glad. Now won't you do just as if you were at home? I want you to be completely at home with us—now and always. You must feel very much the want of your old home in England! being so far from it, too."

"Heaven is my home," said Eleanor cheerfully; "I do not feel the loss of England so much as you think. That other home always seems near."

"Does it?" said Mrs. Esthwaite. "It seems such an immense way off, to me!"

"I used to think so; but it is near to me now. So it does not so much matter whereabouts on the earth I am."

"It must be nice to feel so!" said Mrs. Esthwaite with an unconscious sigh.

"Do you not feel so?" Eleanor asked.

"O no. I do not know anything about it. I am not good—like you."

"It is not goodness—not my goodness—that makes heaven my home," said Eleanor smiling at her and taking her hands.

"But I am sure you are good?" said Mrs. Esthwaite earnestly.

"Just as you are,—except for the grace of God, which is free to all."

"But," said Mrs. Esthwaite looking at her as if she were something hardly of earth like ordinary mortals,—"I have not given up the world as you have. I cannot. I like it too well."

"I have not given it up either," said Eleanor smiling again; "not in the sense you mean. I have not given up anything but sin. I enjoy everything else in the world as much as you do."

"What do you mean?" said Mrs. Esthwaite, much bewildered.

"Only this," said Eleanor, with very sweet gravity now. "I do not love anything that my King hates. All that I have given up, and all that leads to it; but I am all the more free to enjoy everything that is really worth enjoying, quite as well as you can, or any body else."

"But—you do not go to parties and dances, and you do not drink wine, and the theatre, and all that sort of thing; do you?"

"I do not love anything that my King hates," said Eleanor shaking her head gently.

"But dancing, and wine,—what harm is in them?"

"Think what they lead to!—"

"Well wine—excuse me, I know so little about these things! and I want to know what you think;—wine, I know, if people will drink too much,—but what harm is in dancing?"

"None that I know of," said Eleanor,—"if it were always suited to womanly delicacy, and if it took one into the society of those that love Christ—or helped one to witness for him before those who do not."

"Well, I will tell you the truth," said Mrs. Esthwaite with a sort of penitent laugh,—"I love dancing."

"Ay, but I love Christ," said Eleanor; "and whatever is not for his honour I am glad to give up. It is no cross to me. I used to like some things too; but now I love Him; and his will is my will."

"Ah, that is what I said! you are good, that is the reason. I can't help doing wrong things, even if I want to do it ever so much, and when I know they are wrong; and I shouldn't like to *give up* anything."

"Listen," said Eleanor, holding her hands fast. "It is not that I am good. It is that I love Jesus and he helps me. I cannot do anything of myself—I cannot give up anything—but I trust in my Lord and he does it for me. It is he that does all in me that you would call good."

"Ah, but you love him."

"Should I not?" said Eleanor, "when he loved me, and gave himself for me, that he might bring me from myself and sin to know him and be happy."

"And you are happy, are you not?" said Mrs. Esthwaite, looking at her as if it were something that she had come to believe against evidence. There was good evidence for it now, in Eleanor's smile; which would bear studying.

"There is nothing but happiness where Christ is."

"But I couldn't understand it—those places where you are going are so dreadful;—and why you should go there at all—"

"No, you do not understand, and cannot till you try it. I have such joy in the love of Christ sometimes, that I wish for nothing so much in the world, as to bring others to know what I know!"

There was power in the lighting face, which Mrs. Esthwaite gazed at and wondered.

"I think I am willing to go anywhere and do anything, which my King may give me, in that service."

"To be sure," said Mrs. Esthwaite, as if adding a convincing corollary from her own mind,—"you have some other reason to wish to get there—to the Islands, I mean."

That brought a flood of crimson over Eleanor's face; she let go her hostess's hands and turned away.

"But there was something else I wanted to ask," said Mrs. Esthwaite hastily. "Egbert said—Are you very tired, my dear?"

"Not at all, I assure you."

"Egbert said there was some most beautiful singing as he came up alongside the ship to-day—was it you?"

"In part it was I."

"He said it was hymns. Won't you sing me one?"

Eleanor liked it very well; it suited her better than talking. They sat down together, and Eleanor sang:

> "'There's balm in Gilead,
> To make the wounded whole.
> There's power enough in Jesus
> To save a sin-sick soul.'"

And somewhat to her surprise, before the hymn had gone far, her companion was weeping; and kept her face hidden in her handkerchief till the last words were sung.

> "'Come then to this physician;
> His help he'll freely give.
> He asks no hard condition,—
> 'Tis only, look, and live.
> For there's balm in Gilead,
> To make the wounded whole.
> There's power enough in Jesus
> To save a sin-sick soul.'"

"I never heard anything so sweet in all my life!" said Mrs. Esthwaite as she got up and wiped her eyes. "I've been keeping you up. But do tell me," said she looking at her innocently,—"are all Methodists like you?"

"No," said Eleanor laughing; and then she was vexed at herself that the laugh changed to a sob and the tears came. Was *she* hysterical? It was very unlike her, but this seemed something like it. Neither could she immediately conquer the strangling sensation, between laughter and crying, which threatened her.

"My dear! I'm very sorry," said Mrs. Esthwaite. "You are too tired!—and it is my fault. Egbert will be properly angry with me."

But Eleanor conquered the momentary oppression, threw off her tears, and gave her hostess a peaceful kiss for good night; with which the little lady went off comforted. Then Eleanor sat down by her window, and with tears wet on her eyelashes yet, looked off to the beautiful moonlit harbour in the distance—and thought. Her thoughts were her own. Only some of them had a reference to certain words that speak of "sowing beside all waters," and a tender earnest remembrance of the seed she had just been scattering. "Beside all waters" —yes; and as Eleanor looked over towards the fair, peace-speaking view of Port Jackson, in New South Wales, she recollected the prayer that labourers might be sent forth into the vineyard.

CHAPTER XVI.

> "Know well, my soul, God's hand controls
> Whate'er thou fearest;
> Round Him in calmest music rolls
> Whate'er thou hearest."

"THAT girl is the most lovely creature!" said Mrs. Esthwaite when she rejoined her husband.

"What have you been talking to her about? Now she will not be up in time to take a drive in the Domain."

"Yes, she will. She has got plenty of spirit. But oh, Egbert! to think of that girl going to put herself in those savage islands, where she won't see anybody!"

"It is absurd?" said her husband, but somewhat faintly.

"I couldn't but think to-night as I looked at her—you should have seen her—Something upset her and set her to crying; then she wouldn't cry; and the little white hand she brushed across her eyes and then rested on the chair-back to keep herself steady—I looked at it, and I couldn't bear to think of her going to teach those barbarians. And her eyes were all such a glitter with tears and her feelings—I've fallen in love with her, Egbert."

"She's a magnificent creature," said Mr. Esthwaite. "Wouldn't she set Sydney a fire, if she was to be here a little while! But somebody has been beforehand with Sydney—so it's no use talking."

Eleanor was ready in good time for the drive, and

with spirits entirely refreshed by the night's sleep and the morning's renewing power. Things looked like new things, unlike those which yesterday saw. All feeling of strangeness and loneliness was gone; her spirits were primed for enjoyment. Mr. and Mrs. Esthwaite both watched eagerly to see the effect of the drive and the scene upon her; one was satisfied, the other was not. The intent delight in Eleanor's eyes escaped Mrs. Esthwaite; she looked for more expression in words; her husband was content that Eleanor's mind was full of what he gave it to act upon. The Domain was an exquisite place for a morning drive; and the more stylish inhabitants of Sydney found it so; there was a good display of equipages, varying in show and pretension. To Mrs. Esthwaite's disappointment neither these nor their owners drew Eleanor's attention; she did not even seem to see them; while the flowers in the woods through which part of the drive was cut, the innumerable, gorgeous, novel and sweet flowers of a new land, were a very great delight to her. All of them were new, or nearly so; how Eleanor contrasted them with the wild things of Plassy which she knew so well. And instead of the blackbird and green wren, there were birds of brilliant hues, almost as gay as the flowers over which their bright wings went, and yet stranger than they. It was a sort of drive of enchantment to Eleanor; the air was delightful, though warm; with no feeling of lassitude or oppression resulting from the heat.

There were other pleasures. From point to point, as they drove through the "bush," views opened upon them of the harbour and its islands, glittering in the morning sun. Changes of beauty; for every view was a little unlike the others and revealed the loveliness with a difference. Eleanor felt herself in a new world. She was quite ready for the gardens, when they got through the "bush."

The gardens were fine. Here she had a feast which neither of her companions could enjoy with her in anything like fellowship. Eleanor had not lived so long with Mrs. Caxton, entering into all her pursuits, without becoming somewhat well acquainted with plants; and now she was almost equally charmed at seeing her dear old home friends, and at making acquaintance with the glorious beauties that outshone them but could never look so kindly. Slowly Eleanor went through the gardens, followed by her host and hostess who took their enjoyment in observing her. In the Botanical Gardens Mr. Esthwaite came up alongside again, to tell her names and discuss specimens; he found Eleanor knew more about them than he did.

"All this was a wild 'bush'—nothing but rocks and trees, a few years ago," he remarked.

"*This?* this garden?"

"Yes, only so long ago as 1825."

"Somebody has deserved well of the community, then," said Eleanor. "It is a delicious place."

"General Sir Ralph Darling had that good desert. It is a fine thing to be in high place and able to execute great plans; isn't it?"

Eleanor rose up from a flower and gave Mr. Esthwaite one of her thoughtful glances.

"I don't know," she said. "His gardeners did the work, after all."

"They don't get the thanks."

"*That* is not what one works for," said Eleanor smiling. "So the thing is done—what matter?"

"If it *isn't* done, what matter? No, no! I want to get the good of what I do,—in praise or in something else."

"What is Sir Ralph Darling the better of my thanks now?"

"Well, he's dead!" said Mr. Esthwaite.

"So I was thinking."

"Well what do you mean? Do you mean that you would do nothing while you are alive, for fear you would not hear of it after you have left the world?"

"Not exactly."

"What then? I don't know what you are after."

"You say this was all a wilderness a few years ago—why should you despair of what you call the 'black islands?'"

"O ho!" said Mr. Esthwaite,—"we are there, are we? By a hop, skip, and jump—leaving the argument. That's like a woman?"

"Are you sure?" said Eleanor.

"Like all the women I ever saw. Not one of them can stick to the point."

"Then I will return to mine," said Eleanor laughing;—"or rather bring you up to it. I referred—and meant to refer you—to another sort of gardening, in which the labourer receives wages and gathers fruit; but the beauty of it is, that his wages go with him—he does not leave them behind—and the fruit is unto life eternal."

"That's fair," said Mr. Esthwaite. "See here—you don't preach, do you?"

"I will not, to you," said Eleanor. "Mr. Esthwaite, I will look at no more flowers I believe, this morning, since you leave the time of our stay to me."

Mr. Esthwaite behaved himself, and though a speech was on his tongue he was silent, and attended Eleanor home in an unexceptionable manner. Mrs. Esthwaite was in a dissatisfied mood of mind.

"I hope it will be a great while before you find a good chance to go to Fiji!" she said.

"Do not wish that," said Eleanor; "for in that case I may have to take a chance that is not good."

"Ah but, you are not the sort of person to go there."

"I should be very sorry to think that," said Eleanor smiling.

"Well it is clear you are not. Just to look at you! I am sure you are exactly a person to look always as nice as you do now."

"I hope never to look less nice than I do now," said Eleanor, rather opening her eyes.

"What, in that place?"

"Why yes, certainly. Why not?"

"But you will not wear that flat there?"

Eleanor and Mr. Esthwaite here both gave way in a fit of laughter.

"Why yes I will; if I find it, as I suppose I shall, the most comfortable thing."

"But you cannot wear white dresses there?"

"If I cannot, I will submit to it; but my dear cousin, I have brought little else *but* white dresses with me. For such a climate, what else is so good?"

"Not like that you wore yesterday?"

"They are all very much alike, I believe. What was the matter with that?"

"Why, it was so—" Mrs. Esthwaite paused. "But how can you get them washed? do you expect to have servants there?"

"There are plenty of servants, I believe; not very well trained, indeed, or it would not be necessary to have so many. At any rate, they can wash, whatever else they can do."

"I don't believe they would know how, to wash your dresses."

"Then I can teach them," said Eleanor merrily.

"*You!* To wash a cambrick dress!"

"That, or any other."

"Eleanor, do not talk so!"

"Certainly not, if you do not wish it. I was only putting you to rest on the score of my laundry work."

"With those hands!" said Mrs. Esthwaite expressively.

Eleanor looked down at her hands, for a moment a higher and graver expression flitted over her face, then she smiled again.

"I should be ashamed of my hands if they were good for nothing."

"Capital!" said Mr. Esthwaite. "That's what I like. That is what I call having spirit. I like to see a woman have some character of her own; something besides hands, in fact."

"But Eleanor, I do not understand. I am serious. You never washed; how can you know how?"

"That was precisely my reasoning; so I learned."

"Learned to *wash?* *You?*"

"Yes."

"You did it with your own hands?"

"The dress you were so good as to approve," said Eleanor smiling, "it was washed and done up by myself."

"Do you expect to have to do it for yourself?" said Mrs. Esthwaite looking intensely horrified.

"No, not generally; but to teach somebody, or upon occasion, you know. You see," she said smiling again her full rich smile, "I am bent upon having my white dresses."

Mrs. Esthwaite was too full for speech, and her husband looked at his new cousin with an eye of more absolute admiration than he had yet bestowed on her. Eleanor's thoughts were already on something else; springing forward to meet Mr. Amos and his letters.

Breakfast was over however before he arrived. Much to her chagrin, she was obliged to receive him in the company of Mr. and Mrs. Esthwaite; no private talk was possible. Mr. Esthwaite engaged him immediately in an earnest but desultory conversation, about Sydney,

Eleanor, and the mission, and the prospect of their getting to their destination; which Mr. Esthwaite prophesied would not be within any moderate limits of time. Mr. Amos owned that he had heard of no opportunity, near or far. The talk lasted a good while and it was not till he was taking leave that Eleanor contrived to follow him out and gain a word to herself.

"There are no letters for you," said Mr. Amos, speak ing under his breath, and turning a cheerful but con cerned face towards Eleanor. "I have made every enquiry—at the post-office, and of everybody likely to know about such things. There are none, and they know of none."

Eleanor said nothing; her face grew perceptibly white.

"There is nothing the matter with brother Rhys," said Mr. Amos hastily; "we have plenty of news from him—all right—he is quite well, and for a year past has been on another station; different from the one he was on when you last heard from him. There is nothing the matter—only there are no letters for you; and there must be some explanation of that."

He paused, but Eleanor was silent, only her colour returned a little.

"We want to get away from here as soon as possible, I suppose," Mr. Amos went on half under breath; "but as yet I see no opening. It will come."

"Yes," said Eleanor somewhat mechanically. "You will let me know—"

"Certainly—as soon as I know anything myself; and I will continue to make enquiry for those letters. Mr. Armitage is away in the country—he might know something about them, but nobody else does; and he ought to have left them with somebody else if he had them. But there can be nothing wrong about it; there is only some mistake, or mischance; the letters from Vuliva where brother Rhys is, are quite recent and everything is going on most prosperously; himself included. And we are to proceed to the same station. I am very glad for ourselves and for you."

"Thank you—" Eleanor said; but she was not equal to saying much. She listened quietly, and with her usual air, and Mr. Amos never discovered the work his tidings wrought; he told his wife, sister Powle looked a little blank, he thought, at missing her expected despatches, and no wonder. It was an awkward thing.

Eleanor slowly made her way up to her room and sat down, feeling as if the foundations of the earth, to *her* standing, had given way. She was more overwhelmed with dismay than she would have herself anticipated in England, if she could have looked forward to such a catastrophe. Reason said there was not sufficient cause; but poor Eleanor was to feel the truth of Mrs. Caxton's prediction, that she would find out again that certain feelings might be natural that were not reasonable. Nay, reason said on this occasion that the failure of letters proved too much to justify the distress she felt; it proved a combination of things, that no carelessness nor indifference nor unwillingness to write, on the part of Mr. Rhys, could possibly have produced. Let him feel how he would, he would have written, he *must* have written to meet her there; all his own delicacy and his knowledge of hers affirmed and reaffirmed that letters were in existence somewhere, though it might be at the bottom of the ocean. Reason fought well; to what use, when nature trembled, and shivered, and shrank. Poor Eleanor! she felt alone now, without a mother and without shelter; and the fair shores of Port Jackson looked very strange and desolate to her; a very foreign land, far from home. What if Mr. Rhys, with his fastidious notions of delicacy, did not fancy so bold a proceeding as her coming out to him? what if he disapproved?

What if, on further knowledge of the place and the work, he had judged both unfit for her; and did not, for his own sake only in a selfish point of view, choose to encourage her coming? in that case her being *come* would make no difference; he would not shelter himself from a judgment displeasing to him, because the escape from its decisions was rendered easy. What if for *his own sake* his feeling had changed, and he wanted her no longer? years had gone by since he had seen her; it must have been a wayward fancy that could ever have made him think of her at first; and now, about his grave work in a distant land, and with leisure to correct blunders of fancy, perhaps he had settled into the opinion that it was just as well that his coming away had separated them; and did not feel able to welcome her appearance in Australia, and was too sincere to write what he did not feel; so wrote nothing? Not very like Mr. Rhys, reason whispered; but reason's whisper, though heard, could not quiet the sensitive delicacy which trembled at doubt. So miserable, so chilled, so forlorn, Eleanor had never felt in her life; not when the 'Diana' first carried her away from the shores of her native land.

What was she to do? that question throbbed at her heart; but it answered itself soon. Stay in Australia she could not; go home to England she could not; no, not upon this mere deficiency of testimony. There was only one alternative left; she must go on whenever Mr. and Mrs. Amos should move. Nature might tremble and quiver, and all Eleanor's nerves did; but there was no other course to pursue. "I can tell," she thought,—"I shall know—the first word, the first look, will tell me the whole; I cannot be deceived. I must go on and meet that word and look, whatever it costs me—I must; and then, if it is—if it is not satisfying to me, then aunt Caxton shall have me! I can go back, as well as I have come. Shame and misery would not hinder me—they would not be so bad as my staying here then."

So the question of action was settled; but the question of feeling not so soon. Eleanor's enjoyment was gone, of all the things she had enjoyed those first twenty-four hours, and of all others which her entertainers brought forward for her pleasure. Yet Eleanor kept her own counsel, and as they did not know the cause she had for trouble, so neither did they discover any tokens of it. She did not withdraw herself from their kind efforts to please her, and they spared no pains. They took her in boat excursions round the beautiful harbour. They shewed her the pretty environs of the Parramatta river. Nay, though it was not very easy for him to leave his business, Mr. Esthwaite went with her and his wife to the beautiful Illawarra district; put the whole party on horses, and shewed Eleanor a land of tropical beauty under the clear, bracing, delicious warm weather of Australia. Fern trees springing up to the dimensions of trees indeed, with the very fern foliage she was accustomed to in low herbaceous growth at home; only magnified superbly. There were elegant palms, too, with other evergreens, and magnificent creepers; and floating out and in among them in great numbers were gay red-crested cockatoos and other tropical birds. The character of the scenery was exquisite. Eleanor saw one or two of the fair lake-like lagoons of that district, eat of the fish from them; for they made a kind of gypsey expedition, camping out and providing for themselves fascinatingly; and finally returned in the steamer from Wollongong to Sydney. Her friends would have taken her to see the gold diggings if it had been possible. But Eleanor saw it all, all they could shew her, with half a heart. She had learned long ago to conceal what she felt.

"I think she wants to get away," said Mrs. Esthwaite one night, half vexed, wholly sorry.

"That's what it is to be in love!" said her husband. "You won't keep her in Sydney. Do you notice she has given up smiling?"

"No!" said his wife indignantly; "I notice no such thing. She is as ready to smile as anybody I ever saw." —And I wish I had as good reason! was the mental conclusion; for Eleanor and she had had many an evening talk by that time and many a hymn had been listened to.

"All very well," said Mr. Esthwaite; "but she don't smile as she did at first. Don't you remember?—that full smile she used to give once in a while, with a little world of mischief in the corners? I would like to see it the next time!—"

"I declare," said Mrs. Esthwaite, "I think you take quite an impertinent interest in people's concerns. She wouldn't let you see it, besides."

At which Mr. Esthwaite laughed.

So near people came to it; and Eleanor covered up her troublesome thoughts within her own heart, and gave Mr. Esthwaite the benefit of that impenetrable coolness and sweetness of manner which a good while ago had used to bewitch London circles. In the effort to hide her real thoughts and feelings she did not quite accommodate it to the different latitude of New South Wales; and Mr. Esthwaite was a good deal struck and somewhat bewildered.

"You have mistaken your calling," he said one evening, standing before Eleanor and considering her.

"Do you think so?"

"There! Yes, I do. I think you were born to govern."

"I *am* sadly out of my line then," said Eleanor laughing.

"Yes. You are. That is what I say. You ought to be this minute a duchess—or a governor's lady—or something else in the imperial line."

"You mistake my tastes, if you think so."

"I do not mistake something else," muttered Mr. Esthwaite; and then Mr. Amos entered the room.

"Here, Amos," said he, "you have made an error in judging of this lady—she is no more fit to go a missionary than I am. She—she goes about with the air of a princess!"

Mrs. Esthwaite exclaimed, and Mr. Amos took a look t the supposed princess's face, as if to reassure or inform his judgment. Apparently he saw nothing to alarm him.

"I am come to prove the question," he said composedly; then turning to Eleanor,—"I have heard at last of a schooner that is going to Fiji, or will go, if we desire it."

This simple announcement shot through Eleanor's head and heart with the force of a hundred pounder. An extreme and painful flush of colour answered it; nobody guessed at the pain.

"What's that?" exclaimed Mr. Esthwaite getting up again and standing before Mr. Amos,—"you have found a vessel, you say?"

"Yes. A small schooner, to sail in a day or two."

"What schooner? whom does she belong to? Lawsons, or Hildreth?"

"To nobody, I think, but her master. I believe he sails the vessel for his own ends and profits."

"What schooner is it? what name?"

"The 'Queen Esther,' I think."

"You cannot go in that!" said Mr. Esthwaite turning off. "The 'Queen Esther'!—I know her. She's not fit for you; she's a leaky old thing, that that man Hawkins sails on all sorts of petty business; she'll go to pieces some day. She ain't sea-worthy, I don't believe."

"It is not as good a chance as might be, but it is the first that has offered, and the first that is likely to offer for an unknown time," Mr. Amos said, looking again to Eleanor.

"When does she sail?"

"In two days. She is small, and not in first-rate order; but the voyage is not for very long. I think we had better go in her."

"Certainly. How long is the voyage, regularly?"

"A fortnight in a good ship, and a month in a bad one," struck in Mr. Esthwaite. "You'll never get there, if you depend on the 'Queen Esther' to bring you."

"We go to Tonga first," said Mr. Amos. "The 'Queen Esther' sails with stores for the stations at Tonga and the neighbourhood; and will carry us further only by special agreement; but the master is willing, and I came to know your mind about it."

"I will go," said Eleanor. "Tell Mrs. Amos I will meet her on board—when?"

"Day after to-morrow morning."

"Very well. I will be there. Will she take the additional lading of my boxes?"

"O yes; no difficulty about that. It's all right."

"How can I do with the things you have stored for me?" Eleanor said to Mr. Esthwaite. "Can the schooner take them too?"

"What things?"

"Excuse me—perhaps I misunderstood you. I thought you said you had half your warehouse, one loft of it, taken up with things for me?"

"Those things are gone, long ago," said Mr. Esthwaite in a dogged kind of mood which did not approve of the proposed journey or conveyance.

"Gone?"

"Yes. According to order. Mrs. Caxton wrote, Forward as soon as possible; so I did."

Again Eleanor's brow and cheeks and her very throat were covered with a rush of crimson; but when

Mr. Amos took her hand on going away its touch made him ask involuntarily if she were well?

"Perfectly well," Eleanor answered, with something in her manner that reminded Mr. Amos, though he could not tell why, of the charge Mr. Esthwaite had brought. Another look into Eleanor's eyes quieted the thought.

"Your hand is very cold!" he said.

"It's a sign of"—Mr. Esthwaite would have said 'fever," but Eleanor had composedly faced him and he was silent; only busied himself in shewing Mr. Amos out, without a word that he ought not to have spoken. Mr. Amos went home and told his wife.

"I think she is all right," he said; "but she does not look to me just as she did before we landed. I dare say she has had a great deal of admiration here—"

"I dare say she feels bad," said good Mrs. Amos.

"Why?"

"If you were not a man, you would know," Mrs. Amos said laughing. "She is in a very trying situation."

"Is she? O, those letters! It is unfortunate, to be sure. But there must be some explanation."

"The explanation will be good when she gets it," Mrs. Amos remarked. "I hope somebody who is expecting her is worthy of her. Poor thing! *I* couldn't have done it, I believe, even for you."

CHAPTER XVII.

> "But soon I heard the dash of oars,
> I heard the pilot's cheer;
> My head was turned perforce away,
> And I saw a boat appear."

THE morning came for the "Queen Esther" to sail. Mr. and Mrs. Amos were on board first, and watched with eyes both kind and anxious to see Eleanor when she should come. The little bonnet with chocolate ribbands did not keep them waiting; and the first smile and kiss to Mrs. Amos made *her* sure that all was right. She had been able to see scarce anything of Eleanor during the weeks on shore; it was a refreshment to have her near again. But Eleanor had turned immediately to attend to Mr. Esthwaite.

"This is the meanest, most abominable thing of a vessel," he said, "that ever Christians travelled in! It is an absurd proceeding altogether. Why if the boards don't part company and go to pieces before you get to Tonga—which I think they will—they don't give room for all three of you to sit down in the cabin at once."

"The deck is of better capacity," Eleanor told him briskly.

"Such a deck! I wonder *you*, cousin Eleanor, can make up your mind to endure it. There is not a man living who is worth such a sacrifice. Horrid!"

"We hope it won't last a great while," Mr. Amos told him.

"It won't! That's what I say. You will all be deposited in the bottom of the ocean, to pay you for not having been contented on shore. I would not send a dog to sea in such a ship!"

"Cousin Esthwaite, you had better not stay in a situation so disagreeable to you. You harass yourself for nothing. Shake hands. You see the skipper is going to make sail directly."

Eleanor with a little play in the manner of this dismissal, was enough in earnest to secure her point. Mr. Esthwaite felt in a manner constrained to take his departure. He presumed however in the circumstances to make interest for a cousinly kiss for good bye; which was refused him with a cooler demonstration of dignity than he had yet met with. It nettled him.

"There was the princess," whispered Mr. Amos to his wife.

"Good!" said Mrs. Amos.

"Good bye!" cried Mr. Esthwaite, disappearing over the schooner's side. "*You* are not fit for a missionary! I told you so before."

Eleanor turned to Mrs. Amos, ignoring entirely this little transaction, and smiled at her. "I hope he has not made you nervous," she said.

"No," said Mrs. Amos; "I am not nervous. If I did not get sick I should enjoy it; but I suppose I shall be sick as soon as we get out of the harbour."

"Let us take the good of it then, until we are out of the harbour," said Eleanor. "If the real 'Queen Esther' was at all like her namesake, Ahasuerus must have had a disorderly household."

They sat down together on the little vessel's deck, and watched the beautiful shores from which they were gliding away. Eleanor was glad to be off. The stay at Sydney had become oppressive to her; she wanted to be at the end of her journey and know her fate; and hope and reason whispered that she had reason to be glad.

For all that, the poor child had a great many shrinkings of heart. A vision of Mr. Rhys never came up in one of its aspects,—that of stern and fastidious delicacy,—without her heart seeming to die away within her. She could not talk now. She watched the sunny islands and promontories of the bay, changing and passing as the vessel slowly moved on; watched the white houses of Sydney, grateful for the home she had found there, longing exceedingly for a home once again that should be hers by right; hope and tremulousness holding her heart together. This was a conflict that prayer and faith did not quell; she could only come to a state of humble submissiveness; and she never thought of reaching Vuliva without a painful thrill that almost took away her breath. But she was glad to be on the way.

The vessel was very small, not of so much as eighty tons burthen; its accommodations were of course a good deal as Mr. Esthwaite had said; and more than that, the condition of the vessel and of its appointments was such that Mrs. Amos felt as if she could hardly endure to shut herself up in the cabin. Eleanor resolved immediately that *she* would not; the deck was a better place; and she prevailed to have a mattress brought there for Mrs. Amos, where the good lady, though miserably ill as soon as they were upon the ocean roll, yet could be spared the close air and other horrors of the place below deck. Eleanor wrapped herself in her sea cloak, and lived as she could on deck with her; having a fine opportunity to read the stars at night, and using it. The weather was very fine; the wind favouring and steady; and in the Southern Ocean, under such conditions, there were some good things to be had, even on board the "Queen Esther." There were glorious hymn-singings in the early night-time; and Eleanor had never sung with more power on the "Diana." There were beautiful Bible discussions between her and Mr. Amos—Bible contemplations, rather; in which they brought Scripture to Scripture to illustrate their point; until Mr. Amos declared he thought it would be a grand way of holding a Bible-class; and poor Mrs. Amos listened, delighted, though too sick to put in more than a word now and then. And Eleanor's heart gave a throb every time she recollected that another day had gone,—so many more miles were travelled over,—they were so much nearer the journey's end. Her companions found no fault in her. There was nothing of the princess now, but a gentle, thoughtful, excellent nurse, and capital cook. On board the "Diana" there had been little need of her services for Mrs. Amos; little indeed that could be done. Now, in the fresh air on the open deck of the little schooner, Mrs. Amos suffered less in one way; but all the party were sharers in the discomforts of close accommodations and utter want of nicety in anything done or furnished on board. The condition of everything was such that it was scarcely possible to eat at all for well people. Poor Mrs. Amos would have had no chance except for Eleanor's helpfulness and clever management. As on board the "Diana," there was nobody in the schooner that would refuse her anything; and Mr. Amos smiled to himself to see where she would go and what she would do to secure some little comfort for her sick friend, and how placidly she herself munched sea biscuit and bad bread, after their little stock of fruit from Sydney had given out. She would bring a cup of tea and a bit of toast to Mrs. Amos, and herself take a crust with the equanimity of a philosopher. Eleanor did not care much what she eat, those days. Her own good times were when everybody else was asleep except the man at the wheel; and she would kneel by the guards and watch the strange constellations, and pray, and sometimes weep a flood of tears. Julia, her mother and Alfred, Mrs. Caxton, her own intense loneliness and shrinking delicacy in the uncertainty of her position; they were all well watered in tears at some of those watching hours when nobody saw.

The 'Queen Esther" made the Friendly Islands in something less than a month, notwithstanding Mr. Esthwaite's unfavourable predictions. At Tonga she was detained a week and more; unlading and taking in stores. The party improved the time in a survey of the island and mission premises and in pleasant intercourse with their friends stationed there. Or what would have been pleasant intercourse; it was impossible for Eleanor to enjoy it. So near her destination now, she was impatient to be off; and drew short breaths until the days of delay were ended, and the little schooner once more made sail and turned her head towards Vuliva. She had seen Tonga with but half an eye.

Two or three days would finish their journey now. The weather and wind continued fair; they dipped Tonga in the salt wave, and stood on and on towards the unseen haven of their hopes and duties. A new change came over Eleanor. It could not be reason, for reason had striven in vain. Perhaps it was nature, which turning a corner took a new view of the subject. But from the time of their leaving Tonga, she was unable to entertain such troublesome apprehensions of what the end of the voyage might have in store for her. Something whispered it could be nothing very bad; and that point that she had so dreaded began to gather a glow of widely different promise. A little nervousness and trepidation remained about the thought of it; the determination abode fast to see the very first word and look and know what they portended; but in place of the rest of Eleanor's downhearted fear, there came now an overwhelming sense of shamefacedness. This was something quite new and unexpected; she had never known in her life more than a slight touch of it before; and now it consumed her. Even before Mr. and Mrs. Amos she felt it; and her eyes shunned theirs the last day or two as if she had been a shy child. Why was it? She could not help it. This seemed to be as natural and as unreasonable as the other; and in her lonely night watches, instead of trembling and sinking of heart, Eleanor was conscious that her cheeks dyed themselves with that unconquerable feeling of shame. Very inconsistent indeed with her former state of feeling; and that was according to Mrs. Caxton's words; not being reasonable, reason could not be expected from them in anything. Her friends had not penetrated her former mood; this they saw and smiled at; and indeed it made Eleanor very lovely. There was a shy, blushing grace about her the last day or two of the voyage which touched all she did; indeed Mrs. Amos declared she could see it through the little close straw bonnet, and it made her want to take Eleanor in her arms and keep her there. Mr. Amos responded in his way of subdued fun, that it was lucky she could not; as it would be likely to be a disputed possession, and he did not want to get into a quarrel with his brethren the first minute of his getting to land.

Up came Eleanor with some trifle for Mrs. Amos which she had been preparing.

"We are almost in, sister Eleanor!" said Mr. Amos. "The captain says he sees the land."

Eleanor's start was somewhat prompt, to look in the direction of 'Queen Esther's' figure-head.

"The light is failing—I don't believe you can see it," said Mr. Amos; "not to know it from the clouds. The captain says he shall stand off and on through the night, so as to have daylight to go in. The entrance is narrow. I suppose, if all is well, we shall have a wedding to-morrow?"

Eleanor asked Mrs. Amos somewhat hastily, if what she had brought her was good?

"Delicious!" Mrs. Amos said; and pulling Eleanor's face down to her she gave it a kiss which spoke more things than her mere thanks. She was rewarded with the sight of that crimson veil which spread itself over Eleanor's cheeks, which most people thought it was a pleasure to see.

Eleanor thought she should get little sleep that night; but she was disappointed. She slept long and sweetly on her mattress; and awoke to find it quite day, with fair wind, and the schooner setting her head full on the land which rose up before her fresh and green, yes, and exceeding lovely. Eleanor got up and shook herself out; her companions were still sleeping. She rolled her mattress together and sat down upon it, to watch the approaches to the land. Fresher and fairer and greener every moment it lifted itself to her view; she could hardly bear to look steadily; her head went down for a minute often under the pressure of the thoughts that crowded together. And when she raised it up, the lovely hills of the island, with their novel outline and green luxuriance, were nearer and clearer and higher than they had been a minute before. Now she could discern here and there, she thought, something that must be a dwelling house; then trees began to detach themselves from the universal mass; she saw smoke rising; and she became aware too, that along the face of the island, fronting the approach of the schooner, was a wall of surf; and a line of breakers that seemed to stretch right and left and to be without an interval in their white continuity. Eleanor did not see how the schooner was going to get in; for the surf did not break evidently on the shore of the island, but on a reef extending around the shore and at some little distance from it. Yet the vessel stood straight on; and the sweet smell of the land began to come with the freshness of the morning air.

"Is this Vuliva before us?" she asked of the skipper whom she found standing near.

"Ay, ay!"

"Where are you going to get in? I see no opening."

"Ay, ay! There *is* an opening, though."

And soon, looking keenly, Eleanor thought she could discern it. Not until they were almost upon it however; and then it was a place of rough water enough, though the regular fall of the surf was interrupted and there was only a general upheaving and commotion of the waves among themselves. It was nothing very terrific; the tide was in a good state; and presently Eleanor saw that they had passed the barrier, they were in smooth water, and making for an opening in the land immediately opposite which might be either the mouth of a river or an inlet of the sea. They neared it fast, sailed up into it; and there to Eleanor's mortification the skipper dropped anchor and swung to. She saw no settlement. Some few scattered houses were plain enough now to be seen; but nothing even like a village. Tufts of trees waved gracefully; rock and hill and rich-coloured lowland spread out a variety of beauty; where was Vuliva, the station? This might be the island. Where were the people? Could they come no nearer than this?

Mr. Amos made enquiry. The village, the skipper said, was "round the pint;" in other words, behind a woody headland which just before them bent the course of the river into a sharp angle. The schooner would go no further; passengers and effects were to be transported the rest of the way in boats. People they would see soon enough; so the master of the "Queen Esther" advised them.

"I suppose the natives will carry the news of the schooner being here, and our friends will come and look after us," Mr. Amos said.

Eleanor changed colour, and sat with a beating heart looking at the fair fresh landscape which was to be—perhaps—the scene of her future home. The scene was peace itself. Still water after the upheavings of the ocean; the smell and almost the fluttering sound of the green leaves in the delicious wind; the ripple on the surface of the little river; the soft stillness of land sounds, with the heavy beat of the surf left behind on the reef outside. Eleanor drew a long breath. People would find them out soon, the skipper had said. She was exceedingly disposed to get rid of her sea dress and put on something that looked like the summer morning; for without recollecting what the seasons were in the Southern Ocean, that was what the time seemed like to her. She looked round at Mrs. Amos, who was sitting up and beginning to realize that she had done with the sea for the present.

"How do you do?" said Eleanor.

"I should feel better if I could get on something clean."

"Come, then!"

The two ladies disappeared down the companion way, into one of the most sorry tiring rooms, surely, that ever nicety used for that purpose. But it served two purposes with Eleanor just now; and the second was a hiding place. She did not want to be taken unawares, nor to be seen before she could see. So under the circumstances she made both Mrs. Amos and herself comfortable, and was as helpful as usual in a new line. Then she went to look out; but nobody was in sight yet, gentle or savage; all was safe; she went back to Mrs. Amos and fastened the door.

"Let us kneel down and pray together, will you?" she said. "I cannot get my breath freely till we have done that."

Mrs. Amos's lips trembled as she knelt. And Eleanor

and she joined in many petitions there, while the very stillness of their little cabin floor reminded them they were come to their desired haven, and the long sea journey was over. They rose up and kissed each other.

"I am so glad I have known you!" said Mrs. Amos. "What a blessing you have been to us! I wish we might be stationed somewhere together."

"I suppose that would be too good to hope for," said Eleanor. "I am going to reconnoitre again."

Mrs. Amos half guessed why, and smiled to herself at Eleanor's blushing shyness. "Poor child, her hands were all trembling too," she said in her thoughts. They were broken off by a low summons to the cabin door, which Eleanor held slightly ajar. Through the crack of the door they had a vision.

On the deck of the "Queen Esther" stood a specimen of the native inhabitants of the land. A man of tall stature, nobly developed in limbs and muscles, he looked in his native undress almost of giant proportions. His clothing was only a long piece of figured native cloth wound about his loins, one end falling like a train to the very sloop's deck. A thorough black skin was the only covering of the rest of his person, and shewed his breadth of shoulder and strength of muscle to good advantage; as if carved in black marble; only there was sufficient graceful mobility and dignified ease of carriage and attitude; no marble rigidity. Black he was, this savage, but not negro. The features were well cut and good. What the hair might be naturally could only be guessed at; the work of a skilful hair-dresser had left it something for the uninitiated to marvel at. A band of three or four inches in breadth, completely white, bordered the face; the rest, a very luxuriant head, was jet black and dressed into a perfectly regular and smooth roundish form, projecting everywhere beyond the white inner border. He had an uncouth necklace, made of what it was impossible to say, except that part of it looked like shells and part like some animal's teeth; rings of one or two colours were on his fingers; he carried no weapon. But in his huge, powerful black frame, uncouth hair-dressing, and strange uncoveredness, he was a sufficiently terrible object to unused eyes. In Tonga the ladies had seen no such sight.

"Do shut the door!" said Mrs. Amos. "He may come this way, and there is nobody that knows how to speak to him."

Eleanor shut the door, and looked round at her friend with a smile.

"I am foolish!" said Mrs. Amos laughing; "but I don't want to see him just yet—till there is somebody to talk to him."

The door being fast, Eleanor applied herself to a some what large knot-hole she had long ago discovered in it; one which she strongly suspected the skipper had fostered, if not originated, for his own convenience of spying what was going on. Through this knot-hole Eleanor had a fair view of a good part of the deck, savage and all. He was gesticulating now and talking, evidently to the captain and Mr. Amos, the former of whom either did not understand or did not agree with him. Mr. Amos, of course, was in the former condition. Eleanor watched them with absorbed interest; when suddenly this vision was crossed by another, that looked to her eyes much as a white angel might, coming across a cloud of both moral and physical blackness. Mr. Rhys himself; his very self, and looking very much like it; only in a white dress literally, which in England she had never seen him wear. But the white dress alone did not make the impression to her eyes; there was that air of freshness and purity which some people always carry about with them, and which has to do with the clear look of temperance as well as with great particularity of personal care, and in part also grows out of the moral condition. In three breathless seconds Eleanor took note of it all, characteristics well known, but seen now with the novelty of long disuse and with the background of that huge black savage, to whom Mr. Rhys was addressing some words of explanation or exhortation—Eleanor could not tell which. She noticed the quiet pleasant manner of his speech, which certainly looked not as if Mrs. Amos had any reason for her fears; but he was speaking earnestly, and she observed too the unbending look of the savage in answer and a certain pleasant deference with which he appeared to be listening. Mr. Rhys had taken off his hat for a moment—it hung in his hand while the other brushed the hair from his forehead. Eleanor's eye even in that moment fell to the hand which carried the hat; it was the same,—she recognized it with a curious sense of bringing great and little things together,—it was the same white and carefully looked-after hand that she remembered it in England. Mr. Rhys's own personal civilization went about with him.

Eleanor did not hear any of Mrs. Amos's words to her, which were several; and though Mrs. Amos, half alarmed by her deafness, did not know but she might be witnessing something dreadful on deck, and spoke with some importunity. Eleanor was thinking she had not a minute to lose. Beyond the time of Mr. Rhys's talking to the other visiter on the schooner's deck, there could be but small interval before he would learn all about her being on board; two words to the skipper or Mr. Amos would bring it out; and if she wished to gain that first minute's testimony of look and word, she must be beforehand with them. She thought of all that with a beating heart in one instant's flash of thought, hastily caught up her ship cloak without daring to stop to put it on, slipped back the bolt of the door, and noiselessly passed out upon the deck. She neither heard nor saw anybody else; she was conscious of an intense and pitiful shame at being there and at thus presenting herself; but everything else was second to that necessity, to know from Mr. Rhys's look, with an absolute certainty, where *he* stood. She was not at that moment much afraid; yet the look she must see. She went forward while he was yet speaking to his black neighbour, she stood still a little behind him, and waited. She longed to hide her eyes, yet she looked steadfastly. *How* she looked, neither she nor perhaps anybody else knew. There was short opportunity for observation.

Mr. Rhys had no sooner finished his business with his sable friend, when he turned the other way; and of course the motionless figure standing so near his elbow, the woman's bonnet and drapery, caught his first glance. Eleanor was watching, with eyes that were strained already with the effort; they got leave to go down now. The flash of joy in those she had been looking at, the deep tone of the low uttered, "Oh, Eleanor!—" which burst from him, made her feel on the instant as if she were paid to the full, not only for all she had done, but for all that life might have of disagreeable in store for her. Her eyes fell; she stood still in a sudden trance of contentment which made her as blind and deaf as another feeling had made her just before. Those two words—there had been such a depth in them, of tenderness and gladness; and somehow she felt in them too an appreciation of all she had done and gone through. Eleanor was satisfied. She felt it as well in the hold of her hand, which was taken and kept in a clasp as who should say, 'This is mine.'

Perhaps it was out of consideration for her state, that without any further reference to her he turned to Mr. Amos and claimed acquaintance and brotherhood with him; and for a little while talked, informing himself of various particulars of their journey and welfare; never all the while loosing his hold of that hand, though not bringing her into the conversation, and indeed standing so as somewhat to shield her. The question of landing came up and was discussed. The skipper objected to send the schooner's boat, on the score that it would leave too few men on board to take care of the vessel. Mr. Rhys had only a small canoe with him, manned by a single native. So he decided forthwith to return to the village and despatch boats large enough to bring the missionaries and their effects to land; but about that there might be some delay. Then for the first time he bent down and spoke to Eleanor; again that subdued, tender tone.

"Are you ready to go ashore?"

"Yes."

"I will take you with me. Do you want anything out of this big ship? The canoes may not be immediately obtained, for anything but the live freight."

He took the grey ship cloak from Eleanor's arm and put it round her shoulders. She felt that she was alone and forlorn no more; she had got home. She was a different creature that went into the cabin to kiss Mrs. Amos, from the Eleanor that had come out.

"I've seen him!" whispered Mrs. Amos. "Eleanor! you will not be married till we come, will you?"

"I hope not—I don't know," said Eleanor hurriedly seizing her bag and passing out again. Another minute, and it and she were taken down the side of the schooner and lodged in the canoe; and their dark oarsman paddled off.

CHAPTER XVIII.

"Nor did she lift an eye nor speak a word,
Rapt in the fear and in the wonder of it."

ELEANOR's shamefacedness was upon her in full force when she found herself in the canoe pushing off from the schooner and her friends there. She felt exceeding shy and strange, and with that a feeling very like awe of her companion. A feeling not quite unknown to her in former days with the same person, and in tenfold force now. There was no doubt to be sure of the secret mind of them both towards each other; nevertheless, he had never spoken to her of his affection, nor given her the least sign of it, except on paper, up to that day; and now he sat for all she could see as cool and grave as ever by her side. The old and the new state of things it was hard to reconcile all at once. To do Eleanor justice, she saw as one sees without looking; she was too shamefaced to look; she bent her outward attention upon their boatman. He was another native, of course, but attired in somewhat more civilized style, though in no costume of civilized lands. What he wore was more like a carman's frock at home than anything else it could be likened to. He was of pleasant countenance, and paddled along with great activity and skill.

They had been silent for the first few minutes since leaving the schooner, till at length Mr. Rhys asked her, with a little of the sweet arch smile she remembered so well, "how she had liked the first sight of a Fijian?"

It brought such a rush upon Eleanor of past things and present, old times and changes, that it was with the utmost difficulty she could make any answer at all.

"I was too much interested to think of liking or disliking."

"You were not startled?"

"No."

"That was a heathen chief, of the opposite village."

"He wanted something, did he not?"

"Yes; that the captain of the schooner should accommodate him in something he thought would be for his advantage. It was impossible, and so I told him."

Eleanor looked again towards the oarsman.

"This is one of our Christian brethren."

"Are there many?" she asked, though feeling as if she had no breath to ask.

"Yes. And we have cause to be thankful every day at hearing of more. We want ten times as many hands as we have got. How has the long voyage been to you?"

Eleanor answered briefly; but then she was obliged to go on and tell of Mrs. Caxton, and of Mr. and Mrs. Amos, and of various other matters; to all which still she answered in as few words as possible. She could not be fluent, with that sense of strangeness upon her; conscious not only that one of her hands was again in Mr. Rhys's hold, but that his eyes were never off her face. He desisted at last from questions, and they both sat silent; until the headland was rounded, and "There is Vuliva!" came from Mr. Rhys's lips.

In a little bay curve of the river, behind the promontory, lay the village; looking pretty and foreign enough. But very pretty it was. The odd, or rather the strange-looking houses, sitting apart from each other, some large and some small, intermingled gracefully with trees whose shape and leafage were as new, made a sweet picture. One house in particular as they neared the shore struck

Eleanor; it had a neat colonnade of slender pillars in front, and a high roof, almost like a Mansard in form, but thatched with native thatch. A very neat paling fence stretched along in front of this. Very near it, a little further off, rose another building that made Eleanor almost give a start of joy; so homelike and pleasant it looked, as well as surprising. This was an exceeding pretty chapel; again with a high thatched roof, and also with a neat slight bell-tower rising from one end. In front two doors at each side were separated by a large and not inelegant window; other windows and doors down the side of the building promised light and airiness; and the walls were wrought into a curious pattern; reminding Eleanor of the fanciful brick work of a past style of architecture. Near the shore and back behind the chapel and houses, reared themselves here and there the slender stems of palm and cocoanut trees, with their graceful tufts of feathery foliage waving at top; other trees of various kinds were mingled among them. Figures were seen moving about, in the medium attire worn by their oarsman. It was a pretty scene; cheerful and home-like, though so unlike home. Further back from the river, on the opposite shore, other houses could be seen; the houses of the heathen village; but Eleanor's eyes were fastened on this one. Mr. Rhys said not one word; only he held her hand in a still closer grasp which was not meaningless.

"How pretty it is!" Eleanor forced herself to say. He only answered, "Do you like it?" but it was in such a satisfied tone of preoccupation that Eleanor blushed and thought she might as well leave his meditations alone.

Yet though full of content in her heart, Mr. Rhys and his affection seemed both at a distance. It was so exactly the Mr. Rhys of Plassy, that Eleanor could not in a moment realize their changed relations and find her own place. A little thing administered a slight corrective to this reckoning.

The little canoe had come to land. Eleanor was taken out of it safely, and then for a moment left to herself; for Mr. Rhys was engaged in a colloquy with his boatman and another native who had come up. Not being able to understand a word of what was going on, though from the tones and gestures she guessed it had reference to the disembarkation of the schooner's party, and a little ready to turn her face from view, Eleanor stood looking landward; in a maze of strangeness that was not at all unhappy. The cocoanut tops waved gently a welcome to her; she took it so; the houses looked neat and inviting; glimpses of other unknown foliage helped to assure her she had got home; the country outlines, so far as she could see them, looked fair and bright. Eleanor was taking note of details in a dreamy way, when she was surprised by the sudden frank contact of lips with hers; lips that had no strangeness of their own to contend with. Turning hastily, she saw that the natives with whom Mr. Rhys had been talking had run off different ways, and they two were alone. Eleanor trembled as much as she had done when she first read Mr. Rhys's note at Plassy. And his words when he spoke did not help her, they were spoken so exactly like the Mr. Rhys she had known there. Not exactly, neither, though he only said,

"Do you want this cloak on any longer?"

"Yes, thank you," said Eleanor stammering,—"I do not feel it."

Which was most literally true, for at that moment she did not feel anything external. He looked at her, and exercising his own judgment proceeded to unclasp the cloak from her shoulders and hang it on his arm, while he put her hand on the other.

"There is no need for you to be troubled with this

now," said he. "I only put it round you to protect your dress." And with her bag in his hand, they went up from the river-side and past the large house with the colonnade. "Whither now?" thought Eleanor, but she asked nothing. One or two more houses were passed; then a little space without houses; then came a paling enclosure, of considerable size, apparently, filled with trees and vines. A gate opened in this and let them through, and Mr. Rhys led Eleanor up a walk in the garden-like plantation, to a house which stood encompassed by it. "Not at home yet!" he remarked to her as they stood at the door; with a slight smile which again brought the blood to her cheeks. He opened the door and they went in.

"The good news is true, sister Balliol!" he said to somebody that met them. "I have brought you one of our friends, and there are more to come, that I must go and look after. Is brother Balliol at home?"

"No, he is not; he has gone over the river."

"Then I will leave this lady in your care, and I will go and see if I can find canoes. I meant to have pressed him into my service. This is Miss Powle, sister Balliol."

The lady so called had come forward to meet them, and now took Eleanor by the hand and kissed her cordially. Mr. Rhys took her hand then, when she was released, and explained.

"I am going back to the schooner after our friends—if I can find a canoe—"

And without more words, off he went. Eleanor and Mrs. Balliol were left to look at each other.

This latter was a lady of middle height, and kindly if not fine features. A pair of good black eyes too. But what struck Eleanor most about her was her air; the general style of her figure and dress, which to Miss Powle's eyes was peculiar. She wore her hair in a crop; and that seemed to Eleanor a characteristic of the whole make up. Her dress was not otherwise than neat, and yet that epithet would never have occurred to one in describing it; all graces of style or attire were so ignored. Her gown sat without any; so did her collar; both were rather uncivilized, without partaking of the picturesqueness of savage costume. The face was by no means disagreeable; lacking neither in sense, nor in spirit nor in kindliness; but Eleanor perceived at once that the mind must have a serious want somewhere, in refinement or discernment: the exterior was so ruthlessly abandoned to ungainliness.

Mrs. Balliol took her to an inner room, where the cloak and the bonnet were left; and returned then to her occupations in the other apartment, while Eleanor set herself down at the window to make observations. The room was large and high, cheerful and airy, with windows at two sides. The one where she sat commanded a view of little beside the garden, with its luxuriant growth of fruit trees and shrubs and flowers. A tropical looking garden; for the broad leaves of the banana waved there around its great bunches of fruit; the canopy of a cocoanut palm fluttered slightly overhead; and various fruits that Eleanor did not know displayed themselves along with the pineapples that she did know. This garden view seemed very interesting to Eleanor, to judge by her intentness; and so it was for its own qualities, besides that a bit of the walk could be seen by which she had come and the wicket which had let her in and by which Mr. Rhys had gone out; but in good truth, as often as she turned her eyes to the scene within, she had such a sense of being herself an object of observation and perhaps of speculation, that she was fain to seek the garden again. And it was true, that while Mrs. Balliol plied her needle she used her eyes as well, and her thoughts with her needle flew in and out, as she surveyed Eleanor's figure in her neat fresh print dress. And the lady's eyebrows grew prophetical, not to say ominous.

"She's too handsome!"—that was the first conclusion. "She is quite too handsome; she cannot have those looks without knowing it. Better have brought a plain face to Fiji, than a spirit of vanity. Hair done as if she was just come out of a hair-dresser's!—hum—ruffle all down the neck of her dress—flowing sleeves too, and ruffles round *them*. And a buckle in her belt—a gold buckle, I do believe. And shoes?"—

The shoes were unexceptionable, but they fitted well on a nice foot; and the hands—were too small and white and delicate ever to have done anything, or ever to be willing to do anything. That was the point. No harm in small hands, Mrs. Balliol allowed, if they did not betray their owner into daintiness of living. She pursued her lucubrations for some time without interrupting those of Eleanor.

"Are you from England, sister?"

"From England—yes; but we made some stay in Australia by the way," said Eleanor turning from the window to take a more sociable position nearer her hostess.

"A long voyage?"

"Not remarkably long. I had good companions."

"From what part of England?"

"The borders of Wales, last."

"Brother Rhys is from Wales—isn't he?"

"I do not know," said Eleanor, vexed to feel the flush of blood to her cheeks.

"Ah? You have known brother Rhys before?" with a searching look.

"Yes."

"And how do you think you shall like it in Fiji?"

"You can hardly expect me to tell under such short trial," said Eleanor smiling.

"There are trials enough. I suppose you expect those, do you not?"

"I do not mean to expect them till they come," said Eleanor, still smiling.

"Do you think that is wise?" said the other gravely. "They will come, I assure you, fast enough; do you not think it is well to prepare the mind for what it has to go through, by looking at it beforehand?"

"You never know beforehand what is to be gone through," said Eleanor.

"But you know some things; and it is well, I think, to harden oneself against what is coming. I have found that sort of discipline very useful. Sister, may I ask you a searching question?"

"Certainly! If you please," said Eleanor.

"You know, we should be ready to give every one a reason of the hope that is in us. I want to ask you, sister, what moved you to go on a mission?"

Astonishment almost kept Eleanor silent; then noticing the quick eyes of Mrs. Balliol repeating the enquiry at her face, the difficulty of answering met and joined with a small tide of indignation at its being demanded of her. She did not want to be angry, and she was very near being ready to cry. Her mind was in that state of overwrought fulness when a little stir is more than the feelings can bear. Among conflicting tides, the sense of the ludicrous at last got the uppermost; and she laughed, as one laughs whose nerves are not just under control; heartily and merrily. Mrs. Balliol was confounded.

"I should not have thought it was a laughing matter,"—she remarked at length. But the gravity of that threw Eleanor off again; and the little hands and ruffled sleeves were reviewed under new circumstances. And when Eleanor got command of herself, she still kept her hand over her eyes, for she found that she was just trembling into tears. She held it close pressed upon them.

"Perhaps you are fatigued, sister?" said Mrs. Balliol, in utter incapacity to account for this demonstration.

"Not much. I beg your pardon!" said Eleanor. "I believe I am a little unsettled at first getting here. If you please, I will try being quite quiet for awhile—if you will let me be so discourteous?"

"Do so!" said Mrs. Balliol. "Anything to rest you." And Eleanor went back to her window, and turning her face to the garden again rested her head on her hand; and there was a hush. Mrs. Balliol worked and mused, probably. Eleanor did as she had said; kept quiet. The quiet lasted a long time, and the tropical day grew up into its meridian heats; yet it was not oppressive; a fine breeze relieved it and made it no other than pleasant. Home at last! This great stillness and quiet, after the ocean tossings, and months of voyaging, and change, and heart-uncertainty. The peace of heart now was as profound; but so profound, and so thankfully recognized, that Eleanor's mood was a little unsteady. She needed to be still and recollect herself, as she could looking out into the leaves of a great banana tree there in the garden, and forgetting the house and Mrs. Balliol.

The quiet lasted a long time, and was broken then by the entrance of Mr. Balliol. His wife introduced him; and after learning that he could now render no aid to Mr. Rhys, he immediately entered into a brisk conversation with the new comer Mr. Rhys had brought. That went well, and was also strengthening. Eleanor was greatly pleased with him. He was evidently a man of learning and sense and spirit; a man of excellent parts, in good cultivation, and filled with a most benign and gentle temper of goodness. It was a pleasure to talk to him; and while they were talking the party from the schooner arrived.

Eleanor felt her "shamefastness" return upon her, while all the rest were making acquaintance, welcoming and receiving welcome. She stood aside. Did they know her position? While she was thinking, Mr. Rhys came to her and put her again in her chair by the window. Mrs. Amos had been carried off by Mrs. Balliol. The two other gentlemen were in earnest converse. Mr. Rhys took a seat in front of Eleanor and asked in a low voice if she wished for any delay?

"In what?" said Eleanor, though she knew the answer.

"Coming home."

He was almost sorry for her, to see the quick blood flash into her face. But she caught her breath and said "No."

"You know," he said; how exactly like the Mr. Rhys of Plassy!—"I would not hurry you beyond your pleasure. If you would like to remain here a day or two, domiciled with Mrs. Balliol, and rest, and see the land—you have only to say what you wish."

"I do not wish it," said Eleanor, finding it very difficult to answer at all—"I wish it to be just as you please."

"You must know what my pleasure is. Does your heart not fail you, now you are here?" he asked still lower and in a very gentle way.

"No."

"Eleanor, have you had any doubts or failings of heart at any time, since you left England?"

"No. Yes!—I did, once—at Sydney."

"At Sydney?"—repeated Mr. Rhys in a perceptibly graver tone.

"Yes—at Sydney—when I did not get any letters from you."

"You got no letters from me?"

"No."

"At Sydney?"

"No," said Eleanor venturing to look up.

"Did you not see Mr. Armitage?"

"Mr. Armitage! O he was in the back country—I remember now Mr. Amos said that; and he never returned to Sydney while we were there."

An inarticulate sound came from Mr. Rhys's lips, between indignation and impatience; the strongest expression of either that Eleanor had ever heard from him.

"Then Mr. Armitage had the letters?"

"Certainly! and I am in the utmost surprise at his carelessness. He ought to have left them in somebody else's charge, if he was quitting the place himself. When *did* you hear from me?"

The flush rose again, not so vividly, to Eleanor's face.

"I heard in England—those letters—you know."

"Those letters I trusted to Mrs. Caxton?"

"Yes."

"And not since! Well, you are excused for your heart failing that once. Who is to do it, Eleanor?—Mr. Amos?"

"If you please—I should like—"

He left her for a moment to make his arrangements; and for that moment Eleanor's thoughts leaped to those who should have been by her side at such a time, with a little of a woman's heart-longing. Mrs. Caxton, or her mother! If one of them might have stood by her then! Eleanor's head bent with the moment's poor wish. But with the touch of Mr. Rhys's hand when he returned to her, with the sound of his voice, there came as it always did to Eleanor, healing and strength. The one little word "Come," from his lips, drove away all mental hobgoblins. He said nothing more, but there was a great tenderness in the manner of his taking her upon his arm. His look Eleanor dared not meet. She felt very strange yet; she could not get accustomed to the reality of things. This man had never spoken one word of love to her, and now she was standing up to be married to him.

The whole little party stood together, while the marriage service of the English church was read. It was preceded however by a prayer that was never read nor written. After the service was over, and after Eleanor had been saluted by the two ladies who were all the representatives of mother and sister and friends for her on the occasion, Mr. Rhys whispered to her to get her bonnet. Eleanor gladly obeyed. But as soon as it appeared, there was a general outcry and protest. What were they going to do?"

"Take her to see how her house looks," said Mr. Rhys. "You forget I have something to shew."

"But you will bring her back to dinner? do, brother Rhys! We shall have dinner presently. You'll be back?"

"If the survey is over in time—but I do not think it will," he answered gravely.

"Then tea—you will come then? Let us all be together at tea. Will you?"

"It is a happiness we have had no visiters before dinner! I will see about it, sister Balliol, thank you; and take advice."

And glad was Eleanor when they got away; which was immediately, for Mr. Rhys's motions were prompt. He led her now not to the wicket by which she had come, but another way, through the garden wilderness still, till another slight paling with a wicket in it was passed and the wilderness took a somewhat different character. The same plants and trees were to be seen, but order and pleasantness of arrangement were in place of vegetable confusion; neat walks ran between the luxuriant growing bananas, and led gradually nearer to the river; till another house came in view; and passing round the gable end of it, Eleanor could cast her eye along the building and take the effect. It was long and low, with a high picturesque thatched roof, and the walls fancifully wrought in a pattern, making a not unpretty appearance. The door was in the middle; she had no time to see more, for Mr. Rhys unlocked it and led her in.

The interior was high, wide, and cool and pleasant after the hot sun without; but again she had no time to make observations. Mr. Rhys led her immediately on to an inner room. Eleanor's eyes were dazed and her heart was beating; she could hardly see anything, except, as one takes impressions without seeing, that this answered to the inner room at Mrs. Balliol's and had far more the air of being furnished and pleasantly habitable. What gave it the air she could not tell; for Mr. Rhys was unfastening her bonnet and throwing it off, and then taking her sea-cloak from his arm and casting that somewhat carelessly away; and then his arms enfolded her. It was the first time they had been really alone since her coming; and now he was silent, so silent that Eleanor could scarcely bear it. She was aware his eyes were studying her fixedly, and she felt as if they could see nothing beside the conscious mounting of the blood from cheek to brow, which reached what to her was a painful flush. Probably he saw it, for the answer came in a little closer pressure of the arms that were about her. She ventured to look up at last; she was unable to endure his silent inspection; and then she saw that his face was full of emotion that wrought too deep for words, too deep even for caresses, beyond the one or two grave kisses with which he had welcomed her. It overcame Eleanor completely. She could not meet the look. It was much more than mere joy or affection; there was an expression of the sort of tenderness with which a mother would clasp a lost child; a full keen sympathy for all she had done and gone through and ventured for him, for all her loneliness and forlornness that had been, and that was still with respect to all the guardians of her childhood or womanhood up to that hour. Eleanor's head sank down. She felt none of that now for which his looks expressed such keen regard; she had got to her resting-place, not the less for all the awe and strangeness of it, which were upon her yet. She could have cried for a very different feeling; but she would not; it did not suit her. Mr. Rhys let her be still for a few minutes. When he did speak, his voice was gravely tender indeed, as it had been to her all day, but there was no sentimentality about it. He spoke clear and abrupt, as he often did.

"Do you want to go back to the other house to dinner?"

"Do you wish it?" said Eleanor looking up to find out.

"I wish to see nothing earthly, this afternoon, but your face."

"Then do let it be so!" said Eleanor.

He laughed and kissed her, more gaily this time, without seeming able to let her out of his arms; and left her at last with the injunction to keep still a minute till he should return, and on no account to begin an examination of the house by herself. Very little danger there was! Eleanor had not the free use of her eyes yet for anything. Presently he came back, put her hand on his arm and led her out into the middle apartment.

"Do you know," he said as he passed through this, keeping her hand in his own and looking down at her face,—"what is the first lesson you have to learn?"

"No," said Eleanor, most unaffectedly frightened; she did not know why.

"The first thing we have to do, on taking possession here to-day is, to give our thanks and offer our prayers in company. Do not you think so?"

"Yes—" said Eleanor breathlessly. "But what then?"

"I mean together,—not that it should be all on one side. You with me, as well as I with you."

"Oh no, Mr. Rhys!"

"Why not?—Mrs. Rhys?"

"Do not ask me! That would be dreadful!"

"I do not think you will find it so."

Eleanor stopped short, near the other end of the great apartment. "I cannot do it!" she exclaimed with tears in her eyes, appealing to him. He put his arms round her again, but spoke gravely.

"One can always do what is right."

"Not to-day—" whispered Eleanor.

"One can always do right to-day," he answered smiling. "And it is best to begin as we are going on. Come!"

He took her hand and led her forward into the room at the other end of the house; his study, Eleanor saw with half a glance by the books and papers and tables that were there. Still keeping her hand fast in his, they knelt together; and certainly the prayer that followed was good for nervousness, and like the sunshine to dispel all manner of clouds. Eleanor was quieted and subdued; she could not help it; all sorts of memories and associations of Plassy and Wiglands gathered in her mind, back of the thoughts that immediately filled it. Hallowed, precious, soothing and joyful, those minutes of prayer were while Mr. Rhys spoke; in spite of the minutes to follow that Eleanor dreaded. And though her own words were few, and stammering, they were different from what she would have thought possible a quarter of an hour before; and not unhappy to look back upon.

Detaining her when they arose, Mr. Rhys asked with something of his old comical look, whether she thought she could eat a dinner of his ordering? Eleanor had no doubt of it.

"You think you could eat anything by this time!" said he. "Poor child! But my credit is at stake—suppose you wait here a few minutes, until I see whether all is right."

He went off, and Eleanor sat still, feeling too happy to want to look about her. He came again presently, to lead Eleanor to the dining-room.

In the lofty, spacious, and by no means inelegant middle apartment of the house, a little table stood spread, looking exceeding diminutive in contrast with the wide area and high ceiling of the room. Here Mr. Rhys with a very bright look established Eleanor, and proceeded to make amends for keeping her so long from Mrs. Balliol's table. Much to her astonishment there was a piece of broiled chicken and a dish of eggs nicely cooked, and Mr. Rhys was pouring out for her some tea in delicate little cups of china.

"You see aunt Caxton, do you not?" he said.

"O aunt Caxton! in these cups. I thought so. But I had no idea you had such cooks in Fiji?"

"They will learn—in time," said he shortly. "You perceive this is an unorganized establishment. I have not indulged in tablecloths yet; but you will put things to rights."

"Tablecloths?" said Eleanor.

"Yes—you have such things lying in wait for you. You have a great deal to do. And in the first place, you are to find out the good qualities of these fruits of the land," he said, giving her portions of several vegetable preparations with which and with fruits the table was filled.

"What is this?" said Eleanor.

"Taro; one of the valuable things with which nature has blessed Fiji. The natives cultivate it well and carefully. That is yam; and came from a root five and a half feet long. Eleanor—I do not at all comprehend how you come to be sitting there!"

It was so strange and new to Eleanor, and Mr. Rhys was such a compound of things new and things old to her, that a little chance word like this was enough to make her flutter and change colour. He perceived it, and bent his attention to amuse her with the matters of the table; and told her wonders of the natural productions of Fiji. But in the midst of this Mr. Rhys's hand would come abstracting her tea-cup to fill it again; and then Eleanor watched while he did it; and he made himself a little private amusement about getting it sugared right and finding how she liked it; and Eleanor wondered at him and her tea-cup together, and stirred her tea in a subdued state of mind.

"One hardly expects to see such a nice little teaspoon in Fiji," she remarked.

"Aunt Caxton, again," said Mr. Rhys.

"But Mr. Rhys, your Fijians must be remarkable cooks! Or have you taught them?"

"I have taught nobody in that line."

"Then are they not remarkable for their skill in cookery?"

"As a nation, I think they are; and it is one evidence of their mental development. They have a great variety of native dishes, some of which, I believe, are not despicable."

"But these are English dishes."

"Do justice to them then, like a good Englishwoman."

Eleanor's praise was not undeserved; for the chicken and yam were excellent, and the sweet potatoe which Mr. Rhys put upon her plate was roasted very like one that had been in some hot ashes at home. But everything except the dishes was strange, Mr. Rhys's hand included. Through the whole length of the house, and of course through the middle apartment, ran a double row of columns, upholding the roof. If Eleanor's eye followed them up, there was no ceiling, but the lofty roof of thatch over her head. Under her foot was a mat, of native workmanship; substantial and neat, and very foreign looking. And here were aunt Caxton's cups; and if she lifted her eyes—Eleanor felt most strange then, although most at home.

The taro and yam and sweet potatoe were only an introduction to the fruit, which was beautiful as a shew. A native servant came in and removed the dishes, and then set on the table a large basket, in which the whole dessert was very simply served. Cocoanuts and bananas, oranges and wild plums, bread-fruit and Malay apples, came piled together in beautiful mingling. Mr. Rhys went himself to a sort of beaufet in the room and brought plates.

"Servants cannot be said to be in complete training," he said with a humourous look as he seated himself. "It would be strange if they were, when there has been no one to train them. And in Fiji."

"I do not understand," said Eleanor. "Have you been keeping house here all by yourself? I thought not, from what Mrs. Balliol said."

"You may trust sister Balliol for being always correct. No, for the last few months, until lately, I have been building this house. Since it was finished I have lived in it, partly; but I have taken my principal meals at the other house."

"*You* have been building it?"

"Or else you would not be in it at this moment. There is no carpenter to be depended on in Fiji but yourself. You have got to go over the house presently and see how you like it. Are you ready for a banana?

or an orange? I think you must try one of these cocoanuts."

"But you had people to help you?"

"Yes. At the rate of two boards a day."

"But Mr. Rhys, if you cannot get carpenters, where can you get cooks?—or do the people have *this* by nature?"

"When you ask me properly, I will tell you," he said, with a little pucker in the corners of his mouth that made Eleanor take warning and draw off. She gave her attention to the cocoanut, which she found she must learn how to eat. Mr. Rhys played with an orange in the mean time, but she knew was really busy with nothing but her and her cocoanut. When she would be tempted by no more fruit, he went off and brought a little wooden bowl of water and a napkin, which he presented for her fingers, standing before her to hold it. Eleanor dipped in her fingers, and then looked up.

"You should not do this for me, Mr. Rhys!" she said half earnestly.

But he stooped down and took his own payment; and on the whole Eleanor did not feel that she had greatly the advantage of him. Indeed Mr. Rhys had payment of more sorts than one; for cheeks were rosy as the fingers were white which she was drying, as she had risen and stood before him. She looked on then with great edification, to see his fingers deliberately dipped in the same bowl and dried on the same napkin; for very well Eleanor knew they would have done it for no mortal beside her. And then she was carried off to look at the walls of her house.

CHAPTER XIX.

> "Thou hast found ....
> Thy cocoas and bananas, palms and yams,
> And homestall thatched with leaves."

The walls of the house were, to an Englishwoman, a curiosity. They were made of reeds; three layers or thicknesses of them being placed different ways, and bound and laced together with sinnet; the strong braid made of the fibre of the cocoanut-husk. It was this braid, woven in and out, which produced the pretty mosaic effect Eleanor had observed upon the outside. Mr. Rhys took her to a doorway, where she could examine from within and from without this novel construction; and explained minutely how it was managed.

"This looks like a foreign land," said Eleanor. "You had described it, and I thought I had imagined it; but sight and feeling are quite a different matter."

"I did not describe it to you?"

"No—O no; you described it to aunt Caxton."

He drew her back a step or two and laid her hand upon the post of the door.

"What is this?" said Eleanor.

"That is a piece of the stem of the palm-fern."

"And these are its natural mouldings and markings! It is like elegant carved work! It is natural, is it not?" she said suddenly.

"Certainly. The natives do execute very marvellous carving in wood, with tools that would drive a workman at home to despair; but I have not learned the art.

Come here—the pillars that hold up the roof of your house are of the same wood."

A double row of pillars through the whole length of the house gave it stability; they were stems of the same palm fern, and as they had been chosen and placed with a careful eye to size and position, the effect of them was not at all inelegant. The building itself was of generous length and width; and with a room cut off at each end, as the fashion was, the centre apartment was left of really noble proportions; broad, roomy, and lofty; with its palm columns springing up to its high roof of thatch. Standing beside one of them, Eleanor looked up and declared it a beautiful room.

"Do not look at the doors and windows," said Mr. Rhys. "I did not make those—they were sent out framed. I had only the pleasure of putting them in."

"And how did that agree with all your other work?"

"Well," he said decidedly. "That was my recreation."

"There is the prettiest mixture of wild and tame in this house," said Eleanor, speaking a little timidly; for she was conscious all the while how little Mr. Rhys was thinking of anything but herself. "Are these mats made here?"

"Pure Fijian!"

The one at which Eleanor was looking, her eyes having fallen to the floor, was both large and elegant. It was very substantially and neatly made, and had a border fancifully wrought all round it, a few inches in width. The pattern of the border was made with bits of worsted and little white feathers. This mat covered all the centre of the room; under it the whole floor was spread with other and coarser ones; and others of a still different manufacture lined the walls of the room.

"One need not want a prettier carpet," said Eleanor, keeping her eyes on the mat. Mr. Rhys put his arm round her and drew her off to one side of the room, where he made her pause before a large square space which was sunk a foot deep in the earth and bordered massively with a frame of logs of hard wood.

"What do you think of that?"

"Mr. Rhys, what is it?"

"You would not take it for a fireplace?" he said with a comical look.

"But is it a fireplace?"

"That is what it is intended for. The Fijians make their fireplaces in this manner.

"And you are a Fijian, I suppose."

"So are you."

"But Mr. Rhys, can a fireplace of this sort be useful in an English house?"

"No. But in a Fijian house it may—as I have proved. The natives would have a wooden frame here, at one side, to hold cooking vessels. You do not need that, for you have a kitchen."

"With a fireplace like this?"

"Yes," he said, with a smile that had some raillery in it, which Eleanor would not provoke.

"Suppose you come and look at something that is not Fijian," he went on. "You must vary your attention."

He drew her before a little unostentatious piece of furniture, that looked certainly as if it was made out of a good bit of English oak. What it was, did not appear; it was very plain and rather massively made. Now Mr. Rhys produced keys, and opened first doors; then a drawer, which displayed all the characteristic contents and arrangements of a lady's work-box on an extended scale. Love's work; Eleanor could see her adopted mother in every carefully disposed supply of needles and silks and braids and glittering Sheffield ware, and the thousand and one appliances and provisions for one who was to be at a very large distance from Sheffield and every home source of needle furniture. Love recognized love's work, as Eleanor looked into the drawer.

"Now you are ready to say this is a small thread and needle shop," said Mr. Rhys; "but you will be mistaken if you do. Look further."

And that she might, he unlocked a pair of smaller inner doors; the little piece of furniture developed itself immediately into a capital secretary. As thoroughgoing as the work-box, but still more comprehensive, here were more than mere materials and conveniences for writing; it was a depository for several small but very precious treasures of a scientific and other kinds; and even a few books lay nestling among them, and there was room for more.

"What is this!" Eleanor exclaimed when she had got her breath.

"This is—Mrs. Caxton! I do not know whether she expected you to turn sempstress immediately for the colony—or whether she intended you for another vocation, as I do."

"She sent this from England!"

"It was made by nobody worse than a London cabinet-maker. I did not know whether you would choose to have it stand in this place, or in the only room that can properly be called your own. Come in here;—the other part of the house is, you will find, pretty much public."

"Even your study?"

"That is no exception, sometimes. I am a public man, myself."

The partition wall of this room was nicely lined with mats; the door was like a piece of the wall, swinging to noiselessly, but Mr. Rhys shewed Eleanor how she could fasten it securely on the inside. Eleanor had been taken into this room on her first arrival; but had then been unable to see anything. Now her eyes were in requisition. Here there was even more attention paid to comfort and appearances than in the dining-room. In the simplest possible manner; but somebody had been at work there who knew that elegance is attainable without the help of opulence; and that eye and hand can do what money cannot. Eye and hand had been busy everywhere. Very pretty and soft native mats were on the floor; the windows were shaded with East Indian *jalousies;* and not only personal convenience but tastes were regarded in the various articles of furniture and the arrangement of them. Good sense was regarded too. Camp chairs and tables were useful for packing and moving, as well as neat to the eye; white draperies relieved their simplicity; shelves were hung against the wall in one place for books, and filled; and in the floor stood an easy chair of excellent workmanship, into which Mr. Rhys immediately put Eleanor. But she started up to look at it.

"Did aunt Caxton send all these things?" she said with a tear in her eye.

"She has sent almost too many. These are but the beginning. Look here, Eleanor."

He opened a door at one end of the room, hidden under mat hangings like the other, which disclosed a large space lined with shelves; several articles reposing on them, and on the floor below sundry chests and boxes.

"This is your storeroom. Here you may revel in the riches you do not immediately wish to display. This is yours; I have a storeroom on my own part."

"And what is in those chests and boxes, Mr. Rhys?"

"I don't know! except that it is aunt Caxton again. You will find tablecloths and napkins—I can certify that—for I stumbled upon them; but I thought they had best not see the light till their owner came. So I locked them up—and here are the keys."

"And who put up all these nice shelves?"

"Your head carpenter."

"And have you been doing all this for me?" said Eleanor.

He laughed and took her in his arms again, looking at her with that mixture of expressions.

"I wish I could give you some of my content!" he said.

"I do not want it!" said Eleanor laughing.

"Is that declaration entirely generous?"

Eleanor had no mind, like a wise woman, to answer this question; but she was held under the inspection of an eye that she knew of old clear and keen beyond all others to untie the knot of anybody's meaning. She flushed up very much and tried to turn it off, for she saw he had a mind to have the answer.

"You do not want me to give account of every idle word after that fashion?" she said lightly.

"Hush—hush," he said with a gravity that had much sweetness in it. "I cannot have you speak in that way."

"I will not—" said Eleanor, suddenly much more sober than he was.

"There are too many that have the habit of using their Master's words to point their own sentences. Do not let us use it. Come to my study—you did not see it before dinner, I think."

Eleanor was glad he could smile again, for at that minute she could not. She felt whirled back to Plassy and to Wiglands, to the time of their old and very different relations. She could not realize the new, nor quietly understand her own happiness; and a very fresh vivid sense of his character made her feel almost as much awe of him as affection. That was according to old habit too. But if she felt shy and strange, she was the only one; for Mr. Rhys was in a very gay mood. As they went through the dining-room he stopped to shew and display to her numerous odd little contrivances and arrangements; here a cupboard of rustic, and very pretty too, native work; or at least native materials. There a more sophisticated beaufet, which had come from Sydney by Mrs. Caxton's order. "Dear Mrs. Caxton!" said Mr. Rhys,—"she has forgotten nothing. I am only in astonishment what she can have found to fill your new invoice of boxes."

"Why there are not many," said Eleanor.

He looked at her and laughed. "You will be doing nothing but unpacking for days to come," he said. "I have done what I never thought I should do—married a rich wife."

"Why aunt Caxton sends the things quite as much to you as to me."

"Does she."

"I am sure, if anybody is poor, I am."

"If that speech means *me*," said Mr. Rhys with a little bit of provokingness in the corners of his mouth, —"I don't take it. I do not feel poor; and never did. Not to-day certainly, with whole shiploads coming in."

"I do not know of a single unnecessary thing but your microscope."

"Have you brought that?" he said with a change of tone. "It would be just like Mrs. Caxton to come out and make us a visit some day! I cannot think of anything else she could give us, that she has not given. Look at my book-cases."

Eleanor did, thinking of their owner. They were of plainest construction, but so made that they would take to pieces in five minutes and become packing cases with the books packed, all ready for travel; or at pleasure, as now, stand up in their place in the study in the form of very neat bookcases. They were not large; a Fijian missionary's library had need be not too extensive; but

Eleanor looked over their contents with hurried delight.

The rest of the room also spoke of Mrs. Caxton; in light neat tables and chairs and other things. Here too, though not a hand's turn had apparently been wasted, everything, simple as it was, had a sort of pleasantness of order and fitness which left the eye gratified. Eleanor read that and the meaning of it. Here were contrivances again that Mr. Rhys had done; shelves, and brackets, and pins to hang things; nothing out of use, but all so contrived as to give a certain elegant effect to this plain work-room. Even the book and paper disorder was not that of a careless man. Still it was not like the room at the other end of the house. The mats that floored and lined it were coarser; there were no *jalousies* at the windows; and no easy chair anywhere. One thing it had like the other; a storeroom cut off from it. This was a large one, like Eleanor's, and filled. His money-drawer, Mr. Rhys called it. All sorts of articles valued by the natives were there; Mrs. Caxton had taken care to send a large supply. These were to serve the purposes of barter. Mr. Rhys displayed to Eleanor the stores of iron tools, cotton prints, blankets, and articles of clothing, that were stowed away there; stowed away with an absolute order and method which again she looked at as significant of one side at least of Mr. Rhys's character. He amused himself with displaying everything; shewed her the whole of the new and strangely appointed establishment over which she had come to preside, so far at least as the house contained it; and when he had brought her to something like an apparent share in his own gay mood, at last placed her in a camp chair in the dining-room, which he had set in the middle of the floor, and opened the door of the house. It gave Eleanor a lovely view. The plantations had been left open, so that the eye had a fair range down to the river and to the opposite shore, where another village stood. It was seen under bright sunshine now. Mr. Rhys let her look a moment, then shut the door, and came and sat down before her, taking both her hands in his own; and Eleanor knew from a glance at his face that the same thoughts were working within him that had wrought that moved look before dinner—when she first came. She felt her colour mounting; it tried her to be silent under his eye in that way.

"Mr. Rhys, do you remember preaching to me one day at Plassy—when we were out walking?"

"Yes," he said with a half laugh.

"I wish you would do it again."

"I will preach you a sermon every morning if you like."

"No, but now. I wish you would, so as to make me realize that you are the same person."

"I am not the same person at all!" he said.

"Why are you not?" said Eleanor opening her eyes at him.

"In those days I was your pastor and friend simply. The difference is, that I have acquired the right to love you—take care of you—and scold you."

"It seems to me that last was a privilege you exercised occasionally in those times," said Eleanor archly.

"Not at all! In those days I was a poor fellow that did not dare say a word to you."

Eleanor's recollections were of sundry exceptions to this rule, so marked and prominent in her memory that she could not help laughing.

"O Mr. Rhys, don't you remember—"

"What?" said he with the utmost gravity.

But Eleanor had stopped, and coloured now brilliantly.

"It seems that your recollections are of a questionable character," he said. Eleanor did not deny it.

"What is it you wish me *not* to remember?"

"It was a time when you said I was very wrong," said Eleanor meekly, "so do not call it back."

He bent forward to kiss her, which did not steady Eleanor's thoughts at all.

"Do you want preaching?" he said.

"Yes indeed! It will do me good."

"I will give you some words to think of, that I lived n all yesterday. 'Beloved of God.' They are wonderful words, that Paul says belong to all the saints; and they were about me yesterday like a halo of glory, from morning to night."

Now Eleanor was all right; now she recognized Mr. Rhys and herself, and listened to every word with her old delight in them. Now she could use her eyes and look at him, though she well saw that he was considering her with that full, moved tenderness that she had felt in him all day; even when he was talking and thinking of other things he did not cease to remember *her*.

"Eleanor, what do you know about the meaning of those words?"

"Little!" she said. "And yet, a little."

"You know that *we* were Gentiles, carried away unto these dumb idols—or after others in our own hearts—as helplessly as the poor heathen around us. But we have got the benefit of that word,—'I will call them my people, which were not my people; and her beloved, which was not beloved.'"

"Yes!"

"Then look at our privileges—'The beloved of the Lord shall dwell in safety by him; and the Lord shall cover him all the day long, and he shall dwell between his shoulders.'—Heavenly security; unearthly joy; a hiding-place where the troubles of earth cannot reach us."

Mr. Rhys left his position before Eleanor at this, and

with a brow all alight with its thoughts began to pace up and down in front of her; just as he had done at Plassy, she remembered. She ventured not a word. Her heart was very full.

"Then look how we are bidden to increase our rejoicing and to delight ourselves in the store laid up for us; we are not only safe and happy, but fed with dainties. All things are ready; Christ says he will sup with us; and we are bidden—'Eat, O friends; drink, yea, drink abundantly, O beloved.' 'He that cometh to me shall never hunger, and he that believeth on me shall never thirst.'"

"And then, Eleanor, if we are the elect of God, holy and beloved, what bowels of mercies should be in us; how precious all other beloved of him should be to us; how we should be constrained by his love. Are you? I am. I am willing to spend and be spent for these people among whom we are. I am sure there are many, many children of God among them, come and coming. I seek no better than to labour for them. It is the delight of my soul! Eleanor, how is it with you?"

He had stood still before her during these last words, and now sat down again, taking her hands and looking with his undeceivable gaze into her face.

"I desire the same thing. I dare not say, I desire it as strongly as you do,—but it is my very wish."

"Is it for the love of Christ—or for love of these poor creatures? or for any other reason?"

"I can hardly separate the first two," said Eleanor, looking a little wistfully. "The love of Christ is at the bottom of it all."

"There is no other motive," he said; "no other that will do the work; nothing else that will work true love to them. But when I think of my Master—I am willing to do or be anything, I think, in his service!"

He quitted her hands and began slowly walking up and down again.

"Mr. Rhys," said Eleanor, "what can I do?"

"Are you ready to encounter disagreeablenesses, and hardships, and privations, in the work?"

"Yes; and discouragements."

"There are no such things. There ought to be no such things. I never feel nor have felt discouraged. That is want of faith. Do you remember, Eleanor, 'The clouds are the dust of his feet?' Think—our eyes are blinded by the dust, we look at nothing else, and we do not see the glory of the steps that are taken."

"That is true. O Mr. Rhys, that is glorious!"

"Then you are not afraid? I forewarn you, little annoyances are sometimes harder to bear than great ones. It is one of the most trying things that I have to meet," said Mr. Rhys standing still with a funny face,—"to have Ra Mbombo's beard sweep my plate when I am at dinner."

"What does he do that for?"

"He is so fond of me."

"That is being too fond, certainly."

"It is an excess of affectionate attention,— he gets so close to me that we have a community of things. And you will have, Eleanor, some days, a perpetual levee of visiters. But what is all that, for Christ?"

"I am not afraid," said Eleanor with a most unruffled smile.

"I wrote to frighten you."

"But I was not frightened. Are things no better in the islands than when you wrote?"

"Changing—changing every day; from darkness to light, and from the power of Satan to God. Literally. There are heathen temples here, in which a few years ago if a woman or a child had dared cross the threshold they would have been done to death immediately. Now those very temples are used as our schools. On our way to the chapel we shall pass almost over a place where there used to be one of the ovens for cooking human bodies; now the grass and wild tomatoes are growing over it. I can take you to house after house, where men and women used to be eaten, where now if you stand to listen you may hear hymns of praise to Jesus and prayer going up in his name. Praise the Lord! It is grand to be permitted to live in Fiji now!"—

Eleanor was hushed and silent a few minutes, while Mr. Rhys walked slowly up and down. Then she spoke with her eyes full of sympathetic tears.

"Mr. Rhys, what can *I* do?"

"What you have to do at present," he said with a change of tone, "is to take care of me and learn the language,—both languages, I should say! And in the mean while you had better take care of your pins,"—he stooped as he spoke, to pick up one at her feet and presented it with comical gravity. "You must remember you are not in England. Here you could not spend pin-money even if you had it."

"If I were inclined to be extravagant," said Eleanor laughing at him, "your admonition would be thrown away; I have brought such quantities with me?"

"Of pins?"

"Yes."

"I hope you will not ever use them!"

"Why not?"

"I do not see what a properly made dress has to do with pins."

But at this confession of masculine ignorance Eleanor first looked and then laughed and covered her face, till he came and sat down again and by forcible possession took her hands away.

"You have no particular present occasion to laugh at

me," he said. "Eleanor, what made you first willing to quit England and go anywhere?"

The answer to this was first an innocent look, and then an extreme scarlet flush. She could not hide it, with her hands prisoners; she sat in a pretty state of abashment. A slight giving way of the mouth bore witness that he read and understood it, though his immediate words were reassuringly grave and unchanged in tone.

"I remember, you did not comprehend such a thing as possible, at one time. When was that changed? You used to have a great fear."

"I lost part of that at Plassy."

"Where did you lose the rest of it, Eleanor?"

"It was in London."

He saw by the light in Eleanor's eyes, which looked at him now, that there was something behind. Yet she hesitated.

"Sealed lips?" said he bending forward again to her face. "You must unseal them, Eleanor."

"Do you want me to tell you all that?" she asked questioningly.

"I want you to tell me everything."

"It is only a long story."

"Do not make it short."

An easy matter! to go on and tell it with her two hands prisoners, and those particularly clear eyes looking into her face. It served to shew the grace that belonged to Eleanor, the way that in these circumstances she began what she had to say. Where another woman would have been awkward, she spoke with the simple sweet poise of manner that had been the admiration of many a company, and that made Mr. Rhys now press the little hands closer in his own. A little evident shy reluctance only added to the grace.

"It is a good while ago—I felt, Mr. Rhys, that I

wanted,—just that which makes one willing to go anywhere and do anything; though not for that reason. I expected to live in England always. I wanted to know more of Christ. I wanted it, not for work's sake but for happiness' sake. I was a Christian, I suppose; but I knew—I had seen and felt—that there were things,—there was a height of Christian life and attainment, that I had not reached; but where I had seen other people, with a light upon their brows that I knew never shined upon mine. I knew whence it came—I knew what I wanted—more knowledge of Christ, more love of him."

"When was this?"

"It is a good while ago. It is—it was,—time seems so confused to me!—I know it was the winter after you went away. I think it was near the spring. We were in London."

"Yes."

"I was cold at the heart of religion. I was not happy. I knew what I wanted—more love to Christ."

"You did love him."

"Yes; but you know what it is just to love him a little. I went as duty bade me; but the love of him did not make all duty happy. I had seen you live differently—I saw others—and I could not be content as I was.

"We were in town then. One night I sat up all night, and gave the whole night to it."

"To seeking Jesus?"

"I wanted to get out of my coldness and find him!"

"And you found him?"

"Not soon. I spent the night in it. I prayed—and I walked the floor and prayed—and I shed a great many tears over the Bible. I felt as if I must have what I wanted—but I could not seem to get any nearer to it. The whole night passed away—and I had wearied myself—and I had got nothing.

"The dawn was just breaking, when I got up from my

knees the last time. I was almost giving up in despair. I had done all I could—what could I do more? I went to the window and opened it. The light was just creeping up in the sky—there was a little streak of brightness along the horizon, or of light rather, but it was the herald of brightness. I felt desolate and tired, and like giving up hope and quest together. The dull grey canopy overhead seemed just like my heart. I cannot tell you how enviously I looked at the eastern dawn, wishing the light would break upon my own horizon. I shall never forget it. It was dusky yet down in the streets and over the housetops; the city had not waked up in our quarter; it was still yet, and the breath of the morning's freshness came to me and revived me and mocked me both at once. I could have cried for sadness, if I had not been too down-hearted and weary.

"While I stood there, hearing the morning's promise, I suppose, without knowing it,—there came up from the streets somewhere below me, and near, the song of a chimney-sweep. I can never tell you how it came! It came—but not yet; at first I only knew what he was singing by the notes of the air; but the next verse he began came up clear and strong to me at the window. He was singing those words—

"'Twas a heaven below
My Redeemer to know;
And the angels could do nothing more,
Than to fall at his feet,
And the story repeat,
And the Lover of sinners adore."

"I thought, it seemed that a band of angels came and carried those words up past my window! And the dawn came in my heart. I cannot tell you how,—I seemed to see everything at once. I saw what a heaven below it is, to know the love of Christ. I think my heart was something like the Ganges when the tide is coming in. I thought, if the angels could do nothing more than praise him, neither could I! I fell at his feet then—I do not think I have ever really left them since—not for long at a time; and since then my great wish has been to be allowed to glorify him. I have had no fears of anything in the way."

Eleanor had not been able to get through her "long story" without tears; but they came very much against her will. She could not see, yet somehow she felt the strong sympathetic emotion with which she was listened to. She could hear it, in the subdued intonation of Mr. Rhys's words.

"'Keep yourselves in the love of God.' How shall we do it, Eleanor?"

She answered without raising her eyes—"'The Lord is good unto them that wait for him.'"

"And, 'if ye keep my commandments, ye shall abide in my love.'"

There was silence a moment.

"That commandment must take me away for a while, Eleanor." She looked up.

"I thought," he said with his sweet arch smile, "I might take so much of a honeymoon as one broken day—but there is a poor sick man a mile off who wants me; and brother Balliol has had the schooner affairs to attend to. I shall be gone an hour. Will you stay here? or shall I take you to the other house?"

"May I stay here?"

"Certainly. You can fasten the door, and then if any visiters come they will think I am not at home. I will give Solomon directions."

"Who is Solomon?"

"Solomon is—I will introduce him to you!" and with a very bright face Mr. Rhys went off into his study, coming back again in a moment and with his hat. He went to a door opposite that by which Eleanor had entered the house, and blew a shrill whistle.

"Solomon is my fast friend and very faithful servant," he said returning to Eleanor. "You saw him at dinner —but it is time he should know you."

In came Solomon; a very black specimen of the islanders, in a dress something like that which Eleanor had noticed on the man in the canoe. Solomon's features were undeniably good, if somewhat heavy; they had sense and manliness; and his eye was mildly quiet and genial in its expression. It brightened, Eleanor saw, as he listened to Mr. Rhys's words; to which she also listened without being able to understand them, and wondering at the warm feeling of her cheeks. Solomon's gratulations were mainly given with his face, for all the English words he could get out were, "glad—see —Misi Risi"—Mr. Rhys laughed and dismissed him, and went off himself.

Eleanor was half glad to be left alone for a time. She fastened the door, not for fear, but that her solitude might not be intruded upon; then walked up and down over the soft mats of the centre room and tried to bring her spirits to some quiet of realization. But she could not. The change had been so sudden, from her wandering state of uncertainty and expectation to absolute content and rest, of body and mind at once, that her mental like her actual footing seemed to sway and heave yet with the upheavings that were past. She could not settle down to anything like a composed state of mind. She could not get accustomed yet to Mr. Rhys in his new character. As the children say, it was "too good to be true."

A little unready to be still, she went off again into the room specially prepared for her, where the green *jalousies* shaded the windows. One window here was at the end; a direction in which Eleanor had not looked.

She softly raised the jalousies a little, expecting to see just the waving bananas and other plants of the tropical garden that surrounded the house; or perhaps servants' offices, about which she had a good deal of curiosity.

Instead of that, the window revealed a landscape of such beauty that Eleanor involuntarily pulled up the blind and sat entranced before it. No such thing as servants or servants' offices. A wide receding stretch of broken country, rising in the distance to the dignity of blue precipitous hills; a gorge of which opened far away, to delight and draw the eye into its misty depth; a middle distance of lordly forest, with patches of clearing; bits of tropical vegetation at hand, and over them and over it all a tropical sky. In one direction the view was very open. Eleanor could discern a bit of a pathway winding through it, and once or twice a dark figure moving along its course. This was Vuliva! this was her foreign home! the region where darkness and light were struggling foot by foot for the mastery; where heathen temples were falling and heathen misery giving place to the joy of the gospel, but where the gospel had to fight them yet. Eleanor looked till her heart was too full to look any longer; and then turned aside to get the only possible relief in prayer.

The hour was near gone when she went to her window again. The day was cooling towards the evening. Well she guessed that this window had been specially arranged for her. In everything that had been done in the house she had seen that same watchful care for her pleasure and comfort. There never was a house that seemed to be so love's work; Mr. Rhys's own hand had most manifestly been everywhere; and the furniture that Mrs. Caxton had sent he had placed. But Mrs. Caxton had not sent all. Eleanor's eye rested on a dressing-table that certainly never came from England. It was pretty enough; it was very pretty, even to her notions; yet it had cost nothing, and was as nearly as possible made of nothing. Yes, for she looked; the frame was only some native reeds or canes and a bit of board; the rest was white muslin drapery, which would pack away in a very few square inches of room, but now hung in pretty folds around the glass and covered the frame. Eleanor just looked and wondered; no more; for the hour was up, and she went to her window and raised the jalousies again. She was more quiet now, she thought; but her heart throbbed with the thought of Mr. Rhys and his return.

She looked over the beautiful wild country, watching for him. The light was fair on the blue hills; the sea-breeze fluttered the leaves of the cocoanut trees and waved the long thick leaves of the banana. She heard no other sound near or far, till the quick swift tread she was listening for came to her ear. Nobody was to be seen; but the step was not to be mistaken. Eleanor got to the front door and had it open just in time to see him come.

They stood then together in the doorway, for the view was fair on the river side too. The opposite shore was beautiful, and the houses of the heathen village had a great interest for Eleanor, aside from their effect as part of the landscape; but her shyness was upon her again, and she had a thorough consciousness that Mr. Rhys did not see how the light fell on either shore. At last he put his arm round her and drew her up to his side, saying,

"And so you did not get my letters in Sydney.—Poor little dove!"

It struck Eleanor with a curious pleasure, these words. They would have been true, she knew, in the lips of no other mortal, as also certainly to no other mortal would it have occurred to use them. She was not the sort of person by any means to whom such an appellation would generally be given. To be sure her temper was of the finest, but then also it had a body to it. Yet here she knew it was true; and *he* knew; it was spoken not by any arrogance, but by a purely frank and natural understanding of their mutual natures and relations. She answered by a smile, exceeding sweet and sparkling, as well as conscious, to the face that was looking down at her with a little bit of provoking archness upon its gravity; and their lips met in a long sealing kiss. Husband and wife understood each other.

Perhaps Mr. Rhys knew it, for it seemed as if his lips could hardly leave hers; and Eleanor's face was all manner of lights.

"What has become of Alfred?" he asked in an irrelevant kind of manner, by way of parenthesis.

"I have not seen him—hardly—since you left England. He is not under mamma's care now."

"And my friend Julia? You have told me but a mite yet about everybody."

"Julia is your friend still. But Julia—I have not seen her in a long, long time."

"How is that?"

"Mamma would not let me. O Mr. Rhys!—we have been kept apart. I could not even see her when I came away."

"Why?"

"Mamma—she was afraid of my influence over her."

"Is it possible!"

"Julia was going on well—setting her face to do right. Now—I do not know how it will be. Even our letters are overlooked."

"I need not ask how your mother is. I suppose she is trying to save one of her daughters for the world."

Eleanor's thoughts swept a wide course in a few minutes; remembered whose hand instrumentality had saved her from such a fate and had striven for Julia. With a sigh that was part sorrow and part gratitude, Eleanor laid her head softly on Mr. Rhys's shoulder. With such tenderness as one gives to a child, and yet rarer, because deeper and graver, she was made at home there.

"Don't you want to take a walk to the chapel?"

"O yes!"—But she was held fast still.

"And shall we give sister Balliol the pleasure of our company to tea, as we come back?"

"If you please—if you like."

"I do not like it at all," said Mr. Rhys frankly—"but I suppose we must."

"Think of finding the restraints of society even in Fiji!" said Eleanor trying to laugh, as she brought her bonnet and they set out.

"You must find them everywhere—unless you live to please yourself," said Mr. Rhys, with his sweet grave look; and Eleanor was consoled.

The walk to the church was not very long, and she could have desired it longer. The river shore, and the view on the other side, and the village by which they passed, the trees and the vegetable gardens and the odd thatched roofs—everything was pretty and new to Eleanor's eyes. They passed all they had seen in coming from the landing that morning, taking this time a path outside the mission premises. Past the house with the row of pillars in front, which Eleanor learned was a building for the use of the various schools. A little further on stood the chapel. It was neat and tasteful enough to please even an English eye; and indeed looked more English than foreign on a distant view; and standing there in the wilderness, with its little bell-tower rising like a witness for all that was good in the midst of a heathen land, the feelings of those who looked upon it had need be very tender and very deep.

"This chapel is dear to our eyes," said Mr. Rhys. "Everything is, that costs such pains. This poor people have made it; and it is one of the best pieces of work in Fiji. It was all done by the labour of their hearts and hands."

"That seems to be the style of carpentry in this country," said Eleanor.

"The chief made up his mind on a good principle—that for a house of the true God, neither time nor material could be too precious. On that principle they went to work. The timber used in the building is what we call green-heart—the best there is in Fiji. To find it, they had to travel over many a mile of the country; and remember, there are no oxen here, no horses; they had no teams to help them. All must be done by the labour of the hands. I think there were about eighty beams of green-heart timber needed for the house—some of them twelve and some of them fifty feet long. In about three months these were collected; found and brought in from the woods and hills, sometimes from ten miles away. While the young men were doing this, the old men at home were all day beating cocoanut husk, to separate the fibre for making sinnet. All day long I used to hear their beaters going; it was good music; and when at the end of every few days the woodcutters came home with their timber—so soon as they were heard shouting the news of their coming—there was a general burst and cry and every creature in the village set off to meet them and help drag the logs home. Women and children and all went; and you never saw people so happy.

"Then the building was done in the same spirit. Many a time when I was busy with them, overlooking their work, I have heard them chanting to each other words from the Bible—band against band. One side would sing—'But will God indeed dwell on the earth? Behold, the heaven of heavens cannot contain thee; how much less this house that I have builded.'—Then the other side would answer, 'The Lord hath chosen Zion; he hath desired it for his habitation.' I cannot tell you how sweet it was. There was another chant they were very fond of. A few would begin with Solomon's petition—'Have thou respect unto the prayer of thy servant, and to his supplication, O Lord my God, to hearken unto the cry and to the prayer, which thy servant prayeth before thee to-day: that thine eyes may be open toward this house night and day, even toward the place of which thou hast said, My name shall be there: that thou mayest hearken unto the prayer which thy servant shall make toward this place,'—and here a number of the other builders would join in with their cry—'Hearken unto the prayer which thy servant shall make!' And so in the next verse, when it came near the end the others would join in—'And when thou hearest, forgive!'—"

"I should think you would love it!" said Eleanor with her eyes full of tears. "And I should think the Lord would love it."

"Come in, and see how it looks on the inside."

The inside was both simple and elegant, after a quaint fashion; for it was Fijian elegance and Fijian simplicity. A double row of columns led down the centre of the building; they looked like mahogany, but it was only native wood; and the ornamental work at top which served for their capitals, was done in sinnet. Over the doors and windows triangular pediments were elaborately wrought in black with the same sinnet. The roof was both quaint and elegant. It was done in alternate open and close reed-work, with broad black lines dividing it; and ornamental lashings and bandings of sinnet were used about the fastenings and groinings of spars and beams. Then the wings of the communion rail were made of reed work, ornamented; the rail was a beautiful piece of nut timber, and the balusters of sweet sandal wood. The whole effect exceeding pretty and graceful, though produced with such simple means.

"Mr. Ruskin ought to have had this as an illustration of his 'Lamp of Sacrifice,'" said Eleanor. "How beautiful!—"

"The 'Lamp of Truth,' too," said Mr. Rhys. "It is all honest work. That side was done by our heathen neighbours. The heathen chief sent us his compliments, said he heard we were engaged in a great work, and if we pleased he would come and help us. So he did. They built that side of the wall and the roof."

"Did they do it well?"

"Heartily."

"Do they come to attend worship in it?"

"The chapel is a great attraction. Strangers come to see—if not to worship,—and then we get a chance to tell the truth to them."

"And Mr. Rhys, how is the truth prospering generally?"

"Eleanor, we want men!—and that seems to be all we want. My heart feels ready to break sometimes, for the want of helpers. I am glad of brother Amos coming—very glad!—but we want a hundred where we have one. It is but a few weeks since a young man came over from one of the islands, a large and important island, bringing tidings that a number of towns there had given up heathenism—all wanting teachers—and there were no teachers for them. In one place the people had built a chapel; they had gone so far as that; it was at Koroivonu—and they gathered together the next Sunday after it was finished, great numbers of the people, filled the chapel and stood under some bread-fruit trees in front of it, and stood there waiting to have some one come and tell them the truth—and there was no one. My heart is ready to weep blood when I think of these things! The Tongan who came with the news came with his eyes full of tears. And this is no strange nor solitary case of Koroivonu."

Mr. Rhys walked the floor of the little chapel, his features working, his breast heaving. Eleanor sat thinking how little she could do—how much she would!

"You have native helpers —?" she said gently.

"Praise the Lord for what they are! but we want missionaries. We want help from England. We cannot get it from the Colonies—not fast enough. Eleanor," —and he stopped short and faced her—"a few months ago, to give you another instance, I was beholder of such a scene as this. I was to preach to a community that were for the first time publicly renouncing heathenism. It was Sunday."—Mr. Rhys spoke slowly, evidently exercising some control over himself; how often Eleanor had seen him do that in the pulpit!—

"I stood on the shores of a bay, reefed in from the ocean. I wish I could put the scene before you! On the land side, one of the most magnificent landscapes stretched back into the country, with almost every sort of natural beauty. Before me the bay, with ten large canoes moored in it. An island in the bay, I remember, caught the light beautifully; and beyond that there was the white fence of breakers on the reef barrier. The smallest of the canoes would hold a hundred men; they were the fleet of Thakomban, one of Fiji's fiercest kings formerly, with himself and his warriors on board.

"My preaching place was on what had been the dancing grounds of a village. I had a mat stretched on three poles for an awning—such a mat as they make for sails;—and around me were nine others prepared in like manner. This was my chapel. Just at my left hand was a spot of ground where were ten boiling springs; and until that Sunday, one of them had been the due appointed place for cooking human bodies. That was the place and the preparation I looked at in the still Sunday morning, before service time.

"At that time, the time appointed for service, a drum was beat and the conch shell blown; the same shell which had been used to give the war call. Directly all those canoes were covered with men, and they were plunging into the water and wading to shore. These were Thakombau and his warriors. Not blacked and stripped and armed for fighting, but washed and clothed. They were stopping in that place on their way somewhere else, and now coming and gathering to hear the preaching. On the other side came a procession from the village; and down every hillside and along every path, I could see scattering groups and lines of comers from the neighbouring country. *These*, were the heathen inhabitants, coming up now to hear the truth and profess by a public act of worship that they were heathens no longer. They all gathered round me there under the mat awnings, and sat on the grass looking up to hear, while I told them of Jesus.—"

Mr. Rhys's voice was choked and he broke off abruptly. Eleanor guessed how he had talked to that audience; she could see it in his flushing face and quivering lip. She could not find a word to say, and let him lead her in silence and slowly away from the chapel and towards the mission house. Before entering the plantation again, Eleanor stopped and said in a low voice,

"What can I do?"

He gave her a look of that moved sweetness she had seen in him all day, and answered with his usual abruptness,

"You can pray."

"I do that."

"Pray as Paul prayed—for your mother, and for Julia, and for Fiji, and for me. Do you know how that was?"

"I know what some of his prayers were."

"Yes, but I never thought how Paul prayed, until the other day. You must put the scattered hints together. Wait until we are at home—I will shew you."

He pushed open the wicket and they went in; and the rest of the evening Eleanor talked to Mrs. Amos or to Mr. Balliol; she sheered off a little from his wife. There was plenty of interesting conversation going on with one and another; but Eleanor had a little the sense of being to that lady an object of observation, and drew into a corner or into the shade as much as she could.

"Your wife is very handsome, brother Rhys," Mrs. Balliol remarked in an aside, towards the end of the evening.

"That is hardly much praise from you, sister Balliol," he answered gravely. "I know you do not set much store by appearances."

"She is very young!"

Both looked over to the opposite corner where Eleanor was talking to Mrs. Amos, sitting on a low seat and looking up; a little drawn back into the shade, yet not so shaded but that the womanly modest sweetness of her face could be seen well enough. Mr. Rhys made no answer.

"I judge, brother Rhys, that she has been brought up in the great world,"—Mrs. Balliol went on, looking across to the ruffled sleeve.

"She is not in it now," Mr. Rhys observed quietly.

"No;—she is in good hands. But, brother Rhys, do you think our sister understands exactly what sort of work she has come to do here?"

"She is teachable," he answered with great imperturbability.

"Well, you will be able to train her, if she wants it. I am glad to know she is in such good hands. I think she has hardly yet a just notion of what lies before her, brother Rhys."

"When did you make your observations?"

"She was with me, you know—you left her with me this morning. We were alone, and we had a little conversation."

"Mrs. Balliol, do you think a just notion of *anything* can be formed in half an hour?"

His question was rather grave, and the lady's eyes wavered from meeting his. She fidgetted a little.

"O you know best, of course," she said; "I have had very little opportunity—I only judged from the want of seriousness; but that might have been from some other cause. You must excuse me, if I spoke too frankly."

"You can never do that to me," he said. "Thank you, sister Balliol. I will take care of her."

Mrs. Balliol was reassured. But neither during their walk home nor ever after, did Mr. Rhys tell Eleanor of this little bit of talk that had concerned her.

CHAPTER XX.

"My Lady comes; my Lady goes; he can see her day by day,
And bless his eyes with her beauty, and with blessings strew her way."

The breakfast-table was as much of a mystery to Eleanor as the dinner had been. Not because it looked so homelike; though in the early morning the doors and windows were all open and the sunlight streaming through on Mrs. Caxton's china cups and silver spoons. It all looked foreign enough yet, among those palm-fern pillars, and on the Fijian mat with its border made of red worsted ends and little white feathers. The basket of fruit, too, on the table, did not look like England. But the tea was unexceptionable, and there was a piece of fresh fish as perfectly broiled as if it had been brought over by some genius or fairy, smoking hot, from an English gridiron. And in the order and arrangements of the table, there had been something more than native skill and taste, Eleanor was sure.

"It seems to me, Mr. Rhys," she said, "that the Fijians are remarkably good cooks!"

"Uncommon, for savages," said Mr. Rhys with perfect gravity.

"This fish is excellent."

"There is no better fish-market in the world, for variety and abundance, than we have here."

"But I mean, it is broiled just like an English fish. Isaac Walton himself would be satisfied with it."

"Isaac Walton never saw such fishing as is carried on here. The natives are at home in the water from their childhood—men and women both;—and the women do a good deal of the fishing. But the serious business is the turtle fishing. It is a hand to hand conflict. The men plunge into the water and grapple bodily with the turtle, after they have brought them into an enclosure with their nets. Four or five men lay hold of one, if it is a large fellow, and they struggle together under water till the turtle thinks he has the worst of the bargain, and concludes to come to the surface."

"Does not the turtle sometimes get the better?"

"Sometimes."

"Mr. Rhys, have you any particular duty to-day?"

"I don't see how you can keep up that form of expression!" said he, with a comic gravity of dislike.

"Why not?"

"It is not treating me with proper confidence."

Her look in reply was so very pretty, both blushing and winsome, that the corners of his mouth were obliged to give way.

"You know what my first name is, do not you?"

"Yes," said Eleanor.

"The people about call me 'Misi Risi'———I am not going to have my wife a Fijian to me."

The lights on Eleanor's face were very pretty. With the same contained smile he went on.

"I gave you my name yesterday. It is yours to do what you like with; but the greatest dishonour you can shew to a gift, is not to use it at all."

"That is the most comical putting of the case that ever I heard," said Eleanor, quite unable to retain her own gravity.

"Very good sense," said Mr. Rhys, with a dry preservation of his.

"But after all," said Eleanor, "you gave me your second name, if you please—I do not know what I have to do with the first."

"You do not? Is it possible you think your name is Henry or James, or something else? You are Rowland Rhys as truly as I am—only you are the mistress, and I am the master."

Eleanor's look went over the table with something besides laughter in the brown eyes, which made them a gentle thing to see.

"Mr. Rhys, I am thinking, what you will do to this part of you to make it like the other?"

He gave her a glance, at which her eyes went down instantly.

"I do not know," he said with infinite gravity. "I will think about it. Preaching does not seem to do you any good."

Eleanor bent her attention upon her bread and fruit. He spoke next with a change of tone, giving up his gravity.

"Do you know *your* particular duty to-day?"

"I thought," said Eleanor,—"that as yesterday you shewed me the head-carpenter, perhaps this morning you would let me see the chief cook."

"That is not the first thing. You must have a lesson in Fijian; now that I hope you are instructed in English."

He carried her off to his study to get it. The lesson was a matter of amusement to Mr. Rhys, but Eleanor set herself earnestly to learn. Then he said he supposed she might as well see her establishment at once, and took her out to the side of the house where she had not been.

It was a plantation wilderness here too, though particularly devoted to all that in Fiji could belong to a kitchen garden. English beans and peas had been sown, and were flourishing; most of the luxuriance that met the eye had a foreign character. Beautiful order was noticeable everywhere. Mr. Rhys seemed to have forgotten all about the servants; he pleased himself with leading Eleanor through the walks and shewing her which were the plants of the yam and the kumera and other native fruits and vegetables. Bananas were here too, and the graceful stems of the sugar cane; and overhead the cocoanut trees waved their feathery plumes in the air.

"Who did all this?" Eleanor asked admiringly.

"Solomon—with a head gardener over him."

"Solomon is—I saw him yesterday?"

"Yes. He came with me from Vulanga. He is a nice fellow. He is a Christian, as I told you; and a true labourer in the great vineyard. I believe he never misses an opportunity to speak to his countrymen in a quiet way and tell them the truth. He has brought a great many to know it. In my service he is very faithful."

"No wonder this garden looks nice," said Eleanor.

"I asked Solomon one day about his religious experience. He said he was very happy; he had enjoyed religion all the day. He said he rose early in the morning and prayed that the Lord would greatly bless him and keep him; and that it had been so, and generally was so when he attended to religious duties early in the morning. 'But if I neglect and rush into the world,' he said, 'without properly attending to my religious duties, nothing goes right. I am wrong in my own heart, and no one round me is right.'"

"Good testimony," said Eleanor. "Is he your cook as well as your gardener?"

"I had forgotten all about the cook," said Mr. Rhys. "Come and see the kitchen."

Near the main dwelling house, in this planted enclosure, were several smaller houses. Mr. Rhys at last took Eleanor that way and permitted her to inspect them. The one nearest the main building was fitted up for a laundry. The furthest was a sleeping house for the servants. The middle one was the kitchen. It was a Fijian kitchen. Here was a large fireplace, of the original fashion which had moved Eleanor's wonder in the dining-room; with a Fijian framework of wood at one side of it, holding native vessels of pottery, larger and smaller, and variously shaped, for cooking purposes. Some more homelike iron utensils were to be seen also; with other kitchen appurtenances, water jars and so forth. A fire had been in the fireplace, and the signs of cookery were remaining; but in all the houses, nobody was anywhere visible.

"Solomon is gone to collect your servants," said Mr. Rhys. "That explains the present solitude."

"Did he cook that fish?"

"I have not tried him in cooking," said Mr. Rhys with a gravity that was perfect. "I do not know what he could do if he was tried?"

"Who did it then?"

His smile was wonderfully pleasant—now that it could be no longer kept back—as he answered, "Your servant."

"*You*, Rowland! And the dinner yesterday?"

"Do not praise me," he said with the same look, "lest I should spoil the dinner to-day. I do not expect there will be anybody here till afternoon."

"Then you shall see what I can do!"

"I do not believe you know how. I have been long enough in the wilderness to learn all trades. You never learned how to cook at Wiglands."

"But at Plassy I did."

"Did aunt Caxton let you into her kitchen?"

"Yes."

"I shall not let you into mine."

"She went with me there. I have not come out here to be useless. I will take care of the dinner to-day."

"No, you shall not," said Mr. Rhys, drawing her away from the kitchen. "You have got enough to do to-day in unpacking boxes. There will be servants this evening to attend to all you want; and for the present you are my care."

"Rowland, I should like it."

Which view of the case did not seem to be material. At least it was answered in a silencing kind of way, as with his arm about her he led her in through the bananas to the house. It silenced Eleanor effectually, in spite of being very serious in her wish. She put it away to bide another opportunity.

Mr. Rhys gave her something else to do, as he had said. The boxes had in part been brought from the schooner, and there was employment for both of them. He drew out nails, and took off covers, and did the rough unpacking; while the arranging and bestowing of the goods thus put under her disposal kept Eleanor very busy. His part of the work was finished long before hers, and Mr. Rhys withdrew to his study for some other work. Eleanor, happy and busy, with touched thoughts of Mrs. Caxton, put away blankets and clothes and linen and calicos, and unpacked glass, and stowed on her shelves a whole store of home comforts and necessaries; marvelling between whiles at Mr. Rhys's varieties of power in making himself useful and wishing she could do what she thought was better her work than his—the work to be done in the kitchen before the servants came home. By and by, Mr. Rhys came out of the study again, and found Eleanor sitting on the mat before a huge round hamper, uncovered, filled with Australian fruit. This was a late arrival, brought while he had been shut up at his work. Grapes and peaches and pears and apricots were crowded side by side in rich and beautiful abundance and confusion. Eleanor sat looking at it. She was in a working dress, of the brown stuff her aunt's maids wore at home; short sleeves left her arms bare to the elbow; and the full jacket and hoopless skirt did no wrong to a figure the soft outlines of which they only disclosed. Mr. Rhys stopped and stood still. Eleanor looked up.

"Mr. Esthwaite has sent these on in the schooner unknown to me! What shall I do with them all?"

"I don't know," said Mr. Rhys. "It is the penalty that attaches to wealth."

"But you said you never were poor?" said Eleanor, laughing at his look.

"I never was, in feeling. I never was in an embarrassment of riches, either. I can't help you!"

"But these are yours, Rowland. What are you talking of?"

"Are you going to make me a present of the whole?" said Mr. Rhys, stooping down for a grape.

"No, Mr. Esthwaite has done that. The embarrassment is yours."

"I am in no embarrassment; you are mistaken. By what right do you say that Mr. Esthwaite has sent these to me?"

"Because he sent them to me," said Eleanor. "It is the same thing."

"That is dutiful, and loyal, and all that sort of thing," said Mr. Rhys, helping himself to another grape, and looking with his keen eyes and imperturbable gravity at Eleanor. Perhaps *he* liked to see the scarlet bloom he could so easily call up in her cheeks, which was now accompanied with a little impatient glance at him. "Nevertheless, I do not consider myself to be within the scope of the gift. The disposition of it remains with you. I do not like the responsibilities of other people's wealth to rest on my shoulders."

"But this fruit is different from what we have on the

island; is there not something you would like to have done with it?"

"I should like you to give me one bunch of grapes—to be chosen by yourself."

He looked on, with a satisfied expression of face, while Eleanor's fingers separated and overhauled the fruit till she had got a bunch to her mind; and stood still in his place to let her bring it to him. Then took possession of her and the grapes at once, neglecting the latter however entirely, to consider her.

"What would you like to have done with the rest, Rowland?" said Eleanor, while her face glowed under his caresses and examination.

"This is a very becoming dress you have on!"

"I did not know you noticed ladies' dresses."

"I always notice my own."

Eleanor's head drooped a little, to hide the rush of pleasure and shame.

"But, Rowland," she said with gentle persistence, "what *would* you like to have done with that basket? Isn't there some meaning behind your words about it?"

"What makes you think so?" said he, curling the corners of his mouth in an amused way.

"I thought so. Please tell it me! You have something to tell me."

"The fruit is yours, Eleanor."

"And what am I?"

The tears came into her eyes with a little vexed earnestness, for she fancied that Mr. Rhys would not speak *because* the fruit was hers. His manner changed again, to the deep tenderness which he had shewn so frequently; holding her close and looking down into her face; not answering at once; half enjoying, half soothing, the feeling he had raised.

"Eleanor," he said, "I do not want that fruit."

"Tell me what to do with it."

"If you like to send some of those grapes to sister Balliol, at the other house, I think they would do a great deal of good."

"I will just take out a few for you, and I will send the whole basket over there just as it is. Is there anybody to take it?"

"Do not save any for me."

"Why not?"

"Because I do not want anything more than I have got."

"I suppose I may do about that as I please?" said Eleanor, laughing a little.

"No—you may not. I only want this bunch that I have in my hand, for a poor sick fellow whom I think they will comfort. If you feel as I do, and like to send the rest over to the mission house, I think they will be well and gratefully used."

"But Rowland, why did you not tell me that just at first?" she said a little wistfully.

"Do you feel as I do? Tell me that first."

But as Eleanor was not ready with her answer to this question, of course her own got the go-by. Mr. Rhys laughed at her a little, and then told her she might get the house ready for dinner. Very much Eleanor wished she could rather get the dinner ready for the house; yet somehow she had an instinctive knowledge that it would be no use to ask him; and she had a curious unwillingness to make the request.

"Do you know," she said, looking up in his face, "I do not know how it is, but you are the only person I ever was afraid of, where my natural courage had full play?"

"Does that sentiment possess you at present?"

"Yes—a little."

He laughed again, and said it was wholesome; and went off without seeming in the least dismayed by the intelligence. If Eleanor had ventured that remark as a feeler, she was utterly discomfited. She went about her pretty work of getting the little table ready and acquainting herself with the details of her cupboard arrangements, feeling a little amused at herself, and with many deeper thoughts about Mr. Rhys and the basket of fruit.

They were sitting in the study after dinner, alternately talking and studying Fijian, when Mr. Rhys suddenly asked,

"Of whom have you ever been afraid, Eleanor, where your natural courage did not have full play?"

"Mr. Carlisle."

"How was that?"

"I was in a false position."

"I feared that, at one time," said Mr. Rhys thoughtfully.

"I was a bondwoman—under engagements that tied me—I did not dare do as I felt. I understand it all now."

"Do you like to tell me how it happened?"

"I like it very much. I want that you should know just how it was. I was pressed into those engagements without my heart being in them, and indeed very much against my will; but I was dazzled by a vision of worldly glory that made me too weak to resist. Then thoughts of another kind began to rise within me; I saw that worldly glory was not the sufficient thing I had thought it; and as my eyes got clear, I found I had given no love where I had given my promise. Then that consciousness hampered me in every action."

"But you did not break with him—with Mr. Carlisle?"

"Because I was such a bondwoman, as I told you. I did not know what I might do—what was right,—and

I wanted to do right then; till I went to Plassy. Aunt Caxton set me free."

Mr. Rhys was silent a little.

"Do you remember coming to visit the old window in the ruins, just before you went to Plassy that time?" he said, looking round at her with a smile.

His wife though she was, Eleanor could not help a warm flush of consciousness coming over her at the recollection.

"I remember," she said demurely. "It was in December."

"What were you afraid of at that time?"

"Mr. Carlisle."

"Did you think it was *he* whom you heard?"

"No. I thought it was you."

"Then why were you afraid?"

"I had reason enough," said Eleanor, in a low voice. "Mr. Carlisle had taken it into his head to become jealous of you."

She answered with a certain straightforward dignity, but Mr. Rhys had a view of dyed cheeks and a face which shrank from his eye. He beheld it, no doubt, for a little while; at least he was silent; and ended with one or two kisses which to Eleanor's feeling, for she dared not look, spoke him very full of satisfaction. But he never brought up the subject again.

The thoughts raised by the talk about the basket of fruit recurred again a few days later. Eleanor had got into full train of her island life by this time. She was studying hard to learn the language, and beginning to speak words of it with her strange muster of servants. Housekeeping duties were fairly in hand. She had begun to find out, too, what Mr. Rhys had foretold her respecting visiters. They came in groups and singly, at all hours nearly on some days, to see the new house and the new furniture and the new wife of "Misi Risi."

Eleanor could not talk to them; she could only be looked at, and answer through an interpreter their questions and requests, and watch with unspeakable interest these strange poor people, and admire with unceasing admiration Mr. Rhys's untiring kindness, patience, and skill, in receiving and entertaining them. They wanted to see and understand every new thing and every new custom. They were polite in their curiosity, but insatiable; and Mr. Rhys would shew and explain and talk, and never seem annoyed or weary; and then, whenever he got a chance, put in his own claim for attention, and tell them of the Gospel. Eleanor always knew from his face and manner, and from theirs, when this sort of talk was going on; and she listened strangely to the unknown words in which her heart went along so blindly. When he thought her not needed, or when he thought her tired, Mr. Rhys would dismiss her to her own room, which he would not have invaded; and Eleanor's reverence for her husband grew with every day, although she would not at the beginning have thought that possible.

At the end of these first few days, Eleanor went one afternoon into Mr. Rhys's study. He was in full tide of work now. The softly swinging door let her in without much noise, and she stood still in the middle of the room, in doubt whether to disturb him or no. He was busy at his writing-table. But Mr. Rhys had good ears, even when he was busy. While she stood there, he looked up at her. She was a pretty vision for a man to see and call wife. She was in one of the white dresses that had stirred Mrs. Esthwaite's admiration; its spotless draperies were in as elegant order as ever they had been for Mrs. Powle's drawing room; the rich banded brown hair was in as graceful order. She stood there very bright, very still, looking at him.

"You have been working a long time, Rowland. You want to stop and rest."

"Come here, and rest me," he answered stretching out his hand.

"Rowland," said Eleanor when she had been standing a minute beside him. "Mrs. Balliol wants me to cut off my hair."

Mr. Rhys looked up at her, for with one arm round her he was still bending attention upon his work. He glanced up as if in doubt or wonder.

"I have been over to see her," Eleanor repeated, "and she counsels me to cut off my hair; cut it short."

"See you don't!" he said sententiously.

"Why?" said Eleanor.

"It would be the cause of our first and last quarrel."

"Our first," said Eleanor stifling some hidden amusement; "but how could you tell that it would be the last?"

"It would be so very disagreeable!—" Mr. Rhys said, with a gravity so dryly comic that Eleanor's gravity was destroyed.

"Mrs. Balliol says I shall find it, my hair, I mean, very much in my way."

"It would be in *my* way, if it was cut off."

"She says it will take a great deal of precious time. She thinks that your razor would be better applied to my head."

"Than to what other object?"

"Than to its legitimate use and application. She wants me to get you to let your beard grow, and to cut off my hair. 'It's unekal'—as Sam Weller says."

Eleanor was laughing; she could not see Mr. Rhys's face very well; it was somewhat bent over his papers; but the side view was of unprovokable gravity. A gravity however which she had learned to know covered a wealth of amusement or of mischief, as the case might be. She knelt down to bring herself within better speaking and seeing distance.

"Rowland, what sort of people are your coadjutors?"

"They are the Lord's people," he answered.

Eleanor felt somewhat checked; the gravity of this answer was of a different character; but she could not refrain from carrying the matter further; she could not let it rest there.

"Do you mean," she said a little timidly, but persistently, "that you are not willing to speak of them as they are, *to me*?"

He was quite silent half a minute, and Eleanor grew increasingly sober. He said then, gently but decidedly,

"There are two persons in the field, of whose faults I am willing to talk to you; yours and my own."

"And of others you think it is wrong, then, to speak even so privately and kindly as we are speaking?" Eleanor was very much chagrined. Mr. Rhys waited a moment and then said, in the same manner,

"I cannot do it, Eleanor."

He got up a moment after and went out of the room. Eleanor felt almost stunned with surprise and discomfort. This was the second time, in the few days that she had been with him, that he had found her wrong in something. It troubled her strangely; and the sense of how much he was better than she—how much higher his sphere of living than the one she moved in—pressed her heart down almost to the ground. She stood by the writing-table where she had risen to her feet, with her eyes brimful of tears, but so still even to her eyelids that the tears had not overflowed. She supposed Mr. Rhys had gone out. In another moment however she heard his step returning and he entered the study. Eleanor moved instantly to leave it, but he met and stayed her with a look infinitely sweet; turned her about, and made her kneel down with him. And then he poured out a prayer for charity; not merely the kindness that throws a covering over the failings of others, or that holds back the report of what they have been; but the overabounding heavenly love that will send its brightness into the dark places of human society and with its own richness fill the barren spots; and above all, for that love of Jesus the King, that makes all his servants dear; for that spirit of Christ that looks with his own love and forbearance on all that need it. And so, as the speaker prayed, he shewed his own possession of that which he asked for; so revealed the tender and high walk of his own mind and its near familiarity with heavenly things, that Eleanor thought her heart would break. The feeling, how far he stood above her in knowledge and in goodness, while it was a secret and deep joy, yet gave her acute pain such as she never had felt before. She would not weep; it was a dry aching pain, that took part of its strength from the thought of having done or shewn something that he did not like. But Mr. Rhys went on to pray for her alone; and Eleanor was conquered then. Tears came and she cried like a little child, and all the hard pain of pride or of fear was washed away; like the dust from the leaves in a summer shower.

She was so far healed, but she would have run away when they rose from their knees if he had permitted her. He had no such intention. Keeping fast hold of her hand he brought her to a seat by the window, opened it, for the day was now cooling off and the sea-breeze was fresh; and taking the book of their studies he put her into a lesson of Fijian practice; till Eleanor's spirits were thoroughly restored. Then throwing away the book and taking her in his arms he almost kissed the tears back again.

"Eleanor——" he said, when he saw that her eyes were wet, and her colour and her voice were fluttering together.

"What?"

"You must bear the inconvenience of your hair for my sake. Tell sister Balliol you wear it by my express orders."

Eleanor's look was lovely. She saw that the gentleness of this speech was intended to give her back just that liberty she might think was forbidden. Humbleness and affection danced in her face together.

"And you do not object to white dresses, Rowland?"

"Never—when they are white—" he said with one of his peculiar smiles.

"Rowland," said Eleanor, now completely happy again, "you ought to have those jalousie blinds at these windows. You want them here much more than I do."

"How will you prove that?"

"By putting them here; and then you will confess it."

"Don't you do it!" said he smiling, seeing that Eleanor's eye was in earnest.

"Please let me! Do let me! You want them much more than I do, Rowland.'

"Then you will have to let them stand; for they are just *where* I want them."

"But the shade of them is much more needed here."

"I could have had it. You need not disturb yourself. There is a whole stack of them lying under the shelves in your store-room."

"Why are they lying there?" said Eleanor in great surprise.

"I did not want them. I left them for you to dispose of."

"For me! Then I shall dispose some of them here."

"Not with my leave."

"May I not know why?" said Eleanor putting her hand in his to plead for it.

"I do not want to fare too much better than my brethren," he answered with a smile of infinite pleasantness at her. Eleanor's face shewed a sudden accession of intelligence.

"Then, Rowland, let us send the other jalousies to Mr. Balliol to shade his study—with all my heart; and you put up mine here. I did not think about that before. Will you do it?"

"There are plenty of them without taking yours, hild."

"Then, O Rowland, why did you not do it before?"

"I have an objection to using other people's property —even for the benefit of my neighbours"—he said with the provoking smile in the corners of his mouth.

"But it is yours now."

"Well, I make it over to you, to be offered and presented as it seems good to you, to brother Balliol, or to sister Balliol, for his use and behoof."

"Do you mean that I must do it?"

"If it is your pleasure."

"Then I will speak of it immediately."

"You can have an opportunity to-night. But Eleanor,—you must call her, sister Balliol."

"I can't, Rowland!"

Silence fell between the parties. Mr. Rhys's face was impenetrable. Eleanor glanced at it and glanced at it; got no help. Finally laid her hand on his shoulder and spoke a little apprehensively.

"Rowland—are you serious?"

"Perfectly." So he was, outwardly.

"Do you think it matters really whether I call her one thing or another? If it were Mrs. Amos, I should not have the least difficulty. I could call her sister Amos. What does it matter?"

"Why can't you use a Christian form of address with her as well as with me?"

"Do you consider it a matter of *principle?*"

"Only as it regards the feelings of the individual, in

either case." Mr. Rhys's mouth was looking very comical.

"Would she care, Rowland?"

"I should like to have you try," he said, getting up and arranging his papers to leave. And Eleanor saw he was not going to tell her any more.

"What is the opportunity you spoke of, Rowland?"

"This is our evening for being together—it has hardly been a Class before this, we were so few; but we met to talk and think together, and usually considered some given subject. To-night it is, the 'glory to be revealed.'"

"That is what Mr. Amos and I used to do on board the schooner; and we had that subject too, just after we left Tonga. So we shall be ready."

"We ought to go there to tea; but I have to go over first to Nawaile; it will keep me till after tea-time. Do not wait for me, unless you choose."

Eleanor chose, and told him so. While he was gone she sat at the door of the house watching and thinking; thinking of him especially, and of things that his talk that afternoon had brought up. It was a pleasant hour or two. The sea-breeze fresh from the sea; the waving broad banana leaves; the sweet perfume of flowers, which were rarely profuse and beautiful in their garden; the beautiful southern sky of night, with the stars which Eleanor had learned to know as strangers coming over in the ship, and now loved as the companions of her new home. Stillness, and flapping of leaves, and sweet thoughts; until it was time to be expecting Mr. Rhys back again, and Eleanor made the tea, that he might at least not miss so much refreshment. She knew his step rods off, and long before she could see him; his cup was all ready for him when he stepped in. He drank it, looking at Eleanor over it; would stop for nothing else, and carried her off.

"I had a happy time," he said as they went through the plantations. "I have been to see an old man who lies there dying, or very near it. He has been a Christian two years. He is very glad to see me when I come, and ready to talk; but he will not talk with his neighbours. He says he wants to keep his thoughts fixed on God; and if he listened to these people they would talk to him of village affairs, and turn his mind off."

"Then, if you had a happy time, I suppose *he* is happy?"

"He is happy. How beautiful upon the mountains are the feet of him that bringeth good tidings, that publisheth peace! Think of old Cæsar, going to glory from the darkness of Fiji. He said to me to-night—'I am weak, and I am old; my time is come, but I am not afraid to die; through Jesus I feel courageous for death. Jesus is my Chief, and I wish to obey him: if he says I am yet to lie here, I will praise him; and if he says I am to go above to him, I will praise him. I do not wish to eat; his word is my food; I think on it, and lean entirely on Jesus.'—Do you know how good it is to be a missionary, Eleanor?"

They exchanged looks; that was all; they were at the door and went in. The party there were expecting and waiting for them, and it was more than a common welcome, Eleanor saw, that was given to them. She did not wonder at it. After exchanging warm greetings all round, she sat down; but Mr. Rhys began walking the floor. The rest were silent. There was a somewhat dim light from a lamp in the room; the windows and doors were open; the air, sweet with flowers and fresh from the sea, came in gently; the soft sounds of leaves and insects could be heard through the fall of Mr. Rhys's steps upon the matted floor. The hour had a strange charm to Eleanor.

Silence lasted, until Mr. Rhys interrupted it with

kneeling down for prayer. Then followed one of those prayers, in which it always seemed to Eleanor as if somebody had taken her hand, who was leading her where she could almost look in at the gates of that city which Bunyan called the Celestial. Somewhere above earth it took her, and rapt her up as Milton's angel is said to have descended, upon a sunbeam. One came to earth again at the end of the prayer; but not without a remembrance of where one had been.

"Sister Balliol," said Mr. Rhys, "will you put us in mind concerning our subject this evening?"

"It is the glory to be revealed; and I find that it is a glory to be revealed *in us*," Mrs. Balliol made answer. "Sufferings come first. It is a glory that goes along with sufferings in the present life; but it is so much greater than the sufferings, that no comparison can be made of them. For my part, I do not think the glory would be half so much glory, if it were not for the sufferings going before."

"To suffer with Christ, and for him, that is glory now," said Mr. Rhys; "to have been so honoured will always be part of our joy. If any man suffer as a Christian, let him not be ashamed, but rather let him glorify God on this behalf. Those be tears that Christ's own hand will wipe off; and what glory will that be!"

"The word of God fails to express it," said Mr. Amos, "and calls it 'riches of glory.' Riches of glory, to be poured into vessels prepared to receive it. Surely, being such heirs, none of us has a right to call himself poor? we are heirs of an inheritance incorruptible, and undefiled, and not subject to decadence or failure. We may well be content with our penny earnest in this life, who have such an estate coming in."

"I feel poor very often," said gentle Mrs. Amos; "and I suppose that must be my own fault; for the word says, 'Riches and honour are with me; yea, durable riches, and righteousness.'"

"Those are riches that none but the poor come into possession of," said Mr. Rhys. "The poor in spirit inherit the kingdom, and nobody else. It is our very emptiness, that fits us for receiving those unsearchable riches. But having those, sister Amos, it is no deprivation of this world's good things that would make you feel poor?"

"O no, indeed!" said Mrs. Amos. "I did not mean *that* sort of poor."

"The rich he will send empty away"—Mr. Rhys went on.

"So in the matter of suffering," said Mr. Balliol taking up the word. "If we are partakers of Christ's sufferings now, we are told to rejoice. For when his glory is revealed, the word is, that we shall be glad also, and with exceeding joy. When his glory is revealed here, a little, now, we are glad; our joy seems to be exceeding, now, brother Rhys. I wonder what it will be when God calls it exceeding joy!"

There was a pause; and then Mrs. Amos, for the sake simply of starting Eleanor, whose voice she knew in it, began softly the song, "Burst, ye emerald gates!" She had her success, for Eleanor with the others took up the words, and carried it—Mrs. Amos thought—where Mr. Rhys's prayer had been. When the song ceased, there was silence; till Mr. Rhys said, "Eleanor!"—It was her turn to speak.

"I do not believe," she said speaking low and slowly, —"that either sufferings, or promises, or duties, will bring the hope of glory into the heart; until Jesus himself brings it there. And if he brings it, it hardly seems to me that sufferings will enhance it—except in so far as they lead to greater knowledge of him or are the immediate fruit of love to him; and then, as Mr. Rhys says, they are honour themselves already. The riches of the glory of this mystery, is *Christ in you, the hope of glory.*"

Mr. Rhys was standing at the back of Eleanor's chair, leaning upon it. He bent his head and whispered to her to tell her story that she had told him. At that whisper, Eleanor would have steadily gone through the fire if necessary; this was not quite as hard; and though not for her own sake caring to do it, she told the story and told it freely and well. She told it so that every head there was bowed. And then there was silence again; till Mr. Rhys began, or rather went on with what she had been saying; in a voice that seemed to come from every heart.

"Whom having not seen, ye love; in whom, though now ye see him not, yet believing, ye rejoice with joy unspeakable and full of glory."

"Friends, we have the present honour, of being Christ's ambassadors. Do we know what honour that is? 'Whosoever shall receive this child in my name, receiveth me; and whosoever shall receive me, receiveth him that sent me.' That is honour under which we may tremble!"——And standing there at the back of Eleanor's chair, Mr. Rhys began to talk; on the joy of carrying Christ's message, the honour of being his servants and co-workers, and the gladness of bringing the water of life to lips dry and failing in death. He told the instance of that evening which he had told to Eleanor; and leaving his station behind her, he walked up and down again, speaking as she had sometimes heard him speak, till every head was raised and turned, and every eye followed him. With fire and tears, speaking of the work to be done and the joy of doing it, and the need of more to do it; and of the carelessness people have of that glory which will make men shine as the stars for ever and ever.

"Ay, we shall know then, brother Balliol, when the great supper is served, and Christ shall gird himself, and make his faithful servants sit down to meat, and he shall come forth and serve them—we shall know then, if we are there, what glory means! And we shall know what it means to have no want unsatisfied and no joy left out!—when the Lamb that is in the midst of the throne shall feed them, and shall lead them to living fountains of waters."

Mr. Balliol answered—

"If any man serve me, let him follow me; and where I am, there shall also my servants be: if any man serve me, him will my Father honour."

Mr. Rhys went on—"Feed the flock of God which is among you, taking the oversight thereof, not by constraint, but willingly; not for filthy lucre, but of a ready mind; neither as being lords over God's heritage, but being ensamples to the flock. And when the chief Shepherd shall appear, ye shall receive a crown of glory that fadeth not away."

They knelt together again, and then separated; and the tropical moon lighted home the two who did not belong to Mrs. Balliol's household.

THE END.

CPSIA information can be obtained
at www.ICGtesting.com
Printed in the USA
LVHW040029180422
716440LV00005B/344